Praise for
THE DEMON CROWN

P9-DDN-447

"Rollins' latest Sigma Force novel is one of
the best in the series. " —*Booklist* (★Starred Review★)

"Bone-chilling." —*Publishers Weekly* (★Starred Review★)

"Rollins has crafted a perfect thriller that never
fails to enlighten and entertain."
—BookTrib.com

"Riveting…plot revelations keep coming
and the pace never slows."
—*The Wall Street Journal*

"Action and adventure fans can do no better than
James Rollins' latest Sigma Force thriller, *The Demon Crown.*"
—*The Oklahoman*

"Not for the faint of heart." —*Iron Mountain Daily News*

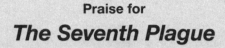

JAMES ROLLINS

THE DEMON CROWN

A Σ SIGMA FORCE NOVEL

wm
WILLIAM MORROW
An Imprint of *HarperCollins*Publishers

Excerpt from *Crucible* copyright © 2018 by James Czajkowski.

"Ghost Ship" copyright © 2017 by James Czajkowski.

"Ghost Ship" was originally published as an e-book novella October 2017 by William Morrow, an Imprint of HarperCollins Publishers.

First William Morrow premium printing: July 2018
First William Morrow paperback international printing: December 2017
First William Morrow hardcover printing: December 2017

Print Edition ISBN: 978-0-06-238174-3
Digital Edition ISBN: 978-0-06-238175-0

Cover illustration by Tony Mauro
Cover photographs © Voyageriz/Dreamstime (background);
© Jakub Gojda/Dreamstime (fire)
Stepback photograph © Hecktic Travels

Maps provided and drawn by Steve Prey. All rights reserved. Used by permission of Steve Prey.

17 18 19 20 21   QGM   10 9 8 7 6 5 4 3 2 1

For Mama Carol,

For all she gave to those around her,

selflessly and lovingly throughout her life

ACKNOWLEDGMENTS

This book has so many fingerprints upon each page, most of those from a certain circle of critics who have been there since the beginning of my writing career, back when I was a full-time practicing veterinarian, writing short stories that are now safely buried in my backyard. So first and foremost, let me thank that close-knit bevy of readers who serve as my initial editors: Sally Ann Barnes, Chris Crowe, Lee Garrett, Jane O'Riva, Denny Grayson, Leonard Little, Judy Prey, Caroline Williams, Christian Riley, Tod Todd, and Amy Rogers. And as always, a special thanks to Steve Prey for the great maps . . . and to David Sylvian for both keeping me grounded and pushing me to greater heights . . . and to Cherei McCarter for the many significant historical and scientific tidbits found within these pages . . . and Hiroaki Endo, who helped with the Japanese translations (though any errors are my own) . . . and Paulina Szylkiewicz, for allowing me to use her father's map in this book, and Monica Szczepa, for facilitating this connection. Finally and reluctantly, I must thank Steve Berry for his assistance with some of the historical details surrounding the Smithsonian, as, inadvertently, we were both working on stories involving that fine institution. And of course, a big note of appreciation to everyone at HarperCollins for always having my back, especially Michael Morrison, Liate Stehlik, Danielle Bartlett, Kaitlin Harri, Josh Marwell, Lynn Grady, Richard Aquan, Tom Egner, Shawn Nicholls, and Ana Maria Allessi. Last, of course, a special acknowledgment to the people instrumental to all levels of production: my esteemed editor who has been with me since my first book was published two decades ago, Lyssa Keusch, and her industrious colleague Priyanka Krishnan; and for all their hard work, my agents, Russ Galen and Danny Baror (along with his daughter Heather Baror). And as always, I must stress that any and all errors of fact or detail in this book, of which hopefully there are not too many, fall squarely on my own shoulders.

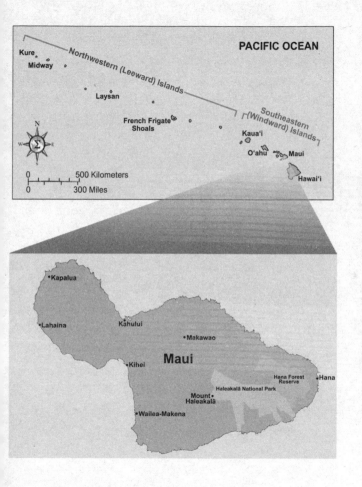

NOTES FROM THE HISTORICAL RECORD

Sigma Force has its roots buried beneath the Smithsonian Castle, a massive and turreted red sandstone structure built in 1849 at the edge of the National Mall. From that one venerable building, the sprawling complex of museums, research facilities, and laboratories of the Smithsonian Institution was born. But before all that and throughout the Civil War, this single building housed the entirety of the Smithsonian's collections.

But where did this shining testament to science get its true start?

Oddly enough, it wasn't an American who founded the institution, but rather an eccentric British chemist and mineralogist named James Smithson. Upon his death in 1829, he bequeathed a half-million dollars to the United States (about twelve million in today's value, or roughly 1/66th of the federal budget at the time) to found "an establishment for the increase and diffusion of knowledge among men."

Still, to this day, there remains a cloud of mystery surrounding this benefactor. For one, James Smithson never set foot on American soil, yet he left his fortune and a substantial mineral collection to this new nation. Furthermore, during his life, Smithson never spoke of his intention to bequeath such a largesse upon the United States, and oddly after his death, his nephew buried him in Genoa, Italy, rather than in England. One of the reasons little is known about the man today is that near the end of the Civil War, in 1865, a devastating fire broke out at the Castle. While the lower levels were spared (only sustaining water damage), the upper levels were torched. Most of Smithson's handwritten papers—including his diaries and research journals—were destroyed. In that one fiery act, the man's lifelong work was forever lost to history.

But the intrigue surrounding Smithson didn't end with his death. In the winter of 1903, the famous American inventor Alexander Graham Bell traveled to Italy against the expressed wishes of the Smithsonian Board of Regents and broke into Smithson's grave in Genoa. He collected the man's bones into a zinc coffin and fled back to the United States aboard a steamship. Upon his return, Bell interred Smithson's remains at the Castle, where they remain today.

So why did the inventor of the telephone defy the wishes of his fellow Smithsonian board members to secure Smithson's body in such a harried manner? Was it merely, as claimed by most, that Smithson's grave was being threatened by the expansion of a neighboring Italian quarry? Or was there something more going on concerning the eccentric James Smithson—first, his out-of-the-blue donation, then the mysterious fire that destroyed his heritage, and finally the strange journey by Alexander Graham Bell to secure his bones?

For the shocking truth about a dark American secret, keep reading . . .

NOTES FROM THE SCIENTIFIC RECORD

Palaeovespa florissantia, a paper wasp that lived 34 million years ago. Image credit: National Park Service

What's the deadliest animal on the planet? Let's take score. Sharks kill about six people a year, while lions account for roughly twenty-two deaths. Surprisingly, attacks from elephants cause five hundred fatalities each year. Snakebites double that number with a thousand deaths annually. We humans, of course, outdo that considerably by slaughtering four hundred thousand of one another every year. But the true assassin of the animal world is much smaller and far deadlier. Namely, the lowly mosquito. As vectors for a slew of diseases—malaria, yellow fever, West Nile, and now Zika—these flying bloodsuckers alone account for more than a *million* deaths each year. In fact, mosquito bites are the leading cause of mortality in children under five.

Still, other tiny beasts also vie with the mosquito

for this deadly crown. Tsetse flies cause ten thousand deaths each year. The aptly named assassin bug (*Reduviidae*) does a bit better with twelve thousand. Ultimately, some insect will kill one person out of sixty every year.

Why is this important? It serves as a cautionary reminder that we are *not* living in the Age of Man, but rather—as has been true for more than 400 million years—in the Age of Insects. While humans have been on this planet for a paltry 300,000 years, insects existed eons before the dinosaurs, multiplying and spreading, filling every environmental niche. In fact, it is now hypothesized that insects contributed—if not led—to the extinction of the dinosaurs. How? From analysis of recent fossil records, it has been discovered that these tiny predators attacked those lumbering saurians while they were compromised and weakened by the climatic changes at the end of the Cretaceous Period, contributing significantly to their demise through predation, disease transmission, and sickness. At that opportune moment in prehistory, insects took advantage to finally rid the planet of their main competitor for all those new plants and flowers—and in one fell swoop, ended the Age of Dinosaurs.

Which, of course, begs the question concerning the insect's latest competitor for the earth's dwindling natural resources: *Could we be their next target?*

I cannot persuade myself that a beneficent and omnipotent God would have designedly created the *Ichneumonidae* [parasitic wasps] with the express intention of their feeding within the living bodies of caterpillars. . . .

—CHARLES DARWIN,
in a letter written May 22, 1860,
to botanist Asa Gray

They're seriously misunderstood creatures.

—J. K. ROWLING,
Harry Potter and the Goblet of Fire

Prologue

11:07 A.M. CET
December 31, 1903
Genoa, Italy

With time weighing heavily upon its passengers, the carriage climbed recklessly up from the snow-swept city of Genoa. It jolted hard around a sharp twist in the narrow street.

Seated in the back, Alexander Graham Bell groaned. He was still recuperating from a fever following the transatlantic voyage with his wife. To make matters worse, upon arriving in Italy two weeks ago, nothing had gone smoothly. At every turn, Italian authorities thwarted his plans to secure the remains of James Smithson, the man who had founded the Smithsonian Institution. To facilitate this bit of grave robbing, he had been forced to act as both spy and ambassador, doling out bribes and deceit in equal measure. It was a game for a much younger fellow, not a man in his midfifties. The stress had taken its toll.

His wife clutched his wrist. "Alec, perhaps we should ask the driver to slow down."

He patted her hand. "No, Mabel, the weather is

turning. And the French are breathing hotly down our necks. It's now or never."

Three days ago, just as he had secured all the proper permits, some distant French relatives of Smithson had wormed out of the woodwork to stake a claim on his body, little knowing what truly was at stake. Before this French roadblock could become entrenched, he had argued with Italian authorities that since Smithson had left the *entirety* of his estate to the United States, such an endowment must surely encompass his very body. He solidified his position with fistfuls of lire plied into the right hands, while at the same time categorically declaring—falsely—that President Theodore Roosevelt supported his mission.

Though he had prevailed in this subterfuge, he could not count on it lasting much longer.

It's indeed now or never.

He placed a palm over his breast pocket, where a fragment of paper was folded, its edges still charred.

Mabel noted his hand. "Do you believe it could still be there? In his grave, buried with his body?"

"We have to be sure. Someone came close to destroying this secret half a century ago. We can't let the Italians finish the job."

In 1829, James Smithson was buried by his nephew in a small cemetery atop a seaside promontory in Genoa. At the time, the graveyard was owned by the British, but the Italians had retained a claim to the ground beneath it. Over the past few years, a neighboring quarry had been slowly eating its way through this hill, and now the company wanted to take it all down, including the cemetery.

Upon learning of the threat to the bones of the founder of the Smithsonian, the museum's board of regents had debated whether to rescue those remains before they were blasted into the sea. It was during that time that an old letter came into Alexander's possession. It was written by the Smithsonian Institution's first secretary, Joseph Henry, the man who oversaw the building of the Castle and who would eventually die within its walls.

"Henry was no fool," he mumbled to himself, stroking his thick beard.

"I know how much you admired him," Mabel consoled. "And valued his friendship."

He nodded.

Enough to follow his instructions to this gravesite in Italy.

In the letter written the year before his death, Henry told a tale that traced back to the Civil War, when the tides were turning against the South. Henry had come upon a strange notation in one of Smithson's old diaries. He only stumbled upon it because he had been seeking additional documentation concerning Smithson's endowment, trying to discern *why* the man was so generous to a country he had never even visited. During that inquiry, he came across a single exception to the estate, something *not* bequeathed to the United States. While the man's entire mineral collection—his lifetime work—was preserved at the Castle, one artifact was held back. It was an object that Smithson ordered his nephew to bury with his body upon his death.

The oddity drew Henry's interest, enough for him to diligently search the man's journals and diaries. He eventually found one reference to it, to something Smithson called *The Demon Crown*. Smithson expressed regret at unearthing it during a trip to a salt mine near the Baltic Sea. He claimed it could free something horrific.

"*'The very hordes of Hell upon this World . . .'*" Alexander whispered, quoting from a page of Smithson's diary.

"Do you truly believe that's possible?" Mabel asked.

"Somebody believed it enough during the Civil War to try to burn the Smithsonian to the ground."

Or so Henry had thought.

Upon discovering Smithson's secret, Henry had discussed it with some fellow board members, even wondering aloud if this artifact might be used as some form of weapon. Then three days later, the mysterious fire broke out at the Castle, which seemed to specifically target Smithson's heritage, both his papers and his mineral collection.

From the timing of this act, Henry suspected someone at the Smithsonian had betrayed his fears to the Confederacy. Luckily, Henry had kept Smithson's journal that referenced the artifact in his own office, so it had been spared the worst of the flames, though the cover was charred and sections lost. Still, Henry decided it best to keep this recovery under wraps, informing only a trusted circle of allies. The group formed a covert cabal within the museum, and over the passing years, they were entrusted with the Smithsonian's darkest secrets, information often kept even from the president.

One example of that was the mysterious symbol discovered tattooed upon the wrist of a scoundrel whom Henry finally connected to the fire. The man died before he could be questioned, slicing his own throat with a dagger. Henry had sketched a copy of that symbol in his letter, serving as a warning for future generations.

It looked like a variant of the masonic symbol, but no one knew what group this particular incarnation represented. Decades later, when Smithson's grave was threatened, Henry's group approached Alexander and showed him Henry's letter. They recruited him to their cause, knowing it would take someone of his prominence and notoriety to pull off this bit of skullduggery on Italian soil.

Though Alexander was not sure what he would find—if anything—in Smithson's grave, he had agreed to undertake this task, even using his own money to finance the mission. No matter the outcome, he couldn't refuse.

I owe it to Henry.

The carriage bumped around the last turn and

reached the summit of the promontory. The vantage offered a wide view across Genoa to its harbor, which was crowded with coal-laden winter barges, so many that it looked as if you could cross the bay by hopping from one to the other. Closer at hand, the small cemetery beckoned, surrounded by white walls crowned with shards of broken glass.

"Are we too late?" Mabel asked.

He understood her concern. A corner of the cemetery was already gone, tumbled away into the neighboring marble quarry. As Alexander climbed out of the carriage into the bitter wind, he spotted what could only be a pair of coffins shattered below. He shivered, but it was not from the cold.

"Let us be quick," he warned.

He led his wife through the cemetery gate. Ahead, he spotted a clutch of men huddled in thick coats. The party consisted of a few government lackeys and a trio of laborers. They gathered near a prominent sarcophagus cordoned off by a spiked iron fence. Alexander hurried over, bending against the wind, one arm around his wife.

He nodded to the American consul in attendance, William Bishop.

Bishop stepped closer and tapped his watch. "I heard a French lawyer is on a train from Paris. We should be prompt here."

"Agreed. The sooner we're aboard the *Princess Irene* with the bones of our esteemed colleague and headed back to America, all the better."

As snow began to fall, Alexander stepped toward the gravesite. A gray marble pedestal bore a simple inscription.

Sacred
to the
Memory
of
James Smithson, ESQ
Fellow of the Royal Society
London
who died at Genoa
the 26th June 1829.
aged 75 Years.

Bishop crossed to one of the Italian representatives and spoke briefly. In short order, two of the laborers set about using crowbars. They cracked the seal on the tomb's marble lid and lifted it free. Nearby, the remaining worker readied a casket made of zinc. Once Smithson's bones were transferred into it, the box would be soldered shut for its transatlantic voyage.

As the men worked, Alexander stared again at the inscription, his frown deepening. "That's odd."

"What is?" Mabel asked.

"It states here that Smithson was seventy-five years old when he died."

"So?"

He shook his head. "Smithson was born June fifth, 1765. By my calculation, that means he was only sixty-four when he died. That inscription is wrong by eleven years."

"Is that significant?"

He shrugged. "I have no idea, but I imagine his nephew would have known his uncle's true age, especially as he was setting it into stone here."

Bishop waved Alexander closer to the tomb as the sarcophagus's lid was finally carried off. "Perhaps you should do the honor."

While he appreciated the gesture, he considered balking, but he had already come too far to turn back now.

In for a penny, in for a pound.

He joined Bishop before the open tomb and peered inside. The wooden casket inside had long rotted away, leaving a blanket of heavy dust over what was clearly a set of bones. He reached reverently inside, parted the debris, and lifted the skull, which was surprisingly intact. He almost expected it to crumble as he gripped it.

Stepping back, he stared into the eye sockets of the Smithsonian's founder.

As stated on the inscription, Smithson was an esteemed fellow of the British Royal Society, one of the world's most distinguished scientific groups. In fact, the man was tapped to join this society the same year he graduated from college. Even at such a young age, his scientific talent had been well regarded. Afterward, as a chemist and a mineralogist, he spent much of his life traveling throughout Europe collecting mineral and ore samples.

Yet, so much remained unknown about the man.

Like why he left his fortune and collection to the United States?

Still, one fact was indisputable.

"We owe you so much," Alexander murmured to the skull. "It was your generosity of spirit that changed forever our young country. It was your legacy that taught America's greatest minds to set aside petty ambitions and work together for the collective good."

"Well spoken," Bishop said, holding out his gloved palms. The weather was growing harsher by the minute, and the consul clearly wanted this matter finished.

Alexander didn't argue. He handed over the skull so it could be transferred to the zinc casket and returned his attention to the tomb. He had already noted a rectangular shape in one corner.

Reaching in again, he waved away the dust to reveal a small metal chest.

Could this be the source of such consternation?

It took all his strength to lift the box out of the tomb. It was dreadfully heavy. He hauled it aside and balanced it atop a nearby gravestone. Bishop ordered the workers to finish transferring the bones, then returned to his side, as did Mabel.

"It that it?" his wife asked.

Alexander turned to Bishop. "Let me remind you again. There is to be no official or unofficial mention of this object. Is that understood?"

Bishop nodded and glanced to the rest of the party, who were busy at work. "You've paid well for their silence."

Satisfied, Alexander unlatched and opened the lid of the chest. Inside, a bed of sand cradled something the size and color of a pumpkin. He stared at it breathlessly for a moment.

"What is it?" Mabel asked.

"It . . . it appears to be a chunk of amber."

"Amber?" Bishop's voice held a note of avarice. "Is it valuable?"

"Somewhat. Though nothing exceptional. It's basically fossilized tree sap." Frowning, he leaned closer. "Bishop, would you ask that worker if we could borrow his lantern?"

"Why—?"

"Just do it, man. We don't have all day."

Bishop rushed over.

Mabel stood at his shoulder. "What do you think, Alec?"

"I can make something out. Through the amber. But just barely."

Bishop returned, lantern in hand.

Alexander took it, twisted the flame brighter, and brought it close to the translucent chunk of amber. It glowed a rich honey, revealing what it hid at its heart.

Mabel gasped. "Are those bones?"

"I believe so."

It seemed Smithson's tomb held more than just his own moldering remains.

"But what are they?" Bishop asked.

"No idea. But surely something prehistoric."

He leaned closer, squinting. At the heart of the amber rested a small, fist-size triangular skull bearing a prominent row of sharp teeth. It looked distinctly reptilian, maybe those of a small dinosaur. A halo of smaller bones floated within the glowing stone. He pictured ancient tree sap flowing over this creature's old grave, stirring up its bones and forever trapping them in this position.

The tinier bones had come to form a ghastly halo above the skull.

Like a crown.

He glanced to Mabel, who took a deep breath as she recognized the pattern. She knew, too, that this must be what Smithson wrote about—what he aptly named the Demon Crown.

"Impossible," his wife whispered.

He nodded. In his pocket, he held a burned page from Smithson's diary, upon which the man had scribbled a remarkable claim about this artifact.

It had to be *impossible*, as his wife said.

He pictured Smithson's words, what the dead man had written concerning this artifact.

Be warned, what the Demon Crown holds is very much alive . . .

Alexander felt an icy trickle of terror.

. . . and ready to unleash the very hordes of Hell upon this world.

"Careful of the rats," James Reardon warned at the entrance door to the tunnel. "Some real bruisers down here in the dark. One bit off the end of a worker's thumb last month."

Archibald MacLeish suppressed a shudder of disgust as he hung his jacket on a hook next to the door. He wasn't exactly outfitted for an excursion underground, but he had been late getting here, as an evening meeting at the Library of Congress had run long.

He stared down the five steps that led to the old subterranean tunnel connecting the Smithsonian Castle to its neighbor across the mall. The newer museum, the Natural History building, was completed in 1910, when ten million objects had been ferried by horse-drawn cart from the Castle to their present home. For a decade afterward, the two buildings had shared utilities via this seven-hundred-foot-long tunnel, but with later modernizations, the passageway was eventually closed off and seldom tread, except by the occasional maintenance crew.

And apparently some overgrown vermin.

Nevertheless, Archibald had believed there might

be a new use for this abandoned tunnel. As the current Librarian of Congress and head of the Committee for the Conservation of Cultural Resources, he had been tasked to secure the nation's treasures at the start of World War II. Fearing bombing raids like those that had beset London during the Blitz, he had personally overseen the shipment of priceless documents—the Declaration of Independence, the Constitution, even a copy of the Gutenberg Bible—to the safety of Fort Knox. Likewise, the National Gallery of Art had transferred their most prized masterpieces to the Biltmore House in North Carolina, while the Smithsonian had buried the Star-Spangled Banner deep in Shenandoah National Park.

Still, Archibald had hated the piecemeal approach to these important efforts. Indeed, back in 1940, he had advocated for building a bombproof shelter beneath the National Mall as a more permanent solution. Unfortunately, Congress had shot down his idea due to the expense.

Despite this setback, Archibald had never given up on his idea—which was why he found himself in the basement levels of the Smithsonian Castle, where temporary bomb shelters had been secured for museum personnel. Three weeks ago, Archibald had hired a pair of engineers to conduct a feasibility study, to explore if such a vault could be constructed in secret, branching off this very tunnel. Then two days ago, during their surveys, the pair had discovered a side door in the tunnel, halfway across the Mall. It was hidden behind some pipes and bricked over.

Archibald had immediately informed James Reardon, the current undersecretary of the Smithsonian. As a longtime friend, James had supported Archibald's efforts for the construction of a bombproof vault. The pair hoped that this discovery might stoke a renewed interest in the shelter, especially considering *who* had apparently hidden this room. His name was found inscribed on a plaque affixed to the steel door after its layer of bricks had been removed.

Alexander Graham Bell.

The notice came with a warning.

What lies beyond this door is both a wonder and a danger like no other. It could alter the course of mankind forever, or in the wrong hands, it could equally doom us all. We the undersigned deem this artifact too treacherous to come to light, but we dare not destroy it — for at its heart lies the possible key to life beyond death.

It was a remarkable claim, but the message was supported by the signatures of five regents of the Smithsonian board. James had verified the names. They were all deceased now, and no other record could be found concerning the circumstances that led Bell and these five to secure something beneath the National Mall, not to mention keeping such an effort from the other regents at the time.

Respecting that level of secrecy, Archibald had limited the knowledge of the door's discovery to only his friend James. The two engineers had been sworn to secrecy and now waited below, ready to break the lock and see for themselves what required such subterfuge almost four decades ago.

"We should hurry," James said, checking his pocket watch.

Archibald understood. They were already running an hour behind schedule due to his tardiness in getting here. "Lead the way."

James ducked through the door and down the steps. He moved spryly, while it took Archibald more time to maneuver the steep, narrow stairway. Then again, James was fifteen years younger and spent more time on his feet doing fieldwork as a geologist. Archibald was a fifty-four-year-old poet who had been coerced by FDR into taking a desk job—or as Archibald had described this assignment at the time, *the president decided I wanted to be Librarian of Congress.*

He entered the dank tunnel. The way ahead was lit by a string of caged electrical bulbs running along the low roof. Several were broken or missing, leaving long gaps of darkness.

James clicked on a thick flashlight and set off down the tunnel.

Archibald followed. Though the passageway was tall enough for him to walk upright, he kept his back hunched and his head low, well away from the run of dark pipes along the ceiling. Especially upon hearing the occasional sound of nails scratching and bodies scurrying up there.

After a few minutes, James suddenly stopped.

Archibald almost bumped into him. "What's wr—?"

A series of sharp *cracks* echoed from the passageway ahead.

James glanced back, his eyebrows bunched together with concern. "Gunfire." He doused his flashlight and freed a Smith & Wesson pistol from a holster under his work jacket. Archibald hadn't known the man was armed, but considering the size of the vermin down here, the presence of the weapon made sense.

"Go back." James passed him his flashlight, then cupped both hands around the grip of his weapon. "Get help."

"From where? The Castle's deserted at this hour. By the time I raise an alarm, it'll be too late." Archibald lofted the long-handled flashlight like a club. "We go together."

A muffled explosion decided the matter.

James grimaced and headed forward, keeping close to one wall and staying in the shadows as much as possible. Archibald followed his example.

Within a few steps, a cloud of dust rolled over them, blown forth by the blast. Archibald fought against coughing, but the air quickly cleared. The same couldn't be said for the passageway. A smattering of dark forms sped across the floor and along the pipes.

Rats . . . hundreds of them.

Archibald had to stifle back a scream as he flattened along one wall. Something dropped from overhead, landed on his shoulder, and bounded away with a sharp squeak. Other bodies pattered over his shoes. A few scrabbled up his pant legs as if he were a tree in a flood-swept river.

Ahead, James seemed unfazed and continued on, oblivious to the squirming bodies underfoot.

Gritting his teeth, Archibald waited until the worst of the horde fled past him, then hurried to catch up.

As the two reached a dark stretch of broken bulbs, a glow appeared ahead, marking a pair of lanterns resting on the floor. The pool of light revealed a body.

One of the engineers.

Other shadowy shapes stepped into view, appearing from the left.

Three masked men.

James dropped to a knee and immediately fired. The loud blast made Archibald jump, deafening him in turn.

One of the intruders spun and struck the wall.

James gained his feet and fired again, running forward. Archibald froze a breath, then gave chase, too. In the tumult that followed, lit by the camera-bulb flashes of gunfire, he watched one of the masked men try to haul his wounded companion to his feet, but James refused to relent, squeezing his trigger over and over again as he ran. Rounds sparked off the nearby pipes and concrete walls.

The third intruder fled down the tunnel with a heavy satchel in one hand, blindly returning fire over his shoulder. The shots went wild as the man was plainly more intent on escaping. His companion finally followed, forced by James's barrage to abandon the slumped form on the ground.

As James and Archibald closed the distance, another explosion knocked them both back. Flames blasted out an open doorway to the left and washed into the tunnel.

Archibald shielded his face with an arm.

As the fire guttered out, James led the way again. Archibald quickly took in the damage as they

reached the doorway. The engineer who lay crumpled at the threshold had been shot in the back
of the head. The other was dead in the neighboring room, his clothes on fire from the blast. More
flames raged at the rear of the small concrete chamber, turning it into a furnace, fueled by a burning bookshelf and the tomes that once rested there.
Fiery pages still floated in the air, drifting through
the smoke-choked air.

Nearby, James checked the assailant slumped
on the ground. He swatted at the man's burning
clothes, then set about searching his body.

Archibald kept his full attention on the neighboring room. A waist-high marble plinth stood in
the center. A small metal chest lay toppled and open
at its foot, likely blown off its pedestal by the blast.
The box appeared to be empty, except for a pile of
sand that had spilled out as it struck the floor.

He pictured the heavy satchel in the hands of the
fleeing thief. With a sinking heart, he knew that
whatever Bell and his cohorts had hidden here was
gone. Still, he lifted his arm over his mouth and
nose and ducked into that wall of heat, drawn by
something he spotted poking out of the sand.

He stepped around the dead engineer to reach
the chest. Dropping to a crouch, he grabbed what
was exposed and pulled it free. It appeared to be
the remains of an old field notebook or journal. Its
leather cover had been blackened by a fire far older
than what raged here now. A quick flip revealed
most of the pages were charred or missing—but
not all.

He imagined the thieves must have failed to spot

the remains of this old journal hidden in the sand at the bottom of the chest. Sensing some significance to this discovery, he retreated with his prize.

"Look at this," James said as he returned to the tunnel.

James sat back on his heels. He had peeled away the thief's woolen face mask.

Archibald took in the sight, shocked by what was revealed. "My god . . . it's a woman."

But that wasn't the only surprise. The thief had black hair and wide cheekbones, and from the pinched squint to her dead eyes, there was little doubt to the figure's heritage.

"She's Japanese," Archibald mumbled.

James nodded. "Likely a Jap spy. But this is what I wanted you to see." He lifted her lifeless arm to reveal something tattooed on the thief's inner wrist. "What do you make of this?"

Archibald leaned closer, frowning as he studied the mark.

"Any idea what this might mean?" James asked.

Archibald glanced back to the burning room. Its door lay crookedly to one side, blown off its hinges. The inscribed metal plaque glowed in the firelight, as if emphasizing the warning about what was once hidden here.

. . . *a danger like no other.*

"No," Archibald said, "but for the sake of our nation—and maybe the world—we need to find out."

FIRST

COLONIZATION

1

The dead man lay sprawled facedown, half in the sand, half in the grass.

"Poor bastard almost made it back to his boat," Professor Ken Matsui noted.

He stepped aside to allow the team's doctor—a young woman named Ana Luiz Chavos—to examine the body. Anyone officially setting foot on Ilha da Queimada Grande, an island some twenty miles off the coast of Brazil, was required to be accompanied by a medical doctor, along with a representative from the Brazilian navy.

Their military escort, First Lieutenant Ramon Dias, checked the small motorized skiff that was camouflaged and hidden among some rocks a few yards away. He snorted derisively and spat into the waves. "*Caçador furtivo . . . idiota.*"

"He says the man must've been a poacher," Ken explained to his postgraduate student. The two of them had traveled together from Cornell University to this remote Brazilian island.

Oscar Hoff was twenty-seven, shaven headed,

with a sleeve of tattoos down his left arm. His exterior gave him a hardened, street-tough look, but it was all show for that occasional young coed who mistook the book for the cover. From his presently sallow complexion and the sickened twist to his lips, it was clear this was the first body the student had stumbled across. Of course, the state of the deceased likely didn't help matters. The body had been picked and scavenged by birds and crabs. A black stain soaked the sand in a wide pool around the body.

Dr. Chavos seemed little bothered by the condition of the deceased. She examined one bare arm, then the other, then sat back on her heels. She spoke matter-of-factly in Portuguese to Dias, then to the waves as she stared toward the sun hanging low in the sky. Sunset was only a couple of hours off.

"Dead for at least three days," Ana Luiz assessed aloud and pointed to the man's left arm. From the elbow to his wrist, most of the flesh was blackened and necrotic. A flash of white bone shone through the melted tissues. "Snakebite."

"*Bothrops insularis*," Ken surmised as he glanced up the neighboring rocks and toward the rain forest that crowned the heights of this hundred-acre island. "The golden lancehead pit viper."

"It is why we call this place Snake Island," Diaz said. "This is *their* island. And you'd do wise to respect that."

It was the pit vipers' dominance on the island—and their endangered status—that restricted access to Queimada Grande to the Brazilian navy. They came once every two months to service the lone lighthouse here. Even that beacon was automated after the first family of lighthouse keepers—a wife, husband, and three children—were all killed one night when snakes slipped inside through an open window. The family tried to flee but were bitten by more vipers hanging from branches along the forested path to the beach.

Since then, tourists were forbidden from setting foot here. Only the occasional scientific team was allowed to visit, but even they had to be accompanied by a doctor armed with antivenom and a military escort.

Like today.

With the substantial backing of his Japanese financiers, Ken was able to wrangle this last-minute trip, tucking it in before a storm that was due to strike the region tomorrow. He and his student had to rush from their hotel in the small coastal village of Itanhaém in order to take advantage of this opportunity. They barely made the boat in time.

Ana Luiz stood up. "We should collect and secure your two specimens and head back to the mainland before we lose the light." Their Zodiac pontoon boat was beached in a neighboring sandy cove. "You don't want to be here after dark."

"We'll be quick," Ken promised. "It shouldn't take long considering the sheer number of lanceheads roaming this island."

He slipped out a long-poled hook and turned to Oscar, giving the student some final instructions. "There's about one snake for every square yard of this island. So stay back, and let me take the lead. And keep in mind that at any time you're only a step or two away from death hiding in a rock or lounging in a tree."

Oscar glanced to the body on the beach. That was likely reminder enough to be extra cautious. "Why . . . why would someone risk coming here alone?"

Ana Luiz answered, "A single lancehead fetches upwards of twenty thousand dollars on the black market. Sometimes more."

"Wildlife smuggling is big business," Ken explained. "I've run across a few such biopirates in different corners of the world."

And this body is certainly not the first I've seen as a consequence of such greed.

Though only a decade older than his postgraduate student, Ken had spent most of his time in the field, traveling to various corners of the world. He had dual PhDs in entomology and toxicology, blending the two degrees into the field of *venomics*, the study of compounds found in poisonous animals.

The combination of disciplines was especially fitting considering his own mixed background. His father was first-generation Japanese and had spent time as a child in an internment camp in California, while Ken's German mother had emigrated as a young girl after the war. A common joke while growing up was that their family had created its own mini-Axis stronghold in the middle of suburbia.

Then, two years ago, the pair had passed away, dying within a month of one another, leaving behind their blended heritage in Ken's pale complexion, dense dark hair, and slight squint to his eyes.

Likewise, his mixed-race background—what the

Japanese called *hafu*—had undoubtedly helped him acquire his current grant. The research trip to Queimada Grande was partially funded by Tanaka Pharmaceuticals, out of Japan. The goal was to discover the next wonder drug hidden in the cocktail of toxins found in the venom of this island's inhabitants.

"Let's get going," Ken said.

Oscar swallowed hard and nodded. He fumbled with an extendable set of snake tongs. While such a tool could securely grab a serpent, Ken preferred a simple hook. It caused less stress to an animal. If the tongs were used too aggressively, a snake could react to the threat and lash out.

As the group set off from the beach, they stepped carefully with their calf-high leather boots. Sand quickly turned into a rocky stretch, studded with low bushes. Fifty yards upslope, a dark fringe of rain forest beckoned.

Let's hope we don't have to go in there to find our specimens.

"Search under the bushes." Ken demonstrated by reaching out with the hooked tip of his pole and lifting the lowermost branches. "But don't try to secure them there. Let them slither into the open before attempting to grab them."

Oscar's tongs shook as he tried to follow Ken's example on a nearby bush.

"Take a deep breath," Ken encouraged. "You know how to do this. Just like we practiced at the zoo back home."

Oscar grimaced and probed his first bush. "All . . . all clear."

"Good. Just one step at a time."

They continued with Ken in the lead. He attempted to ease his student's tension by keeping his voice light. "It was once believed that the lanceheads were brought to the island by pirates looking to protect their buried treasure."

Ana Luiz chuckled, while Dias merely scowled at the thought.

"So not pirates, I guess," Oscar said.

"No. This particular set of vipers got stranded on this island some eleven thousand years ago, when sea levels rose and flooded the land bridge that once connected the island to the coast. Isolated, they had no true predators and reproduced rapidly. But the only food source was up in the trees."

"Birds."

"The island is on a major migratory path, so the snake's bounty is refilled every year. But unlike land-bound prey, birds proved to be trickier. Even after climbing trees, the snakes couldn't exactly run down a bird that took flight after being bitten. So they evolved a more toxic venom, five times stronger than their cousins on the mainland."

"In order to kill the birds more quickly."

"Exactly. Lancehead venom is truly unique, bearing a cornucopia of toxins. Poisons that not only melt flesh but also cause kidney collapse, heart failure, brain hemorrhages, and intestinal bleeding. In fact, it's those very hemotoxic components in their venom that show high promise for developing drugs to combat heart disease."

"And that's why we're here," Oscar said. "Hoping to find the next captopril."

Ken smiled. "At least, that's what the fine folks at Tanaka Pharmaceuticals are counting on."

In fact, it was not a foolhardy gamble on their part. Captopril—Bristol-Myers Squibb's bestselling hypertension drug—was isolated from a close cousin to the golden lancehead: *Bothrops jararaca*, another Brazilian pit viper.

"And who knows what else we might discover buried amid all the poison found here?" Ken added. "Prialt is a powerful pain reliever that just came on the market from Elan Pharmaceuticals. It was derived from a toxin found in poisonous cone snails. Then there's a protein discovered in the venom of Gila monsters that is being investigated as a miracle drug for Alzheimer's. More and more, companies around the globe are investing significant resources into venom-based drug discovery programs."

"Sounds like it's a good time to be a toxicologist specializing in poisonous animals." Oscar grinned over at him. "Maybe we should go into business ourselves. Venoms 'R' Us."

Ken playfully poked at his student with his snake hook. "Concentrate on catching your *first* specimen, then we'll talk about a partnership."

Still smiling, Oscar moved over to another thorn-encrusted bush. He bent down and eased its lower branches. Something shot out from under the fringes and skated across the rocks. Oscar yelped and stumbled back. He bumped into Ana Luiz and knocked them both to the ground.

The two-foot-long snake aimed straight for their warm bodies.

Ken jabbed out and scooped the serpent by its

midsection. He lifted it high, careful not to over-compensate and send it flying. The snake's body went immediately slack within the loop, its tiny head swiveling, tongue lashing.

Oscar tried to crawl back farther.

"Don't worry. It's just another of Queimada Grande's inhabitants. *Dipsis indica.* Also known as Sauvage's Snail Eater." He shifted the snake away. "Totally harmless."

"I . . . I thought it was trying to attack me," Oscar said, his face flushing with embarrassment.

"Normally this little Snail Eater is docile. Admittedly it's strange it came after you." Ken glanced along its intended trajectory. "Unless it was merely trying to get to the beach."

Like the poacher . . .

Frowning at this thought, he glanced in the opposite direction, toward a ridge of rock ahead and the forest beyond. He returned the snake to the rock and let it dash away, continuing its flight toward the sand.

"C'mon," Ken urged and climbed up the slope.

Beyond the top of the ridge, a sand-strewn bowl opened. Shocked, Ken stopped at the edge, surveying the impossible sight before him.

A tangle of yellow-golden bodies covered most of the rocks and open stretches of sand. There were hundreds of them. All golden lanceheads, the island's kings.

"My god . . ." Oscar gasped, visibly shuddering.

Ana Luiz crossed herself, while Dias lifted his shotgun and pointed it down into the sandy hollow. It was an unnecessary precaution.

"It looks like they're all dead," Ken said.

But what killed them?

None of the meter-long golden lengths appeared to be moving. And it was not just the vipers. Another body lay at the bottom, facedown and motionless.

Dias spoke to Ana Luiz in Portuguese. She nodded. Ken understood enough of the Brazilian language to surmise that this must be the partner to the poacher on the beach. Or at least the two men were similarly dressed.

Still, despite the lack of immediate danger, everyone remained rooted by the sheer horror of the sight.

Oscar was the first to speak. "Is that guy still breathing?"

Ken squinted. *Surely not.* But his student's eyes proved to be sharper than anyone else's. The man's chest indeed rose and fell, though shallowly, haltingly.

Ana Luiz swore under her breath and started down into the bowl, already freeing her medical pack from her shoulder.

"Wait," Ken urged. "Let me go first. Some of the lanceheads might still be half-alive. And even dead snakes can bite."

Ana Luiz glanced back at him, her brow crinkling in disbelief.

"There are countless stories of people decapitating a rattlesnake or cobra, only to get bitten when they picked up its head. Even hours later. Many ectothermic—cold-blooded animals—share these same postmortem reflexes."

He shifted ahead of her, lifting and moving each snake's body out of their path with his hook. He worked slowly down the slope. All of the lance-heads appeared to be truly dead. They showed no response to his passage or presence, which was significant considering the aggressive nature of the species.

As he continued down, a strange stench grew around him. There was the expected reek of meat left too long in the sun, but it was undercut by a sickly sweetness, like a flower growing in rot.

For some reason, the scent immediately set his heart to pounding harder, as if triggering some innate sense of danger.

With his senses heightened, he finally noted that the neighboring rain forest was disturbingly quiet. No birdsong, no chirp of insects, only the rustle of leaves. He stopped and lifted an arm.

"What is it?" Ana Luiz asked.

"Get back."

"But . . ."

He retreated a step, then another, herding her behind him. He focused on the body on the ground. He now had a good angle on the man's face. His eyes were gone. Black blood thickly caked his nose, clotted over his nostrils.

This was a corpse.

Still, the torso moved—but it was clearly not driven by any last breaths.

Something's inside him, something alive.

He hurried faster. Still, he feared taking his eyes off the body. Behind him, he heard Ana Luiz reach the others atop the ridge. From the rain forest before him, a new noise intruded. A low hum wafted out from the shadows, setting his hairs on end. It was accompanied by a strange hollow knocking. He wanted to blame it on branches bumping one another, but there was no wind.

Instead, he pictured bones rattling.

He swung away and bounded the last few yards up the slope.

As he neared the top, he gasped breathlessly. "We have to get off this isl—"

An explosion cut him off. A fireball rolled into the sky to his right, rising from the cove where their Zodiac was beached. A small black helicopter sped through the trail of smoke. Gunfire chattered from its undercarriage. Rounds sparked across the rocks, ripping through the sand.

Oscar fell first, his throat gone in a bloody ruin.

Diaz attempted to return fire, but his body went flying backward.

Ana Luiz turned to run, only to get struck in the back.

Ken flung himself back into the bowl. He was a moment too slow. His shoulder erupted with fire. The impact sent him spinning through the air. As he struck the ground, he rolled down the slope, tangling himself with the cold bodies of the dead lanceheads.

Once he came to a stop, he remained where he was, half-buried in snakes, keeping still. He heard the attack helicopter rush overhead, then come sweeping back in a low arc.

He held his breath.

Finally, it retreated to the beach, likely double-checking that the Zodiac was destroyed. He listened as the thumping of its rotors faded farther away.

Was it leaving?

Ken feared to move, even as the nagging hum rose again from the rain forest, louder now. He shifted his chin enough to view the nearest fringe of trees. A mist—darker than the shadows—sifted through the branches, rising through the canopy. That weird clacking grew louder, more furious.

Something's coming . . .

Then the world became fire.

Great blasts rose from the forest, casting up spiraling gouts of fire. The cannonade of explosions spread in succession across the forested highlands of the island. Fiery pieces of shattered tree trunks and branches rained down around him. Black smoke rolled across the rock, choking and bitter, consuming the remainder of the island.

Ken crawled, coughing and gagging.

He tasted a bitter chemical tang on the back of his tongue.

Napalm . . . or maybe some other fiery defoliant.

Lungs burning, he crabbed out of the bowl and rolled down toward the beach. He aimed for the water, for the small skiff camouflaged among the rocks by the poachers. He prayed the smoke hid his escape. Though half-blind, he felt his hands reach cool water. He slid into the sea and worked his way toward the lone boat.

Behind him, fire continued to spread and consume the island, slowly burning it to the bedrock.

He reached the skiff, clambered over the side,

and collapsed on his back. He would wait until sunset before risking the open water. By then the pall of smoke across the waves and the cover of darkness should help hide his flight from any eyes still in the sky.

Or at least, so he hoped.

In the meantime, he used the pain in his shoulder to keep him focused, to stoke a desire that burned with as much heat as the firestorm beyond the boat.

He hugged his thick bag to his chest.

It held one of the dead lanceheads, collected before he fled.

I will know what happened here.

2

The old man knelt in the temple garden. He sat formally, in the traditional *seiza* manner, with his back straight, his legs folded under him on the stone path. He ignored the deep ache in ninety-year-old knees. Behind him, the ancient pagoda of Kan'ei-ji was dusted in the last of the spring's cherry blossoms. The height of the celebrated season had passed three weeks ago, when tourists flocked to Tokyo's parklands to ogle and photograph the beautiful harmony of the peak blossoming.

Takashi Ito preferred these last days of each season. There was a melancholy to the air that echoed the sadness in his own heart. He used a small fan to waft away the dried, brittle petals from the waist-high stone before his knees.

His efforts disturbed the tendrils of smoke rising from a small incense burner at the base of the stone. The fragrance rose from a mix of *kyara*, a type of fragrant agarwood, and *koboku*, an extract from magnolia bark. He fanned the tendrils of smoke toward himself, seeking the blessing and mystery to be found there.

As often in this moment, a snatch of poetry from Otagaki Rengetsu, a nineteenth-century Buddhist nun, sifted through his thoughts.

A single line of
Fragrant smoke
From incense stick
Trails off without a trace:
Where does it go?

His gaze followed a lone black streak of smoke into the air until it vanished, leaving only its sweet fragrance behind.

He sighed.

Like you did so many years ago, my dearest Miu.

He closed his eyes in prayer. Each year, he came here on the anniversary of his marriage, when Miu tied her heart to his in secret. They had been only eighteen at the time, so full of hope for their life together, bound as much by love as purpose. For ten years, the two had trained together, honing skills that would be needed. During that brutal time, they had celebrated their successes and nursed the bruises from punishments inflicted upon them by their hard masters. They were paired because of their complementary talents. He was unyielding stone; she was flowing water. He was thunder and force; she was silence and shadow.

They thought themselves invincible, especially when together.

His lips scowled at such youthful foolishness.

He opened his eyes and inhaled one last breath of smoke rising from the burner. The *kyara* chips had turned to ash by now. *Kyara* was more expensive by weight than pure gold. Even its name in ancient Japanese meant "precious."

Each year, he burned *kyara* in memory of Miu.

But this anniversary was special.

He stared down at the smoldering sticks of *koboku* on the mica plate. They were new to this ritual. The burning of *koboku* was a centuries-old tradition of Samurai warriors, to cleanse mind and body prior to battle. In this manner, he imbued his love of Miu with an old promise.

To avenge her death.

He stared at the stone before him, inscribed in lines of ancient script. It was not his wife's gravestone. Her body was forever lost to him ages ago. Instead, Takashi chose this block of granite to serve as her makeshift headstone, because of the words found here, written in 1821, by her great-grandfather, Sessai Matsuyama.

Her ancestor had placed this marker in these Buddhist gardens to console the spirits of those he had killed. Sessai had been a great benefactor to the sciences and commissioned many volumes and texts, including the *Chuchi-jo*, an anatomical study of insects that was now considered a national treasure for its artistically rendered drawings of butterflies, crickets, grasshoppers, even flies, proving beauty could be found in the smallest creatures. To achieve this great accomplishment, many insects had been caught, pinned, and died for the sake of this science. Out of guilt, Sessai Matsuyama had erected this memorial to their memory, honoring their contribution and perhaps seeking to lighten his karmic burden for their deaths.

Miu had dragged Takashi here many times, her face shining with pride. She had hoped to eventually follow in her great-grandfather's footsteps, inspired by his passion. But even such a simple dream became nothing more than smoke, destroyed in a moment of gunfire.

He slipped the sleeve of his shirt higher to expose his inner wrist. His skin was now paper-thin, unable to hold the ink that had marked him with the same symbol that once graced Miu's soft flesh in the same spot. It represented a set of tools framed around a crescent moon and a black star. It was an honor to bear such a mark, proof that they had survived the training of their masters, the elusive *Kage*. He remembered kissing her wrist after they had been tattooed, his lips seeking to draw the sting of the needle. The act had bound them as thoroughly as their secret marriage.

But now even this connection to Miu was fading.

He dropped his sleeve and stared again as fire consumed the last of the incense, the aromatic trails vanishing into the air.

Where does it go?

He had no answer. All he knew was that Miu was lost to him forever. She had died during their first mission, to steal a treasure from under the noses of their enemy. Shame burned through him as he recalled fleeing from her body through a dark tunnel, forced away by both gunfire and the need to make her sacrifice mean something.

In the end, the mission had been successful. Later, when he eventually learned the true nature of what had been recovered from that cursed tunnel, he took it as an omen. His gaze swept the lines written on the ancient monument. While Miu could never follow in her ancestor's footsteps, Takashi had taken up that mantle for her.

With a small bow, he rose to his feet. His two retainers tried to come to his aid, but he took it as a matter of pride to wave them back and stand on his own. Still, he did accept his cane once he was upright. Bony fingers clutched the rose gold handle, sculpted into the beak and fiery cowl of a phoenix.

It had taken him decades of study and financing, but finally he would exact his revenge and return Japan to its former glory—and to achieve it, he would use the very treasure that had cost Miu her life.

Satisfied, he turned and headed across the garden toward the pagoda, his cane thumping along with his hammering heart. The temple of Kan'ei-ji was founded in the seventeenth century. Its grounds had once encompassed all of neighboring Ueno Park, where the city's zoo and national museums now resided. The temple's downfall began in 1869 when the Japanese emperor attacked the last of the Tokugawa shoguns who had sought to usurp his reign and who had taken refuge within the temple. Bullets from that siege could still be found imbedded in sections of the wooden walls.

Few seldom visited this lonely temple now, its bloody past nearly forgotten.

But I will make this nation humbled by war remember its former glory.

He rounded the pagoda and crossed under the boughs of a large cherry tree. His passage disturbed the last of the clinging blossoms. Petals floated around him, as if Miu were blessing him. He smiled softly and continued to the street to await his limo. Leaning on his cane with one hand, he rubbed the faded tattoo on his wrist with a thumb.

It will not be much longer.

Soon he would join Miu—but not yet, not before he exacted his revenge and elevated Imperial Japan to its rightful place as masters of this world.

While he sat, his mind drifted into the past, as it did more often with each passing year. He and Miu had both been bastard children of aristocratic families. Shunned for sins that were not their own, they had been cast aside by their respective families and ended up within the *Kage*. In Miu's case, she had been sold to them. Takashi had sought them out of bitterness.

At the time, the public knew little about the *Kage*, whose name simply meant "shadow." Rumors and whispers abounded. Some believed they were descendants of a dishonored clan of ninjas; others even considered them ghosts. But eventually Takashi learned the truth, that the cabal's lineage went far back in time. They bore many names, assuming different faces across the globe. Their purpose, though, was to grow stronger, to root deeper into all nations, to use dark alchemies and later science to achieve their ends. They were the shadows behind power.

Here in Japan, as war broke out, the *Kage* briefly came more into the open, discovering opportunity in the chaos. In particular, the *Kage* were drawn to the blood and pain flowing from a series of secret Japanese-run camps, where morality held no sway. The Imperial Army had constructed covert research facilities in northern China—first at Zhongma Fortress, then in Pingfang—specializing in biological and chemical weapons development.

To fuel this project, the army collected subjects from local Chinese villages, along with bringing in captured Russians and Allied POWs. From there, three thousand Japanese scientists set about experimenting on the unwilling subjects. The researchers infected patients with anthrax and bubonic plague, then surgically gutted them without anesthesia. They froze the limbs of patients to study frostbite. They raped and exposed women to syphilis. They tested flamethrowers on men tied to stakes.

At these facilities, the *Kage* worked in the shadows, seemingly to help, but mostly to gain whatever advantage they could from the knowledge gleaned by these ghastly experiments.

It was then that word reached *Kage*'s masters of the discovery of a secret that was believed to have been lost to them forever. They had attempted to secure it nearly a century ago—a potential weapon like no other—but failed. Now they had another chance as word sifted forth from the United States. Near the end of 1944, a small acquisition team, fluent in English, was dispatched to secure it.

The mission proved successful, but it had cost Miu her life.

Unfortunately, afterward, the war came too quickly to an end when two bombs were dropped on Japan, one at Hiroshima, the other at Nagasaki. Takashi always wondered if the motivation for such an extreme action by the Americans could be traced to that theft in a tunnel beneath their capital.

Ultimately it didn't matter.

After the war, Takashi secured what was stolen: a boulder of amber. The secret it preserved remained too dangerous to wield at the time. It would take many decades for science to advance enough to take advantage of the prize, long enough for even the *Kage* to finally meet its end.

A few years back, the Americans had exposed the cabal and dragged it into the light, where shadows always withered and died. By that time, Takashi had risen enough in the ranks of the *Kage* to learn its other names, including the one used by the Americans.

The Guild.

During the resulting purge, most of the various factions of the shadowy cabal had been rooted out and destroyed, but some fragments survived. Like a ninety-year-old man who few thought could be a threat. Other stray pieces also scattered and went into hiding. Since then, Takashi and his grandson had been gathering these seeds in secret, building their own Samurai force, while biding their time.

And now, after much study—both in remote labs and in select field tests abroad—they had nursed and developed a weapon of incalculable strength and malignancy.

They had also settled upon a first target, both as a demonstration to the world and a strike against the very organization that had destroyed the Guild.

Specifically, *two* agents who were instrumental to its downfall.

As his limo glided through the traffic to the curb, Takashi smiled. He felt weightless, knowing that the location *where* the pair currently holed up was a significant omen, too. It was the same place Imperial Japan had struck its first devastating blow against a sleeping giant—and where Takashi would do the same again now.

The devastation would far outshine what had befallen those islands in the past. This first attack would herald the end of the current world order and christen the painful birth of a new one, one in which Imperial Japan would rule for eternity.

Still, he pictured his two intended targets.

Lovers, like Miu and I.

Though the pair didn't know it, they were equally doomed.

3

This is the life . . .

Commander Grayson Pierce lounged on the sunbaked red sands of Kaihalulu Bay. It was Hawaii's off-season and late in the day, so he had the small cove of red-black beach to himself. Plus this particular location was mostly known only by the locals and required a bit of a treacherous trek to reach.

Still, it was worth the effort, both for the spot's privacy and its unspoiled beauty.

Behind him, a steep-walled cinder cone, its flanks thickly forested with ironwood trees, cradled the cove. Over the centuries, its iron-rich cliffs had crumbled to red sand, forming this unique beach before vanishing into the deep-blue waters of the bay. A short distance offshore, heavy waves crashed against a jagged black seawall, casting mist high into the air, catching the brilliance of the setting sun. But closer at hand, sheltered by the reef, the water lapped gently at the sand.

A naked shape rose from those waves, bathed in sunlight, her face lifted to the sky. The drape of her black hair reached to mid-back. As she waded toward shore, revealing more of her body, seawater coursed over her pale almond skin, tracing rivulets along her bare breasts and down her flat stomach. A single emerald stud decorated her navel, sparkling as brightly as her eyes as her gaze settled on him.

No mischievous grin greeted him. Her features remained stoic to the undiscerning eye, but Gray noted the slight tilt to her head, the barest arch to her right eyebrow. She moved toward him with the sultry grace of a lioness stalking its prey.

He propped himself up on his elbows to better appreciate the sight. His legs still toasted in the day's light, but shadows cloaked the rest of his naked body as the sun sank into the cliffs behind him.

Seichan climbed the hot sand and closed the distance. As she reached him, she stepped a leg to either side. She climbed over his body and loomed above him. She came to a stop at the shadow's edge, still bathed in sunlight, as if trying to make the day last just that much longer.

"Don't," he warned.

She ignored him and shook the cape of her soaked hair, scattering cold droplets over his sprawled form. His tanned skin immediately prickled from the chill. Her gaze never left his face, but the arch of her brow rose higher.

"What?" she asked. "Too cold for you?"

She sank down upon his waist, settling atop him, stirring him with the heat found buried there. She dropped forward, a hand landing to either side of his head. She stared into his eyes, her breasts brushing his chest, and rumbled low, "Let's see about warming you up."

He grinned and reached around her. He glided his palms down to the middle of her back, then tightened his arms in an iron grip. He cocked a knee for leverage and rolled her under him.

"Oh, I'm plenty warmed up."

An hour later, shadows had swallowed the two of them, along with the rest of the beach. Still, bright daylight cast forth rainbows through the mists rising from the jagged seawall out in the bay.

Gray and Seichan huddled together, still naked under a blanket, spent and exhausted. The fading heat of their passion warmed through them, making it hard to tell where one began and the other ended. He could stay this way forever, but it would soon be dark.

He craned toward the cliffs framing the cove. "We should head out while we can still see the trail." He glanced over to the two wetsuits drying on the sand nearby and the toppled stack of scuba equipment they had used to explore the reefs around Ka'uiki Head. "Especially if we want to haul all our gear out of here."

Seichan made a noncommittal noise, plainly unconvinced to leave yet.

They had rented a small cottage south of the small town of Hana on Maui's picturesque east coast, a region of lush rain forests, waterfalls, and isolated beaches. They had planned on staying only a couple of weeks, but three months later, they still were here.

Prior to that, they had been traveling for half a year, moving place to place with no itinerary in mind, all but circling the globe. After leaving D.C., they had spent time in a walled-off medieval village in France, taking residence in the attic of a former monastery. Then they flew to the savannas of Kenya, where for a fortnight they shifted from tent camp to tent camp, moving with the timeless flow of animal life found there. Eventually, they found themselves amid the teeming sprawl of Mumbai, India, enjoying humanity at its most riotous. Afterward, seeking isolation again, they jetted off to Perth, Australia, where they rented a truck and drove deep into the wilds of the Outback. After that long desert trek, to cleanse the dust off their bodies, they continued to a hot-springs resort nestled deep in the mountains of New Zealand. Once recharged, they worked their way slowly across the Pacific, hopping island to island, from Micronesia to Polynesia, until they finally settled here, in a place that was a veritable Eden.

Gray sent the occasional postcard to his best friend, Monk Kokkalis, mostly to let those back in D.C. know that he was still alive, that he hadn't been kidnapped by hostile forces. Especially since he had left so abruptly, with no warning and no permission from his superiors. He had worked for more than a decade with Sigma Force, a covert group tied to DARPA, the Defense Department's research-and-development agency. Gray and his teammates were all former Special Forces soldiers who had been drummed out of the service for various reasons, but because of exceptional aptitude or talent, they had been secretly recruited by Sigma and retrained in diverse scientific disciplines to serve as field agents for DARPA, protecting the United States and the globe from all manner of threats.

According to his own dossier, Gray's expertise was an amalgam of biology and physics, but in truth his training went deeper than that, courtesy of his time spent with a Nepalese monk, who taught him to search for the balance between all things, the Taoist philosophy of yin and yang.

At the time, such insight helped Gray come to terms with his own troubled childhood. Growing up, he had always been stuck between opposites. His mother had taught at a Catholic high school, instilling a deep spirituality in Gray's life, but she was also an accomplished biologist, a devout disciple of evolution and reason.

And then there was his father: a Welshman living in Texas, a roughneck oilman disabled in midlife and forced to assume the role of a housewife. As a result, his father's life became ruled by overcompensation and anger.

An unfortunate trait passed on to his rebellious son.

Over time, with help from Painter Crowe, the director of Sigma Force, Gray had slowly discovered a path between those opposites. It was not a short path. It extended as much into the past as the future. Gray was still struggling with it.

A few years back, his mother had been killed in an explosion, collateral damage from Sigma's battle with the terrorist organization known as the Guild. Though blameless, Gray still struggled with guilt.

The same couldn't be said for his father's passing. Gray had a direct hand in that death. Bedridden and failing, his father had languished in the debilitating fog of Alzheimer's, slowing losing more and more of himself. Finally, obeying his dad's frail request for release (*Promise me . . .*), Gray had delivered a fatal overdose of morphine.

He felt no guilt for that death, but he couldn't say he had come to terms with it, either.

Then Seichan had offered him a lifeline, encouraging him to set aside his responsibilities for a time, to escape from everything and everyone.

He grabbed her hand and did just that.

Seichan had her own reasons to vanish, too. She was a former assassin for the Guild, trained from a young age to serve them. After several run-ins with Sigma, she was eventually turned and recruited by Painter Crowe. She had been instrumental in bringing down the Guild, but her past crimes forced her to forever remain in the shadows. She was still on many countries' most-wanted lists; the Mossad even maintained a kill-on-sight order.

Though Sigma offered this former assassin some cover, she was never fully free from her past.

So they had fled together, using the time to heal, to discover each other and themselves. No one tried to reach him, even after Gray failed to show up for his father's funeral. They simply respected his need to vanish.

For the past nine months, the two had been traveling under false papers, but he was under no misconception. He knew Sigma kept track of his whereabouts, both for professional and personal reasons. The team was in many ways a family.

Gray appreciated them giving him this leeway.

I've certainly earned it.

Still, a part of him knew this entire trip was an illusion, a momentary respite before the real world came crashing down around them again. Lately, a vague pressure had been building, a tension whose source he couldn't pinpoint. It was less a sense of imminent danger than it was a feeling that they were nearing an end to this sojourn.

He knew Seichan felt it, too.

She had grown moodier, less settled or satisfied. If she had been a lion in a cage, she would have been pacing the bars. He knew one other certainty. She wasn't dreading this trip coming to an end—she was looking forward to it.

And so am I.

The world was calling to them.

Unfortunately, it didn't wait for them to answer.

A rumbling noise intruded upon their quiet moment on the beach.

Gray sat straighter, his breath quickening with the hair-trigger training from his years with the Army Rangers. While there was no outright threat, his body was tuned from countless tours of duty in sand-blasted deserts to monitor every detail around him. It was an instinct drilled into his bones. Tiny muscles tightened, and his vision sharpened, preparing himself to move at a moment's notice.

Across Kaihalulu Bay, a trio of prop planes—Cessna Caravans from the look of them—headed toward shore. While it wasn't unusual for such small aircraft to be hopping between islands, it struck Gray as strange that they seemed to be flying in a tight formation, as if the pilots had military training.

"That's not a sightseeing group," Seichan said. She must have noted Gray's tension and what had drawn his attention. "What do you think?"

As the trio neared the island, the two flanking aircraft split away to right and left. The center plane continued its trajectory straight for their cove. Gray took in several details at once. The aircraft weren't Cessna Caravans, but the company's sleeker and smoking-fast single-piston brothers, a model known as the TTx. Each of these hellcats also carried large barrels fixed to their undercarriage.

Before Gray could fathom what was happening, a black-gray mist jetted from those tanks, streaming out under high pressure and leaving a thick contrail in each plane's wake. It built into a wide, dark cloudbank hanging over the water. The strong trade winds rolled those heavy mists toward shore, toward their tiny cove.

The centermost plane continued directly at them. By the time it cruised over the seawall in the bay, it had expended the last of its load. It continued to shore and screamed low overhead, not slowing. Gray expected it to bank up and over the heights of Ka'uiki Head behind them.

Instead, the aircraft smashed nose-first into the forested red cliffs.

The explosion shattered trees and blasted rocks high into the air. A fireball rolled into the sky, carried aloft by a column of oily smoke. Gray huddled with Seichan, using their beach blanket like a makeshift shield against the rain of flaming debris and hail of pebbles and sand.

Echoes of other crashes reached him, marking the demise of the other two aircraft. Closer at hand, a large boulder struck the water near shore, casting up a high flume.

Still, Gray ignored the immediate danger and kept his attention fixed on that wide black cloudbank rolling toward them, driven by the prevailing trade winds.

A single white-plumed egret, frightened by the crash, took wing from the neighboring forest to the right. It fled from the smoke and fire, heading out toward the bay. Still, it must have sensed the menace posed by that ominous cloud. Wings beat faster as it strove to climb above it.

Smart bird.

It successfully crested over the mists—but not high enough. A dark gray tendril wafted skyward, as if sensing the passing prey. The egret's path jerked violently as the bird brushed against that threat. Its wings flapped in a panicked beat. Its body contorted, wringing a cry from its neck. Then it plummeted in a tight spiral toward the sea. Its body vanished into the thick of the cloudbank.

"Poison," Seichan said matter-of-factly, recognizing the reality of the situation.

Gray wasn't so sure of her assessment. He pictured the coil of mist seeking out the bird. But no matter the true threat, they were in trouble.

He searched right and left. The trio of planes had

left a swath of mist across the eastern shoreline, at least a mile wide, if not more.

And we're at the center of it.

As the dark fog rolled closer, a faint humming drone rose above the crash of waves. Seichan cocked her head, plainly hearing it, too.

Gray frowned.

What the hell?

He squinted at the threat. As he watched, the buzzing cloud appeared to shift and billow independently of the prevailing trade winds . . . revealing it to be a living thing.

A swarm, he realized.

Taking this new detail into account, he weighed their options. Even if they could traverse the precarious trail along the cliffs, they'd never reach cover before the swarm swept over them. They'd be swallowed up as surely as that unlucky egret.

Gray had to accept the inevitable.

They were trapped.

SCOUT

With a sleek body built for speed, it led the others toward the coastline. Small wings beat frenetically at the air, but it was instinct that truly drove it forward. Mindless to all else but what was written in its genetic code millennia ago, it raced toward the scent of green leaf and fresh water.

Purpose defined its form. It bore the longest antennae of its brethren, splaying out at the ends with friable hairs, better to pick up the slightest vibrations. Its faceted eyes encompassed most of its head, staring unblinking toward their objective. While its wings might be shorter, its thorax was larger, more muscular, granting the scout greater maneuverability and agility in the air. Behind the thorax was a smaller-than-normal abdomen, packed with pheromone glands, but bearing no stinger, for it was no fighter.

Its short existence had one goal: to absorb sensory input. Fine hairlike sensillae covered its entire body, making it acutely sensitive to chemical changes and temperature fluctuations. The hairs even assisted with hearing, though large membranes stretched over a hollow cavity on either side

of its head served that function better. Additional
sensillae in its mouth absorbed odors from the air,
sniffing out food or water, along with monitoring
the flow of pheromones from those around it.

As it flew, it sensed those nearest neighbors, fixing their position in its brain.

It absorbed more and more information until a
threshold was reached. Unable to contain it any longer, data blasted out of its body. It transmitted to
its closest neighbors, communicating via bursts of
pheromones, then further refining the information
through changes in cadence of its wings or by saw-
ing its hind legs noisily.

Information quickly flowed back to others, where
it was absorbed, shared, and spread in a growing
cascade.

Soon, what it knew, they all knew. But it was rewarded for its efforts, as information flowed back to
its body, molding its awareness to a finer edge. After
a time, the scout's body was absorbing as much as it
was transmitting.

It began to lose any sense of individuality.

As it winged onward, the outpouring and feed-
back accelerated, becoming a torrent that flooded
throughout the swarm, binding it together, building toward a perfect harmony of intent.

As the swarm swept over the rolling water, the
goal ahead grew into focus. Details filled in, piece by
piece, dot by dot, coming from its own sensory ap-
paratus and those around it. Viewed through thousands of eyes, the coastline's image grew clearer. A
wall of rock rose from the pounding waves.

The scent of leaf and rot grew stronger as the swarm descended toward its new nesting ground. Other life roosted there already, evident from their movements, their calls, even their breaths. But they were no threat.

This certainty was as much a part of its genetic code as its wings or antennae.

With its role and purpose ending, the scout slowed its path and began to falter. It drifted back into the swarm. Several of its smaller brethren, spent by their duty, tumbled into the salty water.

They were no longer needed.

As landfall neared, the next line of workers drew forward, filling the leading edge of the swarm. This new caste had their own genetically driven purpose: to assess any dangers and clear the way forward from here.

One of the new workers buzzed past overhead. It was far larger, its abdomen already menacingly curled, exposing a jagged stinger and the ripe venom gland at its base.

The duty from here fell to this new class of hunter/killers.

The soldiers.

4

Seichan recognized they were out of time.

"Forget the wetsuits," she warned, tugging up the bottom half of her bikini. Her eyes remained fixed on the swirling swarm as it swept shoreward.

Gray dropped the suit he had been about to climb into. He already had his swim trunks on. After the past weeks under the sun, his skin glowed with a rich tan, while his ash-brown hair—unkempt and long to the collar—had bleached shades lighter, accenting the brightness of his blue eyes. He also hadn't shaved in a few days, leaving the hard planes of his face roughened by shadowy stubble.

His eyes flashed at her as he hauled up a scuba tank from the sand. It was already strapped to its buoyancy vest. He hung the gear over one shoulder, then picked up the other set.

Seichan hurried toward him. She nabbed her mask from the sand and snugged it atop her head, then took the second tank. She hefted the equipment to her back and climbed into the vest. The weight dug into her bare shoulders as she rushed across the red sand with Gray.

Out in the bay, the swarm crested over the sea-wall. The black cloud rose high, filling the breadth of the cove. The droning had grown into a low roar. The winds carried a strange, sickly sweet scent to the beach, like lavenders growing in filth. She tasted it now as much as smelled it.

An inadvertent shudder of revulsion shook through her.

At her side, Gray flinched, ducking his head and swatting at the air.

Something struck Seichan in the upper arm. It hurt like being snapped by a rubber band. She glanced down. A wasplike insect clung to her bicep, wings fluttering to a buzzing blur. It was huge—as long as her thumb. Its black, glossy abdomen bore jagged stripes of angry crimson. Momentarily shocked by the monstrosity of its size, she was slow in reacting.

It stung her before she could knock it away.

The pain was immediate, like someone drove a lit match into an open cut.

Then it got worse.

She gasped, dropping to a knee. Fiery agony exploded up her arm. Muscles tore off bone—or at least it felt that way.

To the side, Gray tried to stamp the wasp into the beach with his heel. He managed to break its wings, but its hard body merely sank into the sand. The stubborn wasp immediately scrabbled free and raced overland toward Seichan. She lurched back, but Gray kicked it into the water before it could reach her.

By now, Seichan's arm had gone limp and hung

uselessly at her side. Still, the pain spiked higher. Tears rolled down her cheeks. She had never experienced such agony. If she had an ax, she would have chopped off her own limb.

With trembling lips, she forced out a breath. "Gr . . . Gray . . ."

He hauled her up, tank and all. "We have to get underwater."

That had been their plan: to use their scuba gear to escape the threatened cove.

She wanted to obey, but her legs refused to cooperate. She wobbled, growing disoriented. The world wavered. She felt the first convulsion as she toppled face-first toward the sand.

Gray caught her and dragged her quaking form into the waves.

More wasps suddenly fell out of the air, raining down like fiery black hail.

Their tiny bodies struck the sand, shot past her face, and pelted into the bushes and leaves. To escape the onslaught, Gray wrapped her in his arms and flung them both underwater.

But even in the cold depths, her body continued to burn.

6:37 P.M.

C'mon, baby, hold on . . .

Gray tugged his mask in place and rolled Seichan under him as he kicked for deeper water. The weight of their combined gear pulled them down along the seabed. Desperate and fearing the worst, he used his free hand to secure her mask over her nose and eyes. He then scooped up her loose regulator, tilted the lower edge of her mask, and blew a blast of air under there to clear it before securing it in place again.

Seichan's body tremored beneath him, but the worst of the spasms seemed to have subsided. He studied her face as he worked the regulator's mouthpiece between her lips. Her eyes were open, but her pupils rolled. She was plainly still dazed.

He reached to her hand and was relieved to feel her fingers squeeze back.

She was coming around.

He shifted her hand up to her regulator. *Can you manage on your own?* he asked with an exaggerated lift of his eyebrows.

She seemed to understand and nodded.

Good.

He swung an arm to hook his regulator and bring it to his mouth. Once breathing on his own, he glanced up. The sun was near to setting, but the sea was bright enough to discern small black dots peppering the water. Eddies marked where several bodies squirmed. Most appeared tiny, but a few were larger, marking the presence of those monstrous wasps.

Growing up in the hill country of Texas, he had his share of run-ins with bees and heard stories of neighbors dealing with Africanized swarms. The latter species would notoriously hunt you down if you disturbed their nest. Even jumping in a pool or lake was no guarantee of safety. The bees would hover over the water, waiting until you popped your head up, then attack again.

He stared at the swarm.

This species seemed to be following the same game plan.

But luckily we don't have to come up for air.

At least, he hoped that was true.

Before he continued, he adjusted his float position in the water by filling the air bladders in his buoyancy vest, then helped Seichan do the same. He kept them hovering six feet below the surface. Satisfied, he herded Seichan farther out into the cove, while keeping a close watch on her. He didn't know what other surprises might be lurking in the wasp's venom.

He remembered Seichan's agonized expression. In the past, he had seen her shot, knifed, even pierced through the gut by an iron spear. Nothing slowed her down. For the pain of a wasp's bite to bring her to her knees, the bastard must be packing some potent venom. He suspected a few more stings and her heart might have stopped.

Respecting this danger, he continued away from shore. He passed the seawall and aimed for the brighter water beyond the cliffs of Ka'uiki Head. He periodically checked over his shoulder. Through the diffraction of the water, he could still make out a shadowy haze of the swarm up there. While the mass had made landfall, the bulk seemed to be hugging the coastline, hanging back cautiously.

Maybe they were letting the big wasps clear the way first.

Gray had to admit the tactic worked on them.

He continued straight out, trying his best to escape the swarm's shadow. Unfortunately, the sun eventually set. The resulting twilight made it difficult to tell if the horde still churned overhead.

Gray considered surfacing and using his LED dive light to scan the skies, but even if he had cleared the swarm's edge, he worried the shine might draw its attention.

So he kept going, using his wrist compass as a guide.

Better safe than sorry.

Still, he couldn't continue this way forever. Without wetsuits, the chill of the water would wear them down, especially Seichan. She had been steadily slowing, her left arm dragging behind her. He needed to get her out of the ocean and someplace warm. Knowing that, he turned them in a southerly direction, aiming for the beach a mile away where their seaside cottage stood atop a volcanic cliff.

As he pressed on, the waters slowly darkened. Soon he could barely see his hands, let alone Seichan. He finally relented and tugged out his dive light from a vest pocket and squeezed its button. The brightness through the water was momentarily blinding. Inwardly, he winced, fearing he was lighting a beacon for the swarm to follow.

No choice.

As his eyes slowly adjusted, the midnight world beneath the waves revealed itself. Ridges of reefs stretched below and outward. Everything seemed to be in motion. Bright yellow and red anemone waved in the current, while the prickly black spines of urchins shifted slowly below. Ahead, a school of blue Hawaiian flagtails fled from their path, skirting around a slower-moving eagle ray. As he crossed a wall of coral, a white tip reef shark suddenly darted away with a muscular flick of its tail.

Beyond the light's glow, other larger shadows moved.

He imagined they were sea turtles, which were abundant around Maui, but he kept a wary watch for some of the true predators that prowled these waters. Tiger and bull sharks occasionally attacked swimmers or snorkelers around Maui. He didn't intend to become one of those statistics.

He glanced to Seichan. She had fallen farther behind. He slowed and drew alongside her. He raised a hand and inquired about her status by signaling her with an okay sign. She lifted her stung arm enough to return the sign, but she did so weakly. The worst of the poison must be clearing, but it had plainly taken its toll, as had the long swim.

She waved him on, grimacing at him—not in pain, but in irritation.

Her stubborn determination was easy to read.

Keep going already. I'll keep up, goddammit.

He shifted around and continued, but he stayed alongside her now. Stubbornness only got you so far.

Slowly, each kick and paddle propelled them farther from the beleaguered section of shoreline and closer to their destination. He periodically checked the compass strapped to his wrist.

Shouldn't be much farther.

Still, it took them another thirty minutes to finally reach the shallows of their beach. Gray popped his head up first. They were nearly out of air. The gauges on their tanks were deep in the red zone. He checked to make sure the skies were clear, then helped Seichan clamber up to the thin rocky beach. They happily shed their tanks at the water's edge.

With an arm still around her waist, he felt her shiver. He had to all but carry her toward the cliff face ahead. Their cottage perched at the top, where a glowing window beckoned.

Seichan pushed out of his grip and sank to her knees in the sand. She lifted an arm toward the cottage. "Go . . ." she gasped out.

"I'm not leaving you. I'll haul you the whole way if I have to."

It was a promise he didn't know if he could carry out. His own legs felt like rubber.

"No . . ." She scowled at him, breathing hard. She waved an arm toward the north. "Ball . . . ballpark."

He shook his head, not understanding—then it struck him.

Oh, no.

His body stiffened. Adrenaline pumped steel back into his legs.

This morning, they had parked their Jeep along Uakea Road, between a community center and the Hana Ball Park, which consisted of a freshly mowed baseball diamond, a soccer field, and a couple of tennis and basketball courts. Seichan had commented on a sign posted outside the park, announcing a Little League tournament set for this evening. She had suggested grabbing hot dogs and watching the game.

He pictured its location.

As a crow flew, the park was only a quarter mile inland from the red sand beach.

He imagined the commotion from that game.

All the music, cheering, lights . . .

"Take one of our bikes," Seichan said. "You gotta warn them."

He stared up toward the cottage. They had rented a couple of motorbikes so they could explore trails too thin and treacherous for a regular vehicle.

He glanced back to Seichan, who must have read the concern on his face.

She frowned at him. "I'll get up there on my own. May take me some time, but I'll alert Sigma, get them mobilizing a local response." She pointed again. "Go. Before it's too late."

He nodded, knowing she was right.

He checked his watch. The game was scheduled to start in ten minutes. He'd never make it there in time, but he had to do what he could. Clenching his jaw, he sprinted for the switchback that led up the cliff to the cottage.

As he reached the trailhead, he glanced back. Seichan was on her feet. Her legs shook but her face was stony with determination. Their eyes met. Both knew the danger Gray was rushing toward—and one other certainty.

Their vacation was over.

5

Painter Crowe had been expecting this call for months.

Trouble always had a way of finding Commander Gray Pierce. It was why Painter, as the director of Sigma Force, had been keeping tabs on the errant agent during the man's long walkabout around the globe. Still, Painter could never have imagined or predicted *how* this particular trouble would have presented itself.

A swarm of wasps?

Exhausted but strung taut by tension, he combed fingers through his black hair, tucking a lock that had gone snowy white behind one ear. He had ended his call with Seichan ten minutes ago and sent an alert up the chain of command, both to his superiors at DARPA and to the appropriate authorities in Hawaii. As he sat at his office desk, he pondered the strangeness of the situation, taking to heart Seichan's warning before she had hung up.

This was no random act of Mother Nature. It's a biological assault.

A knock at his open door drew his attention forward. A slim shape whisked into the room. Captain Kathryn Bryant was his second-in-command. Despite the time being after midnight, her shoulder-length auburn hair was combed and braided in the back, as conservative as her attire: navy blue suit, crisp white blouse, black leather pumps. Her only flash of color was a jeweled pin on her lapel, a tiny gold-enameled frog. She'd been awarded the gift by an amphibious team she had joined during a marine recon operation for naval intelligence. One teammate from that mission had never come back. She continued to wear the pin in his memory.

After her stint with the military, Painter had recruited Kat as an analyst for Sigma. She quickly grew to be as essential to operations here as the directorship—maybe even more so.

"We've got a far larger problem brewing on those islands," she said brusquely.

"What do you mean?"

Kat reached his desk and tapped at an e-tablet in her hand, then pointed to one of the three flat-screen monitors mounted to the walls of his office. A topographic map of the Hawaiian Islands bloomed on the screen. He swung his chair back from his desk to better view the image. Small red dots peppered three of the largest islands.

"It wasn't just Maui that was attacked." She stepped over and tapped a red zone along the island's eastern shore, where Seichan had reported the attack. "We've also got reports of similar assaults on Oahu and the big island of Hawaii."

Painter stood and joined her. He had hoped to attribute all of this to some lone attack, perhaps ecoterrorists trying to prove a malicious point.

On the map, Kat pointed to the state's capital, Honolulu. "A Cessna crashed near Diamond Head, about the same time as the three on Maui." She then shifted her finger to the largest Hawaiian island. "Over in Hilo, a hospital sent out a broadcast for emergency help. They've been overrun by people suffering from varying degrees of stings. Including a few fatalities."

Painter remembered Seichan's warning.

This was no random act. . . .

It seemed she was right. This attack had been coordinated.

Kat continued, "So far we've heard nothing from Kauai or any of the other smaller islands, but I suspect it's only a matter of time. I have Jason scanning all newsfeeds, social media, and law enforcement chatter across Hawaii."

"Why out there?" Painter pondered aloud. "Why those islands?"

"We don't have enough intel yet to make any suppositions." She studied the topographic map. "But perhaps Hawaii's remoteness is part of the reason. Beyond the immediate danger to the populace, the introduction of an aggressive foreign species could wreak havoc to the state's isolated ecosystem."

It was a chilling thought, but such long-term concerns would have to wait. They had a more immediate question to answer.

"What exactly are we facing?" he asked. "*What* was unleashed on those islands?"

Kat turned back to him. "I've already placed a call to an entomologist over at the National Zoo. Dr. Samuel Bennett is a leading expert, respected around the globe. From Seichan's description, there can't be many wasps that big."

"Good. The sooner we know what we're dealing with, the better."

That was one of the key advantages to having Sigma's command center buried beneath the Smithsonian Castle. The group had ready access to the many labs and research centers of the Smithsonian Institution, which included the National Zoo.

From this location, Sigma could also tap into the neighboring halls of power, both at Capitol Hill and the White House. Painter had no doubt his immediate superior at DARPA, General Gregory Metcalf, was already alerting the powers-that-be and ramping up a federal emergency response.

But those cogs and wheels moved too slowly.

It was why Sigma Force existed: to lead surgical strikes when necessary. They were the front line against the chimeric and shifting threats of new technology. With the cutting edge of science changing so rapidly and in so many unexpected directions around the globe, the United States needed a team that could respond as quickly and with as much agility. That was the core of Sigma Force's mission statement: *to be there first.*

Kat's phone chimed. She glanced down at the number. "Seems our entomologist keeps late hours. It's Dr. Bennett."

"Put him on speakerphone."

She nodded, tapped her phone's screen, and held

the device between them. "Thank you for return-ing my call so promptly, Dr. Bennett."

"My assistant called and shared your urgency, which certainly got my attention. I don't get a lot of emergency calls from DARPA. Not in my line of work. And not in the middle of the night.

"Still, we appreciate your cooperation." She nod-ded to Painter. "In fact, I have my boss on speaker with us."

"Oh, okay. So what's this all about?"

"Did you get my description of the wasp that I forwarded?"

"I did indeed. That's the other reason I returned your call so quickly and can answer your question so promptly. I received a similar inquiry about a month ago, someone asking about a wasp like you described. Over three inches. Black body with jagged crimson stripes across its abdomen."

Painter leaned closer to the phone. "Who con-tacted you?"

"Someone out of Japan. Working for a phar-maceutical company. Hang on. Let me get to my desktop, and I can pull his name from his last email."

As they waited, Kat stared at Painter and cocked her head.

So much for Sigma always being there first.

Bennett spoke as he searched for the informa-tion. "Like I told this other researcher, there's no *Hymenoptera* species that matches such a classifica-tion. The closest is the Asian giant wasp, which can grow to be three inches long, but its patterning comes in yellow and black. A close second is our native tarantula hawk wasp out of New Mexico. It's a whopping two inches long, with a helluva sting, but its body is solid blue-black with orange wings."

Painter grimaced at the thought of being stung by either of those species.

Bennett continued, "Now if I had a specimen, I could learn more. Maybe it's a heterochromatic mutant of one of these known species. In other words, genetically related, but a different coloring."

Kat sighed. "Unfortunately, we may have plenty of specimens for you to study before too much longer."

"I'd certainly love to get my hands on—ah, here's that email!" Bennett cleared his throat. "The researcher's name is Ken Matsui. According to the letterhead, he's a professor at Cornell University. Department of Toxicology."

Painter frowned. "I thought you said the request came from Japan?"

"That's correct. It seems he has a grant with Tanaka Pharmaceuticals. He emailed me from their location in Kyoto. I can text you his contact information there."

"We would appreciate that," Kat said. After thanking the researcher, she ended the call and faced Painter. "What do you think?"

"Clearly someone's encountered this species well before today's attack." He returned to his chair. "We need to speak to this Professor Matsui as soon as possible."

"I'll get on it." She began to turn away, then hesitated. "But what about Gray and Seichan?"

"It'll take some time for emergency services to respond. For the moment, they're on their own."

"What about our guy we have on the ground out there?"

Painter sighed. For the past nine months, he had been not only tracking Gray but also positioning a rotating series of Sigma operatives along his path. At the start, Kat's husband, Monk Kokkalis, had been in Paris finishing up some work with Interpol on an animal smuggling ring, so he was already conveniently near Gray's location in the South of France. After that, Painter had contacted Tucker Wayne—who was at a game park he co-owned in South Africa—and asked him to be ready in case Gray needed any help during his time roaming through the jungles of that dark continent. And on and on from there. It was perhaps a foolish waste of resources, but knowing Gray, trouble would find him or he would find it himself.

It was only a matter of time.

For this latest assignment in Hawaii, it hadn't been hard to persuade agents to assume this duty. While there was no pressing reason to station anyone among those islands, a few weeks of R&R on a beach was an easy sell.

Unfortunately for Gray, the roll of this particular dice had landed on snake-eyes in regard to *which* agent had just rotated out there.

"Kowalski's on the other side of Maui," Painter said sourly. "At a resort in Wailea. I've alerted him, but it'll take him an hour to reach a helicopter and cross the island."

"So Gray and Seichan are truly on their own."

"Perhaps, but knowing Gray, he'll do what he can to help."

"You mean put himself in harm's way."

Painter grinned wryly. "That's what he does best."

6

Hunched low, Gray raced his motorbike north along the Hana Highway. He ignored the speed limit, easily doubling it. The tail of his T-shirt flapped in the wind. He hadn't had time to get properly dressed. He still wore trunks and had shoved his feet into a pair of worn hiking boots resting on the stoop of his rented cottage.

As he passed the Hasegawa General Store, he braked hard, startled by red taillights stretching ahead. Refusing to be caught in that traffic jam, he skirted to the shoulder and sped alongside the line of stalled cars.

The source of the congestion quickly became evident.

Through the muffle of his helmet, he heard sirens. His heart hammered in his throat as he throttled up his engine.

Am I already too late?

Worried, he cut across the lawn of a church to reach the next side street: Hauoli Road. After making the turn, he aimed for the noise and flashing lights. The Hana Ball Park lay a couple hundred yards down the road, where it dead-ended at a native community health-care center. A fire engine stood crookedly in the center's parking lot, along with a couple of ambulances and squad cars. A yellow helicopter swept past overhead as Gray reached the ballpark.

He skidded his bike to a stop, let it drop, and ran the last of the way down the packed road. Onlookers crowded the pavement, gawking at the bustle of the response teams. Confused parents herded children, some in Little League gear, through the throng. The baseball diamond's grandstands were packed, but most of the patrons had their back to the field and stared across the road at the emergency vehicles.

No doubt the game had been canceled or delayed due to all the activity.

Past the baseball diamond, the park's soccer pitch had turned into a makeshift picnic area. Closer at hand, a row of food trucks had parked along Hauoli Road, selling snow cones, hot dogs, even barbecue. Hawaiian music blared from the field's speakers, competing with noise of the sirens.

Gray headed through the circuslike crowds toward the health-care center parking lot. He needed to find someone in authority. Still, he kept an eye on the sky. In the glare of lights, he spotted no evidence of the swarm's presence. In addition, no one around him seemed panicked, only curious.

If there's no swarm, then why all the emergency vehicles?

He followed the helicopter as it swung over the forests behind the community center. The chopper aimed toward Ka'uiki Head. The spear of its lights revealed a faint trail of smoke spiraling into the night sky.

He grimaced as he remembered the Cessna TTx nosediving into the side of Ka'uiki's cinder cone. He now understood *why* the emergency teams were already on hand. Of course, the dramatic crash of a trio of planes had drawn this commotion.

The emergency must have forced the cancellation of the ball game, but before that happened, the crowds had already gathered for the tournament and now stayed to watch the action.

It was a perfect storm of events that could lead to a disaster.

He rushed through the commotion, sidestepping a shouting match between a driver leaning out of one of the traffic-snarled cars and someone at the vehicle's front bumper. As a final retort, the driver lay into his horn, adding to the cacophony.

Gray flinched at the noise, but he kept watch on the sky.

Would all this commotion draw the swarm or hold it at bay?

He finally reached the community center's parking lot. He crossed toward a stocky black man with salt-and-pepper hair who wore blue slacks and a starched white uniform with a prominent badge. He carried a yellow jacket over one arm, a match to the bright yellow truck next to him. Likely the fire chief for Hana. The man huddled beside a large Hawaiian outfitted in baggy fire gear.

Gray caught a part of their conversation as the two men shouted to be heard.

With a radio in hand, the Hawaiian leaned toward the chief. "—lowered Watanabe to the wreckage. He says there's no body."

"So the pilot ditched before the crash?"

The fireman shrugged heavily. "Seems so."

Gray knew that hadn't happened, which meant the planes must have been unmanned, flying like drones. He knew a Cessna TTx had advanced autopilot features, but not enough to pull off this stunt, not without additional engineering.

He stepped close enough to draw both men's attention and took off his motorcycle helmet. "There was no pilot," he said as introduction.

The pair eyed him up and down, their brows furrowing with disdain. He couldn't blame them for this reaction. Unshaven, wild-haired, and wearing only a T-shirt, trunks, and hiking boots, he didn't come off as the most reliable-looking resource. He also knew how insular the locals could be when it came to dealing with a *haole*, a foreigner.

He spoke quickly before he was dismissed. "I was on the red sand beach when the planes crashed." He thrust out his hand. "Name's Gray Pierce, former Army Ranger, now an adjunct commander with DARPA."

That wasn't entirely true, but close enough.

The chief ignored his hand and continued to look at him with a sour expression, but the fireman next to him narrowed his eyes, plainly reassessing this *haole* standing before them.

Gray lowered his arm. "You all have a larger problem. A danger far greater than any spreading fire. Those planes were crashed purposefully, but before doing so, they unloaded swarms of wasps into the air."

"Wasps?" The chief frowned and rolled his eyes.

Whatever credibility Gray had a moment ago faded from the other fireman's face. They must think he was high on a potent strain of locally grown weed, which was practically a staple here.

Gray struggled to find the words to make them understand the threat. "These are *big* wasps. Like nothing I've seen before. The woman I was with got stung by one. Almost instantly incapacitated her." He waved to a clutch of boys in Little League uniforms across the street, chattering and laughing. "I suspect it would only take a sting or two to kill—"

The chief had had enough and shoved a palm at Gray. "We don't have time for this nonsense." He turned to the other. "Palu, get this asshole out of here."

The other hesitated, even glancing skyward.

"I know how this sounds, but you must listen to me." Gray focused on the native fireman, knowing his chief would not listen. Back in the military, Gray had run into obstinate superiors, men too prideful in their position to see past their noses.

Palu seemed torn. "Chief, maybe we'd better at least check his story out."

"Like we have the manpower to chase wild—"

The radio in Palu's hand squawked. All three men looked down as a spat of harsh screaming rose from the tiny speakers.

Palu shoved the radio to his lips. "Say again, Chopper One." He tilted his head, listening for a response, but the answer came from above.

A rhythmic thumping drew all their attentions up. A yellow helicopter with the word FIRE emblazoned on its belly swept into view, canting wildly back and forth—then plunged into the woods behind the community center. The crumpling crash cut through the sirens and music. The crowd went silent as a fireball rolled into the night sky.

The brightness briefly revealed a dark cloud looming above the forest, cresting high, like a black wave about to crash over the town of Hana.

Palu looked to the *haole* at his side, but Gray could only state the obvious.

"It's too late. They're already here."

SOLDIER

With powerful beats of her four wings, the soldier hovered at the head of the swarm. Her hum carried back to the others, full of warning as she assessed the threat and landscape ahead. Rows of tiny spiracles—pinpoint holes along thorax and abdomen through which she breathed—vibrated angrily, casting out a whistling cry to her caste.

Fellow soldiers gathered and packed the swarm's vanguard, communicating by sound and pheromone. All their antennae pointed forward, swiveling at their bases, testing the scents carried on the breeze.

Sweetness . . .

Flesh . . .

Salt . . .

They shared what they learned.

As she waited with the others, she bent the eleven joints at the ends of her antennae, weaving a map of those scents inside her brain. A billowing force built before her, full of the promise of sustenance for the swarm. A cloud of odors rose before her.

The mélange of those smells stoked her hunger,
which in turn triggered a surge of aggressive hormones. Muscles contracted in her abdomen, caus-
ing sharp lances to slide along the grooves on either
side of her stinger, honing her weapon.

She waved her antennae a final time and focused
on the source of this delicious smoke.

Instinct demanded her to possess it.

Her sisters felt the same.

Signaling one another, the soldiers plunged as
one from the swarm's edge and dove toward that
source. As they fell, they drew closer together, becoming a dark arrow pointed toward their goal.

Other senses continued to draw information, refining what she knew.

Large membranes over hollow pockets on either side of her head vibrated to the myriad sounds
that spiked through the fog of odors. In turn, the
swarm's angry buzzing was cast forth, only to re-
bound back with more details of the landscape
ahead. With each wingbeat, she learned more and
shared with the others, as they did with her. Struc-
tures and shapes began to coalesce, constructed of
sound and echo.

As they raced below, she became both fighter and army, both one and many. She closed in on the source of those odors. Propelled by a millennia-old drive for territory, she would not let anything stop her. Ancestral memory, imprinted in her genetic code, erased fear. Her ancient sisters had felled greater foes than any found in this new land so far.

Still, she brought to bear more of her senses, readying herself for the battle.

Two large black eyes—each fractured into several hundred hexagonal facets—studied what lay ahead. She took in color and shape, but her eyes had evolved for one keen purpose: *to detect motion.*

Her gaze fixed to each twitch and flail around her as she whisked through a pall of scents and odors. Everything was in motion, but her brain noted vectors and tides within this chaos. It allowed her to rank the dangers ahead.

She ignored the forces that fled from her path.

They were no immediate threat.

Instead, she knew she must clear away anything that blocked her path, that challenged her dominance. Her wings blurred faster, fueled by aggression, daring any to defy her from reaching her goal.

But her eyes remained alert for the greatest threat.

Movement caught her attention—a flow of motion *toward* her.

She focused on this coming contest, whipping her anger to a boil. An image of this challenger pushed through the bedlam of her senses. It was still more shadow than substance.

She plunged toward it, while still attuned to the other soldiers. Her antennae noted a draft of distress, a flare of pheromone as one of her caste was trampled to her left. Immediately, others raced along the trail of pheromone, drawn by the death, intending to multiply their strength and poison to eradicate whatever killed one of their own.

She ignored it, concentrating on the danger coming straight at her.

The challenger's image grew clearer.

She assessed the figure and hunted for the best place to attack it. She smelled the salt of its sweat and blood, but instinct guided her toward the carbon puffing from its breath. Eons of ingrained experience had taught her to focus her poison there.

She curled her abdomen and readied her stinger.

The threatening form rushed toward her.

She lowered her head, arcing her wings higher, and dove to attack.

7

As Gray ran, he snapped down the face shield of his motorcycle helmet—and not a moment too soon. A large wasp struck the visor hard enough to make the polycarbonate ring. It clung there with its six jointed legs, an inch from his nose. Its wings beat in a furious blur. Its armored abdomen jabbed at the shield, over and over again, hard enough to be heard, like a determined woodpecker on a tree trunk.

Gray stared cross-eyed for a moment, assessing the enemy at close range.

A deep-seated horror froze him momentarily, as if something ancient in his genetic code responded to this threat. And maybe it had. He had read how phobias could change a person's DNA through epigenetics, passing a fear from one generation to another, as a survival instinct against deadly predators.

Gray shuddered at the sight of the sharp stinger, easily a quarter-inch long, striking his visor.

Before he could move, a thick glove swatted at his helmet and knocked the wasp away. "Here!" He turned to find the fireman, Palu, standing there, holding out a silvery fire blanket. "Cover yourself and get to shelter!"

Gray took the lightweight fabric and wrapped it over his shoulders. With one hand, he clutched it to his neck. The blanket only draped to his knees, leaving his calves exposed, but it was better than nothing.

Palu had donned the rest of his full bunker gear. Besides his yellow trousers, turnout jacket, and helmet, he had pulled on a firefighting hood with a clear SCBA mask over his face, leaving little skin exposed. Hauling a white hose over one shoulder, he pointed his other arm toward the community health-care center.

"Go!"

Gray glanced in that direction. In the parking lot, the fire chief sat in his truck, a handheld radio at his lips. His voice boomed from his vehicle.

"SEEK IMMEDIATE SHELTER! WHEREVER YOU CAN. CARS, HOMES, THE COMMUNITY CENTER. GET OUT OF THE OPEN!"

The warning came too late. All around, people fled in every direction. It was pandemonium and bedlam, scored by Hawaiian music blasting from speakers at the ballpark. Screams and curses and crying added to the chorus.

A father ran past Gray carrying a small girl on his shoulder, waving an arm as wasps chased them. The child sobbed, both in panic and from a large red welt on her cheek. The man banged sidelong into a car, where a Good Samaritan inside risked opening the back door and hollered for them to get inside.

Similar scenarios broke out all around him as homes and stores gathered people inside, but there were too many still trapped in the park or streets. Bodies thrashed on the pavement. Parents huddled over their children, shielding them, as wasps hurled down.

The handful of emergency personnel on hand tried to help, dragging whom they could to safety, suffering for their efforts. But even they were too few to save so many.

Not that they were giving up.

"Go!" Palu ordered as he lowered the hose's nozzle to his hips, which ran back to the engine tanker.

Down the street, another fireman had a hose attached to a fire hydrant, while a third rescue worker used a large wrench to unlock its flow. Water suddenly jetted high. The fireman waved the fierce column through the air, trying to drown the swarm out of the sky. But it was like fighting a wildfire with a squirt gun.

A cold certainty firmed inside Gray.

I need to buy them more time.

He gripped Palu's arm and shouted through his face shield. He pointed back to the engine tanker. "Is that a CAF system?" he asked.

Palu nodded.

As Gray had hoped, the fire engine was outfitted with compressed air foam, a thick knockdown retardant for fighting fires.

And hopefully more.

"Follow me!" Gray shouted.

As he turned away, he shook wasps from his silvery blanket. For now, the reflective fabric seemed to confuse the insects.

Let's hope it stays that way.

Gray headed across Uakea Road toward where he'd dropped his bike. He prayed his plan would work—and that Palu's hose had a long enough reach.

A glance over his shoulder showed the stout Hawaiian keeping pace with him, digging with his legs to haul the heavy white hose by himself.

Gray sped up, leaving Palu to follow as best he could. He reached the row of food trucks parked along Hauoli Road and crossed to one selling Hawaiian shave ice. It was shut tight with a pack of people and children inside.

"Can't fit anyone else in here!" the proprietor yelled through the screen door. The mesh was thick with giant wasps, which appeared to be chewing at the fine wire, trying to get inside.

"That's okay." Gray panted and shifted over to a sliding service window. "Pass me your bottles of your syrup."

"What?"

"Just do it!"

Gray glanced to a snow cone smashed in the grass a few yards away. A thick clot of wasps covered the slush.

The window slid open and someone handed him a bottle of blueberry-flavored syrup. He took it, twisted to the side, and threw the glass bottle like a Molotov cocktail. It flew high over a neighboring fence and exploded against the blacktop of an empty tennis court.

He turned back to the truck. "More!"

As those inside fed him bottle after bottle, he flung them into the same court. His efforts were soon rewarded. Wasps started flocking in that direction, drawn by the bright smell of sugar. Even the cluster crawling over the truck's screen door gave up their efforts to chew their way inside and flung themselves off, buzzing toward the promise of an easier bounty.

Gray had hoped his lure would work. In the past, countless family picnics had been plagued by persistent hornets, wasps, and bees. He remembered his father once swallowing a yellow jacket that had fallen into his beer can. Gray suspected these creatures would be no different than their smaller cousins.

I mean, who doesn't like dessert?

He didn't know what fraction of the swarm would be diverted, but any portion he could pull away from attacking those left outside would buy time for emergency personnel to get additional people to shelter.

"That's all I have!" the proprietor shouted, drawing back his attention.

Gray nodded and retreated a few steps, where he met Palu. "Wait until there's a good swarm at the tennis court . . . then let 'em have it."

"You are one lolo buggah," Palu said in native pidgin. It was likely an insult but the big man's wide grin suggested he was also impressed. "Now get your okole somewhere safe."

"Not yet." Gray stared at thick trails of wasps streaming high above.

Some of these bastards might not have a sweet tooth.

He hunched deeper into his silvery blanket and rushed to the next food truck. The side was painted with a dancing hot dog in a bun. He repeated the same maneuver, this time flinging torn-open packages of wieners into a nearby basketball court.

As he tossed the last of the dogs, a huge flume of white foam arced high to his right. He followed it back to where Palu was down on one knee, aiming the nozzle toward the tennis court. The fireman showered it across the hovering mass of wasps in the air, coating them heavily and driving them down to the thick carpet of churning bodies feasting amid the broken bottles of syrup.

Palu noted Gray's attention. "I got it, brah! You go!"

Gray considered doing more, but he was dissuaded when a wasp latched on to his bare calf and stung him. He danced backward as if that would do any good. A second lance of pain brought him to his senses. He used his hiking boot to scrape it off and stamp it into the pavement, which only seemed to irritate it. It took grinding his heel atop its armored body to finally get a satisfying crunch.

By then, his other leg had become a tower of fire.

He tried to limp down the street, but whether the swarm noted his distress or were drawn by the odor of their crushed comrade, wasps pelted his fleeing form. His helmet rang with the impacts, and he felt strikes against the silvery blanket.

Agony climbed to his hip, making it harder

to keep moving. His breath gasped between his clenched teeth. His vision wavered with tears. His entire world became pain. All he wanted to do was fall to the ground and scream.

Still, he forced himself to continue along the street, looking toward the community center's glass doors. It seemed an impossible distance.

Never make it.

With each fiery step, he became more convinced. He no longer had control of his right leg. He fell sideways and caught himself on the hood of a Ford Taurus. Faces inside stared at him with concern, but they were packed tight in there.

No more room at the inn.

He pushed off to continue toward the community center. But he had exposed his hand for too long. Before he could tuck it under the blanket, a wasp landed on his wrist. Gray flung his arm, dislodging it before it could sting him, but he also lost his tenuous balance.

He toppled toward the curb, his arms swinging, which only drew more wasps.

He prepared to curl into a ball and do his best to pull his limbs under the fire blanket—but a force struck him in the middle of the back and rolled him across the pavement for a couple of panicked heartbeats.

He gasped as his vision whited out. It took him a full breath to realize his helmet's visor was coated in foam, as was most of his body. Palu must have drenched him. An arm hooked his waist and pulled him upright.

Gray swiped his face shield to clear it.

Palu had hold of him. "We go!"

Gray felt no need to argue.

The fireman dragged him along, while still manning the hose with his other arm. As he half-carried Gray past the basketball court, he blasted foam across the wasps gorging on the piles of hot dogs over there.

Then the hose sputtered, and the arc of foam collapsed to a dribbling stream.

The tanker must be out of CAF.

Palu dropped the hose and firmed his grip on Gray, readying for a final run for the community center. Then a new noise intruded.

Sharp, insistent barking.

It drew both their attentions to the left. A scruffy terrier hid behind the baseball diamond's home plate. A red leash ran back to a small boy crumpled on his side at the bottom of the backstop fence. His head lolled back, froth bubbling at the corners of his lips. His limbs twitched convulsively.

He was going into anaphylaxis.

Gray pulled in that direction, but the tall backstop blocked the way. They'd have to circle far around the fence to reach the child. Such a delay could mean his death, but Gray had to make the attempt.

Palu tried to restrain him—perhaps also recognizing the futility of this rescue attempt—then swore and followed Gray toward a gate fifteen yards away.

We're never going to make it in time.

Already the boy's limbs had stopped moving, and the dog's barking had turned into a forlorn whine.

Gray tried to hurry, but adrenaline and desperation did little to dampen the fiery pain. Wasps bombarded their every step. Foam still coated most of Gray's exposed limbs, but a determined wasp burrowed through the thick coating and stung the soft flesh behind his left knee.

Fresh agony flared, drawing a cry to his lips.

At his side, Palu did the same and swatted at his own belly. One of the bastards must have found its way under the hem of his fire jacket. Panicked, Palu let Gray fall and ripped open his coat and smacked the culprit off his chest, but pain dropped him to his hands and knees.

They were both on the ground now. Gray's limbs tremored and quaked, overwhelmed by the poison. He stared toward the boy. He caught the terrier's desperate gaze, begging for help.

Sorry, buddy, there's nothing—

Then movement drew his attention farther out into the diamond. A thick, snaking shadow uncoiled from the sky and draped down to the pitcher's mound.

Gray blinked, trying to make sense of the sight.

A rope.

He stared up its length to a large shadow hovering high overhead. It was a helicopter running without lights, likely to avoid drawing the swarm.

A large shape plummeted down the line and reached the ground. A pair of boots pounded into the dirt mound. The giant figure straightened, decked out in a full wetsuit, including a hood, mask, even a tank on his back. Through the faceplate of the mask, a familiar grizzled face scowled at the situation.

Gray could not comprehend the sudden arrival of someone he knew, but it didn't matter. He yelled with all his strength and pointed toward the backstop fence.

"Kowalski! Grab that boy!"

9:17 P.M.

Twenty minutes later, Gray stood behind the sealed glass doors of the community center. He stared out at the aftermath of the swarm's attack. He counted more than a dozen bodies still sprawled in the outfield or soccer pitch. And there were likely more victims beyond his range of view.

Rescue teams had begun to arrive, dropping people in protective gear. But the situation remained dire. Eddying dark swirls of wasps still swept across the park and empty streets, while the larger shadowy mass of the swarm hung higher, hovering above.

Kowalski strode up to him. "Kid's going to be okay according to the doc. Dog, too."

"Thanks to your timely arrival."

Gray pictured the gorilla of a man throwing the boy over his shoulder, then grabbing the dog by the scruff. He helped Gray and Palu over to the community health-care center, where a team of local nurses and doctors did their best with their meager resources to attend to the injured.

Kowalski had already explained how he had come to be here. It appeared Painter had been keeping tabs on Gray's travels. Normally he would have resented being babysat, even from a distance, but considering a boy now lived because of the director's caution, Gray could hardly complain.

"You just can't keep your ass out of trouble, can you?" Kowalski said. The big man had stripped out of his protective wetsuit and wore boots, a pair of knee-length cargo shorts, and a Tommy Bahama shirt. He waved sourly at his attire. "There I was, about to head to a nice dinner at the Four Seasons with Maria, when I get this call to pull your butt out of the fire."

It seemed Kowalski had used this babysitting assignment as a paid Hawaiian vacation, bringing along his girlfriend, Dr. Maria Crandall, a geneticist from Georgia who had helped Sigma in the past. The pair made an odd couple, but then again, her work dealt with Neanderthals. So clearly she had a type.

"Of course, maybe it's just as well. Maria wanted to go to some restaurant that served raw food." Kowalski shook his head. "What's the point of paying to go to a place that's not going to cook your stuff? It's stupid, I tell you."

"Then it sounds like you'd fit right in."

Kowalski scrunched his heavy brow. "What do you mean by—?"

They were interrupted as two figures approached from an office. It was Hani Palu and his battalion chief, Benjamin Renard.

Palu had gotten rid of his heavy fire jacket, but still wore baggy yellow trousers held up by bright red suspenders. The Hawaiian clapped Kowalski on the back. The two could almost be brothers from another mother. Palu stood shoulder-to-shoulder with Kowalski, both standing well over six feet. The pair had dark hair, razored nearly to the scalp. But the Hawaiian's face was rounder than Kowalski's and certainly less scarred.

The two were also worlds apart in attitude.

Palu smiled broadly and often, even in these grim circumstances. Whereas Kowalski wore a perpetual scowl, as if expecting the worst at any moment.

Chief Renard pushed forward and held out a cell phone toward Gray. "You have a call. From a Director Crowe."

"Thanks." He took the phone and stepped a yard away. He was not surprised Painter had managed to hunt him down here.

He cradled the phone to his ear. "So what's the situation?"

"I was hoping you could tell me . . . at least in regard to events out there. It seems Maui was not the only target of this attack. Honolulu was also hit, as was Hilo on the big island of Hawaii."

Gray turned to the glass doors, trying to imagine such a poisonous swarm boiling into major population centers on those two islands.

"Kat also suspects the city of Lihue on Kauai might have been targeted, but a sudden downpour with high winds may have spared the place, driving the swarm out to sea."

"If that's so, how do you know Lihue was even a target?"

"A Cessna washed up on a beach not far from the city. With no pilot."

"A Cessna TTx?"

"Exactly."

Painter let the implication hang in the air. Gray was surprised after nine months how easily he fell right back into sync with the director. He also knew the director was holding something back and began to get an inkling of what it might be.

"Were any other sites on Maui attacked?" Gray asked.

"No, just Hana."

Gray considered this detail. Maui had larger population centers, both the city of Kahului—where the international airport was located—and the more touristy stretch on the far side of the island.

"Then why only hit such a small place like Hana?" Gray pondered aloud.

"That's a good question."

Gray pictured the trio of aircraft aiming for shore, with the centermost one bearing directly toward the red sand beach.

"Unless they weren't just targeting Hana," he suddenly realized. "They could've been trying to take us out, too."

Two birds with one stone.

He stared past the doors to the bodies in the fields.

Were they all dead because of me?

"We suspected the same," Painter admitted. "If we're right, that means someone knows you were out there. Someone close enough to know you were at that beach."

Gray cringed inwardly.

If they should learn we survived . . .

He swung his gaze to the south, remembering who was out there all by herself.

Seichan . . .

8

From the porch of the old cottage, Seichan watched the trespasser creep through the fence row and along the garden path. The movements were furtive, keeping to the darkest shadows, approaching in short, lightning-fast advances. This predator clearly knew how to stalk its prey.

She waited near the doorway.

She had been expecting this visit all night.

Seichan slipped down to a knee. She did not want to put the other on guard.

The intruder glided low to the porch steps, vanishing momentarily from Seichan's line of sight.

C'mon, already . . .

As if hearing her summons, the figure leaped into view and landed lightly atop the porch planks. Glassy eyes reflected the meager glow slipping through the shaded kitchen window. They fixed Seichan with a steady stare.

"About time," she whispered to her guest.

A plaintive meow answered her.

Seichan lowered the plate of minced ahi tuna.

The black cat looked to the offering, then away.

She stretched her long legs, splaying her paws, feigning disinterest.

"That's all you're getting."

After another moment of hesitation, the cat swished her tail and stalked forward. She sniffed the plate, nosed the food, then began to eat, tentatively at first, then with more gusto.

Seichan risked stretching out a hand and scratching a single finger atop its head. A low growl flowed, though the cat never stopped eating. The creature was clearly feral, but over the past three months, Seichan had coaxed it closer and closer. She had noted the swollen mammary glands, suggesting the cat had a litter of kittens hidden somewhere out there.

Gray had scolded her for feeding the stray, counseling her on the devastation wrought by the wild cat population on the island, how they were endangering many bird species.

She ignored him. She remembered all too well what it was like to live on the streets after escaping the orphanage in Laos. She had been as feral as this cat, doing what she could to survive. Eventually the Guild had found her and trained her to hone those same street skills into deadlier pursuits.

She stared at the hungry cat. Though she was free of the Guild, a part of her could never fully escape her past. So she fed the stray, while trying to ignore the deeper motivations behind her actions.

Gray has enough on his mind.

After his father's death, he had needed this escape from the real world. While he had accepted his role in ending his father's life, sparing the proud man of needless suffering and loss of dignity, she knew a part of Gray remained haunted. She caught him often staring blindly into the distance. He never talked about his father, but his ghost hovered at his shoulder. Many nights he tossed and turned or simply slipped from their bed to sit on the porch.

She let him have those moments to himself.

With a sigh, she straightened and let the cat finish her meal. She rubbed her upper arm, trying to massage away the residual numbness from where she'd been stung. The fire had subsided in her arm, but a dull headache had settled between her eyes. This pain, though, was from tension and not an aftereffect of the venom.

She stared to the north, toward the source of her nervousness.

What's taking you so long?

Earlier, Gray had called after reaching the community center in Hana, letting her know he was okay. But since then, nothing. He had warned her to stay at the cottage, as the situation in the small town remained chaotic. She imagined he was coordinating with Sigma back in the States, especially considering the unexpected arrival of Joe Kowalski.

Still, she remained on edge, anxious for an update.

The distant echo of sirens from Hana had faded a while ago, but the silence afterward only heightened her sense of misgiving.

She paced barefooted to the cottage's porch rail. It creaked when she leaned on it. According to the caretaker, the cottage had been built in the mid-forties, around the time the last sugar plantation had closed here. The thatch-roofed homestead sat a hundred yards off the highway, perched atop volcanic cliffs. The wooden structure was raised on stilts and ribbed by thick bamboo supports, harvested locally from a nearby forest. The furniture inside was all crafted of native koa wood. The old patina almost glowed.

For the past sleepy weeks, Gray and Seichan had the surrounding hundred acres all to themselves. Most of the grounds were untouched, a piece of unspoiled Hawaii, but closer at hand, the landscape was a paradise of papaya and banana trees, set amid towering palms. Wild gardens abounded, flowering with red ginger, yellow plumeria, and pink hibiscus.

Her gaze lingered on a plank swing hanging from a nearby mango tree. She and Gray had spent many hours there, lost in their own thoughts, watching the late-afternoon shadows stretch into evening.

She inhaled the night's perfume, drawing it deep.

The place reminded her of her home back in a small village in Vietnam. The jungles here were different, but there remained a similar sense of timelessness and connection to the natural world that harked to her childhood. Her fingers found the small dragon pendant at her throat, a gift from her mother before the woman was ripped from her life. Seichan had been loved back then, a love that infused their small hovel, transforming it into a magical place.

And maybe that was what truly made this cottage feel like home now.

She stared at the swing, remembering Gray's fingers entwined in hers as they sat together.

He had made this place a home.

She paced again, unable to escape a sense of trepidation, a feeling that everything was coming to an end. It was not his love she mistrusted, only her continuing capacity to accept it. These months on the road had been wonderful, beyond anything she could have imagined with another person. But at the same time, this was a dreamlike sojourn, one from which she'd have to eventually awaken.

And then what?

Under the harshness of reality, could this last? Or even should it?

The cat growled, drawing Seichan's attention around.

"Quit complaining. There's no more—"

The cat had her back to the plate, staring out toward the forest of palm trees. The deep-throated growl faded to a low hiss as the cat slunk warily to its belly.

Seichan followed the example and crouched. She shifted away from the glow of the kitchen window.

Someone's out there.

9:38 P.M.

Gray dialed the number for a third time. He was holed up in the community center's office, using their landline to try to reach Seichan. Unfortunately, the remote location of the cottage offered no cell service, which limited his communication options.

He listened as the connection rang once—then nothing but dead air.

He slammed the receiver down.

Earlier, he had reached Seichan by phone, but the emergency here must have finally overloaded the local systems. He cursed himself for abandoning his satellite phone when he left the States, but the device was Sigma property. Back then, he had wanted privacy and feared the phone would be used to track him.

Fat lot of good that did.

He stared out the office door at Kowalski. Clearly Painter had still managed to keep tabs on Gray.

Knowing he would have no better luck with the phone, he headed to the lobby. Kowalski straightened from where he was leaning against a wall. He had the stub of an unlit cigar clenched between his molars. A large nurse behind a desk stared daggers at him, as if daring him to try to light it.

Gray interrupted their standoff. "No luck reaching her. I'm going to make a run for my bike and head out there myself."

"Could be worrying over nothing," Kowalski groused. "And if there's trouble, knowing her, she'll handle it just fine."

Gray knew both statements were roughly true, but he wasn't taking any chances. If he and Seichan had been specifically targeted as part of this attack, he planned on facing any repercussions at her side.

"You hang here, while I check on her." He spotted a familiar broad-chested figure by the main doors and crossed over. "Palu, do any of your men have gear that might fit me? A jacket, maybe trousers?"

Palu must have understood his intent. "You planning on going back out there?"

"A friend of mine might be in trouble."

"Okay, then I'll go wit' you."

"Thanks, but there's not enough room on my bike."

"Who says we take your little bike?" Palu lifted an arm. A set of keys dangled from a finger. "I have a better ride."

The big Hawaiian nodded outside to a bright yellow SUV parked a few yards away. The words BATTALION CHIEF were emblazoned on the side door. Clearly it belonged to his boss, who was currently preoccupied with a radio interview.

"Plus I know a shortcut," Palu added. "Get you there *wikiwiki*."

Gray nodded, happy to accept the offer. "Let's go."

A gruff voice at Gray's shoulder startled him. Kowalski had followed him over, moving with surprising stealth for someone so large. "If he's going, I'm going."

Palu shrugged. "Mo' better."

"Fine." Gray waved to the door. "We all go."

Kowalski paused long enough to light his cigar, glaring back at the nurse behind the desk. They then rushed out the glass doors and through a cloud of smoke rising from a smoldering barbecue set up at the entrance. The acrid pall was meant to guard against the wasps still buzzing out there.

At least the worst of the attack seemed to have passed. Stars twinkled above. The majority of the swarm had rolled off into the dense rain forest that climbed the northeasterly flank of Mount Haleakala, a dormant volcano that formed half of Maui. While the immediate danger had dissipated, Gray suspected this was only the tip of the proverbial iceberg.

But dealing with such a threat would have to wait for now.

They reached Chief Renard's truck—a Ford SUV equipped with sirens and a light bar—and clambered inside. Palu hopped behind the wheel, while Gray joined him in front. Kowalski simply sprawled across the backseat.

Palu started the engine and got them moving.

A familiar buzz rose near Gray's ear. He ducked and glanced back. A large wasp landed and climbed across the inside of the window behind him.

Kowalski took his cigar and casually stubbed its lit end onto the wasp. Its body exploded with a sizzling pop. He then returned the stogie to his mouth.

Gray settled back to his seat.

Okay, maybe the guy has his uses.

9:44 P.M.

Crouched low, Seichan watched the black cat dash down the cottage's porch steps and vanish into the flowering shrubbery. That wasn't an option for her. At least, not yet. She had to assume that whoever was out there had the place surrounded.

She considered her options.

Shadow or *fire*.

The Guild had grilled those two approaches into her whenever she found herself cornered. *Shadow* involved staying calm, using stealth and subterfuge to slip out of a snare. Or she could *fire* up her adrenaline for a direct assault, breaking the snare by force.

Unfortunately, she had no firepower to blast her way out of here. As arbitrarily as she and Gray had moved from country to country, they hadn't been able to transport any sidearms. Traveling as civilians, they had no way of circumventing customs laws, and they had spent too brief a time in places to bother securing weapons through the black market.

Still, she wasn't totally unarmed. She had a sheaf of daggers, throwing knives, and a well-balanced Chinese cleaver secured in a leather roll. Only one customs official ever questioned her collection. To justify her possession of such an assemblage of cutlery, she had claimed to be a freelance chef and carried around a forged Diplôme de Cuisine from Le Cordon Bleu as proof.

Sadly, the knives were currently secured in the

back bedroom on the cottage's far end, and she dared not expose herself long enough to get inside.

Which left her no option but to follow the path of the *shadow*.

This decision was made in a single breath—with the next, she was already in motion.

9

"Anyone have eyes on her?"

Atop the cliff above the pounding waves, Masahiro Ito listened as each of his *genin* reported in from their positions around the thatch-roofed cottage. Fifteen minutes ago, the strike team had arrived by pontoon boat. They had paddled to shore, running dark, and scaled the cliffs fifty yards north of their goal to keep their arrival quiet and unseen.

Masahiro cursed whoever had alerted their target. He had ordered the others to stay hidden, to await the return of the American. His grandfather wanted both the woman and the soldier dispatched this night.

But now the situation had changed. Their target—the Eurasian woman, a traitor to the *Kage*—had disappeared just as the team had moved into position. One moment she appeared to be feeding a cat, and then she simply vanished off the porch. With the element of surprise gone, they could no longer hold back. The woman must be dispatched before she notified her partner of the ambush.

"Negative, *Chūnin* Ito," Masahiro's second-in-command radioed in. "No one has her in sight."

Masahiro clenched his jaw.

All five of his men were former *Kage* assassins, recruited by his grandfather after the destruction of the organization. As the hierarchy was brought low, few in the Echelon—the upper levels of the *Kage*—survived the global purge. As far as Masahiro knew, only his grandfather managed to avoid notice.

Who would give an elder of ninety years more than a second glance?

It was a mistake.

As the *Kage* collapsed, Masahiro's grandfather shielded him, not by hiding his grandson in some hole, but by pushing him further into the limelight. Masahiro became vice president of R&D for Fenikkusu Laboratories, a company founded by his grandfather decades ago. He was even granted a board position.

Still, his grandfather had assigned him another duty, one unknown to the board: to covertly gather the *genin*—or lower men—of the *Kage*, those who had scattered after the organization's fall. He was to take them under his wing and build them into a smaller but deadlier force.

Following his grandfather's guidance, he patterned this new group upon the *shinobi*, the secretive warriors of feudal Japan, a group who would later be bastardized and mythologized under the name *ninja*. His grandfather, Takashi, believed in the older ways, when Japan was at its most glorious. Though over ninety years of age, Takashi was the new group's *jōnin*, or leader. Masahiro was granted the title of *chūnin*, or "middle man." All the *genin* reported directly to Masahiro.

It was an efficient means of organization, one that had served the *shinobi* for centuries. Even their ancient training was honored, used to further hone the skills of the *genin* under him.

To that end, Masahiro carried a traditional *katana*, the sword sheathed over his back. He also bore a *kusarigama*—a steel sickle attached to a length of weighted chain—coiled at his waist.

While these were old weapons of the *shinobi*, Masahiro had updated their arsenal with modern tech. He and the others wore dark green camouflage with lightweight Kevlar body armor beneath and were armed with stubby 9mm Minebea machine pistols equipped with suppressors and night-vision scopes.

Still, each member of the strike team also wore the traditional *tenugui*, a length of cloth used to hide one's features, but which could also serve as a belt or even a rope for a quick climb.

Masahiro adjusted his *tenugui* higher on the bridge of his nose.

Where is this woman?

Frustrated, he knew he could wait no longer.

"Close in now," he ordered. "Kill on sight."

9:47 P.M.

Seichan crouched in the bower of a hundred-year-old mango tree. Its crown stretched thirty feet wide above her head, creating a pool of darker shadows below. She balanced barefooted on a limb as thick as her thigh.

Moments ago, she had leaped headlong over the porch rail, careful not to brush the rickety wood. Anticipating the enemy might be equipped with night vision or infrared, she rolled under the porch and past the stilts that supported the cottage. She used the wooden bulk to hide her passage, then darted back out into the thickest patch of garden, running low, until she could clamber up the nearest tree, seeking higher ground.

She expected focus to be on the cottage or the grounds.

Hopefully, not up.

She kept frozen on her perch. Her only movement was the silent breath in and out her nose. Then a rustle of dried leaves alerted her. A darker patch of shadows slipped under the wide bower below her. As she waited for her moment, she searched for anyone else in the immediate vicinity.

No one.

She took in this detail and judged the spread of the combatants. From there, she extrapolated the number necessary to surround the cottage and estimated a team of five to seven.

Not great odds, but she'd handled worse in the past.

Of course, back then she had been armed—with more than just a mango.

It'll have to do.

She gently tossed the ripe fruit to the left.

Below, the figure swung in that direction, one eye fixed to the gun's scope. With the target's back turned, she reached down to the rope knotted around the tree limb under her. It trailed down to the old swing where she and Gray had idled for many lazy hours. She hauled the line up, tilting the plank seat and drawing it higher.

Before the figure could turn back around, she dropped quietly off her perch. As she fell, she tossed a loop of rope over the man's head—then landed on the crooked seat with both feet. Her weight snapped the noose tight around her victim's neck. Still balanced on the plank, she twisted and grabbed the man's skull and finished what the rope had failed to do.

Vertebrae broke, and the man's limbs went limp.

She stepped off the swing and relieved the man of his weapon.

So much for *shadow*.

She hefted the submachine gun to her shoulder.

Now it's time for *fire*.

9:52 p.m.

A volley of blasts drew Masahiro's attention toward the cottage. The assault was under way. The suppressed gunfire sounded little louder than the clapping of hands. He shifted away from his position at the top of the cliff.

His team must have finally rousted the woman out of hiding.

Only a matter of time now . . .

He listened for two more breaths as the night went quiet again. He heard the soft *shush-shushing* of the waves behind him. Then another spate of gunfire erupted, only from a new direction, closer to his position.

Suspicion rankled through him. He crouched and touched the microphone buried in the folds of the *tenugui* covering his lips. "Status report?"

As he waited, his heart pounded. He sensed something was wrong.

Another short burst reinforced this.

Then Jiro, his second-in-command, radioed. He sounded winded, his voice strained. "She's secured a weapon. Took out three others."

More gunfire interrupted the conversation, followed by a sharp rattling cry.

Make that *four* . . .

Masahiro's chest tightened with fury.

Jiro spoke again, his voice hushed now: "*Chūnin* Ito, it is best you retreat to the boat."

Before he could refuse, a new voice cut in over the radio, sultry and calm, her Japanese flawless. "Or you can wait for me to join you."

Masahiro clenched the grip on his weapon. It seemed the woman had secured more than just a gun off one of his teammates.

She taunted him. "Or are you too much of a *koshinuke*?"

He bristled at the insult. He was no coward. Yet he also recognized she was goading him to act rashly. He took a deep breath, then spoke calmly.

"I will secure the boat and wait for you there, *Genin* Jiro."

"Understood. I will find her."

A snort of derision answered this challenge. "Then let us play."

9:56 P.M.

Seichan stood with her back to a palm tree as the exchange ended. She had her eyes closed, the stolen radio earpiece in her hand. She had heard the whisper of Jiro's last words rising somewhere to her left.

While her interruption had failed to spook the others or get them to overreact, she had managed to get a bearing on the gunman sharing the forest with her. She had already estimated that the group had arrived by boat, likely beaching somewhere north of the cottage's location. The coastline to the south was too jagged with rocks and pounded by heavier surf.

She weighed the odds of reaching the beachhead before the leader escaped by sea. Earlier, she had used the advantage of surprise and her knowledge of the local terrain to defeat four of the men, but the final target blocking her—the one called Jiro— would be wary and ready.

So be it.

She accepted the fact that she could not reach the leader in time and put all her attention into capturing Jiro alive. She planned on interrogating the man, picturing her knives rolled up in the cottage nightstand.

I will get him to talk.

She set off to the left, passing through a thicket

without stirring a branch. She paused periodically to use her gun's night-vision scope. Each peek illuminated the landscape in bright shades of gray. Her ears strained for every creak, rustle, and snap.

She had memorized the grounds, as she always did with any new surroundings. It was as instinctual as breathing after so many years. She knew every bush, tree, and rock. So when she spotted a stationary boulder amid a grove of papaya trees forty yards to her left, she knew it didn't belong there.

She settled to a knee behind a hibiscus bush, took aim, and fired two rounds dead center, avoiding a head shot if possible. She kept an eye on her scope. The bullets shredded through camouflage fabric and toppled the target over—revealing nothing beneath it but a frame of crossed branches.

A decoy.

Biting back a curse, she leaped headlong to the right. The hibiscus bush exploded under a spray of automatic fire. She landed on a shoulder and rolled to her feet. She kept firing blindly in the direction of the attacker as she ran. She didn't expect to hit him, only to drive him into cover.

She gritted her teeth as she fled. She would not underestimate her opponent a second time. She abandoned any pretense of capturing the clever man alive. When faced by such an adversary, there was only one safe play.

Kill or be killed.

Unfortunately, she failed to fully comprehend the game being played.

As she flew around an outcropping of volcanic rock, she found a figure already waiting there, with a weapon leveled at her chest. It was a trap. She had been flushed here on purpose. She immediately knew the man was not Jiro.

But rather his leader.

The bastard had not fled back to his boat after all.

She pictured the grin hidden behind his mask—as he fired at her.

10:02 P.M.

Masahiro savored the kill.

Unfortunately, he was premature. The woman was still in motion when she flew into view. She used that momentum to pirouette sideways, slimming her profile, her arms high. His first volley of rounds ripped past her stomach, close enough to tear through her blouse.

Before he could adjust his aim, she hammered her arm down. The butt of her stolen gun struck his wrist. Pain burst there, and he lost hold of his pistol.

Fortunately, the impact also jarred the weapon from the woman's grip.

They stared at each other for a half-breath—then both moved at the same time.

The woman lashed out with a roundhouse kick, while dropping low to retrieve her weapon. He leaped back to avoid the strike and grabbed the hilt of the katana sheathed across his shoulders.

As she scooped the pistol, he yanked the short sword from its scabbard and swept it at her face. She leaned back at the last moment, the blade slicing past her nose.

Though he had failed to draw blood, the damage was done.

Following the ways of the *shinobi*, he had packed the top of his scabbard with a powerful irritant. In the past, warriors had used powdered red peppers to subdue their victims; he updated the formulation with ground ghost pepper and dry bleach.

The effect was instantaneous.

The woman gasped as a waft of powder struck her eyes. The reflex drew the irritant deep into her nose and lungs.

She fired blindly, hacking and choking as she retreated.

He sheltered behind the rock and waited until she emptied the weapon's magazine. When the volley ended, he retrieved his pistol and gave chase. He intended to run his prey down himself.

But she remained fast, even incapacitated.

Within a few yards, a form burst alongside him out of the forest.

Jiro.

Masahiro pointed after the woman, and they set off together, both eager for the kill.

Blind and breathless, she had no hope of escape.

10:04 P.M.

With tears streaming down her cheeks, Seichan ran. She held her arms out before her. Each gasp seared her lungs. Her eyes felt like two hot coals in her skull.

It was as if she fled through the heart of a forest fire.

Only these woods remained watery and dark.

Her shoulder struck the bole of a tree and sent her careening to the side. She absorbed the impact, flowing with it to keep her footing. She dared not fall. She heard branches breaking behind her and the footfalls of her pursuers.

Through the pain and tears, she focused on the blurry glow through the darkness ahead, a beacon in the night. The lighted window of the cottage. She needed to reach shelter and buy herself enough time to secure her knives and hopefully a balm for her eyes.

No other choice.

She forced one leg after the other, racing toward that light. She used the flow of the ocean breeze and the slope of the ground to further guide her. Branches and thorns tore at her. Sharp volcanic stones ripped at the soles of her bare feet. Still, she sought to run faster as the others closed in on her.

She expected at any moment to feel rounds pound into her back.

Finally, the air opened up around her. The bushes and low tree branches stopped dragging at her body. She must have cleared the forest and entered the cottage gardens. The glow of the kitchen window beckoned, as bright as the sun to her inflamed eyes.

So close.

Then her world exploded.

Two supernovas burst to her right, circling the cottage on that side, coming straight at her.

Blinded by the glare, she froze, a deer in headlights.

Headlights . . .

A voice boomed at her, impossibly loud.

"Seichan! Drop flat!"

She obeyed, trusting the man who held her heart. She stumbled a few steps into that radiance, then sprawled on her belly. The twin supernovas ran up and over her. The gust of a large vehicle's passage whipped her torn blouse. She smelled exhaust as it cleared her.

Gunfire erupted behind her.

Then the heavy thud of metal hitting flesh.

She remained where she was, too exhausted and in pain to move.

Car doors slammed, and then a form dropped to his knees next to her.

"Are you okay?" Gray asked.

"I am now." She rolled with a groan, barely able to make out Gray's features. "Did . . . did you get both of 'em?"

"Only one. He managed to shove the other guy out of the way at the last moment."

She pictured this act and knew what it meant.

Jiro had sacrificed himself to save his leader.

"Kowalski went after the bastard, but he vanished into the dark. Even if we don't find him, I don't think he'll be back."

She stared off into the woods.

At least, not yet.

10:12 P.M.

Masahiro raced the pontoon boat away from the shoreline. He rounded a volcanic peninsula to put rock between him and the cliffs near the cottage. He had already radioed the float plane to rendezvous with him and prepare for the voyage away from these islands.

He sighed as he glanced back to shore.

The bio-attack had gone as planned. The only exception was in Kauai, when a sudden storm had waylaid operations there. Otherwise, matters had been set in motion on the other islands, and nothing could stop what would happen from here.

He faced the open ocean again.

Despite the success, he burned with shame.

He had failed in his grandfather's vendetta. The two most involved in the downfall of the *Kage* still lived.

And it is my fault.

Still, he intended not to repeat this failure, but to learn from it.

In the meantime, he would have to be satisfied to see these islands burn—especially as it would be the Americans themselves who would destroy Hawaii.

They would have no choice.

Once the truth revealed itself, the world would demand it.

He smiled within the folds of his *tenugui*.

Until then, the suffering here will be glorious to behold.

SECOND

EMERGENCE STAGE

10

Twelve hours after the attack in Hawaii, Kat Bryant paced the length of Sigma's communication nest. A tall Starbucks cup warmed her hands. She'd had no sleep overnight, except for a short nap. She was running on caffeine and adrenaline.

Not unusual, not for this job.

She finally stopped in the center of the circular room. The ambient light was kept low, like the control room for a nuclear submarine. All around, technicians manned computer stations, their faces lit by the glow of their monitors. The nest served as Sigma's digital eyes and ears. Information flowed into and out of this room, carrying feeds from various intelligence agencies, both domestic and foreign.

She was the master of this domain, the spider of this digital web.

Movement drew her attention to the door leading out to the hall.

Painter strode in, looking harried. He must have just returned from his meeting with their boss, General Metcalf, over at DARPA.

"What's the latest?" he asked.

"We have an updated casualty report."

Painter grimaced, clearly girding himself. "How bad is it?"

"Bad." She picked up an e-tablet from a workstation. "Across the islands, the number of fatalities stands at fifty-four, but there are over a thousand others hospitalized in various conditions. So, the death count will surely rise."

Painter shook his head. "And there's no telling how many more will be injured or killed in the days ahead as the swarm establishes itself across those islands."

"It'll be chaos for sure. Especially as local emergency services have no protocol for dealing with such an attack. Everyone is still scrambling for what to do."

"Has anyone claimed responsibility yet?"

"Not so far. But I expect the usual suspects will soon latch on to this disaster and try to take credit."

Which would only further complicate the investigation.

"What about the forensics on the crashed Cessnas?" he asked.

"All pilotless drones. Each of the aircraft—at least those that weren't burned beyond recognition—was reported stolen from sites around the globe, stretching back over the course of two years."

"So someone's been prepping for this attack for a long time."

"It would appear so."

Kat set down her coffee, tapped at the workstation keyboard, and brought up a map of the Pacific Ocean on a monitor. A translucent red circle swallowed the chain of Hawaiian Islands, along with a wide swath of the surrounding ocean.

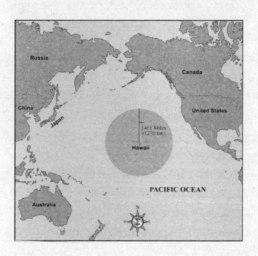

"The maximum flight range for a Cessna TTx is just shy of thirteen hundred nautical miles." She pointed to the circle. "Which means they were launched from somewhere in this zone."

Painter leaned closer to the map. "Unless the planes refueled along the way and originated from a greater distance."

Kat turned and raised a brow. "A fleet of pilotless Cessnas? I think such a sight would draw attention." She stared back at the screen. "No, I wager there must be a staging ground for this assault somewhere in this zone."

"That's a lot of ocean to cover."

"Almost seven million square miles. That's over *twice* the size of our lower forty-eight states."

Painter frowned at the screen. "There must be hundreds of islands in that region."

"More if you count atolls, islets, and shoals. But the number could be narrowed to only those places large enough to accommodate an airstrip." Kat sighed. "Admittedly, that still leaves plenty of potential sites."

"Do Hawaii's radar records offer any further guidance?"

"Unfortunately not. Their land-based systems only extend some two hundred miles out to sea. By the time the planes entered radar range, they were coming from every direction."

One of her techs pushed back from his seat and turned to her, looking hesitant to interrupt.

"What is it?" she asked.

"I have a call for you coming in on our secure channel."

"Who is it?"

"He says his name is Professor Ken Matsui. Claims you asked him to contact you."

Kat glanced over to Painter. "The Cornell toxicologist," she reminded him. "The one who made an inquiry with Dr. Bennett at the National Zoo."

Painter gave her a questioning look. "You mean the ghost?"

"Seems like he's come back from the dead."

Overnight, she had prepared a dossier on the scientist. According to a report out of Brazil, the professor—along with a student and two Brazilian nationals—had gone missing and were presumed dead after being caught in a storm at sea.

"We should take the call in my office," Kat offered.

She retrieved her cup of coffee and led Painter to the neighboring room. Her office was efficient and Spartan, much like herself. Her only personal effects were a scatter of pictures of her two young girls, Penelope and Harriet. The centermost photo showed her husband, Monk, balancing the two kids on his knees. The stocky man grimaced, appearing to be suffering under the weight of the five-year-old and seven-year-old. With his thick arms and wide chest bulging under a Green Beret T-shirt, he could easily have juggled the pair—which, considering the girls' rambunctious temperament, was a necessity every now and then.

Kat's eyes lingered there as she crossed to her desk. Monk had taken the girls to a camp up in the Catskills. She had planned to join them until the current emergency pinned her down in D.C.

Maybe I'm not the spider of this digital web after all, but more like a fly trapped here.

Still, she knew Monk would take good care of Penny and Harriet. Though it pained her to admit it, she had been leaning more and more on him of late to cover for her. Not that he ever complained. Still, a part of her envied the sabbatical that Gray and Seichan had taken, to carve out an uninterrupted swath of time. She owed that to Monk, to her family.

Yet, another part of her knew she could never give up this regular adrenaline fix.

She took a sip of her coffee.

Or all the caffeine . . .

The tech spoke over the intercom. "I have the caller on line two."

She set her cup down and put her desktop phone on speaker. "Professor Matsui, thank you for returning my call."

"I don't have much time. What's this all about?"

Though the international connection was a bad one, she easily heard the suspicion in the other's voice. She glanced to Painter, who waved for her to take the lead.

She pretended not to know about the professor's presumed death. "We got your name from an entomologist here in D.C. You contacted him in regard to an unusual species of wasp."

There was a long pause. Whispering could be heard in the background, as if he were consulting with someone before speaking.

She shared a glance with Painter.

What's going on over there?

"Yes," Matsui said, returning to the line. "But I think we all know we're too late."

"What do you mean?"

"The *Odokuro* have been released."

"The *Odokuro*?"

"That's what I've been calling this species of *Hymenoptera*. Named after a Japanese demon— *gashadokuro*. Trust me, it's a most fitting name. I've been studying the species for the past two months. Its life cycle is beyond anything imaginable."

"Wait. You've been studying this organism? Where? In Kyoto?" She recalled that the professor's last address was a research facility for a Japanese pharmaceutical company.

"I'm not in Kyoto any longer," he said.

"Where are you then?"

"Headed to Hawaii. Aboard a Tanaka corporate jet. We should be landing within the hour."

"Why are you going there?"

"To evaluate the colonization firsthand. It's the only way I'll know for sure."

"Know what?" she asked, as a cold dread settled over her.

"Whether or not you'll need to nuke those islands."

9:28 A.M. HST
Airborne over North Pacific Ocean

Ken Matsui stared out the window of the corporate HondaJet 420. He waited for the shock of his words to subside. Two over-the-wing engines raced them toward their destination in Honolulu. Though the aircraft was the fastest jet in its class, they had to refuel on Midway Atoll. The brief delay on the ground there had him pacing the small four-seater cabin.

I should never have agreed to stay silent.

He glared across the cabin at the slim figure of Aiko Higashi. She claimed to be with Japan's Public Security Intelligence Agency. The PSIA oversaw and investigated national threats and monitored local extremist groups. But Ken suspected there was more to this woman's background.

She certainly carried herself as someone with military training. Her haircut was trimmed in straight lines across her forehead and neck. Her navy blue suit was starched as stiff as her upper lip. Her expression seldom changed from its stern countenance as she had shadowed him these past months.

Finally, Kathryn Bryant returned to the conversation. Ken equally questioned whether the woman on the line was someone simply working for DARPA. Especially when word reached him about her request to speak to him. He had wanted to ignore the inquiry, but Aiko had insisted he take her call. Even now, she eavesdropped on the exchange, leaning imperceptibly forward from her seat.

"What makes you think such a drastic action might be necessary?" Bryant asked.

"Because I've seen firsthand the devastation wrought by the *Odokuro*."

"Where? How?"

Ken stared over at Aiko, who offered the smallest of nods. She had already told him to be forthright with this caller, as if she knew the woman on the line and trusted her enough to receive this information.

Ken, on the other hand, didn't know whom to trust. His parents had instilled in him a healthy suspicion of governments. The two had experienced firsthand how easily one could be chewed up or rolled over by those in power. His father had told him tales of the harsh, dehumanizing conditions found behind the barbed wire of the Japanese internment camps, where his dad was detained as a boy. The camp was located in the bucolic foot-hills of the Sierra Nevada mountains, not far from the small town of Independence, a name his father found both ironic and disheartening. Likewise, his German mother had her own experiences in her home country during the war. Though she seldom spoke of that time, she had taught Ken to question authority and stand up for the oppressed.

Still, despite his ingrained distrust, he knew his story needed to be told.

Especially now.

"It happened eight weeks ago . . ." he started, his voice catching in his throat.

Has it been only that long?

It seemed like ages ago now.

He pictured the smirking face of his postgraduate student Oscar Hoff. The memory of gunfire echoed in his head. He closed his eyes, pushing back the pain and terror of that trip. Still, guilt knotted his gut. He held a fist clenched to his stomach, mirroring that tension.

"What happened?" Bryant pressed.

He swallowed before speaking, then slowly told the story of what happened on Ilha da Queimada Grande, the cursed place that First Lieutenant Ramon Dias named "Snake Island." As he continued his story, his words became more rushed as the panic of that day returned. He described the dead bodies—both the smugglers and the swath of snakes—followed by the helicopter attack.

"They firebombed the island, burned it to the bedrock. But I escaped . . . and not empty-handed. I took a specimen, one of the lanceheads. Under the cover of night, I fled to the coast, to a small Brazilian village. Once there, I was afraid if anyone learned I survived . . ."

"You would've been killed," the caller said matter-of-factly.

He found himself surprisingly relieved by this confirmation. He knew a good portion of his shame and remorse had less to do with Oscar's murder than with his own silence afterward. The knot of guilt loosened the tiniest fraction. He unclenched his fist and let his arm relax.

He tried to explain his rationale. "I knew I had to return with what I'd taken from the island, to understand why this had happened. So I reached out to a colleague, someone I trusted at Tanaka. I needed the company's deep pockets to extract me from Brazil and get me somewhere safe before anyone knew I was alive."

"So Tanaka supplied you with false papers."

He glanced over to Aiko, who nodded again, further proving there was more to these two women than either pretended.

"They did. I made it safely to Kyoto, where I holed up at a research lab to study what I'd found. The snake's body was full of larva—the early instars of this species."

"Instars?"

"Stages of insect development," he explained. "The instars were devouring the snake from the inside."

He pictured the gruesome sight when he sliced into the lancehead at the quarantine lab. White larvae had boiled out of the body.

But that wasn't even the worst of it.

"Let's get back to the matter of the island," Bryant said. "It sounds like that isolated place was a test run by whoever orchestrated the attack on Hawaii."

"You're probably right, but I never imagined they had such ghastly plans. I assumed the island was merely home to a secret lab, one that lost control of its research, and as a fail-safe, they purged the place afterward, covering everything up."

"Yet, you just happened to stumble upon that island by accident?"

"I thought so at first," he admitted. Back then, he had dismissed this coincidence as a matter of being at the wrong place, wrong time.

Or so I tried to convince myself.

"But you have your doubts now?"

He stayed silent. Over time, he had indeed grown suspicious. It had left him feeling isolated and wary, especially on foreign soil. Sensing he was trapped, he had risked emailing a colleague, an entomologist at the National Zoo, to inquire if the man knew anything about this species. It had ended up being a dead end, but he'd had to try.

The woman on the phone spoke again. "You said Tanaka Pharmaceuticals funded most of your research through corporate grants. Was it the company who directed you to obtain venom samples from that island?"

"Yes," he said hesitantly.

He stared over at Aiko, who didn't blink.

"It makes me wonder," Bryant said, "if Tanaka suspected a competitor was at work on that island and sent you to investigate."

It was as if the woman were reading his own paranoid fears. He had never voiced it aloud, but he had come to wonder if he had ended up on that island as a pawn in some game of corporate espionage. In Japan, business was a blood sport, with operations often playing out in the shadows. Had someone at Tanaka heard a rumor of what was going on on Queimada Grande?

Was I sent in blindly to check it out?

It was a chilling thought.

But the woman wasn't finished.

"If I'm right, this suggests Tanaka's corporate spies directed you to that island based on intel from another company, one likely based in Japan."

"Wh—why Japan?"

"From the choice of target for last night's attack."

Ken suddenly understood her train of thought.

Why didn't I think—?

Aiko waved for him to pass the satellite phone to her.

He hesitated but obeyed.

She leaned over the phone. "*Kon'nichiwa*, Captain Bryant. It's Aiko. Aiko Higashi. Sorry I didn't alert you that I was aboard the jet with Professor Matsui. I wanted to see if you'd come to the same conclusion as our agency did."

"Aiko, hello." The woman on the line didn't miss a beat, seemingly taking the presence of the intelligence officer in stride. "The conclusion was an easy enough leap to make, especially as I was suspicious from the start." Her next words stunned Ken. "This might be Pearl Harbor all over again."

Aiko agreed. "A *biological* Pearl Harbor."

Ken turned to the window as the jet raced toward the chain of islands rising out of the ocean directly ahead.

If they're right, am I flying straight into a war zone?

3:55 P.M. EDT
Washington, D.C.

Kat led the director out of her office and across the communication nest.

She had finished the satellite call, which was rushed at the end as the jet made its final approach to the islands. She had instructed them to divert their aircraft from its intended destination of Honolulu and to land at Kahului Airport on Maui. From there they'd be airlifted to Hana to join Gray and company to evaluate the colonization of the swarm on that island.

The exact details of the threat remained frustratingly unclear as the call was cut short, but Kat already prepped an action plan. She ran it past her boss, turning to Painter.

"Aiko said she'd forward Professor Matsui's research on the *Odokuro* species as soon as they land. If it's okay with you, I'd like to consult Dr. Bennett, the entomologist at the National Zoo, to get his take on all of this."

"We can definitely use his expertise." Painter touched her arm as they reached the door out to the hall. "But how well do you trust this woman, Aiko Higashi?"

Kat took in a deep breath. "I know her on a professional basis, but not much beyond that. We ran up the ranks of our respective intelligence services around the same time. When I was in Naval Intelligence, she was working for the Japanese Ministry of Justice and was recruited by the Public Security Intelligence Agency. But she vanished from radar about two years ago, only to resurface again under the same PSIA banner."

"And what do you think that implies?"

"A few months before Aiko disappeared, a pair of Japanese captives were killed by Islamic militants in Syria. After that, the prime minister came under pressure by the military. Currently their constitution—written after World War II—limits espionage activity on foreign soil. But many in power are trying to amend the constitution to centralize and expand Japan's intelligence operations."

"You're thinking this woman could be an agent in some newly formed organization."

"I'm suspicious. Knowing how fragmented Japan's intelligence agencies are, it would take years for them to train handlers and field agents to run operations abroad."

"So you suspect they've already started that process in secret while the slow wheels of government turn."

"It's what I would do." Kat shrugged. "Plus, the Japanese are notoriously secretive, even more so than the British, where the existence of MI6 wasn't officially admitted until 1994."

"And if Aiko Higashi is part of this secret intelligence agency, what does that suggest as to her trustworthiness?"

Kat waved Painter toward the hall. "Same as me. Push comes to shove, she'll put her country's interest first."

Painter nodded. "We'll need to keep that in mind."

Kat prepared to let the director return to his office, but before she could turn away, the communication tech gave her a wounded look and held aloft a phone receiver.

"What is it?" she asked.

"Another call," he said. "Sounded urgent."

She checked her watch. Surely Aiko's plane hadn't already landed.

"It's from Simon Wright," the tech informed her.

Painter stepped to her side. "The curator of the Castle?"

Kat frowned at the unusual call. Simon—known as the "Keeper of the Castle"—was the only staff member of the museum above them who knew about Sigma's buried headquarters.

"What does he want?" she asked.

The tech's gaze flicked toward Painter. "He's asking for the director to come to a meeting at the Regents' Room of the Castle. The request was passed through him by Elena Delgado, the Librarian of Congress."

With a baffled expression, Painter crossed over and took the phone. "What's this all about, Simon?"

Kat had followed her boss over and overheard the curator's response.

"Dr. Delgado says she has information concerning events in Hawaii, something that harks back to the founding of the Castle itself."

Painter looked flabbergasted. "What information? What is she talking about?"

"I don't know for sure, but she claims to have knowledge about what was released in Hawaii. Along with a warning from the past."

"A warning from whom?"

"From Alexander Graham Bell."

11

Standing in the sunlit parking lot, Gray watched a small helicopter land in the neighboring soccer field. Another aircraft—a medevac chopper—sat in the middle of the baseball diamond. In the trampled outfield, temporary medical tents fluttered in the stiff morning breeze.

All around, a fleet of emergency vehicles lined the roads. They had arrived throughout the night, traversing the twisted and torturous Hana Highway, which hugged the rugged coastline. Bullhorns continually shouted orders, adding to the noisy chaos.

By now, the dead had been removed, but the injured were still being triaged. The worst afflicted were being shipped and distributed to various hospitals in Maui, some critical cases even to other islands. But with both Honolulu and Hilo attacked, beds were running low.

Out in the soccer field, a pair of figures climbed from the helicopter's cabin. Gray lifted an arm. They spotted him and headed over, bowing beneath the spinning blades.

As they approached, Gray recognized them from Director Crowe's description.

Professor Ken Matsui clutched a leather messenger bag to his chest as he hurried across the field. The toxicologist appeared to be in his mid-thirties, but from his tanned features and sun crinkles at the corner of his eyes, he had spent a good measure of his research time in the field. He also looked ready to work, dressed in khaki pants, boots, and a utility vest over a long-sleeved shirt.

He was trailed by an agent from Japanese intelligence. Aiko Higashi was whip-thin and crisply dressed. Her gaze swept across the commotion. Gray didn't doubt she absorbed everything in that single glance.

He had also been informed as to *why* the pair had been sent here: *to evaluate the threat level posed by the swarm's colonization.*

Gray's job was to make sure they accomplished this as quickly as possible—which meant first getting them clear of the chaos in Hana and circumventing any red tape that might slow them down.

When Professor Matsui reached Gray, they shook hands, but the man's eyes remained on a patient being stretchered toward the medevac helicopter. "What are they doing? This whole area should already be under quarantine."

"It's too late for that, Professor," Aiko said as she joined them. "A local quarantine would be a waste of resources at this juncture, especially with multiple islands affected. Later, if your evaluation proves as dire as anticipated, federal emergency services will need those resources—and more."

Gray frowned at her. "What do you mean?"

"Hawaii will need to be under quarantine, even blockaded. At that point, no one must be allowed to leave these islands."

Gray took in this grim news as he led the pair toward his Jeep. Earlier, Painter had informed him about the professor's belief that the only solution to this danger could be a nuclear one.

And if no one's allowed to leave these islands . . .

Gray stopped the professor at the Jeep. "How long will it take for you to make your initial assessment?"

"Less than a day. But if I confirm my worst fears, we'll have no more than three days before we'll be faced with the inevitable."

The professor looked hard at Gray, leaving no doubt as to what he was talking about.

"Trust me," Matsui said as he turned to the Jeep, "if we reach that point, those left on the island will be begging for us to drop those bombs."

A doctor in blue scrubs caught the tail end of the conversation as he passed their group. He looked quizzically back at them.

Not wanting to create a panic, Gray hustled everyone into the Jeep.

Palu was already behind the wheel. Gray had needed someone who knew the local terrain and had recruited the Hawaiian fireman. Palu agreed after Gray explained the seriousness of the situation. It hadn't been hard to convince the big man. He had a wife and two children in town.

As soon as everyone was aboard, Palu took off. He drove them cross-country toward the rental cottage, skirting the main highway. They traveled dirt tracks and, at one point, cut straight through a coconut farm owned by a local nursery.

Professor Matsui clung to the door handle in the back as he was bounced about, but his gaze remained on the verdant landscape of lush green meadows and vast stretches of rain forest climbing up to the clouds that hugged the top of Mount Haleakala.

"Dear God, I hope I'm wrong," he mumbled to himself.

As do we all.

The Jeep finally reached the cottage. Palu parked at the foot of the porch. Kowalski sat there with his boots on the rail, the satellite phone crooked by his ear. He nodded to Gray as the group climbed out, but he didn't let their arrival disturb his call.

"I paid good money for it," Kowalski said. "Tell the bastard that the poolside cabana is yours. If he gives you any trouble, I'll take one of those beach umbrellas and shove it where there's no goddamn sun to worry about."

His girlfriend, Maria, had offered to stay nearby in Wailea. With her background in genetics, her expertise could prove useful during this crisis.

It seemed a prudent precaution at the time—but now that Gray had learned the true level of threat posed by the swarm, he might be needlessly risking the geneticist's life.

Seichan appeared in the doorway. She squinted between swollen eyelids at the pair of strangers. Her focus lingered on Aiko Higashi, clearly sizing her up and evaluating this potential adversary.

While Seichan had recovered her sight from the attack, her skin was a patchwork of bruises, all criss-crossed with scrapes and cuts.

Gray mounted the steps to join her. "We have drinks and food inside," he informed the others. "We can compare notes while you fuel up. I want to be back on the road within the hour."

Professor Matsui nodded. "The sooner, the better."

With everyone on the same page, Gray made introductions all around.

The professor shook Seichan's hand. "You can call me Ken. Especially considering what we'll be facing together."

He extended this invitation to the group by glancing around, but his gaze settled back on Seichan. She had that effect on most men, not to mention a few women.

To clarify matters, Gray slid an arm around her waist as they went inside. It was for the professor's own good.

She'd eat you alive.

Gray led the group to a narrow dining table constructed of koa wood. A wicker ceiling fan slowly churned the warming air. As everyone settled, Gray remained standing, leaning on the back of one of the chairs. He fixed the professor with a stare.

"What exactly are we facing here?" he asked.

11:28 A.M.

Ken opened his bag and removed a laptop and folders. He shuffled through them, buying himself time to collect his thoughts. He felt the scrutiny of these strangers and the weight of his responsibility.

Where to start . . . ?

He finally settled on a folder of photos and read its tab.

"I've named this species *Odokuro horribilis*. And while I don't know everything about this creature, what I do know is indeed *horrible*."

Seichan shifted in her seat, wincing slightly. "I recognize the name *Odokuro*," she said, her voice hoarse after whatever injuries she had sustained. "That's a monster out of Japanese mythology."

He nodded. "*Gashadokuro* is an ancient spirit, said to rise from battlefields, a skeletal giant made of the disarticulated bones of the dead. The only warning of its approach is the rattle of bones."

Ken looked down at the folder again, drawn back against his will to Queimada Grande. He pictured the dark mist rising above the island's rain forest. He remembered the strange hollow knocking that had accompanied the swarm's appearance. He recalled even thinking at the time that it reminded him of rattling bones.

But that wasn't the only reason he picked that monster's name.

"Once *gashadokuro* has your scent," Ken continued, "it will hunt you down, letting nothing stop it. Made up of loose bones, it can even break up into smaller pieces to squeeze through tight spaces, only to re-form again on the other side."

"Like a swarm," Gray mumbled.

Ken nodded. "And after it catches you, there's no appeal, no way to stop it. It will devour your skin, organs, and blood, and add your bones to its own at the end."

The big man named Kowalski leaned back in his chair with a groan. "Something tells me I'm not going to like the rest of your story."

No, you're not.

"Enough with ghost stories," Gray said. "Tell us about these wasps."

"Right." Ken cleared his throat. "First of all, this species wasn't born in any lab. From my initial study of its DNA, it doesn't appear to be a genetically engineered monster, but a natural predator, something ancient, likely prehistoric. Wasps have been found in the fossil record going back to the Jurassic Period. Since then, the species has diversified and multiplied. Today there are over thirty thousand different species. Which proves how supremely agile they are at surviving. To accomplish that, they've adapted all sorts of strategies, often incorporating other insect traits and skills into their own arsenal."

"And this species?" Gray pressed.

"I've never seen one so versatile and resourceful. For example, most wasp species can be divided into social animals or solitary hunters." He noted their confused expressions and tried to explain. "*Social* wasps—like hornets and yellow jackets—build nests, have a queen who lays eggs, and employ a whole slew of drones that forage for food or are involved in mating or in protecting the hive. The venom of their stings is usually defensive, meant to induce pain as a warning to back off."

The Hawaiian, Palu, rubbed his stomach. "Yep, got that message loud and clear."

"Exactly. And if you ignore that warning for too long, additional stings can pump enough toxin into you to turn deadly."

Gray grimaced. "As we witnessed last night."

"But social wasps are relatively tame compared to *solitary* wasps." Ken found himself staring at Seichan, somehow sensing this woman could relate to such a species. "These lonely hunters have developed a unique and deadly survival strategy. They don't have nests or swarms like social wasps. Instead, the hunters of these species—all females—use their stingers for two purposes. The most important being the task for which the stinger was originally designed."

"What do you mean?" Seichan asked.

Ken backtracked a little to clarify. "The stinger of all *Hymenoptera* species—whether a bee, a hornet, or a wasp—was originally an ovipositor, a biological syringe meant to poke through tough tissue and inject eggs beneath it. But over time, the ovipositor evolved into a weapon."

"How?" Palu asked, still rubbing the spot on his belly.

"Once a queen became the exclusive egg layer for a hive, the other female wasps had no need for an egg sac at the base of their ovipositors. Instead, they transformed those sacs into a more useful purpose: to inflict damage."

Gray understood. "By filling those sacs with *venom* instead of eggs."

"Precisely. It's also why you don't have to worry about male bees or wasps. Being non–egg layers, they have no stingers."

Kowalski shrugged heavily. "I'm not about to look under a wasp's skirt to decide if it's a boy or a girl. If it lands on me, I'm squashing it."

Gray waved to Ken. "Go on. Back to these solitary wasps. With no hive queens, I'm assuming these female hunters continue to use their stingers—their ovipositors—to inject eggs."

"They do. Like I said before, their stingers serve two purposes. To lay eggs, but also to inject a poison that subdues their host. Such a venom is seldom painful. In fact, sometimes it can trigger a euphoric high that leaves the host entranced. There are caterpillars who fall so deeply under the spell that they'll willingly allow themselves to be dragged down a hole and buried alive. But the toxin's effect varies by species. Some paralyze a host. Others can trigger a baffling neurologic effect, where the host will actually fight to protect the larva inside it. But all these different venomous strategies have the same purpose."

"Which is what?" Seichan asked.

"To leave the host alive." He saw the others understood the implication, but filled in the blank anyway. "Once those eggs hatch, the larvae inside have a ready-made meal."

Sickened expressions spread around the table.

Better they know the truth now.

He pictured the storm of white larvae boiling out of the dissected lancehead.

"And the species dumped onto these islands?" Gray asked. "I'm assuming from its arrival as a swarm that we're dealing with a *social* species."

"No." Ken slowly shook his head. "This species is *both*."

"But wait? How can that be?"

"As I said before, this is an *ancient* species, one that likely existed before wasps differentiated into those two camps. Instead, this species shares characteristics of both evolutionary pathways." He let that sink in before continuing. "And despite the damage wrought last night, you've not seen the worst that this species can do."

Gray straightened. "What do you mean?"

"The swarming behavior of this species has one goal, one purpose."

"Which is what?"

"To seek out and establish a *lek*."

Kowalski frowned. "What the hell's a *lek*?"

"It's a mating territory." He swept his gaze across those gathered at the table. "Which we must not let happen."

Gray frowned at him. "Why?"

Ken allowed the group to see his seriousness and terror. "Because once that happens, this place will become hell on earth."

BREEDER

The tiny drone was nearly blind and deaf. Two pinpoint black eyes, no more than a dozen facets apiece, strained for visual cues, but the world remained a colorless blur, shaded in grays. Only when close to an object could he see any details.

Instead, his head was dominated by a pair of antennae, each longer than his body and feathered at the end with puffs of delicate sensillae. As he flew, he waved those perceptive tools that he used to define his world by gradients of smells.

He lit upon a petal, drawn by the sweet nectar. His antennae probed for the source, pulling his head deeper into the flower. Lacking the strong mandibles of the others, he extended a long tongue and lapped at the richness found buried in the heart of the petals.

As he took his fill, he was content. The swarm had settled into a dense, shadowy forest—though to his weak senses, he could barely hear their hum and buzz. As he emptied the flower, he climbed to the edge of the petal and groomed the pollen from his limbs, fluttering his wings clean.

He must be ready.

Then he sensed it—faint at first, then undeniable.

A pheromone that his fine sensillae had evolved to detect. His blind head turned, tugged by his antennae. He leapt in that direction, unable to refuse. Chemicals fired the tiny knot of ganglions in his head. He drove faster. His wings buzzed with ferocity, threatening to burn through the reserve of nectar in his body.

He did not care.

He followed the trail of pheromones. The complex broth of hormones and scents overwhelmed him, filled his drab world, forming a cloudy image in the distance.

He raced others like him for the prize. They collided, rebounded, fought their way toward the source. Each struggled to be there first. The aroma fueled him as much as the sugar in his abdomen. Muscles in his thorax became fire.

Ahead, scent became shadowy shape.

Then, once close enough, those tiny eyes perceived the target—and shape became substance.

A hundred times his size, she hovered ahead, exuding a pheromone of receptiveness, fluttering in a haze of evolutionary demand. He and the others dove through that miasma to reach her. They came from all directions, climbing atop her, scrabbling over her.

He landed among them and clung with his hindmost legs, a pair of barbed claspers. Others crashed atop him, even broke his wings. Still, he dug his claspers deep into the jointed armor of her abdomen and held fast.

In turn, she fought them. She flung and contorted. Legs kicked and scraped.

Finally, their combined weight and interference with her wings drove her into a tumbling spin through the leafy bower and into the soft litter on the ground.

He and the others jostled and battled for position. From her flanks, pheromones continued to flow, rising like steam from scores of small pores lining her abdomen. He shifted to the nearest, intoxicated and drawn by that scent.

Once there, hormones forced his own abdomen to contract, extruding his phallic aedeagus. He jabbed it through the pore and into one of her countless oviducts. Locked into her now, his entire body clenched. He emptied everything into her until he was a hollow husk.

With nothing left to offer, he jackknifed his powerful claspers against her flank and threw himself off. The violence ripped the aedegus from his body, leaving it as a plug in her oviduct.

He fell, broken and wingless, into the soil.

Others did the same, shedding from her great body.

Though empty, his duty was not yet done.

Out of the haze and murk of his weak vision, a shadow pushed closer, becoming clearer to his tiny eyes. He recognized what approached.

A set of mandibles.
He knew what he still owed her.
She was hungry.

12

Gray leaned on the dining table. He stared as Professor Matsui pulled a set of photos from a folder marked ODOKURO and spread them across the patina of the old wood. Each picture showed a different wasp: some small, others quite large.

Gray struggled to comprehend what he was seeing.

"These are all incarnations of the same wasp species," Ken explained as he organized his work. "The level of differentiation of these adults is fascinating. Their anatomy dictates their function. Each one serves a specific role in the swarm."

Moments ago, Ken had explained how he came to study these wasps, how he had harvested larvae from a snake discovered on a Brazilian island and grown them in a lab in Kyoto. There he had watched his subjects molt through a series of larval stages, instars, until the final pupae produced the adults in the photos.

Ken shifted one of the pictures closer. It showed a tiny wasp with elongated antenna, its body covered in tiny hairs. "Take for instance these tiny scout drones. Their anatomy seems built solely to gather sensory data and share it with the swarm. I'm guessing they're the group's surveyors, evaluating and judging territory."

Gray examined the photo. "I think I saw a bunch of these dead in the water when Seichan and I escaped the beach."

"Really?" Ken rubbed his chin. "Perhaps they had served their purpose once the swarm made landfall, and died off. That's interesting."

To you maybe.

Still, the professor's surprise was a reminder of how little they knew about their enemy. With only two months to study this species, Ken had made significant progress, but much remained unknown, especially as the professor's research was all conducted in a lab versus in the field. Though considering the gruesome state of that Brazilian island, maybe keeping his investigation confined to a lab was smart.

Ken tapped another picture. This one showed a larger wasp pinned to a board. For perspective, a small ruler rested beside it. The armored body, striped in black and crimson, measured three inches across.

"I know you encountered this one," Ken said.

Gray winced and nodded.

"This sterile female's stinger wields a cornucopia of toxins in its venom. Unfortunately, I've not had enough time to fully assess all of its components. But this worker's purpose is obvious."

Gray could guess that answer. "To clear the way for the swarm."

"And defend any *lek* it forms afterward."

Gray frowned. "You warned us about that before, about the swarm seeking a mating territory."

"Yes. It's best you understand what's at stake." Ken searched through his photos. "Those first two photos illustrate what I had mentioned before, how this species acts like typical social wasps. They demonstrate swarming behavior, with drones serving different functions. Some are built to be searchers; others, defenders. But there are also what I call *harvesters* and *gardeners*. All typical of a swarm's differentiation of duties."

Ken finally found what he was looking for and slid two new photos toward Gray. "But this pair is different. They reveal that rather than a single queen ruling this hive, the breeding of this swarm is conducted by a collective of solitary wasps. And once a satisfactory *lek* is found, breeding will begin."

Gray studied the two pictures. One was a blowup of a very tiny wasp, barely larger than a typical ant.

"That's a male," Ken explained. "He'll mate with the larger female in the other photo."

Kowalski whistled between his teeth. "She looks like an aircraft carrier next to that little bugger."

It was an apt analogy. This breeding female was even larger than the stinging attackers from last night, well over five inches.

Luckily, none of us here were stung by that specimen.

Ken's next words reinforced this sentiment.

"She is a veritable egg factory," he explained. "I've never seen anything like her. She'll mate with hundreds of males at the same time to collect enough spermatheca for her load. Afterward, she consumes the spent males."

"She eats them?" Kowalski shook his head with disgust. "Remind me never to complain when Maria wants to cuddle afterward."

Palu concurred. "Amen, braddah, amen."

Professor Matsui ignored the pair. His expression was one of scientific curiosity rather than revulsion. "This species does not waste resources needlessly." He pointed to the posterior of the female. "Look at its stinger. Almost a half inch long. In her abdomen, the eggs are on a conveyor-belt-like system. Once she finds a host, she'll stitch that needle all over the body, injecting thousands of eggs. And note her thick hind legs; they're extremely powerful. She can crack them together, like you might snap your fingers. When they do that as a group, it creates a weird rattling sound. And it's loud, about the same decibels reached by cicadas."

"Why do they do that?" Seichan asked.

"I . . . I think it acts as a crude form of sonar."

She narrowed her sore eyes. "Sonar?"

"Even modern wasps deploy such a technique. They use sonar to scan a potential host for the presence of larvae, evaluating whether or not a target has already been parasitized by another female."

"So," Gray said, "she goes knocking to see if anyone's home."

Ken swallowed, his gaze momentarily distant. "It's a disturbing noise. And heralds the beginning of the end."

"Why?" Seichan asked.

"Because I've not told you the worst. You've not

asked me the most obvious question about this prehistoric organism."

Seichan frowned. "What question?"

Gray could guess and asked it out loud. "If this species is so ancient, where did it come from? How come these wasps are still alive today?"

Unfortunately, Ken knew the answer. "Because they don't die."

11:58 A.M.

And I almost missed it . . .

Ken knew if he hadn't stumbled upon this final detail concerning this species' life cycle, they would already be doomed. No one would know the true threat posed by the colonization of these wasps. He had to get authorities here to understand the extent of the danger, which started with this motley group connected to DARPA.

He paced the length of the table, trying to shed his anxiety. "I warned earlier about how efficiently wasps have evolved since their first appearance during the Jurassic Period, how wasp species have developed clever strategies to survive, carving their own unique niche in an environment. Some pick only one host in which to lay their eggs, while others are generalists, choosing whatever organism is handy. Many modern wasps can even multiply without mating. In fact, there are a few species of wasps that have no known males."

"Sounds okay to me," Seichan mumbled.

"What about *these* wasps?" Gray asked.

"The *Odokuro* deploy several strategies for propagating their numbers. Like some of our modern wasps, each of their eggs produces multiple larvae. All of them appear pluripotent, meaning they are capable of becoming *any* of these adults." He waved a hand across the spread of photos. "I still don't understand what environmental signals or stressors drive a larva toward one adult version versus another. But this method is very robust at growing a swarm rapidly. From egg to adult takes about two weeks. And the species likely breeds continuously. I estimate the swarm's size would grow exponentially, limited only by the amount of food and the number of viable hosts for its eggs."

Ken tried to emphasize the significance. "Normally a colony's *size* is limited by its sole queen. When the environment turns hostile—like during the cold of winter—the colony dies off. Only the queen survives. She digs in and hibernates during the freeze, but come spring, she emerges again, full of eggs, ready to establish a new colony."

Gray's face grew grim. "But that's not the case here."

Ken shook his head. "The *Odokuro* swarm will simply grow and grow."

"But earlier, you mentioned a timeline of *three* days. Why? If these wasps take two weeks to mature, why is three days a deadline?"

Kowalski snorted. "And you said before that these buggers don't *die*? I squashed a bunch of 'em. Looked pretty dead to me."

Ken nodded. "The answer to both of your questions is the same. It's the other way the swarm ensures its survival. Similar to those all-female wasp species, the *Odokuro* can multiply asexually. A process they do continuously during the larval stage, specifically when they reach their third instar, the third level of development."

"Which I'm guessing must happen around day three," Gray said.

"And I came close to missing it. Let me explain. An egg hatches almost immediately upon implantation and releases a load of the first instar larvae. They're ravenous and will eat nonstop, eventually shedding their skin within a day, and becoming the second instar. The process repeats again until another molt produces the third. Then the larvae do something unique. They're still small enough at that stage to drill into the bones of their hosts and nest in the marrow."

Kowalski gave a shudder of revulsion. "I knew I wasn't going to like this story."

"You have to understand that all wasps are very clever at using a host's own resources to hide their larva, even sometimes allowing a host to crawl around, completely oblivious of its own infestation until it's too late."

"What happens once the larvae are in those bones?" Gray asked.

"At first, I thought they were just feeding on the rich marrow, but when I examined the tissue microscopically, I found some strange debris left behind. I was ready to dismiss it as *frass*, or larval excrement, but the particles were too regular and abundant. Here, let me show you."

Ken shuffled through the photos until he came

upon an electron micrograph of one of these particles and passed it around.

"It looks like a crazy egg of some sort," Palu said.
"With lots of blisters on it."

Gray squinted at the picture. "What is it?"

"Palu is basically correct. It's a desiccated cyst,
about a tenth of the size of a grain of rice. It's full
of those blisters. Well over a thousand. Each blister
holds a miniature genetic clone of the third instar,
only with tiny nubby claws."

Ken showed them a scanning electron micrograph of it.

"Remember when I told you how wasps sometimes incorporate the strategies of other insect
species?" He tapped the picture. "This is an example."

"I don't understand," Gray said. "What strategy is it borrowing?"

"Are you familiar with tardigrades?"

Heads shook around the table.

"They look much like what's shown here. They're sometimes called 'water bears' because of their pudgy appearance, but they're basically micro-animals, little larger than 0.05 millimeters."

"And what do they have to do with these wasps?" Gray asked.

"Tardigrades are far older than wasps, almost twice as old, rising sometime during the Cambrian period. But today you can find species of tardigrades in every environment because they're extraordinary survivors. When environmental conditions grow harsh, they can undergo a deathlike hibernation—known as *cryptobiosis*. They curl up into a dried-out ball, called a *tun*. In this suspended state, they can withstand temperatures close to absolute zero and as high as 300 degrees Fahrenheit. Not to mention crushing pressures or the vacuum of space. They can even survive massive doses of radiation. They are virtually indestructible."

Ken pointed to the cyst in the photo. "Back in 1948, scientists in Japan showed that *tuns* could come back to life after one hundred and twenty years of *cryptobiosis*. And newer research suggests they could survive many times that, if not nearly forever."

Gray lifted the photo of the cyst. "And you believe these wasps borrowed this survival skill from these tardigrades?"

"Why not?" Ken shrugged. "Even tardigrades learned this trick from other species. Almost eighteen percent of their genome comes from prehistoric plants and fungi. Including what's been deemed the dark matter of life."

"Dark matter of life?"

Ken nodded. "The term refers to bacteria that exist in the boundary between life and death. They've only recently been identified, described as Lazarus microbes. Like *Natronobacterium*, which came back to life after being encrusted in crystals for a hundred million years. Or colonies of *Virgibacillus*, which were revived after lying dormant inside formations for two hundred and fifty million years. And those are only a few. There are likely many more examples yet to be found."

"And you believe these wasps incorporated some of these ancient survival strategies." Gray turned to Ken. "Why? To what end?"

"I believe it's an evolutionary safeguard. They leave behind this indestructible genetic trail, hidden and protected in the bones of their dead hosts. Perhaps to wait until those bones turn to dust, allowing the cysts to be blown far and wide, hopefully to be inhaled or ingested by some unsuspecting animal. Once inside a suitable host, they would hatch and continue their life cycle through the fourth and fifth instars, eating their way through that host until they burst forth as adults, allowing the swarm to be reborn again."

Aiko Higashi spoke for the first time. "Like a phoenix rising from the ashes."

Ken noted the ruminative quality to her statement, as if this detail struck her as significant. Still, she ignored his questioning glance, so he continued.

"By day three," he said, "the swarms on these islands will become entrenched into the environment, down to its very *bones*, rooted so deeply there will be no eradicating it. And that's not even the end of it."

"What do you mean?" Gray asked.

"Remember that these wasps keep their hosts *alive*. So, while parasitized with larva, birds will take wing and spread it. Rodents will burrow away. Animals will migrate."

"And people will travel," Gray added dourly.

"If we don't create a firebreak here," Aiko warned, "it will quickly spread worldwide."

"Wreaking environmental havoc." Ken tried to express what was coming. "During my brief time with these wasps, I tested to see if they showed any pickiness in regard to the hosts they're willing to parasitize."

Seichan leaned forward. "Were they?"

"No." He pulled forward the photo of the egg-laden female. "This stinger evolved during the Jurassic Period. Besides being a half-inch long, it's forged of sclerotized tissue, nearly as hard as steel. It was meant to pierce tough hides, even penetrate between the armored plates of dinosaurs. Compared to prehistoric creatures, life here is an easy bounty. And worst of all, we've no natural defenses against this ancient species."

"Meaning we're sitting ducks," Kowalski said.

Gray slowly nodded, plainly absorbing all this. "There's certainly plenty of modern examples of the damage done by invasive species. Pythons in the Everglades. European rabbits in Australia. Asian carp in our lakes."

"And those were merely species moving from one continent to another. We're talking about a creature not seen in this world for eons." Ken grew frustrated at his inability to convey the true extent of this threat. "I saw what was left on Queimada Grande. These wasps will lay waste to anything that crawls, slithers, or flies. It won't even care if it burns out the local environment."

"Because it has a backup plan to survive." Gray shoved the photo of the cyst away. "So we stop that before it happens."

Ken sighed.

Easier said than done.

Gray stood up. "Tell us what we should do."

He turned toward the window, toward the midday brightness shining across the gardens. "First, we need to find where the swarm settled."

Gray stepped over to the credenza and returned with a topographic map of the island. "Do you have any idea *where* we should begin looking?"

"From my brief study, the *Odokuro* don't appear to be nest builders like social wasps. I suspect they're more like solitary wasps in this regard, too. If so, they'll seek burrows to create underground shelters."

Palu leaned over the map. "Trade winds blow this way." He drew a line from Hana into the forests that climbed the slope of Mount Haleakala.

He stared for a long breath, then tapped a spot on the map.

The big Hawaiian turned to the others, grinning broadly. "I think I know where these *li'i* buggers could be."

13

Painter crossed through the octagonal-shaped rotunda on the second floor of the Smithsonian Castle. Doors led to various offices, but he aimed for the set that opened into the illustrious Regents' Room. Voices echoed out through the half-open door.

"Let's see what this summons is all about," Painter whispered to Kat.

He kept his voice hushed, not out of secrecy, but out of respect for the history of the old building. The churchlike quality of the place, with its grand spaces, private chapels, and long galleries, weighed upon one's sense of time. He could picture the first secretary, Joseph Henry—whose bronze statue graced the front of the Castle—walking these halls. There were even rumors the place was haunted. In fact, a séance was once conducted in the Regents' Room, overseen by Henry himself, done at the bequest of Lincoln to convince his wife, Mary Todd, that spiritual mediums were frauds.

Painter found himself smiling at such a scene, his love of this place warming through him. He and Kat had ridden up in the hidden elevator from their subterranean headquarters to enter the Castle proper. The museum had closed thirty minutes ago, so the lower halls were only occupied by a handful of docents and a scatter of janitorial staff. He always enjoyed these after-hour moments in the museum, when he had the place mostly to himself. He would sometimes even wander the halls after midnight, using the quiet to help settle his thoughts. It allowed him to see problems more clearly, to un-clutter his mind. The place also served as a stony testament to the respect for science, for the lessons taught by history. It reminded him of the important duty of Sigma.

Kat lowered her phone as they neared the entrance to the Regents' Room. "Dr. Bennett confirmed he received Professor Matsui's research notes. He texted that he'll review them immediately."

Painter nodded. He had spoken briefly with Gray before heading up to this meeting and had gotten a sketchy account of what had been released on the Hawaiian Islands. He hoped the entomologist at the National Zoo could shed further light on this threat.

Especially with the deadline set by Gray.

Three days.

With such a narrow window, he bristled at this summons, not wanting to waste any time. Still, he could not discount his own curiosity concerning this meeting. What light could the Librarian of Congress shed on any of this? How could it be connected to the founding of the Castle or even more unlikely, with Alexander Graham Bell, the inventor of the telephone?

Only one way to find out.

Painter knocked on the door and pushed it the rest of the way open. He waved Kat in first, then followed.

The Regents' Room was dominated by a large circular table with the sunburst seal of the Smithsonian at the center. All around, velvet curtains framed the windows that overlooked the Mall and the rest of D.C. It was here that eighteen members of the Board of Regents met every quarter.

Currently, though, there were only two people present.

The curator of the Castle, Simon Wright, circled around to greet them. The man was in his mid-fifties with hair that had gone white at a young age. He wore it to his shoulders, brushed back like an aging rock star.

"Director Crowe, thank you for coming. And Captain Bryant, it's always a pleasure to see you again. How are your girls?"

Kat shook the man's hand and smiled at his genuine warmth. The three of them knew one another going back well over a decade. "I shipped them off to camp with Monk."

"No kids? No husband? Then I must apologize for disturbing what normally must be a rare moment of R&R for you."

"Considering the circumstances, I understand."

Simon introduced them to the chamber's other occupant, Elena Delgado, the current Librarian of Congress. His manner grew more formal. She had been appointed to the post only four months ago, the first Hispanic woman to hold this office. So none of them were well acquainted with her.

Still, Painter respected her curriculum vitae. She was the youngest of four daughters, born to migrant parents in California. Her academic and athletic prowess earned her a dual scholarship to Stanford. There she earned a doctorate in American history, while also winning both a silver and a gold medal at the Munich Olympics for swimming. Afterward, her interest in history kept her ensconced in library stacks, enough that she had earned a second PhD from the nearby University of Maryland in library sciences.

Painter happily shook her hand. Her grip was firm. It appeared, despite being sixty-four, that she kept her Olympic physique. Her only concession to age was the pair of reading glasses hanging around her neck by a thin silver chain that also bore two small crucifixes.

"I know your time is valuable," she said abruptly and drew them to the table. "But I believe this is important."

On the table before her rested two books. One was bound in thick leather, but the cover had been cracked and blackened, as if someone had tried to burn it. The other looked newer, with an elastic strap sealed around it, but the binding appeared hand-sewn, suggesting it was at least a few decades old.

She placed a palm on one of the books, almost possessively. "These volumes are from a special collection sustained by each successive Librarian of

Congress. Few know of this private stack. Over the centuries, books have been disappearing from various museum's racks, so it was decided to conserve a special library of texts important to our nation, books that might not necessarily be priceless—such as our copy of the Gutenberg Bible—but were of significant worth to keep secure nonetheless."

Simon nodded. "Elena is right. As curator, I can attest that a good portion of the Smithsonian collection has a tendency to drift away. In total, about ten percent of our artifacts and books have vanished. And not just small objects. We're talking about almost three dozen Tier Four items, each worth a million dollars or more."

Kat looked shocked. "Were they stolen?"

Simon shrugged. "Some. Others were checked out, never to return. And I'm sure a good portion were simply miscataloged, lost somewhere at our Suitland storage facility."

Painter knew about the site he was talking about. The Museum Support Center over in Suitland, Maryland. Its five buildings, each the size of a football field, warehoused 40 percent of the Smithsonian's collection, more than fifty million items.

"Still," Elena continued, "as you can imagine, the need arose to preserve those books that others might overlook, books that on face value might not merit being locked up under tight security, but were still too important to risk losing. Consider it our version of the Vatican Archives."

Painter waved at the books on the table. "And these two are from that collection."

Elena smiled, which it appeared she did easily.

She pulled the newer book toward her. "In fact, the author of this book founded our archive. Archibald MacLeish, the ninth Librarian of Congress, who served during World War II. He had been assigned the task during the war to preserve our national treasures, dividing our most important pieces of history and hiding them around the country. Afterward, when he resigned as librarian and became the assistant secretary of state, he saw the need for some continuance of this project and left behind this legacy for the Smithsonian libraries, a special secret collection."

"Starting with his own book?" Painter asked.

"And many others," Elena corrected. "Though I think he did this to further bury these two volumes from the public eye."

Kat clasped her hands, as if holding them back from grabbing the books to examine them. "What do they have to do with what's going on now?"

"Everything . . . or maybe nothing. I don't know. But when I told Simon about the story of these books, he thought I should share them with you two." Elena eyed Painter and Kat with no small amount of suspicion. "Two members of DARPA, as I'm supposed to understand."

Simon had kept mum about Sigma but he wasn't a very good liar. The librarian clearly suspected there was more to this introduction.

Painter sidestepped the issue for now. "So what's this story?"

"First, I should explain that I only stumbled upon these books out of personal interest. My doctoral thesis was on the Civil War, concentrating on the role of Lincoln's cabal of close confidants, which included Joseph Henry, the first secretary of the Smithsonian, back when its collections were housed in this one building."

Painter knew of the close relationship between those two men, again imagining the séance that had occurred in this very room.

Elena settled to her seat. "The story starts with Joseph Henry and a fire that almost burned down the Castle during the Civil War."

From there, she told a fantastic tale concerning James Smithson, the man who left his fortune to the young nation, a legacy that would start the institution named after him. Most of her story was recounted in MacLeish's journal on the table, how Joseph Henry had learned of an artifact buried in Smithson's tomb in Genoa, something called the Demon Crown. Decades later, Alexander Graham Bell was sent on a secret mission, both to preserve the remains of Smithson and to secure this object, an artifact rumored to be dangerous, maybe even a weapon.

"What did he find?" Kat asked.

"According to MacLeish, Bell discovered a boulder of amber with the preserved bones of a reptile inside, maybe a small dinosaur. Like Smithson, the inventor left behind a cryptic note, warning that it was both dangerous and perhaps miraculous."

Painter frowned. "Miraculous? How?"

"Bell claimed the object could hold the secret to life after death. But he never elaborated how he came to such a wild assertion."

Painter glanced over to Kat. She had also heard

Gray's account of the threat posed by the ancient wasps plaguing Hawaii and how they could go into a state of suspended animation, what was termed *cryptobiosis*, and seed dormant cysts into the bones of their victims as a means of resurrecting their swarm centuries later.

Elena must have noted their silent exchange. "Does this mean something to you two?"

"Maybe, but go on. What became of the artifact?"

"Bell thought it best—perhaps following Smithson's example—to rebury the object. But on American soil."

"Where?" Kat asked.

"In a hidden chamber off the old utility tunnel that connects the Castle to the Museum of Natural History across the mall."

Despite the seriousness of the matter, Painter could not help but be amazed.

All this started in our own backyard?

"MacLeish had been investigating the construction of a bomb shelter to protect our national treasures during the Second World War."

"And he found Bell's chamber."

"But unfortunately, this discovery did not go unnoticed. MacLeish suspected afterward that one of the engineers involved in surveying the project had let the information slip out. The news reached the ears of our enemy at the time, who could not help but be interested in Bell's warning about the buried object."

Kat leaned closer, clearly fascinated. "What happened?"

"There was a firefight in the tunnel. The amber

object was stolen by Japanese spies." Elena stared significantly at the two of them, as if she also wondered if this attack on Hawaii could be some echo of Pearl Harbor. "MacLeish also copied down a symbol he found tattooed on one of the attacker's bodies. He claimed the same symbol was somehow connected to a conspirator involved in the fire at the Castle almost a century earlier, as if the same group tried to erase evidence of this object in the past."

"What symbol?" Painter asked.

"I can show you." Elena lifted her reading glasses, while reaching for the book. "But it looks vaguely Masonic."

"Masonic?" Painter swallowed hard, while Kat sat back, her expression worried. "By any chance, did the symbol frame a moon and a star at its center?"

Elena lowered her glasses and frowned deeply at them. "It did. How did you know?"

Kat closed her eyes and swore under her breath.

Painter shared her sentiment.

No wonder Gray and Seichan were targeted.

The librarian looked between them. "Maybe it's time *you* two started telling your story."

6:33 P.M.

Elena waited for an explanation. A familiar obstinate streak hardened inside her. She had been condescended to most of her life—from a father who insisted on her getting married and having a household of little *niños* . . . to professors who believed she only earned her place in the academic world through affirmative action.

At her age, after raising a daughter by herself and surviving breast cancer, she did not suffer fools lightly, and she certainly wasn't going to be kept in the dark any longer.

What's really going on here?

She was already suspicious when the museum curator, Simon Wright, had insisted she meet with these two representatives from DARPA at the Regents' Room of the Castle.

Why here?

She eyed the young woman—Captain Kat Bryant, who looked like a well-made bed, all crisp lines and military tautness. Elena sensed an ally in her, especially when the woman gave her boss a stern look, as if to say *let's be up front with this lady.*

But Director Crowe appeared as stubborn as Elena, his back stiffening, the muscles of his jaw tightening. Upon first meeting him, she had been momentarily taken aback by his striking looks, his penetrating blue eyes and dark hair—which included a snowy lock tucked behind one ear, which inexplicably intrigued her. She guessed he had some Native American blood in his background.

Still, he was getting in her way.

Kat must have sensed the growing impasse and offered a compromise. "Before we tell *our* side, perhaps you can finish yours." She waved to the journal on the table. "Clearly Archibald MacLeish's tale didn't end with the theft of Smithson's artifact. That book looks mighty thick."

Elena hesitated, then sighed loudly, accepting that this might be the best recourse.

For now.

"You're right about MacLeish's story," she said. "Archibald found the chamber in November 1944 . . . and a week later, the man resigned. Right in the middle of the war. The tides were turning against the Germans, but Japan remained a major threat in the Pacific. MacLeish feared what the Japanese might do with what was stolen, so he went searching for the truth about it."

"Like *where* it came from?" Kat guessed. "And *why* Smithson feared it?"

"Exactly. MacLeish intended to follow in Smithson's footsteps, but it proved to be a difficult trail." She pointed to the charred volume. "The man's burned journal offered no clue to its origin, and most of Smithson's personal papers were destroyed by that fire. Still, MacLeish was determined. He went to Europe, a continent still at war, and sought out anyone who knew the man in the past. Friends, fellow colleagues, relatives. He tried his best to backtrack from that grave."

"What did he find?" Painter asked.

"More mysteries. You can read about it in detail, but the trail ended in Estonia, at the city of Tallinn neighboring the Baltic Sea."

Kat's expression sank with defeat. "So MacLeish never discovered the artifact's origin?"

"He did not, but he heard a story from a geologist, an old man near his deathbed. Decades earlier, when the geologist was first starting his career, he ended up sharing drinks with Smithson at a tavern in Tallinn. Smithson was tipsy enough to tell a drunken tale, one that the geologist believed was pure fancy."

Painter's brow crinkled. "What story?"

"A harrowing tale of a group of miners who broke into a rich deposit of *amber*." Elena touched Smithson's charred journal, acknowledging the significance of such a discovery. "As they were digging, something was unleashed in that mine. A horrible disease carried by stinging insects. Giant wasps. They were said—and I quote—*born right out of the bones of the rock.* The only way to stop them from escaping was to firebomb the mine with the workers still down there and bury it afterward."

Kat glanced to her boss, suggesting this story might not be as outlandish as it first sounded.

Painter leaned back. "You said MacLeish's search ended there in Tallinn. I'm guessing he must have assumed this story was all an old wives' tale and gave up his pursuit."

"Maybe partly for that reason . . . but mostly because he was told this story on August sixth, 1945."

Painter looked momentarily confused.

Kat explained. "The day the bomb was dropped on Hiroshima."

Elena nodded. "Following this event, MacLeish grew less worried about some vague threat by the Japanese. He figured it was all a moot point by then."

Painter shook his head. "Apparently he was wrong."

"Which brings us back to the attack on Hawaii," Elena said. "If there truly is a connection that trails from Smithson's discovery to a terrorist attack in

Hawaii, then perhaps someone needs to continue MacLeish's work and find out where that artifact came from."

"You're right." Kat turned to her boss. "If Professor Matsui was correct about the danger posed by this ancient species, then knowing its origin could be important."

"Why?"

"Because these wasps went *extinct* in the past." She must have noted his bewilderment and explained. "Why aren't these wasps still around? Why don't they dominate the world today? What stopped them from running amok in the past? Something must've driven this aggressive species into a state of *cryptobiosis*—basically into hiding."

Elena didn't follow all of this, but she knew when to stay quiet.

Painter looked at the books on the table. "So if we could find out what stopped them before . . ."

"Then maybe we could use it to stop them again."

As the pair seemed to come to a mutual understanding, Elena knew it was time to press her advantage. "If you intend to pursue such an undertaking—to look for clues in Tallinn, in Estonia—you'll need to know everything about MacLeish's journey there." She laid her palm atop the former Librarian of Congress's book. "And where this goes, I go."

Painter shifted to his feet, plainly ready to dismiss her. "There's no need to risk those historic texts. A simple copy will do."

Elena picked both books off the table. "Not if you

hope to succeed." She stared the man down. "You'll likely need more than what can be found within these pages. You'll want someone who knows every detail about these authors, especially Smithson."

"In other words, *you*?" Painter asked skeptically.

Kat touched his arm. "Remember, we only have three days."

Elena knew nothing about such a deadline, but she appreciated Kat's support in this matter.

In the end, it was the curator, Simon Wright, who broke the stalemate. He cocked an eyebrow at Painter. "Sounds to me like it's time you gave our new Librarian of Congress the *full* tour of the Castle."

7:05 P.M.

Fifteen minutes later, Kat held open the door to the security elevator. She enjoyed the look of surprise and wonder on Elena Delgado's face as she stepped into the subterranean complex buried beneath the Castle.

"I never suspected such a place existed . . ." she mumbled, her eyes huge. "I feel like Charlie entering the chocolate factory."

Painter smiled, leading the way, plainly warming up to the willful librarian. "Then I guess that makes me Willy Wonka."

Elena blushed. "Sorry. I guess I spend too much time with my two granddaughters. I must have that movie memorized by now."

Kat knew all too well that particular circle of hell, the nonstop loop of a children's film playing in the background of one's life.

"I'll take you to my office," Painter offered, "while Kat settles everything for the trip."

"Jason has a jet prepping as we speak," Kat said. "We should be wheels up within the hour."

Elena glanced back, still struggling with all of this. "So soon?"

Kat nodded.

Welcome to Sigma.

She broke away from the pair as they reached the threshold of the communication nest. "I'll join you in a few moments," she said. "I want to make sure Jason is up to speed before I leave."

As the two headed away, Kat spotted her second-in-command, Jason Carter. The young man, whose straw-blond hair had a perpetual cowlick, was bowed between two technicians.

"Well?" she asked.

He didn't need any further direction and spoke without looking her way. "I just finished with Dr. Bennett. He's agreed to join you two. He says he'll need forty minutes to pack up all of Professor Matsui's notes and meet you at the airport."

"Good."

For any hope of success, they would need to scramble every resource they could—which included bringing along their own entomologist. If there was some clue as to what held these wasps in check in the past, then Dr. Bennett's expertise could prove invaluable at discovering it.

"Have you heard any further word from Gray?" she asked.

"No, not yet. The last update was that he and the others were following a lead on the swarm." Without turning, he pointed an elbow at a tall Starbucks cup. "Vanilla latte. Double shot."

She crossed to it, both hands out. Her fingers curled around its welcoming warmth. "Only a double?"

He eyed her sidelong. "Really?"

She ignored him and took a sip to clear the cobwebs. "What about the attacker who ambushed Seichan and escaped by boat?"

"Vanished. No telling where he might be now. But I've alerted intelligence agencies across the Pacific."

Kat clenched her jaw, running a thousand details through her head. She hated to abandon her station with everything up in the air. She was leaving Jason with a herculean task. Not only would he have to coordinate operations on two sides of the world, but he would need to keep Painter fully updated, so the director could orchestrate what had to be done both politically and possibly militarily.

Let's hope it doesn't come to the latter.

Jason turned to her, easily reading her. "Don't worry, boss. I got this."

She nodded.

Of course he did.

Still, she went over some last details, making sure Jason had everything he needed. Once satisfied, she gave the room a final glance, then returned her attention to her second-in-command.

"Okay, the shop's all yours." She pointed at him. "Just don't break anything."

"Wow, I drop one coffee mug and you never let me forget it."

"It was my favorite," she mumbled and headed out.

As she crossed down the hall, she cradled the hot cup in her palms. She sensed she had forgotten something. Voices drew her ahead, toward Painter's open office door.

She entered without knocking—then stopped.

Ah, that's what I forgot . . .

A stocky man leaned against Painter's desk, grinning at something Elena had said. He was showing the librarian his prosthetic hand, demonstrating the latest in DARPA technology. He had disarticulated the hand from his wrist and was wiggling the disembodied fingers.

Elena expressed amazement. "You can control it remotely."

"And it has a built-in camera under the thumbnail," the owner said proudly. "There's even a small packet of plastic explosives wired under the palm for those special occasions when a simple handshake won't do."

"Monk?" Kat crossed farther into the room, flabbergasted at finding him standing there. "How . . . what are you doing here?"

He straightened sheepishly. He was dressed in shorts and a hoodie that showed a pine tree and the words CAMP WOODCHUCK.

"I figured you might need an extra hand." He lifted his prosthetic, trying to make a joke. When she continued to frown, he snapped it back onto its titanium wrist sheath. "Plus, I figured this was the only way I'd get to spend any quality time with my wife."

"Where are the girls?"

He swiped a palm over his shaved scalp. "I imagine terrorizing camp counselors about now. Which means they're as happy as two hyperactive clams."

Kat turned to Painter, suspecting the director had a role in arranging all of this.

He admitted as much. "Didn't think you should be the only one chaperoning Dr. Delgado and Dr. Bennett to Estonia."

Monk grinned. "Think of it as an all-expense-paid European vacation."

Kat rolled her eyes.

Only, in this case, the fate of the world was at stake.

14

From the front passenger seat, Palu pointed ahead. "Take the next left."

"What left?" Gray leaned over the wheel, squinting at the wall of ferns and ironwood trees. Branches scraped both sides of the rental Jeep.

They had been crawling and bouncing along a series of mud tracks that constituted a road through an unmapped section of the Hana Forest Reserve. They had left the highway's blacktop nearly an hour ago, taking a detour off of Mill Place near the Hasegawa General Store. From there they had been forced to dodge stray cattle and skirt around taro fields.

Gray had wanted to cut straight across those fields, but Palu had shaken his head, deeming it *pō'ino*, or bad luck: "*Taro come from the body of the Father Sky and Mother Earth's first son. It gives life.*"

So Gray had taken the recommended detour, not wanting to tempt fate.

"How much farther?" Kowalski complained. His large frame was folded into the backseat next to Professor Matsui, who was otherwise alone.

Aiko Higashi had stayed behind at the cottage to coordinate with Kat on some new details regarding this threat, a connection going back to World War II, one possibly involving the Guild.

Gray's gaze flicked to the rearview mirror. Seichan trailed behind them on one of the motorbikes. They might need such a nimble vehicle for the rugged terrain ahead. After learning of a potential Guild connection in all of this, she had gone unusually quiet. Then again, she had become more reticent of late. Something was clearly bothering her, but he knew her well enough to give her the space she needed to work through it.

After consulting a compass, Palu called back to answer Kowalski's question. "Another mile . . . maybe two, brah. That's if the road's not washed out from last week's rain."

Kowalski groaned, voicing Gray's own concern.

Palu shoved an arm across the dashboard. "There's the turn."

Gray spotted it at the last second. He yanked the wheel hard, forcing the SUV into a sharp skid to enter the break in the forest. An even narrower track led ahead from here.

A glance behind revealed Seichan had managed the same turn. The cycle expertly swung onto the path, the rider hunkered low over the handlebars.

As he forged ahead, the windows to either side were swiped by massive fronds of tree ferns, known as *hapu'u*. It was as if they were driving through a prehistoric car wash. And maybe they were. The forest here looked untouched, with some of the huge trees likely thousands of years old.

A lacy frond smacked the front windshield as if warning them away.

Palu noted the affront and grinned. "Forest don't like you *haole*. Only *kama'aina* know where I take you."

Gray took him at his word. While tourism was a major source of income for the islands, the native-born Hawaiians still carved out places exclusively for themselves and defended them diligently. Like how the multimillion-dollar construction of a new telescope atop Mauna Kea was being held up by protests due to the site's sacred history.

Across the islands, lines were literally being drawn in the sand.

Gray understood the local's concern. After three months here, he recognized the deep bond between the island and its people. Their history was imbued into every rock, animal, and plant.

As if reading his thoughts, Palu stared out at the forest of tree ferns. "We use the golden hair—the *pulu* of the *hapu'u*—for stuffing pillows and mattresses. You can even eat the leaves and core." He glanced over and grimaced. "Not good, though. Tastes bad."

Gray wondered if Palu's ongoing discourse about life here was more than nervous chatter, but rather an attempt to share with them what was at stake. If they didn't stop the scourge unleashed on these islands, everything could be lost—not just the land, but its very history.

Knowing he couldn't let that happen, Gray drove deeper into the forest. As they climbed the rugged flank of Mount Haleakala, the canopy grew higher.

Occasional breaks allowed glimpses to the coastline behind them. From this height, the commotion around Hana was muted, the chaos muffled by both distance and the looming countenance of the mountain ahead.

As they gained elevation, the mists trapped beneath the canopy grew denser, wet enough to occasionally require a swipe of the vehicle's wipers. Around them, the forest took on a ghostly character.

Professor Matsui spoke from the back, his voice hushed, perhaps overwhelmed by a sense of reverence. "Are those koa trees?"

He pointed toward a grove of tall hardwoods, the branches tipped with yellow flowers.

Palu smiled. "Yah, brah. Once, all of Haleakala was covered in koa forests. Only patches remain. Like this one." He glanced back to the others. "It's another reason we don't tell *haole* about this place."

Ken leaned forward. "Still, where we're headed now—the collection of old lava tubes you described—such a place would be just what the *Odokuro* need. A perfect place to establish a *lek*." He looked out the window. "They'd want a deep central burrow, shaded by a canopy, with an ample water source. And look at all the nectar-rich flowers around here."

"Not to mention, plenty of hosts," Gray added.

The rain forest around them teemed with life: birds, mammals, other insects.

Ken nodded soberly and settled back to his seat.

Gray tried to picture their destination. Three weeks ago, he and Seichan had visited Ka'eleku Cave on the northern outskirts of Hana. The touristy cave was a large and easily accessible lava tube, decorated with stalactites and chocolate-colored formations. Skylights—sections that had collapsed and were open to the blue sky—helped illuminate the long cavernous tunnel. It was a popular tourist attraction, reminding visitors of Haleakala's fiery past, when flows of basaltic lava—both surface *a'a* and subterranean *pāhoehoe*—had formed Maui.

Many other lava tubes wormed throughout the flanks of Haleakala, most hidden by dense forest, their locations known only to the locals. Palu was taking them toward where a braided knot of tubes had collapsed long ago, opening a maze of tunnels, shafts, and caves. If the swarm had journeyed inland along the route of last night's trade winds, this spot would be in their direct path.

On the ride up here, Gray had watched for any sign of the wasps, but so far, nothing. It was as if the entire mass had vanished, perhaps swept out to sea.

If only we could be so lucky . . .

Palu pointed ahead. "End of the road. Have to hike from here."

That was obvious. The pair of rutted tracks ended at a sprawling banyan tree. Its crown rose seventy feet high and spread fifty yards wide. It was all draped and supported by hundreds of aerial roots, forming a woody curtain under the leafy bower.

"That can't be good," Kowalski said.

Gray recognized the same.

An old VW van sat parked alongside the tree.

"Somebody's already up here," Gray mumbled.

Palu scowled. "That's Emmet Lloyd's camper. Runs a tour company out of Makawao. Takes tourists on overnights. That *kanapapiki* should know better than to bring anyone up here."

Gray stared beyond the banyan at the mist-shrouded forests.

Especially now.

1:31 P.M.

Emmet hollered at his trio of charges. "Not so fast!"

He clambered down the slippery volcanic rock, grabbing at the towering poles of bamboo on either side to keep his footing. After packing their campsite higher up the flank of Haleakala, he had set a hard pace. All night long, a slew of helicopters had winged across the mountaintop. With no cell service, they were in the dark as to the situation, but something was definitely wrong. Whatever was going on was more than an ordinary search-and-rescue operation.

But at least we're not far from where I parked.

Maybe another mile or so.

He used this small chunk of bamboo forest as a trail marker. It was not as extensive as the growth found to the southeast, but that area of Haleakala was trafficked by lots of day hikers. Such a place certainly didn't match his tour company's motto, which was painted on the side of his van.

To truly get off . . . get off the beaten track.

He half-slid down a mud-slick section of the trail, balancing on his feet, reminding him of his former glory as a surfer. He had been a champion in his heyday, but that had been a lifetime ago. Still, at fifty-two, he refused to give up his passion, financing his life on Maui by taking tourists—those with a more rough-and-ready bent—on camping trips deep into the forests around Haleakala.

He had spent three nights with his current group, a husband and wife, along with their eleven-year-old son, Benjamin.

"Slow it down, Benjie!" Paul Simmons warned, breathing hard, trying to match his son's goatlike nimbleness.

The Simmonses owned a tech start-up out of San Rafael. Both parents were gym-fit. The husband was a CrossFit addict; the wife, Rachel, practiced yoga daily. Emmet had enjoyed watching her go through her poses the first night at the edge of a moonlit pool, the surface dappled by a thin waterfall. Her body was lithe; her long auburn hair, tied in a tail, swished with her every transition. When she bent backward, propped on her hands and feet, her breast pointing high . . .

He smiled at the memory.

Not a bad perk of the job.

He finally reached the parents, while their son raced ahead with the boundless energy of youth. Benjie vanished around a bend in the bamboo forest.

Emmet grew concerned, knowing how treacherous this particular terrain could be. This area was riddled with mossy holes and fern-covered drop-offs.

He pointed ahead. "Hey, you'd better rein your kid in."

Paul suddenly yelped and swatted at his neck.

His wife turned, more exhausted than concerned. "Jesus, Paul. What's the matter?"

Paul waved at something in front of his face—then his shoulders jerked to his ears, a gasp turned into a cry of pain. He fell to his knees, both palms clasping his neck.

Rachel grabbed his arm. "Paul!"

Emmet backed a step and searched around. Normally this bamboo forest had a magical quality to it, with its endless march of stout green poles, umbrellas of dripping foliage, all woven together by snaking threads of heavy mist. But now the place seemed suddenly eerie, a foreign landscape where they were unwanted intruders.

This sense of dread was enhanced by a low hum, one he hadn't noted before because of his own panting. Now with his breath held, he heard it more clearly.

What is that?

He turned in a circle as Rachel got her husband back on his feet.

All around, sections of the mists stirred, swirled by some invisible force. The infernal humming set his hairs on end. He had never heard such a sound. Then he made out small black shapes buzzing through the mists, coming from all directions, heading for them.

"*Run!*" he warned.

He didn't know the exact nature of the threat, but he knew they were in danger.

Rachel's attention was on her trembling husband, who looked unsteady on his feet. "W-what?"

Emmet shoved past them and continued down the trail. Something smacked into his arm, landing on the long sleeve of his shirt. He gawked at the sight. A giant wasp or hornet sat there, wings vibrating. Shocked, he swung his arm against a bamboo trunk and knocked the creature off.

Fuuuuck . . .

"Wait!" Rachel cried after him as he fled. "Help me!"

Then Paul screamed again—and a moment later, a wail from Rachel.

Despite appearances, he wasn't abandoning them. They were adults and knew the way down. They'd have to fare as best they could.

Instead, he ran toward his other responsibility.

Benjie.

He skidded around a bend in the trail, coming close to flying headlong over a short cliff. He regained his balance, relying on muscle memory from his surfing days, and sped down the trail.

Where the hell is this kid?

He cupped a hand to his mouth. "Benjie!"

Then he spotted the boy—not on the trail but in the woods to the left. Either the kid had lost the path or something had drawn him astray.

Either way . . .

"Get back over here," he yelled.

Benjie looked scared, frozen in place. He must have heard his parents' cries. He stared at Emmet, clearly hesitant to trust this near-stranger.

"C'mon, kid! We need to get off this mountain!" Emmet forced his voice away from its edge of panic. "Your mom and dad are right behind me. So how about you get back on the trail."

Benjie's gaze flicked all around. Finally he sagged and hurried toward the path.

Good going, kid.

Then on his third step, the boy vanished, swallowed up by the ground.

A cry of surprise burst from Emmet's lips, echoed in a higher octave by the boy.

Panicked, Emmet shoved toward the spot. He crashed between teetering poles of bamboo, setting their lengths to swinging. They knocked hollowly all around him.

Like the rattle of so many bones.

EGG-BEARER

After feasting on the males, she waited in the cool darkness. She reserved every motion after breeding, her entire being centered on her laden abdomen. Her antennae were curled atop her head, her four wings folded along her back.

Satiated, her senses had dulled.

Her large eyes remained unblinking.

The swarm had found refuge earlier and led her to this spot with trails of pheromones. She had settled into the welcoming darkness with those like her. As she readied herself, her legs tasted the water dripping over the rock wall. She sucked at the moisture occasionally.

It was all she needed for now.

Ganglions behind her eyes responded to the change of light—from brightness to complete blackness. Hormones surged through her, letting her know it was safe. She responded in kind and fertilized her thousand eggs with subtle contractions of her oviducts. The cells inside divided and divided again, packing each egg to bursting.

Once finished, her abdomen thrummed with demand.

A droplet of poison formed on the tip of her stinger.

Then an alarm spread, rising from the distant edge of their territory.

Threat . . . and possibility.

With the *lek* settled, the soldiers at the edges resisted their natural urge to attack anything that moved. Their aggression was tempered now by the need of the swarm. They allowed creatures to enter their domain, those who could serve the swarm's needs. They let them draw close, only attacking enough to herd their prey in closer, goading them forward with pain.

She extended her antenna and monitored the trap by sound and smell.

Her abdomen curled and uncurled, loosening her eggs and driving them toward her sharp ovipositor. Still, she waited. Across the walls, others did the same. Some fluttered their wings, expressing desire. A few snapped their thick, sclerotized hind legs. Each crack resonated down the tunnel. The echoing helped give shape to the passageway.

Then a new note alerted her.

She listened to the change in cadence of the swarm's buzz. The muscles of her legs tightened. She crouched on the wall. Driven by instinct, she kicked out her hind legs, joining the chorus of clacking.

Finally, her antenna picked up two scents: the pheromone of conquest and the carbon of breath.

It was enough.

She leaped into the air, wings buzzing to lift her heavy form. She headed toward the puffing exhalations. All around, those like her took flight or snapped their legs. The echoing allowed her to easily perceive obstacles in the pitch dark.

Though her eyes were still blind, the membranes over the hollow sockets on either side of her head were stretched taut and picked up every vibration. She trailed along streams of pheromones. Chitinous lancets honed her stinger, already lubricated with poison.

Her eggs would have to wait for now.

She clacked her legs together as she flew, casting out a sharp wave of sound ahead of her flight. As it rebounded back, it filled her head and gave shape to darkness. But she also began to hear something more within that cloud of exhalations.

A vibration, one she could not resist.

It echoed to her, drawing her faster. She must be there first. Light grew ahead, but she ignored the brightness and concentrated on the trembling in the air.

It grew clearer.

Becoming a rhythmic pulsing, beating fast.

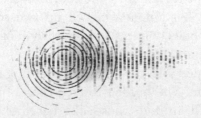

She lowered her head, antennae stretched, and raced straight for it. The brightening tunnel crackled with more sharp snaps, triggering her to flick her own hard legs together, adding her cadence to the chorus.

Ahead, a thrashing shape appeared.

Panicked beats drew her toward it.

The reverberation of the swarm now penetrated flesh. Through a cage of bones, she watched a chunk of muscle pound and pound. She followed the cloud of carbon gasping from her target and dove through it.

She landed on soft skin, much more tender than ancient memories in her genetic code remembered. She had once sought out larger prey, those whose flesh had hammered with deafening beats, all guarded over by armor.

She easily slipped her stinger into that tenderness. Muscles at the base of her abdomen convulsed, pumping her poison deep. Her prey did not react. Her venom was not meant to bring pain— only control.

Once empty, she leaped away but stayed near, fluttering over her target. She wafted a net of pheromones over her prey, marking it as her own. Those laden with their own eggs fled out into the brightness, searching for other hosts.

She hovered in place.

Her antennae weaved the air as she waited.

She continually snapped her legs, evaluating her prey, making sure its flesh was uncorrupted by a previous incursion. Her abdomen held thousands of eggs. In turn, each egg nestled many larvae. Their hunger was her hunger. They would need plenty of meat, blood, bone.

To ensure that, she waited for her poison to fully take effect.

Her venom was meant to fell much larger prey, so it didn't take long.

As she listened, the panicked beating slowed, then slowed again, becoming fainter.

In that cage of bone below, the chunk of flesh quivered, convulsing unsteadily.

It was time.

She dropped through the cloud of puffing carbon once again and landed on soft skin. She arched her abdomen. Eggs surged into position. Each sting would deliver scores of her progeny.

And with her prey subdued—she could stab over and over again.

She would not stop.

There was plenty of meat.

15

No doubt this is the right place.

Five minutes ago, Gray had parked the Jeep next to the banyan tree, only to hear faint screams echoing down the forested slope of the mountain. Fearing the worst, he had left the team to organize and grab their gear, while he and Seichan took off on the motorbike.

He leaned over the handlebars of the Yamaha off-roader, challenging the bike's knobby tires and suspension for the precarious climb along a narrow trail.

Seichan clutched an arm around his waist. Her other limb balanced a large pack over her shoulder, crammed with fire blankets and a med kit, which included EpiPens.

He prayed they could reach the campers in time, but even before he and Seichan had reached the trailhead, the screaming had eerily stopped.

Too suddenly.

He gritted his teeth and goosed more speed out of the bike's four-stroke engine. He expertly bobbled up the rocky trail, all but hopping from rock to rock, sometimes balancing on the rear tire. The motor growled in complaint, and mud flew behind them.

Gray searched the trail ahead.

Palu had given them vague directions to the old lava tubes.

Follow the trail. Watch where the forest turns into bamboo.

The Hawaiian had also warned them of the precarious nature of the upcoming terrain. A series of collapses had broken into a knotted labyrinth of old tunnels, riddling the slope with hidden chasms and fissures. The main entrance, the largest hole—what Palu called a *puka*—was near a small spring-fed pond.

The team would rendezvous there.

Behind the bike, Palu and Kowalski followed on foot, each carrying a pair of propane tanks outfitted with spark-igniters and timers, all courtesy of the fireman's connections with his department.

Still, it had been Professor Matsui who had laid out this course of action. The plan was to dump those tanks down various skylights into the tunnels. If the swarm had gone to ground down there, the team's goal was twofold: do as much damage as possible to the swarm, while also chasing off any survivors. By unsettling the wasps, Ken hoped to delay them from establishing a *lek*.

For now, it was a decent plan.

It could buy the island some time.

That is, if it's not already too late . . .

With only one way to find out, Gray fought his bike higher up the mountainside. After another minute, he rounded a sharp switchback, and the forest miraculously changed. Hardwoods and ferns fell away, replaced by an endless stretch of green bamboo. The stout poles marched in all directions ahead. Mists hung heavy among the lilting emerald fronds.

Gray gaped at the sudden transformation.

With his attention distracted, he missed a figure stumbling out of the forest to his right. The man fell across the path, his shoulders slamming into the bamboo on the far side. His form crumpled to the ground.

Gray braked hard.

To avoid hitting the man, he jerked the bike off the trail and crashed into a tall thicket of ferns. The cycle toppled and threw off its riders. He rolled, compromised by the beekeeper's coverall he wore, a precaution recommended by the professor. He and Seichan had donned the protective clothing before making the trek up here.

Gray quickly regained his feet and adjusted the veiled hood.

Seichan dragged her pack out of the lush under-brush.

They then converged toward the man on the trail.

Gray reached him first and dropped to a knee. The man appeared to be in his mid-fifties, balding with a mustache. Likely the tour operator, Emmet Lloyd. The man's head lolled. Ropes of drool hung from his lips.

Gray grasped his cheeks. "Mr. Lloyd, where are the others?"

Emmet seemed to hear him, but the man's eyes fought to focus. His pupils were huge.

Drugged or a concussion . . .

Seichan pushed next to him. She had the med kit open and an EpiPen in hand. She jabbed the injector into the man's neck, shooting epinephrine into his system.

Professor Matsui had studied the toxins found in the venom of these wasps. It was his specialty. He had warned them of the poison carried in the stingers of the large breeding females.

A potent neurotoxin.

While epinephrine was no cure, Ken had said it should counteract some of the effect.

"Mr. Lloyd," Gray repeated.

The pupils seemed slightly more responsive, but the man remained dazed and loopy.

"Gray," Seichan warned.

He noted her tone and turned. She stood up and pointed out into the misty forest. Through the fog, columns of dark smoke—dozens of them—wafted up from the ferns carpeting the ground. A droning hum filled the forest's undercarriage.

The swarm.

The wasps were abandoning their subterranean lair, likely drawn by the noisy approach of the bike. Gray pictured the knotted maze of lava tubes beneath the ground, all interconnected.

He glanced to the right.

More shadows curled into the white mists.

They were out of time.

He turned to Emmet and slapped his face.

Then twice more.

Finally, the man's lips curled with irritation.

"Where are the others?" Gray pressed.

After a long moment, a tremoring arm lifted and waved at the trail ahead. Slurred words slipped from slack lips. "Up . . ."

"How many?"

To answer seemed to take all his effort. "Two . . ." he forced out. "Husband, wife . . ."

"We don't have enough time to search for them," Seichan said dourly.

She was right, but how could they abandon them?

A new crashing noise intruded, coming from behind them. They both turned. Palu appeared, half-running in his beekeeper's getup. He hauled a propane tank in each hand, carrying them as effortlessly as a couple of pillows. The only sign of exertion was a sheen of perspiration glowing over his tanned features.

Despite the situation, he wore a big grin. "There you are, brah."

Kowalski came puffing up behind him, gasping and looking close to keeling over. He dropped the tanks and leaned on his knees. A continual string of curses followed. "Christalmightymotherfuck . . ."

Gray waved to the swarm swirling forth from fissures and holes all around. "Get to planting those charges. Five-minute timers. We can't let more escape."

A good portion of their plan counted on catching the swarm while the majority remained underground. According to the professor, wasps were attracted to the sweet stench of propane gas and often nested near pilot lights. While the gas was normally odorless, companies added the odor to alert homeowners of a leak.

The plan was to open those tanks, drop them into the labyrinth of tunnels, and let the heavy gas spread throughout the lava tubes before the ignition set it all on fire. If they could get those spewing tanks underground fast enough, the odor might lure the swarm closer—hopefully near enough to be caught in the explosion.

Kowalski hauled up his tanks with a groan. "Let's do this."

Palu hesitated. "Where are those campers?"

Gray pointed to the path. "Up there. A husband and wife."

"I know this trail." Palu nodded to Kowalski. "We drop these in the tunnels, then go find them."

Gray pictured the coming firestorm. "Five minutes," he reminded the big men. "Whether you reach them or not, you haul ass off this slope before those timers run out."

As they headed away, Gray hooked an arm around Emmet. He bent at the waist and hauled his slack form over a shoulder. As he straightened, he watched Kowalski lumber toward one of the smoky columns, waving wasps from his path. Once close enough, he lobbed a tank toward a fissure hidden there.

Palu followed this example, and the two men moved farther upslope, seeking new sites to plant their second charges.

Gray hefted his own burden and started down the trail.

Seichan headed to the bike.

Before Gray could take three steps, Emmet stirred, thrashing weakly. "No, wait . . ."

Gray stopped and turned, cheek to cheek with the man. "What?"

"Another . . . a boy . . . Benjie . . ." An arm pointed toward where Emmet had stumbled out of the forest. "Fell down hole."

Seichan heard this and let out an exasperated sigh. "I'll go look for him."

Gray hesitated, but she scowled at him.

"Get moving." She tapped her wristwatch. "I know."

He checked his own watch as he headed down.

Five minutes . . . and counting.

2:07 P.M.

Seichan clambered through the dense underbrush. It was like wading through a bog. Ferns grasped at her, thorns tried to tear her tough nylon-blend suit, and mud sucked at her rubber boots.

Frustrated, she was tempted to rip away the cumbersome outfit, but this was no bog and those weren't mosquitoes buzzing through the air. She swatted wasps from her veil and slapped at bigger ones on her arms or chest. There was a limit to her trust in this suit. She recalled Matsui's account of these creatures, how the wasps' usual prey in the prehistoric past had been far better armored than her.

She also only had to look around to be reminded to be extra cautious. Small birds littered the ground, some wings still twitching. Off to the right, antlers poked above the brush, marking where a speckled deer had met a similar fate. And what she thought was a mossy boulder to the left was actually a collapsed wild boar, evident from the curl of its yellowed tusks.

Clearly the wasps had been busy.

Respecting the danger, she slipped a Maglite from a pocket of her backpack and twisted it on. She did her best to hurry from one smoky column to another.

Where the hell are you, kid?

She kept an eye on her watch.

Three minutes left.

She didn't want to be here when those tanks exploded. Still, she pictured a delirious child trapped in those fiery tunnels and growled deep in her chest. She cursed his parents for putting him in harm's way—not that they could've anticipated this exact situation.

But still . . .

She forged to the next fissure and pushed into the humming, battering cloud around it. She poked her flashlight through a break in the undergrowth. Her beam revealed a good-sized hole. She pointed her light through the skylight and into the tunnel. The floor lay twelve feet below.

Nothing but more wasps, crawling over every surface.

She turned away—but as her beam flashed across

the far rim of a hole, she spotted a small print in the mud. Maybe a sneaker. The edge of the fissure looked freshly crumbled.

Swearing under her breath, she returned to studying the tunnel. From her vantage, she could only spy the immediate area below. The boy, frightened and panicked, could have crawled deeper into the system. Even a few yards and he'd be out of her direct line of sight.

Only one way to find out.

While she could have easily hopped down, she needed a way to climb back up. She had rope in her pack, but unspooling and rigging it would take too long.

Instead, she reached to her waist. After being caught unarmed back at the cottage last night, she had come fully prepared this time. Under her suit, daggers and throwing knives were hidden in wrist and ankle sheaths. For this chore, she snapped free a large Chinese cleaver from her belt.

She picked a bamboo stalk as thick as her wrist. With her blade freshly honed, she felled the trunk with one strong strike. She caught the pole as it toppled, then shouldered it to the hole and dropped one end to the floor below.

Two minutes.

She grabbed the green shaft, swung around it, and slid down its dewy length. Her feet crunched into a mat of wasps. She ignored the swarm's alarmed and vigorous response at her intrusion. Wasps exploded off the walls and rose from deeper in the tunnels.

She crouched against their assault.

She pointed her beam down the tunnel.

First one direction, then the other.

Through the swirling cloud, she caught a flash of white skin and a small red sneaker.

Benjie.

She reached with her rubber glove, snatched his ankle, and pulled his gangly frame toward her. She didn't have time to check to see if he was still alive. She simply picked him up and draped his small body across her shoulders in a fireman's carry.

She crouched and leaped up. Her hands latched on to the pole, while her legs tucked. Using her boots as grips, she shoved higher. All would have gone well, but the freshly cut end of the bamboo slipped and danced wildly across the uneven damp floor below.

She crashed sideways, hitting the wall hard. She managed to keep hold of the bamboo, but the end of the pole skittered below for a long terrifying breath—until it finally found its grip again.

She hung there for another moment to be sure. The internal timer still counted down in her head.

Less than a minute.

She started her ascent again.

Only another four feet to go.

Then pain flared in her side, fiery and explosive.

Surprised, she slid down the pole's length. Before her boots hit the ground again, her fingers clamped hard, stopping her fall. As she balanced the limp boy, she glanced to her side. She spotted a triangular tear in her suit.

Must've ripped it on the sharp stone when I hit the wall.

A wasp—one of the large soldiers—crawled out the tear and buzzed away, its work done.

Tears welled as agony racked through her.

She stared up as best she could.

So far . . .

Her only hope of escaping was to drop the boy and climb as swiftly as she could.

Still, she could feel the boy's heartbeat pounding against her neck, as if begging her not to abandon him.

I'm sorry . . .

2:11 P.M.

From under the bower of the banyan tree, Gray stared up at the forested flank of Haleakala. He didn't need to check his watch. With each passing second, his heart hammered harder in his throat.

Off to the side, Ken knelt next to a dazed Emmet, who sat with his back to a tree trunk. The professor pressed two fingers to the tour operator's neck, monitoring his pulse.

A crashing sound rose from the forest ahead.

Gray stood straighter as two large shapes burst into view, running headlong, ignoring the trail.

Kowalski and Palu.

They each had someone tossed over a shoulder.

"Found 'em," Kowalski gasped as he skidded to a stop, breathing as heavily as a bull.

The professor waved them over. "Bring them here!"

Kowalski either ignored him or his strength gave

out. He lowered a woman—the missing wife—to the leafy ground, then dropped to his backside. "How 'bout you come here."

Palu unshouldered his burden beside the woman.

Gray moved toward them, but his gaze remained on the forest. "Where's Seichan?"

Kowalski sat up straighter. "Whaddya mean?"

Gray realized the men had left before Seichan had gone to look for the boy.

Palu's brow furrowed deeply, following Gray's gaze. "We saw no one when we came down. But we were going *wikiwiki* . . . very fast."

Gray stepped toward the forest.

Then where the hell are—?

A resounding explosion cut off his silent question.

2:12 P.M.

Seichan rolled across a bed of damp ferns, purposefully soaking herself against a blast of searing heat. Two yards behind her, a spiral of blue-orange fire shot into the sky.

She remained low, gaping at the maelstrom around her. Swirling columns of flames exploded everywhere. She pictured the subterranean conflagration sweeping through the tangle of tunnels below and bursting forth through its many skylights and fissures.

She crawled away, nearly deaf, her retinas seared. The ground trembled under her with aftershocks. The volcanic rock of the slope was honeycombed with tunnels and caves. The concussive force of the trapped explosions must have further weakened the substructure.

As she fled, new chasms cracked open, expelling smoke, flickering with residual flames. Trees toppled and bamboo poles waved through the air.

She fought her way back to the trail. At some point, she must have lost her beekeeping hood, but the smoke and heat seemed to have driven off the swarm. She finally reached the path, doing her best to shield the boy with her own body.

Abandoning the child was never an option for her. Especially not now.

Earlier, not knowing if she would survive, she had silently expressed her regret. (*I'm sorry . . .*) But her apology was meant for Gray, for making this choice to risk everything, including their lives together, for the sake of this boy.

Though, down deep, she knew she had risked much more and felt a twinge of guilt. She had no right to—

The ground jolted again, reminding her she was far from safe.

She firmed her arm around the boy and dragged him along with her. Ahead, she spotted a glint of metal and a black rubber tire.

The motorbike.

She left the boy on the trail, dragged the cycle up, and leaned it against a tree—then collected the kid again. Moments later she was seated with the boy cradled in her lap, his head rolled back on her shoulder. She hugged her arms around him to reach the handlebars.

Hang in there, Benjie . . . just a little longer.

It took her three tries to get the engine to turn over. She felt like crying with relief when the cylinders finally ignited and the motor growled under her. Before she could take off, the mountain shook violently, almost unbalancing her. She glanced to the right and watched the slope collapse in on itself, creating a massive smoking sinkhole.

The chasm grew rapidly as she watched, spreading toward her.

She leaned over the boy, throttled the engine up, and sped away.

As she outran the sinkhole, the world around her grew both hazy and too bright. She shook her head, which only set her vision to whirling. Colors bled around her. The path and forest shattered into a kaleidoscope of fractured images, spinning into and out of focus.

She could no longer tell if she was riding up or down.

Or even moving at all.

As the world lost all meaning, she held on to the boy.

I'm sorry . . .

This time, her apology was for the child.

She had failed him.

2:24 P.M.

Even before the explosion had echoed away, Gray had started up the mountainside with Kowalski and Palu. As they climbed, thick smoke rolled down from above, filling the lower forests and making it harder to see. The ground continued to tremble underfoot, and volcanic rock cracked with thunderous claps, as if the mountain were tearing itself apart.

Panic set his heart to pounding in his ears.

Then a familiar rumbling whine rose from up ahead.

Gray stopped on the trail.

Out of the pall, a motorcycle shot into view. It raced toward them. At first, Gray thought Seichan was hunched over the handlebars with her usual fierce determination. Then he saw her body roll crookedly in her seat. One arm hugged a boy in her lap; the other weakly grasped the handlebar's grip.

She looked barely conscious, likely keeping upright only by instinct and the gyroscopic balance of the bike's momentum.

As the distance narrowed, she failed to acknowledge them, even when Kowalski called out and waved. Her cycle continued to fly toward them, gaining even more speed downhill.

Her luck—and consciousness—were not going to last much longer. Even worse, Gray and the others had just scrambled up a steep cliff face, climbing a series of precarious switchbacks to reach the top.

The bike aimed straight toward the cliff's edge.

"Off the trail!" Gray yelled.

Kowalski and Palu shoved to the side.

Gray stepped with them, but stayed close to the path. He bunched his legs, tensing his muscles. He'd have only the one chance.

As the bike sped up to his position, he lunged out and dove across the cycle. He shouldered into

Seichan, hooking an arm around her and the boy. He knocked them both out of the seat. They crashed headlong in a rolling tangle across a bed of ferns on the far side. Unmanned, the motorcycle continued down the trail, still impossibly upright—then flew over the cliff. It sailed far before finally dipping and dropping into the woods below.

Gray quickly checked Seichan and the boy.

Both seemed unharmed but unconscious.

Kowalski and Palu joined him, wearing matching expressions of concern.

Gray waved down the mountain. "Help me get them back to the Jeep."

Palu took the boy, while Kowalski and Gray slung Seichan between them. In minutes, they were back at the banyan tree.

Ken rushed to them. "Thank God, they're okay."

But were they?

Gray lowered Seichan. "Professor, what's wrong with them?" He waved to include the entire dazed group.

Ken glanced to the others, then back to Seichan. "Definitely the neurotoxin from the sting of a female breeder. They should recover with time."

Gray sensed the man was holding back. "What else?"

"While you were gone, I . . . I examined Mr. Lloyd's body with a magnifying glass. His skin is peppered with stings. But the sites don't show the typical red welts that surround a soldier's painful stings."

Gray understood, remembering the professor's description of the breeding female's pattern of needling a host multiple times to implant her full load of eggs. "You're thinking he's been parasitized."

"Maybe the others, too."

Gray glanced to Seichan.

Ken must have read his thoughts. "The others were up there awhile, unconscious and immobilized. The female wasp would wait until her host was subdued before parasitizing them."

So there's hope.

Gray began to kneel next to Seichan—when a monstrously large wasp crawled out of a rip in her suit. It perched at the edge, its wings humming in a frenzied blur.

Gray recognized the creature from the professor's photo collection.

A breeding female.

Kowalski kicked it to the side, then stamped it into an oily black puddle.

Gray looked at Ken. The professor's despairing expression answered his unspoken question.

There was no hope now.

16

Safely back at the cottage, Ken stood on the porch, his arms crossed with worry. An ocean breeze carried the promise of a late-afternoon rain, along with the perfume of the gardens. The bucolic setting stood in stark contrast to the dark pall clinging to the flank of Haleakala.

While the quaking had stopped and the flames were subdued by the wet forests, Ken knew the true threat to the island remained. He anxiously waited to learn the extent of the danger, but other matters needed to be attended to first.

An ambulance turned on the gravel drive and headed for the highway. It carried the Simmons family and the tour operator. Palu had radioed for the paramedics to meet them here as the group frantically rode down the mountainside. By the time the Jeep reached the cottage, the neurotoxin's effect had begun to wear off. Still, the afflicted needed further medical attention.

Palu had coordinated with his battalion chief to make sure the group was put into a quarantined ward at the local medical center. The extent of their parasitation still needed to be evaluated and monitored.

He tightened his arms, picturing the boy's scared face, his tears. The family had clung dazedly together. He hadn't explained to them the true nature of their medical state.

That could wait for now.

Still, he knew his reticence was born more out of cowardice than true compassion—and not a small measure of guilt.

If I had raised the alarm about this threat earlier . . .

The screen door opened behind him.

Gray poked his head out. "Seichan is awake enough to answer some questions, if you're ready."

"I . . . I am."

Ken crossed to the door. As he entered, Gray gave Ken's upper arm a reassuring squeeze, as if to say *we're all in this together.* He appreciated the gesture, but he knew only *one* of their group was uniquely threatened.

Seichan sat at the dining table. Her skin looked ashen, her eyes glazed. Her palms clutched a mug of coffee. Earlier, Ken had been honest with her. She had demanded it, already suspecting the worst as she fought through the toxin's haze.

Ken had urged her to go with the others in the ambulance, out of concern for her health, along with the danger she could potentially pose.

In three days.

She had refused.

Gray settled into the chair next to her, staying close. "Tell Ken what you told me."

She stared into the steaming depths of her mug.

"When I went looking for the boy, I saw animals lying prone all around. Deer, wild pigs, hundreds of birds."

"Dead or alive?" he asked.

"Not sure about most of them. But some were still moving."

"That's not good, but also not surprising." Ken slowly sat down, absorbing this information. "Like I said before, the *Odokuro* are generalists. They're not selective in their choice of hosts. From what you described, we'll have to assume a fair amount of the fauna up there is already contaminated."

"What do we do?" Gray asked.

Ken frowned. "Teams will need to go up there immediately. Any bodies should be burned, but I don't know how much good it will do. By now, most of the afflicted animals will have shaken off the neurotoxin's effect and scattered. Worse, the surviving members of the swarm will eventually seek a new shelter and start the process all over again."

"So what are you saying?" Gray asked.

The answer came from Aiko Higashi. The Japanese intelligence officer stood straight-backed on the table's far side, her expression unreadable. "He's saying it's too late. With the wasps already breeding, the countdown must begin. In three days, we will have no choice but to turn these islands into a firebreak. The organism cannot be allowed to spread beyond these shores."

Ken pictured the Brazilian island swirling with flames.

Gray's face hardened, clearly not willing to give up. "Professor, is there any way of eradicating the larvae from the environment? Any weaknesses we can exploit to buy us more time."

Ken noticed Gray's hand resting on the thigh of the woman next to him. The question was clearly one of personal concern, too.

"Again, I only had a short time to investigate this species. I tried the usual drugs. Like Ivermectin, a medication effective against a wide range of internal parasites." He shook his head. "It had no effect. Nothing I tried worked."

Seichan fixed her gaze on Ken. "What's going to happen?"

Ken looked away. He was tempted to sugarcoat the situation, but he knew the woman wanted brutal honesty.

"I examined your skin while you were unconscious." He tried to keep his voice clinical, but his words cracked. "I . . . I found over a hundred stings. I estimate the number of implanted eggs to be well over several thousand."

He glanced at her apologetically.

"Go on," she said.

"The eggs likely hatched within minutes of implantation. Each producing a score of first instars. They'll be microscopic as they burrow deeper. So you'll likely not experience any clinical signs for most of the day."

"And tomorrow?"

"They'll molt into their second stage. The larvae by then will be about the size of a grain of rice.

That's when they'll begin to inflict real damage. Luckily, they seem to avoid anything vital, shying away from the central nervous system and heart. Though I'm not sure how they do this." He locked his gaze with hers. "Still, it will be painful—but not as excruciating as the third day."

"When they start moving into my bones," she said stoically.

Ken pictured the test rats he had used as hosts at the Kyoto lab. When they reached this stage, they had contorted in agony, biting at themselves. Some even ripped their bellies open, as if trying to reach the source of the pain. Opioids did little to relieve the torture. In the end, he had anesthetized his subjects and kept them asleep throughout the remaining gruesome stages.

"It will get worse and worse," he told her.

"And at the end?" she asked.

Ken shook his head. He couldn't be that honest. He shut his eyes but failed to block the image of the rats' bodies as they finally succumbed. The fourth and fifth instars had laid waste to their hosts, hollowing them out before finally killing them. Afterward, the husk housed and protected the incubating pupae. Within days, the fledgling adults broke from their cocoons and ate their way out of their dead hosts.

He had unfortunately witnessed examples of that awful birth. It was something he could never unsee. The rats' bodies had churned from the inside, as if still alive. What came next made him shudder where he sat.

Gray must have noted his distress. "We need to stop this from ever getting that far."

Ken swallowed. "Like I said, nothing I tried worked. Even if I had more time, I'm not sure I would've been any more successful. Once parasitic larvae are entrenched, drugs are often useless." To make this clear, he asked a question. "Are any of you familiar with screwworms?"

Palu scrunched his brow. "Screwworms?"

"They're the larvae of blow flies. *Cochliomyia hominivorax*. The flies lay their eggs in wounds, and the maggots take root and start consuming tissue. Without prompt treatment, they can kill you."

"What's the treatment?" Gray asked.

"Only surgery. Digging them out. No drugs can touch them."

Gray stared toward Seichan. "Then maybe with surgery . . ."

Ken squashed the man's hope. "Screwworms only burrow *shallowly*. Not like these larvae, which dig deep and spread wide, beyond the reach of any scalpel."

He watched despair set in.

Aiko stepped forward, as if she had been waiting for this moment. She leaned on the back of a chair. "As Professor Matsui has admitted, he's only worked with the *Odokuro* for two months. But if the story out of Washington is true—about an artifact stolen during World War Two—then someone has possessed this scourge for *decades*. Which begs the question. *Why* wait to release the wasps until now?"

No one answered.

"Because something's changed," she said. "They must have learned a way to control this monster's biology. Maybe even developed a cure."

She looked at Seichan.

Ken frowned. "But if you're right, where do we even begin to look?"

Aiko offered a small smile. "I have an idea."

"What?" Gray asked.

"Let me begin by stressing that what I'm about to tell you is based on assumptions that could easily be wrong."

Kowalski scoffed. "So, in other words, real solid ground."

Aiko ignored him. "I discussed this all with Captain Bryant while you were gone."

"You spoke with Kat?" Gray asked.

Aiko nodded. "We put our heads together. We know the range of the Cessnas used to distribute the swarms. Likewise, we suspect a Japanese connection behind all of this. So I compiled a database of Japanese companies who hold leaseholds or who have financial ties to any of the islands within the Cessna fleet's range."

"And?" Gray asked.

"There was a surprising number of possibilities. Asia invests heavily across Polynesia, with China and Japan hotly competing. But one site raised a significant red flag. A pharmaceutical company bought a small island. An atoll, to be precise."

She pulled a map out of her pocket and unfolded it onto the table. The legend read NORTHWESTERN HAWAIIAN ISLANDS. It appeared to be a long chain of tiny islands that spread in a thousand-mile arc across the Pacific, stretching all the way to Midway Island and beyond.

Aiko explained. "The atoll is too small to be shown on this map, but it's located near the island of Laysan."

She tapped the spot on the map.

Palu shifted closer. "I know those islands. My bruddah and I sail out there sometimes. Very pretty. Very private. No one goes out there much."

Aiko concurred with his assessment. "Most of the islands are uninhabited."

Gray joined the Hawaiian in studying the map. "But why does this raise a red flag?"

"First, the company in question is a competitor with Tanaka Pharmaceuticals, the company who funded Professor Matsui's work."

Aiko glanced at him, but Ken needed no reminder that his ill-fated research trip to Queimada Grande might have had a darker purpose, turning him into an unwitting pawn in a game of corporate espionage.

Aiko moved on. "Second, the atoll in question once housed an old U.S. Coast Guard LORAN station. All that's left of it is an unmaintained airstrip and some abandoned buildings."

"Which if modernized," Gray admitted, "would make for a convenient staging ground."

"But which Japanese company are you referring to?" Ken asked.

"One that's been on our radar for a few years. But for reasons that don't seem connected to any of this. Black market deals. Financial malfeasance." Aiko shook her head, clearly exasperated. "We could never build a strong case. Mostly because Japanese law tends to favor corporations."

Ken knew that was certainly true. "So what's the company's name?"

Aiko lifted an eyebrow. "Fenikkusu Laboratories."

Ken sat back in his chair. He recognized the name. Only now it had more meaning and significance.

"What?" Gray asked.

"The name *Fenikkusu*," Ken explained. "In Japanese, it means *phoenix*."

Aiko nodded. "An immortal creature reborn from its own ashes."

Kowalski snorted. "Wonder where they got the idea for that name, huh?"

Aiko shrugged. "But like I said, all of this is circumstantial and possibly coincidental. We can hardly raid facilities owned by Fenikkusu Laboratories based on this."

"Not until you have more evidence," Gray said.

Aiko stared down at the map. "Which perhaps we could find on a small island in the middle of the Pacific."

"Then we head over there," Gray decided. Ken could see the wheels already turning in his head.

"I should go with you," Palu interjected. "I know those islands. Even have cousins out in Midway, who might lend us a boat. Make good cover."

Gray slowly nodded, clearly willing to accept this offer.

Seichan stood up. "I'm going, too."

Gray's gaze sharpened. "Maybe it's better if—"

"I'm going."

Ken tried to intervene, knowing firsthand what was coming. "For now, you should remain under quarantine. If not at the medical center, then at least here."

Seichan swung her scorching gaze upon him. "Am I contagious right now, Doc?"

He tilted away. "Well, no."

"Then I've got three days."

She stormed off, slapping open the door to the porch.

As the screen slammed shut behind her, Kowalski held up both palms. "Just so you all know, I'm fine with her going."

4:44 P.M.

Gray slipped gingerly out onto the porch. He had waited for Seichan to stop pacing before coming out. It had taken her a full half hour to finally settle to a seat on the top step.

Still, he took measure of the storm clouds hovering over her shoulders.

"Hey," he said.

She ignored him, keeping her back to him.

Not good.

He moved slowly, afraid to spook her. He extended an offering as he reached her side, his version of an olive branch.

"I minced up some fresh ahi." He stared off into the gardens. "Since we're leaving in an hour or so, I thought you might want to feed your stray cat one more time."

She sighed heavily and took the plate.

He dropped to a seat next to her, but he kept a few inches between them as a buffer zone for now.

She mumbled, "What about your warning not to feed strays?"

"I think we're way past worrying about one cat's threat to the island's biosphere."

"That's certainly true."

Still, she refused to look at him.

"Seichan . . ."

"You're not leaving me behind."

"I know, but—"

"If I'm going down, I'm going down fighting."

"I understand. We'll find a cure." He held out a hand, palm up. "Together."

She sagged, releasing some of the tension in her shoulders, and reached over. She entwined her fingers with his. As he squeezed back, he felt a tremor in the fine muscles of her hand.

"You'll be okay," he promised her.

"It's not *me* I'm worried about." She finally turned to him, her cheeks streaked with tears. "I should have warned you before now."

Gray's brow knit with concern. He knew something had been bothering her for nearly a month. "What is it?"

She stared at him with fear shining in her eyes.

"I'm pregnant."

THIRD

THE AMBER ROAD

17

Takashi Ito ignored his quiet visitor and knelt before a low table. It was a traditional *kotatsu*, which consisted of a wooden frame above a recessed alcove, all covered over by an antique quilt. Beneath the blanket, sand covered the sunken section of floor and supported a small coal brazier.

His thin, arthritic knees rested under the edge of the *kotatsu*, warmed by the heat of the coals. While it was already spring, the elevation of the resort town along the banks of Lake Kawaguchi kept the air cool. The lake rested eight hundred meters up the northern flank of Mount Fuji.

Kawaguchi was one of five lakes surrounding the sacred mountain, but it was the most famous due to its magnificent view. For centuries, artists had come to try to capture the beauty of the towering snow-capped summit reflected in the mirror-flat waters.

And always failed.

To truly appreciate it, one had to make the pilgrimage here.

Takashi stared out the wall of glass at the peak. It was why he chose this site several kilometers away from the bustle of the town's many hotels and restaurants to build the latest research complex of Fenikkusu Laboratories.

The view was spectacular.

The shining summit of Fuji—a perfectly symmetrical cone—hung serenely in the sky. It transformed throughout the day as the sun coursed its path, from a crystalline diamond to a purple bruised shadow. According to Shinto mythology, it was home to the undying god Kuninotokotachi. Even its name, *Fuji*, was synonymous with *immortal*.

Takashi also appreciated the dichotomy of this mountain, serene yet turbulent. Fuji was an active stratovolcano that had laid waste to the surrounding area multiple times throughout history. The last eruption, back in 1701, rained burning cinders over a wide swath, destroying homes and temples, and blanketed Tokyo in ash, which led to a decade-long famine.

Yet the same peak was also the source of water for most of this land, irrigating rice fields and farms.

It was this clash of temperament that made Fuji the soul of Japan, representing its people's capacity for great wisdom and serenity, while also demonstrating its willingness to destroy everything around it when agitated or threatened.

In the past, ancient samurai had even used this mountain to house their great training facilities. The land upon which this research laboratory sat was once home to the Tokugawa shoguns. It was those same warriors who had died in the temple of Kan'ei-ji back in Tokyo. Takashi pictured the stone memorial behind the temple, where he burned incense every year in memory of his beloved Miu.

So how could I not choose this site for my facility?

Also, there was a more practical reason. The town of Fujikawaguchiko lay only a hundred kilometers from Tokyo, where the corporation's main headquarters was located. The facility's proximity to the capital was convenient while maintaining its own isolation.

As it needed to be.

The staff here were all handpicked for their loyalty, discretion, and scientific knowledge. Average salaries were over sixty million yen, which also ensured lips remained sealed, as did exacting security measures that monitored everyone and every square centimeter of the buildings and its grounds.

Of course, such methods did not keep rumors about this structure from being whispered about by both competitors and anyone who happened to look past the security gates of the walled-off facility.

Perhaps I should have been more conservative in its design.

While there were many outbuildings, the main facility was a wonder of glass and steel, sculpted into the shape of a *gojū-no-tō*, a five-storied pagoda.

He had heard the nickname for this structure, sometimes out of derision, sometimes out of respect.

Kōri no Shiro.

The Ice Castle.

He appreciated the name and took it to heart himself. Especially in the depths of winter, when snow descended from the peak of Mount Fuji to cover the surrounding lands. The glass facility reflected this frozen landscape, becoming part of it, an icy apparition out of Japan's ancient past.

Beyond such beauty, the facility's engineering and design also served a practical purpose. Glass and steel would not burn if Mount Fuji should ever grow angry and rain flaming cinders over the town. Plus, unknown to most, the facility was more than its façade. There were five underground levels, the same number as were shining above. The laboratory bunker below hid the corporation's greatest secret, with the bottommost floor capable of withstanding a nuclear blast.

Soon such secrecy would be rewarded.

His goal was nearing fruition. The horrors to come would serve as revenge for the slaughter of his beloved wife, Miu, to make the world suffer as he had. While at the same time, from this very temple, a transcendent Imperial Japan would be reborn.

As he sat and waited with his silent guest in his private suite—located in the highest tier of the glass pagoda—he occupied his time with a hobby practiced from his youth. Upon the quilted surface of the *kotatsu* rested a flat piece of glass that served as his worktable. A laptop stood open near his elbow, awaiting the scheduled video call from his grandson, but his focus was upon a folded piece of paper.

With great care, he made two more creases, pressing crisp lines. He had taken up origami as a boy, before being cast out by his family, and had never forsaken the art. It was a connection to his past, both personal and cultural—going back to when origami was first practiced in the courts of Imperial Japan. His passion for the art grew greater during his time with Miu. He had folded a menagerie for her, grew a garden of paper flowers, just so he could earn a rare smile from her. He believed this skill was part of the reason he had won her over.

Now he continued the practice for its calming effect, for its ability to exercise his arthritic fingers, even for its mathematical challenge to keep his mind as sharp as the creases in the paper. Over the decades, he had knelt at the feet of origami masters, honing his skills. Akira Yoshizawa had been one of his teachers, before the man died a few years back at the age of ninety-four.

The age I will reach at the end of this year.

He moistened his fingertips on a dampened sponge, employing the wet-folding technique developed by Yoshizawa, to make the final crease in his handiwork. Once done, he propped it on his glass desktop, balancing his work on its paper legs.

It was a praying mantis.

As was usual, he had no intent of his design when he started. He let his fingers dictate the flow and shape, reflecting his own meditative mind. But now finished, he could understand why he chose this particular figure.

He stared across the table to the woman kneeling

silently in the formal *seiza* style. She wore a white kimono tucked into a knotted red *hakama*, along with straw sandals and split-toed *tabi* stockings. Her dark hair was braided and nested atop her head by the artful placement of decorative pins. Her clothing was typical for a *miko*, a Shinto temple maiden.

But Takashi knew the religion she practiced was one of blood and death.

He studied the praying mantis and knew what had inspired this design. It knelt across from him. Like him, the woman was trained by the *Kage* to be an assassin. For the past several years, Takashi and his grandson had been secretly collecting those who had survived the *Kage*'s purge, building and training a small army, a modern version of the *shinobi*, the shadowy warriors of feudal Japan.

This woman, though, had found him instead and had already proven her worth. She had provided information, which was confirmed by his contacts in Japanese intelligence, of an American group headed to Estonia. They were seeking the source of the amber artifact that had cost Miu her life. Wary of such an unusual pursuit, he had already dispatched a team to intercept them. He intended to discover the reason behind this strange trip and eliminate any threat it might pose.

His laptop chimed, announcing an incoming call, and its screen bloomed to life.

He reached over and tapped the phone icon to accept the call from Masahiro. His grandson's face filled the new window. From under a brow shiny with sweat, Masahiro's dark eyes glowered, but his gaze was cast down in shame. His grandson had already reported the events on Maui. While the general operation had proceeded according to plan, one failure blemished the operations.

The two agents of Sigma—the pair who had brought about the downfall of the *Kage*—still lived.

"*Kon'nichiwa, Sofu*," Masahiro said gruffly, his eyes flicking upward. His grandson must have noted the anger shadowing Takashi's face and dropped the informality. Masahiro needed to earn back Takashi's respect before calling him grandfather, *sofu*, again.

"*Jōnin* Ito," Masahiro started again, his head more deliberately bowed as he used the proper title.

"Report on the situation at the base?"

After fleeing Maui, his grandson had flown to the island of Ikikauō. Their base of operations was located on a small atoll, not far from Midway, where the Imperial Japanese Navy had suffered a humiliating defeat during World War II. It was only fitting that this new assault should rise from those same waters.

"*Hai*." Masahiro bobbed his head once. "The data has been collected. The breeding pens are being dismantled. We should be clear for incineration by nightfall."

Takashi noted the slightest shake of the woman's head across the table. She had already shared her counsel. He eyed the woman.

"Are you sure they'll go there?" he asked her.

She lowered her head once. She seemed certain the Americans—specifically the two operatives who survived the attempts to kill them—would track Masahiro back to Ikikauō. It seemed improbable, but Takashi had come to trust her.

Masahiro must have noted this brief exchange, his voice worried. "*Jōnin* Ito, all is on schedule. We can—"

Takashi lifted a palm to silence him. "You lost a good soldier. *Genin* Jiro. Your second-in-command. I am sending you a replacement."

Takashi's eyes flicked toward the kneeling woman.

Masahiro frowned. "But there is no time."

Takashi took in a deep breath.

What does one so young know of time?

"You will continue operations as planned," he ordered. "But you have a new mission on Ikikauō. A chance to redeem your honor."

Takashi shared the details, while the woman waited. Her fingers had come to rest on a dagger hidden in the knot of her *hakama*. She called it an *athamé*, a blade intended for dark purposes. She had her own reasons for wanting the Americans lured into this trap.

As he instructed his grandson, he noted a small picture in the corner of his computer screen. It showed the face of the woman here, but it was nothing like the dark-haired beauty with black eyes and a perfect complexion seated across from him.

The photo showed a ghost. A deathly pale woman with icy blue eyes and hair the color of fresh snow. As if to defy her lack of pigmentation, she had a black wheel tattooed across the right side of her cheek and face. The symbol was presently powdered over and erased, such was her skill. Over her decades with the *Kage*, she had learned to transform that blank canvas into any number of faces, becoming a master of disguise and subterfuge.

No wonder she had survived the purge.

Still, Takashi had learned everything about her.

He read the Russian name at the bottom of her photo: *Valya Mikhailov.*

But even that name failed to describe *who* she truly was.

He nudged the praying mantis perched on the glass, knowing his fingers had instinctively captured her hidden nature.

This is who you truly are.

18

"I think we've fallen into a storybook," Monk said.

Kat understood her husband's sentiment. The city of Tallinn was one of the oldest European capitals, dating back to the thirteenth century. Despite its turbulent history—which saw the country fought over by its many neighbors—much of its medieval heritage had been miraculously preserved.

Especially here in Old Town.

As Monk drove, she stared out at the spread of cobbled streets and twisted alleyways, all framed by quaint red-tiled buildings painted in pastel shades, most dating back to the Middle Ages. The spire of St. Olaf's Church towered above it all, the world's tallest building throughout much of the sixteenth century.

Yet, out the other side of the BMW's windows, a modern city beckoned, a metropolis of glass skyscrapers and angular architecture. In the new millennium, Tallinn had reinvented itself. What had once been a port city on the edge of the Baltic Sea, full of paper mills and match factories, had transformed into the Silicon Valley of Europe. Tallinn had more tech start-ups per capita than anywhere else. Even Skype was founded here.

Still, the people were proud of their history and celebrated it, like the festival under way now. Her group had been warned at the airport about *Tallinna Vanalinna Päevad*, or Tallinn Old Town Days. Men and women in period costumes crowded the medieval streets. Some climbed through the throngs on stilts. One stalked alongside their traffic-stalled vehicle on poles two stories high. All around, open-air stalls added to the congestion, selling local food or handicrafts.

A boy walked alongside their slowly moving sedan and knocked on their window. He held up a basket of Kalev chocolate bars and candy, all made in Estonia. He was dressed in a traditional loose linen shirt and trousers, both embroidered in a colorful pattern.

Monk pointed from behind the wheel. "We should pick up some candy for the girls."

Kat lifted an eyebrow. "You want to give them *more* sugar?"

She suspected he really wanted the candy for himself. The man had an insatiable sweet tooth—and apparently he wasn't the only one.

"Actually, I wouldn't mind some chocolate," Dr. Bennett said from the backseat, gawking at the midday festivities outside his window.

"Me, too," Elena said with a grin.

Kat bowed to the majority and rolled down the window. The smells of sugary baked goods and sizzling meat piqued her own appetite. She bought several candy bars and a bag of caramels. She kept the bag for herself, purely for research purposes, of course, to evaluate the quality of candy manufacturing in Estonia.

As they cleared Old Town, the traffic finally opened back up. Despite the delay, it had taken them less than half an hour to drive from the Tallinn airport to the center of the city. Their destination appeared ahead: the *Eesti Rahvusraamatukogu*, or the National Library of Estonia.

"Impressive," Elena said, eyeing the massive structure.

The sprawling eight-story brick building spanned the entire city block. Its façade looked like a Stalin-era tomb, a featureless gray limestone slab decorated with a single rosette window, all roofed over by a grim pyramid. The utilitarian design made a certain sense as the library's construction had begun when Estonia was still under the iron thumb of the Soviet Union, but it was eventually finished after the country declared its independence in 1988.

The building now stood as a testament to Estonian fortitude.

But for their small group, the library was where they would seek to follow in the footsteps of Archibald MacLeish.

During the eight-hour flight here, Kat had read the former Librarian of Congress's journal. MacLeish had arrived in Tallinn during a tense and bitter time, when the Soviets had come to occupy the city after driving the Nazis out with a series of savage bombing raids. Many civilians had been killed during the attack, including children. MacLeish had recorded the words found scrawled on the firebombed ruins of the Estonian Theatre, written by defiant locals: *Varemeist tõuseb kättemaks!* or *Vengeance will rise from the ruins!* At the time, MacLeish had been struck by the resilience of the people here, and even today the Estonians remained fiercely nationalistic, determined never to fall under occupation again, especially by the Russians.

It was also here where MacLeish had ended his search for the origin of James Smithson's amber artifact—on the same day that "Little Boy" was dropped on Hiroshima. With the Japanese seemingly thwarted, MacLeish had abandoned his quest.

Leaving us to pick it back up again.

As Monk parked the car, Kat stared up at the looming building, momentarily overwhelmed by the enormity of their task. How could they hope to discover where Smithson had acquired his artifact . . . and do so in less than three days?

Elena must have sensed her despair and tried to reassure her. "The National Library is the largest in all the Baltic States. Besides what you see aboveground, there are two basement levels, where its most valuable books are stored. All told, its stacks hold over five million volumes, meticulously preserved in air-conditioned facilities. So, if there are any clues left behind by Smithson, they'll be found here."

As they climbed out, Dr. Sam Bennett craned at the expanse of the façade. He grated his palm over the stubble on his chin. "But where do we even begin to look?"

The entomologist was in his mid-sixties—though his hay-colored hair, sharp blue eyes, and ruddy skin made him look decades younger. Kat knew he still maintained a family ranch back in Montana and definitely looked the part of the cowboy. For the trip, he wore jeans, boots, and a plaid shirt, which he dressed up with a suit jacket.

Kat had noted Elena eyeing the man with not a small measure of interest. The librarian touched Sam's elbow now and pointed toward the entrance. "The facility's director, Gregor Tamm, should be waiting for us. He was kind enough to rally his staff to pull together anything concerning Smithson, especially the time he spent here. Hopefully there'll be some clue as to where to search next."

"Sounds good." Sam smiled his appreciation. "Nothin' like pulling a few strings to speed things along."

Elena shrugged, blushing a bit. "One of the few perks of being the Librarian of Congress."

Kat got them all moving toward the long flight of stairs up to the entrance.

Monk drew alongside her, taking her hand. "Ah, young love . . ." he whispered to her, nodding to the pair in front.

"Shush," she scolded him, but she couldn't hold back a smile.

Once through the imposing doors, a trim middle-aged man in a black suit strode toward them, his arm out toward Elena. His dark hair and thin mustache looked freshly waxed. He could easily pass as a butler in some aristocratic house.

"*Tere tulemast*, Dr. Delgado, welcome." The man touched his chest with a palm. "I'm Director Tamm, we spoke on the phone."

Elena stood straighter as she shook his hand. "Yes, thank you. I'm sorry to call you in the middle of the night and to impose on your staff like this."

"No, no problem, I assure you. We were most happy to gather what you asked. Come with me." He waved to the far side of the lobby. "We have a private reading room reserved for you."

After introductions were quickly made, he guided them past several rare book exhibitions on the way to an elevator. They all piled into the cage. Once they reached the seventh floor, Tamm led them down a long hall flanked by bookshelves. The interior spaces here looked like a medieval castle, with cavernous galleries, tall archways, and bricked vaults. Statuary of mythical beasts graced pedestals and alcoves.

Kat noted a peculiar sculpture of a man with a rat's body.

Before she could inquire about it, Director Tamm glanced back at the group. "I understand the Smithsonian hopes to learn more about its benefactor for an upcoming museum celebration."

"That's right," Elena said haltingly, clearly uncomfortable with lying to a colleague.

Kat relieved her of this responsibility. "Smithson was an avid mineral collector, traveling across Europe to obtain unusual specimens. As you may know, his collection was lost during a fire in the nineteenth century. We're hoping to rebuild his collection for an exhibit celebrating the Smithsonian's founder."

At least, that was their cover story.

"A most ambitious project," Tamm acknowledged. "And what a glorious way to honor the man's life. From what I've been able to glean overnight, Mr. Smithson's esteem as a chemist and mineralogist has been glossed over by history, overwhelmed by his endowment to found your institution."

"That's what we're trying to correct," Elena said, sounding as if she were warming to the story. "To reveal the scientist behind the benefactor."

Tamm nodded and drew them to an arched wooden doorway. Banded and studded with iron, it looked like it could have come from an old Estonian castle. "This is a reading room normally reserved for academic scholars from our local universities in Tallinn. I'd be happy to leave you to review what we've gathered. Or perhaps, as I've taken the liberty of curating much of the material myself, I could help you with your work."

"We'd certainly welcome your assistance," Kat said.

"It would be an honor."

Tamm opened the door and waved them into a room that looked like a medieval cloister. There was even a tarnished suit of armor standing in a corner, guarding tall bookshelves full of dusty volumes along all four walls. A single wooden table divided the room. Before each chair, a reading lamp overlooked a tilted dais meant to hold an open book.

Kat expected to see a crooked-backed monk laboriously working on an illuminated manuscript. Instead, a lone young woman with a braided blond ponytail stood by a computer station next to the room's single window.

Tamm introduced her. "This is Lara. One of our newest researchers." He smiled at her. "And my daughter."

Monk chuckled. "So she's following in her papa's footsteps."

"I couldn't be happier."

Kat noted the man's beaming pride and the daughter's slightly embarrassed expression. Kat suspected Lara preferred to stand on her own merits. Or it could simply be the universal embarrassment daughters of this age felt for a doting father. She wondered when her own daughters would become just as exasperated.

Monk had another worry, whispering to Kat as they all filed inside. "Let's hope the girls don't follow in *our* footsteps. I think we should start pushing them toward a safer career path, perhaps handling pillows."

"Knowing those two, they'd end up smothering one another."

"Well, that's true," Monk said soberly. "So then maybe accounting."

With their daughters' futures still undecided, Kat and Monk followed Tamm to the table. Hundreds of books, periodicals, and newspapers were neatly stacked across its length.

Kat felt a sinking despair at the sheer volume.

"As you can see," Tamm said, "my daughter and I have been quite busy. But perhaps if I knew more about what you were seeking, I might be able to point you in the right direction."

Kat nodded. "We're doing our best to follow

James Smithson's footsteps across Europe as he collected his specimens. We hoped to learn why he
came to Tallinn."

"Ah . . ." Tamm turned to the table, waving his
daughter over to help. "Then you came here to
learn about *merevaigutee*, what you call *amber*."

Kat was glad the director's back was turned, so
he missed her startled expression. Elena and Sam
both glanced at her, just as surprised. Monk simply
looked worried, as if he expected something malicious afoot.

Tamm missed the silent exchange. "You see, I
know exactly *why* James Smithson came to Tallinn." He turned back around. "It was because of a
secret he was keeping involving amber."

1:03 P.M.

How could the man possibly know this?

Puzzled and shocked, Elena took a step back. She
bumped into Dr. Bennett. Sam caught her by the
elbow and steadied her. His firm fingers gave her
the strength to challenge the director.

"What do you mean?"

Tamm lifted a yellowed treatise bound in vel-
lum from the table. "This is one of Mr. Smithson's
scientific papers. Its subject is quite esoteric, but we
preserved a rare copy in our vaults because it per-
tains to our region's history."

Elena gingerly accepted the paper and read the
handwritten title aloud. *"An Account of Experiments*

with the Spirit of Amber." She lowered the treatise. She knew from researching James Smithson that the man performed and recorded many of his own chemical experiments, but this was beyond her. "I don't understand. What was he trying to accomplish?"

Lara answered, glancing down shyly. "I took the liberty of researching the topic. Spirit of Amber was also known at the time as 'acid of amber.'" She pointed to the yellowed pages. "Even Mr. Smithson calls it that in his notes, where he explains how he created his own supply by heating up raw amber and distilling it into a whitish acidic powder. Today we know this compound as *succinic acid."*

Monk cleared his throat, drawing Elena's attention. She knew the man had an extensive medical background through his training with Sigma.

"Does that mean something?" Kat asked her husband.

Monk reached with his prosthetic hand for the treatise. Elena passed it to him. "Definitely want to read this. But I know about succinic acid. It's produced by mitochondria in our cells as part of our body's energy-generating system. It's what keeps us alive."

"But why would Smithson be experimenting with this spirit of amber?" Elena asked.

Kat looked worried and turned to Director Tamm. "Did Smithson perform these experiments here in Tallinn?"

"He did, but I'm afraid, if you read his notes, you'll see he did not learn anything significant. It's

why he likely left these papers here and never officially published them. I believe he was keeping this
all a secret."

Elena knew the director was right. It was the
same secret he took to his grave. Still, she wondered
if Smithson might have left clues in those journals
of his that were destroyed in the Castle fire during
the Civil War.

If so, could he have hidden other clues elsewhere?

Before she could contemplate this, Monk turned
to his wife. "Kat, I can tell you're on to something."

She dropped her voice, turning away from Tamm
and his daughter. "From MacLeish's account, Smithson had shared his drunken story of a mine disaster
with a geologist here in Tallinn. Which suggests he
must have already obtained his artifact *before* coming
to the city."

"Makes sense." Monk nodded. "But why did he
conduct these experiments?"

"What if he was trying to figure out how something trapped in amber could come back to life? I
could easily see him believing some unknown property in the amber itself was life-sustaining and was
trying to figure it out."

"But, of course, he would've failed," Sam interjected. "The physical properties of amber have
nothing to do with sustaining any cryptobiotic cysts
lying dormant in the trapped bones. That miracle
was part of the wasps' genetic makeup already."

"Still, he couldn't know that," Elena said rather
sharply, feeling she had to be Smithson's advocate
here. "And despite his failure, he was wise enough
to recognize the artifact was too dangerous to be-

queath to the United States—yet, at the same time, too miraculous to destroy."

"He acted like a true scientist," Kat admitted. "Both safeguarding and preserving the knowledge for future generations."

Elena nodded. "Which was also his goal—only on a grander scale—when he financed the founding of the Smithsonian."

Sam frowned. "But why set it in America? I always wondered about that."

She shrugged, only able to guess at Smithson's motivation. "He was born to an aristocratic family, but because his parents fell into financial hardship, he was never truly accepted by his peers. Due to that, I think he rankled against the rigid caste structure in Europe and knew his best hope for fostering a new period of enlightenment was in the New World, where ideas wouldn't be strangled by the strictures of status and class."

Elena had experienced herself the gifts of such a free society, rising from a family of migrant workers to become the Librarian of Congress.

Had Smithson envisioned and envied such a world?

Monk drew them back to the matter at hand. "That's all fine and good, but if Smithson had already obtained his artifact before reaching this city, where did it come from?"

Tamm and his daughter had clearly tried to give them their privacy, but Monk's question drew the director closer to their group. From the suspicious squint to the man's eyes, he was beginning to wonder about their true purpose in coming here.

"I don't mean to pry," he said carefully. "But as

I mentioned before, I do know *why* Mr. Smithson came to Tallinn. Perhaps such knowledge could help with whatever it is you seek."

Elena glanced to Kat. For the moment, the director seemed willing at least to cooperate. She suspected her station as the U.S. Librarian of Congress had something to do with that.

Just as well I came on this trip.

Kat must have felt the same way. She nodded to Elena, clearly wanting her to press onward from here with the authority of her position.

"Director Tamm, I'm going to be honest with you," she said. "We're seeking to track down the origin of one of Smithson's mineral specimens. It was a large chunk of amber. About seventeen pounds."

She also held out her hands to demonstrate its approximate two-gallon size.

Tamm's eyes grew larger. "Such an outstanding specimen. I can see why you would want a piece like that for your new collection."

"Ideally," Kat added, "we'd also like to acquire a sample from the same site where Smithson obtained his . . . for the purpose of authenticity."

"Indeed. But Baltic amber is the best," Tamm said with a measure of pride. "In the prehistoric past, these lands, even the neighboring sea, were covered by vast pine forests. It was from the sap of those giant trees that the rich amber deposits formed around here. Since then, pieces continually get churned up from the seafloor and wash ashore, but older veins run deep underground, some even several meters thick." He stared at them. "Just imagine that."

Elena found herself looking at her feet, trying to picture such vast golden flows.

"So, then is it any wonder," Tamm continued, "that Mr. Smithson should come to this region looking for a perfect specimen of amber? Since ancient times, people have been coming to these shores to collect our amber. Both for its gemlike quality and its magical properties."

Elena frowned. "Magical?"

"Indeed. Throughout history, amber has been valued for its healing properties and as a ward against evil, a way to keep beasts and monsters at bay."

Elena shared a glance with Kat, wondering if Smithson had heard these same stories. If so, it would support Kat's supposition that Smithson had conducted his experiments for a reason, perhaps to test such wild claims with science. Maybe Smithson wasn't just looking for the presence of a life-sustaining healing chemical, but also testing the amber to see if it could be a ward against evil.

Could his experiments have been a search to find a cure against what was hidden inside?

Tamm continued again, drawing back her attention. "While I can't tell you *where* Mr. Smithson discovered such an outstanding specimen, I do know the path he took to get here." He turned away. "Let me show you."

1:27 p.m.

Kat followed the director over toward his daughter.
Let's hope this leads somewhere.

Tamm glanced back to their group. "Are you familiar with the Silk Road?"

Kat frowned at the abrupt change of subject. "As in the ancient trade route, between Europe and China, where silk and other goods were shipped?"

"Precisely. But there is another trade road, one far older, tracing back five thousand years."

What is he talking about?

Tamm turned to his daughter and spoke rapidly in Estonian. Lara nodded, tapped at the computer keyboard, and brought up a map of the eastern half of Europe on her monitor.

They all gathered around.

Tamm pointed to the dotted line coursing across the map. "This is known as the Amber Road. Along this route, cargos of precious amber traveled from St. Petersburg—where there are large deposits of amber—all the way down to Venice, Italy. From there, ships carried this treasure across the Mediterranean." He looked at the group. "In fact, did you know that the breast plate of Tutankhamen is decorated with pieces of Baltic amber?"

Pride shone from the director's face as he recounted this illustrious history of the region's native gemstone.

Tamm continued, "Even the ancient Greeks prized Baltic amber, especially due to its mystical properties. Some twenty-five hundred years ago, Thales of Meletos rubbed a piece of cloth over a chunk of amber and produced sparks. He called this strange new force *electricity*, derived from the Greek word *electron*, which was their name for amber."

"That's interesting," Monk said. "But what does all this have to do with James Smithson?"

"Everything." Tamm's eyes twinkled as he nodded to the map. "Mr. Smithson started his journey in Venice and traveled northward along the Amber Road. He intended to go all the way to St. Petersburg, but he ended his sojourn here in Tallinn. Though I can't say why he stopped."

Kat could guess. After his experiments had failed to produce any usable results, he must have forsaken his pursuit.

Tamm tapped the city of Tallinn on the map and ran his finger backward. "I have to imagine that Mr. Smithson must have discovered his specimen somewhere along this route."

Elena glanced to Kat. "He must be right."

She scowled at the map, studying the sheer length of the Amber Road.

If so, how can we hope to find the source in less than three days?

A possible answer came from Lara. "My father is

not entirely correct." She cast an apologetic glance to the director. "While Mr. Smithson was following the route north from Venice, once he reached the Baltic Sea he took a sailing ship along the coast to reach Tallinn's port."

"How do you know this?" Tamm asked, looking surprised.

She touched her computer keyboard. "This morning I took the liberty of searching electronic copies of ship records from the time Mr. Smithson was in our city. I found his name listed on a passenger manifest for a merchant vessel that had arrived from Gdansk, Poland."

Kat leaned closer to the monitor and followed the road back to the Polish city. It sat at the edge of the Baltic Sea.

Monk bent down next to her. "If he traveled from there, that would narrow our search considerably."

"To only *half* the Amber Road." Kat sighed heavily. "But that still leaves a lot of ground to cover."

Monk leaned his shoulder against hers. "We've done a lot more with a lot less."

True.

Kat straightened and turned to Lara. "Were you able to learn anything more about Smithson's travels?"

"No, I'm afraid not." Lara crossed her arms. "But Gdansk has been the center of the world's amber trade for centuries. Back a few years ago, the city started a large amber museum. They have archival records tracing back to the founding of the first guild of amber craftsmen in 1477. Perhaps the museum might have some record of Mr. Smithson."

Monk shrugged. "It's a long shot."

Kat nodded. "But like you said, we've done far more with less."

As preparations were being made for their departure, Elena paced the length of the library table. She stared down at the record of life of the Smithsonian's founder stacked on the table. It was as if his body were sprawled there.

Is this all that's left after we're gone?

Smithson had never married, never had children, and while his name was writ large in stone across the National Mall, few knew the man himself. All anyone could do was piece together bits and pieces of his life. She picked up the yellowed handwritten treatise, trying to understand this man who sought to better the world through science.

She returned the paper to the table.

You deserved better.

Sam stepped next to her. "Are you okay?"

She turned to her companion, who stood a head taller than her and a tad closer than she found comfortable. "Just tired," she forced out. "And maybe a little wired at the same time."

"Totally get that." Sam glanced sidelong to their teammates. "Those two do not let any moss grow under their feet."

She smiled.

That's certainly true.

Off to the side, Monk finally ended his call with

their jet's pilot and spoke to his wife. "If we hurry, we can be wheels-up in an hour."

Kat nodded. "Then let's head out. Hopefully the town festival won't bog us down."

Director Tamm noted her concern. "Perhaps I can show you a route to the airport to avoid the worst of the congestion." He stepped smartly toward the thick door. "There's a map in the lobby."

Monk and Kat followed at his heels, drawing Sam and Elena with them.

As they headed to the exit, Sam lifted an eyebrow toward Elena. "See what I mean?"

Tamm hauled open the door. "A festival parade is scheduled—"

A sharp clap cut him off.

The side of the director's neck exploded, showering Kat with blood. His body fell back into the room.

Time slowed.

Lara cried out, sounding far away to Elena's ears.

As if choreographed, Kat dropped and dragged Tamm's body to the side, while Monk shouldered hard into the iron-banded planks of the door and slammed it shut.

A sharp knocking followed, as more rounds pelted the door.

Sam caught Elena around the waist, drawing her back and not letting go.

Monk held the door but called across the room. "Lara, is there another way out of here?"

The director's daughter stood stiff-backed, her hands at her throat, her eyes too wide.

Kat pressed her bare palms against Tamm's neck wound, trying to stanch the flow. "Lara, we don't have much time."

The young woman stared at the spreading pool of blood, her answer a low moan.

"No . . ."

19

Gray stood alone on the foredeck of the dark catamaran. A sickle moon hung low over the midnight waters, casting little light. He checked his dive watch, a steel Rolex Submariner.

Almost time.

Still, he clenched a fist, the cords of his forearm bulging, reflecting his impatience. It had taken the team nearly seven hours to reach their destination, arriving a few minutes before midnight. Back in Maui, they had commandeered the corporate HondaJet owned by Tanaka Pharmaceuticals and flown across the archipelago of the northwestern Hawaiian Islands to reach Midway. There they had rendezvoused with Palu's cousins who owned a fishing catamaran, a Calcutta 390 customized with a pair of 550 Cummins diesel engines, and raced southeast at forty knots to reach these waters.

Gray lifted his binoculars to study their target. From two miles offshore, the island of Ikikauō looked like a forested hump rising from the waves. A handful of lights twinkled on the western side, marking a cluster of decommissioned U.S. Coast

Guard buildings. They bordered a small runway of crushed coral.

Earlier, as their catamaran had neared the island, a small plane had landed there.

So somebody was definitely home.

Knowing that, the group continued to pretend to be a simple fishing charter. They kept well away from the island. Palu and his two cousins—who were shorter, rounder versions of the fireman—had positioned rods around the boat, acting as if they were trolling through the water for a little night fishing.

The others hid down below in the small cuddy cabin. The plan was to wait for the moon to set, then drop overboard in scuba gear and swim ashore. They needed proof that this island was the staging ground for the attack and to try to identify who was behind it.

A tall order . . . especially on hostile territory.

Gray lowered his binoculars and turned to the satellite map of the island. It was tacked to a board near the catamaran's wheel. The thousand-acre island was really an atoll, nearly circular in shape, fringed all around by reefs. But the most unusual feature was the oblong lake resting at its center. It was surrounded by low hills covered in dense rain forest. According to the old Coast Guard records, the lake was over thirty meters deep in spots and very salty, which suggested it communicated with the neighboring ocean.

The slap of bare feet drew his attention around.

Palu climbed from the stern deck to join Gray in the boat's tiny wheelhouse. The big Hawaiian must have noted Gray's focus. He pointed to the map. "That's why we call this island Ikikauō. Means *Little Egg*." He tapped the lake. "See, here is the yolk."

"Got it."

"We name it also because of the life that hatches from here. Finches, ducks, terns, albatrosses. Then there's the water 'round here . . . you can scoop a pail and catch a fish." He grinned. "Maybe not that easy, but pretty close."

Gray suspected Palu was sharing this as a reminder yet again of all that was at risk. The man's mood grew pensive as he stared out to sea.

"According to our myths," he mumbled, "Pele's brother—Kāne Milohai—guards these islands way out here." He glanced over to Gray. "But sometimes even the gods need a little help."

"We'll do all we can," Gray promised.

"I know, I know." Palu returned his attention to the map. "But this place has been threatened long before now. All these islands." He waved to include the entirety of this remote stretch of his native homelands, then pointed to the southwest. "They sit at the fringe of the Great Pacific Garbage Patch."

Gray stared out to sea. He had read of the swirling galaxy of trash that had formed in the nearby vortex of currents known as the Pacific gyre. Covering an area twice the size of Texas, the patch was composed of millions of small trash islands set amid a soup of floating rubber, degraded plastics, old fishing nets, and other debris.

Palu shook his head. "It's slowly poisoning our lands. Washing more and more garbage onto the beaches. Wiping out birds, killing sea turtles. No one pays attention out here." He shrugged. "The Papahānaumokuākea monument helps, but it's not enough."

Gray recognized the name of the protected marine reserve that surrounded the northwestern Hawaiian Islands.

Palu nodded to the map. "Unfortunately, this small island—Ikikauō—and many others sit outside the reserve."

Gray nodded. "It's probably why that corporation leased this place. Being beyond the reach of U.S. Fish and Wildlife, they'd have a free hand to do what they'd like with the place."

"Maybe, but this island is still important to my people." He pointed a thumb at his cousins. "Makaio and Tua say there are some old shelter caves with petroglyphs on the eastern side, even ruins of a *heiau*, an ancient Hawaiian temple."

Gray appreciated the man's heritage, but Palu was sharing this for another reason.

On the map, he pointed to the atoll's eastern shore. "While these *kanapapikis* might not have to worry about Fish and Wildlife, they would know better than to trespass on this side." He looked significantly at Gray. "Which means no one should be around there."

Ah . . .

Gray now understood. "So you're saying that's where we should aim when we swim to shore."

Palu's grin returned. "From there, we catch them with their pants down." He slapped Gray on the rear. "And smack their *okole* good."

Gray rubbed the sting from his own rump and glanced over to the moon.

It had almost set.

Time to get moving.

Gray headed toward the cuddy cabin. "Let's tell the others."

12:12 A.M.

Seichan pretended to be asleep on the tiny bed.

Kowalski, on the other hand, snored on the far side of the cabin, sounding as if he were being strangled. It was so loud she could barely make out Ken and Aiko whispering at a small table in the cabin's kitchenette. But Seichan wasn't trying to eavesdrop on the pair.

Instead, her palm rested on the flat of her stomach.

She tried to gauge what was happening inside her. With her eyes closed, she imagined the microscopic larvae rooting through her like worms in a rotted apple. She felt no sign of their presence, certainly no pain. According to the professor, that would soon change.

Still, her palm sought signs of the other life inside her.

How far along are you?

On the journey here, Gray had tried to question her about the pregnancy, but she only gave terse answers.

Maybe six weeks.

She pictured the baby at that age. From what she

had read, it was about the size of a pomegranate seed. It should have a heartbeat by now—one too quiet to be picked up by any stethoscope, though an ultrasound might reveal its fluttering. Right now, the brain would be dividing into hemispheres and starting to cast out waves of electrical impulses.

Why didn't you tell me?

Seichan recognized Gray's wounded look as he asked this question. She had just shaken her head. She didn't know herself—or maybe she feared the true answer and avoided looking too deeply.

Gray had tried another question.

Do you want to keep—?

She had stopped him with a scathing look and a sharper retort.

For now, it doesn't matter what I want.

And that was the closest to the truth she was willing to admit. The decision could be taken from her at any time—maybe it already had. After all she had been through this past day, how could she know for sure?

It was better not to hope.

And even making a decision required hope.

Instead, she held on to one firm conviction. Her fingers curled on her belly, knotting into a fist.

Hope would not save her child.

The better path forward was one she knew well.

Vengeance.

If there was any hope of a treatment for her affliction—one that could save her and her baby—she would not stop until it was found and the perpetrators of this attack were either captured or killed.

Preferably the latter.

This thought relaxed her fingers. She rubbed her palm over her stomach, as if reassuring what impossibly slept inside her.

My baby . . .

The door to the cuddy cabin opened. Without looking, she knew who ducked inside to join them. She recognized his breath, his scent. Her hand settled to a stop over her lower belly, daring for the briefest moment to hope.

Our baby . . .

12:32 A.M.

Gray fell backward over the starboard rail. He was last to go overboard, letting the scuba tank on his back drag him deep. To mask the group's departure, they exited on the side of the catamaran opposite the island.

Once the dive computer on Gray's wrist registered twenty feet, he balanced his buoyancy compensator. As he floated, he flipped down his DVS-110 diver night-vision system over his mask. Back on Maui, all the necessary equipment for the mission had been coordinated by Painter. Scuba gear had been sent from a Coast Guard station in Wailuku to their corporate jet. Everything had been waiting for them, including weapons and demolition gear.

Gray searched the waters. The other five members of the landing party hung in the darkness. They appeared as dim silhouettes. He signaled them by flicking on a UV penlight and pointing it due west toward the island. He got thumbs-up from everyone.

He would have preferred to swim dark, but with civilians in tow, he considered the lone UV light a reasonable risk. As he set off, he glanced right and left, making sure Ken and Aiko were not panicking. For this mission, the team might need the professor's entomological expertise, and the intelligence agent had refused to be left aboard the boat, insisting she was best suited to gather any incriminating evidence to satisfy Japanese authorities.

Gray had reluctantly agreed. Time was too critical to be cautious. It would be up to Gray, along with Seichan and Kowalski, to do their best to protect the pair, while Palu would act as the team's guide. The Hawaiian was the only one of them to have ever set foot on Ikikauō.

Ready to go, Gray reached to his chest where a ScubaJet was clipped to his vest. The torpedo-shaped propulsion system was only a little longer than his forearm, yet was strong enough to drag a diver at a heady clip through the water.

He made sure the others followed his example and hit the engine's starter. He glided off at low power until they were all coordinated and traveling together like an underwater fighter squadron. Satisfied, he ratcheted up the high-torque motor, setting them to jetting just shy of six miles per hour. The speed should allow them to cross the two miles to the coast in under twenty minutes.

In the meantime, Palu's cousins would slowly motor their catamaran farther out, pretending to be leaving in order to ease any suspicion.

As Gray headed toward the island, he kept an eye on the others, which was hard to do, due to the distractions below. Through the night-vision scopes, the single UV beam ignited the surrounding reefs into an electric kaleidoscope of fluorescent colors. It was as if everything in the sea had instantly evolved its own bioluminescence. Stony coral shone in hues of aquamarine and crimson. Anemones waved incandescent fronds of yellow and lime-green. Runnels of crimson traced the black spines of urchins. A lobster stalked past, shining as brightly as a lamp, while ahead, a manta ray glided at the edge of the glow, leaving behind a shimmering wake before it vanished into the dark.

Despite the wonder of it all, Gray forged ahead.

Occasionally other sights appeared, unnatural objects to this landscape: a ship's anchor half-swallowed by coral growth, a new reef formed by the skeletal remains of an old World War II–era plane, even the barrel of an old bow gun poked out of the sand. They were all ghostly reminders of the fierce Battle of Midway, fought across these islands after Pearl Harbor.

As Gray continued, these sights fell away, vanishing into the darkness behind him. Even the hillocks of coral disappeared, replaced with sand. Soon the seabed began to rise under him, forcing him upward.

They had reached the shallows surrounding the island.

Gray clicked off both his light and the ScubaJet. The world collapsed around him, fading to a monochrome world of dull grays. As he swam onward, he used his compass and GPS to guide him the last of the way to the proper coordinates along the shoreline. He motioned for the others to stay underwater, while he rose and scoped the crumbled wall of rock beyond a thin strand of beach.

A darker shadow marked a cave, the one Palu had told him about, where the man's ancestors had once sheltered while fishing and hunting among these remote islands.

With no alarm raised at his bobbing presence, he waved for the others to follow and headed to shore. They all clambered out of the water, shedding tanks and vests, and carried their gear in a low hustle into the shadows of the cave. They kept their wetsuits on. The drab black covering could help with camouflage.

"That was amazing," Ken gasped breathlessly, still staring out to sea.

"But now comes the hard part," Gray warned, as he huddled with the group. "The old Coast Guard station lies a mile due west. We have to assume they'll be watching the neighboring coast and immediate area. Our best approach will be to haul our gear over the neighboring hills to reach the eastern edge of the inland lake."

"We call it *Make Luawai,*" Palu whispered, his back to the group. "Means *Deadly Well.*"

"That doesn't sound good," Kowalski mumbled.

Palu shrugged. "Just means the water is very salty. Bad to drink."

The Hawaiian stood at the rear of the cavern. A moment ago, after getting an okay from Gray, Palu had flicked on a lighter, shielding the tiny flame with his palm. The soft glow illuminated a scatter of petroglyphs across the back wall. Stick figures with prominent triangular chests had been carved into the stone. Some sat in crude silhouettes of canoes, while others ran across the rock with fishing spears in hand. Dispersed among them were random concentric circles, along with renditions of fishes and sea turtles.

Palu's back was hunched with sorrow.

Kowalski stood next to the big man's shoulder and suddenly jabbed a finger at a petroglyph, his voice far too full of pride. "Look, a whale!"

"*Koholā*, brah," Palu said, smiling, clearly snapping out of his melancholy. "That's our name for 'em. Be respectful. It is my family's *aumakua*, our personal god." He puffed out his chest, thumping a palm there. "Maybe because all us *keikikaneare* grow so big."

Kowalski turned, bumping his head on the cave's roof. He rubbed his skull. "Maybe I better make *Cola* my god, too."

"*Koholā*," Palu corrected.

"Got it. *Cola*."

"Close enough, brah."

Gray waved the two men over and finalized their plan. "Once we reach the lake, we'll proceed underwater again. Only this time we'll be swimming entirely dark."

He glanced over to Ken and Aiko to make sure they were comfortable.

Both nodded, though Ken looked scared.

Can't blame him.

Gray rose out of the huddle. "Hopefully we can

get close enough to figure out what the hell is going on here."

Seichan straightened next to him—then clutched her left side, visibly wincing.

He caught her elbow. "You okay?"

"Just a muscle cramp." She shook her arm free. "That's all."

Worried, Gray glanced to Ken, who looked even more scared now.

FIRST INSTAR

The cream-colored larva burrowed blindly through muscle. Its ten segments were barbed with spines, allowing it to corkscrew through sinew and fat. It was in no hurry as it feasted on blood and tissue. Muscular contractions of its pharynx extruded sharp chitonous mouth parts. It bit a chunk and swallowed the meal into its midgut, which was already full.

Only hours after bursting forth from an egg—one of several larvae packed inside there—it had already grown tenfold in size. It now stretched half a millimeter in length. Sensory nets in its elastic skin responded to the rapid growth. Hormones surged through its body. A new layer of skin had begun to form beneath the old, readying for the molt to come—which would allow it to grow tenfold yet again.

But first it needed more sustenance: *sugar* for the energy to drill deeper, *protein* to expand its length, *fat* as storage for what was to come.

Its hunger was insatiable and bottomless.

As it bored deeper, spines tore open a capillary. Blood bathed its segments. Spiracles along its sides drew oxygen from the hemoglobin, setting fire to its drive. Refueled, it burrowed onward, blind but not senseless.

In its wake, it exuded droplets, a trail of chemicals.

Some contained antimicrobials, meant to keep its macerated path from getting infected.

The meal must live.

Those same droplets also delivered biochemical messages into the host's bloodstream. It used the body's ready-made network of vessels to send information to other larvae who feasted elsewhere, both to coordinate their molts and to stake out territory.

But most important, such a communication warned of areas that were off-limits.

The nerves in its soon-to-shed skin responded to sound, to the heavy thudding of a muscle that kept their host alive. The sound, persistent and regular, reverberated through the tissues.

The four thousand larvae responded to millennia-old instincts to shirk from its source, to not feed from that deep sonorous well.

The meal must live.

The larva reacted and drilled away from that thumping beat. As it chewed deeper, a section of its segments brushed against a thin nerve. Electrical contact contracted the muscles on that side. The larva twisted its length away from that charge. All the while, its body also continually responded to a similar stimulation, one far larger.

Great waves of electrical potential wafted through the host, sweeping down from above.

Again, the larvae knew to ride that tide *away* from its source for the simplest of reasons.

The meal must live.

With its path laid out, it continued, delving ever deeper.

Then, as barbed spines ripped another capillary, a new biochemical warning arrived. Other larvae had detected a second muscular fluttering in its host, one different from the deep thudding. The same spot also cast out tiny waves of neurological activity.

The larva—like all the others—obeyed this new message and drifted away from that region, driven by millennia-old instructions in its genetic code.

Its goal was simple and ancient, driven by rudimentary imperatives.

Eat and grow . . .

Along with . . .

The meal must live.

But that last instruction was only for now.

20

Kat crouched over the body of Director Tamm. Hot blood seeped between her fingers as she did her best to stanch his neck wound. Though unconscious after hitting his head on the stone floor, he still breathed.

But for how much longer?

His daughter, Lara, remained stiff-backed with shock.

Sam stood in front of Elena, shielding her from the bloody sight while he tried to phone for help. A volley of rounds pelted the thick door, pinging off bands of iron on the outside. From the distinct lack of pistol blasts, the attackers' weapons must be equipped with silencers.

"Can't get a signal," Sam said, holding his phone higher.

Kat considered this fact. The thick stone walls could be blocking the connection.

Or else someone's jamming communication.

She looked at the door.

Either way, these were not simple thieves.

The shooting suddenly stopped, which was more

disconcerting than the pinging. She had to imagine the assailants had come prepared to blow their way inside.

Monk must have had the same concern, his brow furrowing deeply. He still braced the door. He had levered down a latch to secure it, but the mechanism looked more decorative than anything, crafted to match the room's medieval décor.

Her husband's gaze swept the room. "Where's a secret passageway when a guy needs one?"

Kat weighed the odds of reinforcing the door by pushing the heavy library table against it and holding the fort until help arrived. She dismissed it, knowing the plan would certainly doom Director Tamm and likely only get more people killed.

Gotta be another way . . .

Both Kat and Monk had holstered sidearms—SIG Sauer P226s—under their light jackets, but a firefight across the library could end with the same result.

She looked across to the room's lone window. She had glanced out it earlier. It overlooked a sheer seven-story drop to an employee parking lot. The building's exterior, though, was limestone bricks with mortar set deep enough for decent finger holds. Two stories down, a thin decorative ledge circled the building.

She calculated the odds.

Maybe with Monk's help . . .

Her husband noted the direction of her attention. When she turned to face him, he easily read her plan.

"It's insane," he said, "but that's one of the reasons I married you."

2:10 p.m.

Elena huddled with Lara under the library table. Next to them, Sam hunched over Tamm's slack body. He had taken over for Kat and had a wadded handkerchief pressed against the director's neck wound. The cloth was already soaked with blood.

We're running out of time.

Kat must have noted the same but for a different reason. The woman straightened from where she had her ear against the latched door. "I can hear them doing something out there."

"Probably planting charges to blow the hinges," Monk warned. He crouched in a corner, struggling to lift an antique suit of armor.

"Then let's go," Kat said. She rushed from the door and retreated along one side of the table.

Monk finally shouldered his burden and barreled past on the other side. The pair converged on the lone window at the back. As Monk reached the table's end, he grunted loudly.

A splintering crash followed.

Though she couldn't see much from where she hid, Elena pictured the suit of armor shattering through the window and sailing in a long swan dive down to the parking lot far below.

"Hurry!" Kat urged as she joined her husband.

Through the broken window, bright music flowed

into the room, rising up from the festival under way in Tallinn's Old Town. The cheery notes were a sardonic counterpoint to the danger they were all in.

"Go, go, go . . ." Kat yelled.

A pair of loud blasts made Elena jump. She twisted around to peer past the chair legs toward the door. Smoke blew toward her as shards of shattered wood pattered the tabletop. A piece of twisted metal shot across the stone floor, bouncing like a skipped stone over water.

With the hinges blown off—as Monk had anticipated—the massive door fell into the room. It slammed hard and rattled once before settling to a stop. Boots pounded across it. Four men entered and spread out.

Elena dropped to her belly and glanced back to the window.

She spotted Monk's hand clamped to the lower sill. His fingers shifted, doing their best to grasp a firmer hold.

She wasn't the only one to spot the desperate movement.

Shouts erupted, both in Japanese and maybe Arabic.

Two of the masked men broke from the others. Flanking either side of the table, they rushed the window.

Elena covered her head, knowing what was coming. She imagined the looks of surprise when the two only discovered a disembodied hand grasped there.

Even though it was expected, the explosion made her gasp. Monk had warned them of the fail-safe built into his prosthesis, a packet of C4 hidden under the palm. The force of the blast tossed the two men's bodies across the room. The entire table shifted forward two feet. Chairs tumbled across the floor. Books and papers flew high.

Without waiting for the dust to settle, Monk and Kat fired from where they hid atop the bookshelves to either side. The pair had counted on the broken window and the earlier splintery crash to draw the attackers' focus.

It appeared to have worked.

Caught in the pair's crossfire, the remaining two masked men crumpled to heaps by the crashed door.

Monk and Kat dropped together to the floor, landing at the same time. Like a choreographed dance, they raced through the chaos to the door, moving in perfect step. They paused in unison at the threshold, then rolled into the hallway, guarding both ways and each other.

As the ballet ended, Kat leaned back into view. "Clear. Let's go."

Elena crawled forward, while Sam reluctantly passed his duty to Tamm's daughter.

"I'm sorry," he whispered.

Elena touched Lara's arm. "We'll get a medical team up here right away."

It was all they could do. She hated to abandon the young woman, but Kat had warned them that if any other assailants were in the area—in the lobby or outside—their continuing presence risked more deaths.

They had to leave.

But not by the front door.

Elena clutched Lara's staff badge by its lanyard. It would allow them to access the library's book elevator at the other end of the hallway. The plan was to drop down to the basement level and exit through the employee parking lot, where hopefully no one was watching.

As Elena fled with Sam at her side, she cast one glance back at the smoky ruins of the room. She ignored the pools of blood, the broken bodies. Her eyes fixed on the handful of fiery pages fluttering down.

It was all that was left of Smithson's legacy here.

All gone.

She turned away and ran after Kat, who took the lead with her husband trailing them all. She clutched the pair of crucifixes hanging from her reading glasses, one for each of her granddaughters. She prayed that the next steps along Smithson's trail were not so bloody.

Still, she held out little hope.

2:44 P.M.

Back out in the bright afternoon, Kat led her group through the crowded heart of Old Town. Music blared, hawkers shouted from streetside shops, children danced around legs. Laughter abounded, some drunken, others in good cheer.

The bloodshed and mayhem at the library seemed nothing more than a bad nightmare. No one at the festival seemed to have noted the commotion, likely due to the fact that the explosions and gunfire had erupted at the back of the hulking building. The only signs of the prior chaos were distant sirens closing in on the National Library.

Kat had alerted authorities as soon as the group had reached the basement and discovered their phones worked again. She also informed the handful of library staff found there about the director's condition. She asked them to help Lara with her father. Suspicion shone in their eyes at the sudden arrival of this clutch of strangers into their midst, but the pistol in Kat's hand had discouraged any probing questions.

Once outside, she had headed immediately for the bustle of the festival. She knew better than to return to their parked sedan, knowing it might be watched. Plus the crowds and commotion in the narrow streets and alleys should hopefully confound anyone tracking them.

For now, putting distance between them and the library was the priority. After that, she would make arrangements to rendezvous with their private jet.

She glanced at her phone's GPS map to make sure they didn't get lost in the maze of medieval streets. She pointed to the next left turn. "That way."

She turned to make sure the others heard her.

Sam and Elena nodded, both far paler than normal.

She had been pushing them hard.

Beyond them, Monk caught her eye. He must have noted the pair's condition, too. He silently warned her that the two researchers were reaching their limit.

She nodded back.

Time to get out of this labyrinth, find a taxi, and head to the airport.

Distracted and worried, she ignored the motorcycle cruising through the crowd. It was not an unusual sight. Only bikes, Vespas, and tiny European two-seaters dared the narrow, cobbled streets of Old Town.

Still, as she swung away, the tiny hairs on the back of her neck stood on end. She had learned long ago to trust this warning, when her body sensed a threat before her mind registered it. The cycle carried two riders, both helmeted, their faces obscured. But these were no festivalgoers; their entire body language read military.

Unfortunately, her gaze lingered on them a fraction too long.

Stupid.

The motorcycle engine screamed and shot forward. She went for her holstered sidearm. Monk noted her motion and twisted sideways, grabbing at his own weapon.

They were both too slow.

The cycle reached them. The driver snapped a kick into Monk, slamming him into a wall. Kat freed her weapon, but the riders were already atop them. Without the bike slowing, the passenger in back lunged out. He hooked Elena around the waist, threw her across his lap, and jabbed her neck with a syringe.

Tires burned rubber on cobbles and spun away.

Kat lifted her freed weapon, but the cycle was already deep in the crowd. She didn't have a clear shot. Still, she ran to where the bike turned into a pedestrian alley.

The cycle zigged and zagged through shoppers, al fresco diners, and street musicians. Confounding the matter, the alley was lined on one side by shops, all covered from the sun by awnings, creating a dark tunnel under them.

She immediately lost sight of the kidnappers.

Monk ran up to her.

She turned and pointed. "Boost me up."

He knew better than to question her. He dropped to one knee and offered her the other. She vaulted atop it and leaped. Monk's hand on her buttock propelled her higher. She landed on her belly atop the nearest awning and used the spring of the taut fabric to gain her feet.

Then ran.

She fled across the continuous spread of stall canopies, leaping the occasional gap. By racing above the crowds, she avoided the congestion below. She prayed for the motorcycle to be bogged down by the pedestrians, enough for her to catch up.

She kept her ear tuned for the whine of the two-stroke engine.

Then heard it.

Up ahead, maybe another twenty yards.

She sprinted, doing her best to close the gap.

Unfortunately, the end of the alleyway appeared ahead, marked by a tile-roofed bridge arching from one side to the other. It was the gate through the medieval city wall. Once the kidnappers left Old Town, the streets would open up for them, and she'd lose them forever.

She ran faster—but quickly saw a problem.

A small square opened before the foot of the gate. The row of canopies ended short of the plaza. Her flight was about to run out of runway.

Still, she didn't slow.

As she neared the end, she caught sight of the motorcycle. It shot into the square, scattering pedestrians. One of the festival's many stilt-walkers—a fellow in motley costume on a pair of two-story-high poles—could not get out of the way in time and got sideswiped. One stilt was knocked loose.

Kat thanked this small bit of luck and shoved her weapon into her belt.

She reached the last awning and leaped headlong over the crowd. She caught the loose stilt as it toppled and used her momentum to turn it into a pole-vaulter's stick. Grasping hard, she levered her body, kicking out with her legs—and sailed high across the square.

She hurdled over the motorcycle as it was forced to slow at the gate's bottleneck. She rolled in midair. People scattered in a panic, allowing her to land in a crouch, absorbing the impact with her legs, facing the bike.

The motorcycle shot straight at her.

She grabbed her pistol from her belt, pointed one arm, and fired.

The round shattered the helmet's visor.

The cycle toppled, skidding on its side across the cobbles, passing her on the left.

The rider in back leaped at the last moment and rolled safely away. She leveled her weapon as he rose, but he twisted around and fled into the stunned onlookers.

Kat rushed forward.

Elena had been knocked free of the cycle when her kidnapper had leaped off the backseat. Elena tried to sit up, but she was clearly dazed—whether from the crash or from whatever was loaded in the syringe.

Likely a sedative to subdue their target.

Kat helped her sit. "Are you okay?"

Elena looked at her limbs, then at the gawking crowd. "I . . . I think so."

Loud honking drew both their attentions back to the alleyway. A small electric-green Mini Cooper jammed into the square. The already panicky crowd fled out of its way.

Kat guarded over Elena and lifted her SIG Sauer—then lowered her weapon when she spotted Monk behind the wheel. He must have commandeered or carjacked the vehicle.

He sped up alongside them and braked hard. Before coming fully to a stop, he yelled out the open window. "Get inside!"

Sam popped the rear door.

Kat hauled Elena up and toppled with her into the backseat. She reached back and yanked the door closed behind her. "Go!"

Monk gunned the engine and set off for the gate. In moments, the small car raced under the arched bridge and out of Old Town.

Kat climbed into the front seat, leaving Sam with Elena.

Monk turned and asked the question plaguing her since the attack. "How did they know we were here?"

Kat had already come to only one conclusion. Besides a handful of people at Sigma, the only others who knew of this planned trip were Japanese intelligence.

And among them, one suspect stood out.

Aiko Higashi.

She reached to her jacket for her sat-phone. "I need to reach Painter."

"Why?"

"To get him to warn Gray."

"About what?"

Kat stared worriedly at Monk. "I think he's about to walk into a trap."

21

Geared up, Gray waded into the brackish water.

It had taken the team twenty long minutes to hike through the densely forested hills to reach the eastern shore of the flat lake at the island's center. They were forced to move slowly, using night-vision scopes to see, careful not to disturb the flocks of nesting birds. Under the dark canopy, bats had swooped at them.

As he entered the lake now, he hoped the bats were the only ones to note their progress. Ahead of him, Make Luawai stretched a quarter-mile wide and twice that in length. The air above the lake stank of brine, while a pall of tiny biting flies and noisome gnats hung heavily over the dark surface. Still, there was life below, evident from the occasional flop of a fish darting up at the clinging cloud of insects.

"Watch your step," Gray warned, as he headed out into the lake. "The bank drops away steeply."

He found himself neck-deep after only two meters. Even through the wetsuit, the lake felt distinctly warmer than the surrounding ocean. Still, it wasn't pleasant, more like wading into lukewarm soup. The strangeness was amplified by the lake's hypersalinity. With a salt content three times higher than the sea, the water buoyed his body unnaturally.

Before ducking below, Gray searched the opposite shore one last time. His night-vision goggles discerned a vague glow rising beyond the fringe of hills on that side, marking the site of the old Coast Guard installation.

All remained quiet over there.

Satisfied, he slipped underwater. Once everyone joined him, he quickly got the group moving. They swam fifty yards out, then returned to gliding through the water, propelled by the muffled hum of their ScubaJets. Only this time he kept their flight path shallower in the water, sticking to a depth of ten feet. At this level, starlight still filtered down, enough for their night-vision goggles to pick up.

Not that Gray needed even that meager illumination. He could've made this swim naked with only his compass, gauging the distance by the count of his blind kicks. But he had to accommodate the civilians in their party. The little bit of illumination should allow them to keep within sight of one another, which would hopefully lessen any chance of panic.

Unfortunately, such a precaution wasn't only for the benefit of the civilians.

As Gray glided, he glanced over his shoulder. During the overland trek, Seichan had tried to mask the pain she was in, but Gray had read the sheen of her skin, the faltering to her sure footing, the heavier panting to her breath. The discomfort seemed to be growing steadily worse. By the time they reached the lake, her jaw muscles had stood out as she clenched her teeth against the visceral pain.

He grew more worried when he couldn't spot her now. He knew she was at the back of the group with Palu, but apparently she had fallen even farther behind.

He felt a pang of regret.

I should've been firmer with her before, insisted she remain on Maui.

Still, knowing her, she would've found a way to follow them. Back in Hana, he had recognized the stubborn set to her stony face. He had seen that look often enough in the past. But in this case, he had also sensed a deeper well to her determination, one possibly due to the extra life she now guarded.

Trusting she would fight to her last breath, he faced forward again—and came within a breath of running his face into a wall. He canted to the side at the last moment. The obstruction was an upended wing of an old plane. As he shot past the wreck, the ScubaJet on his chest brushed the metal, scraping away a layer of algal growth.

Once clear, he switched off the jet and twisted around. The others noted his near collision. Ken and Aiko swept wide to either side. Gray immediately lost them in the murk as their ScubaJets sped them away.

Swearing under his breath, he signaled Kowalski by pushing his body in Aiko's direction and pointing, then he swam after Ken. He trusted he could outkick the man's jet, but as an extra measure, he also clicked on his UV light, using it like a lamp in the dark.

Ken appeared ahead. The man had the wherewithal to switch off his ScubaJet's engine and spotted the light. Gray swam up to him, offered a questioning okay sign, and got a thumbs-up from the man. Still, Ken's eyes were huge behind his mask.

Together, they headed toward where Aiko and Kowalski had vanished. Gray proceeded with caution as the UV light revealed the sprawl of a graveyard around them. The sphere of his glow swept over the tangled wrecks of four or five planes. Pieces were strewn far and wide. Half of a propeller stuck up out of the sand, looking all too appropriately like a cross in a cemetery. Fuselages lay cracked open below. Broken wings pointed crookedly in every direction or were pancaked into the silt.

All the wreckage was coated and draped with mats of algae.

Still, Gray recognized the planes' design, mostly from the prominent circle visible on one wing and the nose of a black torpedo poking out from under a plane. The wrecks were a squadron of World War II Japanese torpedo bombers—Nakajima B5Ns—usually launched from nearby aircraft carriers.

Gray pictured what must have been a pitched aerial battle over this island, part of the four-daylong Battle of Midway. The decisive naval fight dealt a crippling blow to the Japanese Imperial fleet, one from which they would never fully recover.

As he stared across the graveyard, dark shapes appeared out of the gloom.

One small, the other large.

Aiko and Kowalski.

The pair headed for the beacon of Gray's light.

As they closed in, Gray swung in a complete circle.

So where were Seichan and Palu?

In the tumult, Gray had lost track of the two. Were they still behind the rest of the team? Or had they missed the commotion and obliviously sped past this location already?

He had no way of knowing, but the contingency plan in case anyone got separated was to meet at the predetermined coordinates along the western shore, or if compromised, to retreat to the shelter cave.

With no other choice, Gray signaled for his group to continue onward. Still, as an additional precaution, he had them all stick closer together now. He didn't intend to lose anyone else.

As they left the wreckage behind, the lake bottom fell away again, dropping precipitously into a darkness that extended beyond the reach of his glow. It was as if the group were sailing into a vast void.

Feeling exposed as they glided out into that abyss, he doused his light, but not before pointing his beam behind the team, hoping it might act as a last beacon for Seichan and Palu.

That is, if they're even back there.

He finally relented and thumbed his light off.

As if upon this signal, the void below exploded

with a dazzling brilliance. Shocked, he flipped his night-vision goggles off his mask. Still, his overwhelmed retinas remained blinded. It took him two full breaths for the flare of the flash to die down enough for him to see.

Far below, a large complex now glowed across the lake bottom. It had the appearance of a giant circuit board, one that had suddenly sprung to life. He could make out interconnecting clear tunnels that linked an array of glass-domed chambers, creating a multilevel maze. Other darker spots marked the location of steel-walled rooms.

Gray understood what he was seeing.

An underwater lab.

He could also guess its purpose: *What better way to safeguard and quarantine any work done on a dangerous organism?*

Still, the glowing lab was not the major source of the blinding radiance. That came from the nose of a submersible shooting upward toward the trapped group, blazing a cone of brilliance before it.

With no way to outrun such a swift craft, Gray gathered the others. They were in varying degrees of shock and panic—or, in Kowalski's case, sullen resignation.

Gray motioned for the group to head to the surface.

Pools of light shone up there, too, closing in from the western shore. The muffled rumble of motors reverberated through the water.

Boats . . .

His team was being squeezed, from top and bottom.

As Gray reached the surface, he stripped off his swim mask. The others followed suit. A trio of pontoon boats aimed for them. Assault rifles bristled from the shadowy figures aboard.

Gray took a small amount of consolation that they weren't immediately fired upon, but he was not surprised. He expected the island's owners would want to interrogate the trespassers.

But apparently others weren't needed for questioning.

A loud explosion echoed to the southeast.

They all turned and watched a fireball roll into the dark sky.

Kowalski scowled darkly at the sight, knowing as well as Gray the likely source of the explosion.

The catamaran.

Gray was glad Palu was not here to see this. He stared across the dark lake, again wondering where the other two had vanished. While their absence had concerned him earlier, now it gave him hope.

At least they aren't caught in this snare.

Motion drew his attention down into the water.

Meters below, an arrow of brilliance angled away from their bobbing group, marking the passage of the submersible. But rather than descending back to its watery berth, it sped off toward the graveyard of the Japanese planes, sweeping right and left, clearly searching.

Gray prayed the others were safe and well hidden.

Especially with a glowing shark now patrolling these dark waters.

1:52 A.M.

Seichan braced her arms and legs against the fuselage walls, pinning herself within the plane's wreckage. The Japanese bomber had cracked upon impact, splitting the hull in two. She kept her back to the cockpit, where the collapsed skeleton of the pilot still hung in a knot of moldering belts.

The name of the lake—*Deadly Well*—proved all too true for that airman.

Let's hope it's not the case with us.

She stared across the two-meter gap of open water that separated her from the aft end of the aircraft. Palu had crammed his shadowy bulk into that half. It was a tight fit. Due to the dark depths, she could only imagine the strained expression behind his mask.

Moments ago, the two of them had entered the fringes of this sunken graveyard. They had lagged behind the rest of the team—or rather, *she* had. Palu had kept at her side, likely upon Gray's orders.

She had been having difficulty with her ScubaJet. It refused to click into its highest gear, forcing her to compensate with kicks to keep her moving as fast as the others.

Normally it wouldn't have been an issue.

But her current situation was far from *normal*.

Even now, sharp knives of pain carved through her muscles. Her arms trembled as she pressed her palms against the inner hull. Every fiber in her back burned, sculpting her spine with fire.

She took a moment to lean on her Guild training. She quieted her mind, shuttering away the discomfort behind cold walls. She drew deeply upon the oxygen in her tank. She had been taught that pain was the body's early-warning system. It did not necessarily equate to damage or disability, which seemed to be the case here. While everything ached or burned, she sensed her overall strength remained.

For now.

And now was all that mattered.

Gray and the others were in trouble.

As she and Palu had traversed the graveyard, the world ahead had exploded with a silent mushroom cloud of brilliance. The algae-coated debris field stood out starkly against that flare. Her mask's goggles amplified the blaze, burning a temporary hole in her vision.

Still, she had left the night-vision gear in place and instinctively moved into the shadows—where she had lived most of her life. She scouted for shelter, drawing Palu with her, until she came upon the broken plane on the lake's bottom.

They were lucky to have found it so quickly.

As she reached the hiding place, a two-man submersible had risen out of the depths. In the blaze of its lamps, she made out dark motes rising toward the surface.

Gray and the others.

Soon thereafter, bright boats appeared, skating across the roof of this watery world. With their quarry trapped, the submersible swung its nose toward the graveyard and headed this way. Its light swept back and forth.

Does it know we're here or is this search merely precautionary?

Either way, she could not outrun it.

As it entered the graveyard, she studied her adversary. The submersible was really a two-man sled, what was known as a *wet* sub, with its riders outfitted in full scuba gear. A Lexan glass hood covered the bow end but was open to the water at the back. Under the hood, a pilot sat behind the wheel, while a passenger crouched behind. The rider had his legs bunched under him. His hands clutched grips on the bottom of the sled to hold him in place. With his head ducked low, the hood protected the bulk of his body from the sub's draft through the water.

Submersibles like this were used by various militaries to sneak divers into enemy territory. The sub here looked designed for a similar purpose, especially as Seichan noted the speargun poking above the shoulders of the rider in back.

Equally vexing, she also spotted a pair of steel spear points flanking the nose light. It seemed the sub had its own weaponry.

As the craft entered the debris field, the rider dove sideways off the sled. He swam lower, while the sub angled higher. It looked like the diver intended to search the graveyard and either eliminate or drive any potential targets out of hiding.

Unfortunately, only four or five planes had crashed into the lake, so the number of hiding spots was limited. The diver was surely familiar with those spots. He dropped straight for a neighboring wreck. He pointed the light affixed to his speargun through the shattered cockpit window. The fuselage lit up from within, with beams blazing out of cracks in the hull.

Satisfied that no one was inside, the diver aimed for their shattered plane. He led with his light, shining it between the two halves. Both Seichan and Palu retreated deeper into their respective sections of the plane. With the additional illumination, she could now see the Hawaiian's face. She pantomimed by lowering her arms and mimicking a bear hug.

Palu squinted behind his mask, his nose crinkling in confusion.

She had to trust he'd figure it out.

As the waters separating them grew brighter, she readied her two weapons, one in each hand as she braced her legs. She waited for the black-steel tip of the speargun to enter her field of view—then tossed her first weapon out into the gap.

The momentum of the diver carried him forward to meet face-to-face the shock of what she had thrown out of the fuselage.

It was the pilot's skull.

The white bone struck the enemy's face mask.

Reacting with basic human nature—both at the unexpected attack and the nature of the object staring hollowly back at him—the diver twisted away. He swung his speargun toward Seichan's half of the fuselage, while falling back toward the other.

Before he could fire, thick arms grabbed him from behind and pulled him into the aft end, like a trapdoor spider pulling in its prey.

It seemed Palu had finally understood.

Seichan kicked off the cockpit seat and flew across the gap. She risked a fast glance up. The sub's beam searched the wreckage to her left.

Good.

Diving to join Palu, she struck the trapped diver and pressed the barrel of her SIG Sauer against his chest. She angled the barrel up as she fired. The shot was muffled but still loud. She trusted the whining rumble of the sub's engine would mask the noise. Shooting a pistol underwater was problematic. Most handguns could fire one shot before becoming disabled. Even then, the kill range was limited to less than two feet. She counted on that limitation to keep the slug inside the dead man.

While a dagger made more sense in a close-quarter battle underwater, she feared her target might thrash too much. The blood trail from a large gaping wound would be as obvious as a smoke signal to the hunter above.

Instead, she pulled the barrel away and pinched the hole through his rubbery suit. Once satisfied the diver had succumbed, she scraped a wad of algae from the wall and plugged up the bullet hole. She then snapped the flashlight off the speargun, handed it to Palu, and pointed in the direction of the searching sub.

Pretend to be the diver, she willed him.

He nodded his understanding, shimmied past her, and dove low across the sand. He led with the beam of his light. Palu was roughly the same size as the diver. Hopefully the ruse would last long enough.

Once he was away, Seichan ripped off the dead man's mask, which covered his entire face. He also had a radio headpiece. She ripped it away, secured it to her own, and switched masks. By the time she blew out the water to clear the mask, darkness had fallen over the plane's wreckage as the false diver and sub headed away.

She finally abandoned her hiding spot and rose out into the black water.

Despite the pain racking her body, she felt calmer in her natural element, a shadow in the darkness.

A voice whispered in her ear, speaking Japanese. It was the sub's pilot radioing his partner. *"Any sign of the targets?"*

Seichan knew a response was needed. The dead diver looked to be Japanese, so she answered in kind, only gruffly. *"Ōrukuria."*

All clear.

She continued to rise, drawing level with the slowly retreating submersible. She then set off in its wake. Agony flared with each kick, but she focused on her target, drawing slowly closer.

Below, Palu continued his charade, pausing every now and then to inspect the wrecks, which helped keep the sub idling along.

Ahead, the pilot sat under his hood, silhouetted against the brightness of his craft's light. She kicked harder, stirring up those fiery embers in her lower belly and legs.

Finally, she whispered into her radio, her Japanese flawless from her youth spent in Southeast Asia. "Movement five meters ahead. Do you see anything?"

The pilot responded, *"Nothing from up here."*

Counting on the pilot's increased focus below, she swept up behind the back of the sled, pointed the stolen speargun, and fired.

The shaft shot through the open back end of

the glass hood and impaled the pilot through the neck, nearly taking his head off. Blood bloomed and quickly filled the Lexan dome. Unguided now, the sub slumped toward the bottom, spilling a crimson trail behind it.

Out here alone, she didn't fear anyone seeing this particular smoke signal. Still, she sped after it. As she reached the sled, she grabbed one of the handgrips on the bottom and propelled herself forward. She manhandled the pilot out of his seat and tossed his body out the back. With his BC vest deflated, his heavy gear dragged his corpse to the waiting graveyard.

Seichan gained the controls. Though she had some experience piloting such craft, she was rusty. Still, after a few attempts, she got the sub spiraling down toward Palu. The Hawaiian had noted the bloody descent of the pilot and waited not far from the body.

Likely making sure it wasn't me.

Once she was close, he kicked off the bottom and joined her in back.

He pointed up, his expression questioning.

She shook her head and pointed down.

Time to pay the locals a visit.

Before heading off, she took mental inventory. She had an assortment of sheathed daggers hidden all over her body, and her waterlogged SIG Sauer could be dried out and made serviceable again. While it wasn't a lot of firepower, she would manage. To help her, she would lean upon a skill *not* taught to her by the Guild, but instead by the father of her unborn child, a man who was the master of lateral thinking, of shrewd improvisation.

If I intend to rescue Gray, then I'd better act like him.

Still, as she turned the wheel and engaged the thrusters, a flare of fire burned through her limbs. Her vision narrowed to a pinpoint. She bunched over the wheel, one palm on her belly, willing the pain away—not from her body, but what she guarded inside.

She breathed heavily, noting the needle in the red zone of her oxygen meter.

Running out of time.

She sat straighter, knowing how true this was for all of them.

Especially one.

As she aimed the sub down, she made a promise—to Gray, to herself, but mostly to her unborn child.

I won't fail you.

Still, a dark question had been growing steadily inside her over the past hours.

How much am I willing to sacrifice to keep that promise?

22

Now what . . . ?

Painter rode up the security elevator from Sigma command toward the first floor of the Smithsonian Castle. He had been summoned from the bowels beneath the museum by its curator, Simon Wright. Painter didn't have time to waste, but the Keeper of the Castle had insisted Painter would want to see this for himself.

If nothing else, I get to stretch my legs.

He had been buried underground all night, taking a brief hour-long catnap around 5 A.M. He had been coordinating with various agencies around the globe. As soon as he put out one fire, another started.

As the elevator doors opened into a security vestibule manned by an armed guard behind a desk, Painter's phone chimed in his hand. He glanced down and recognized the number. He nodded to the guard, who stood straighter, silently acknowledging Sigma's director. The room was additionally safeguarded by electronic surveillance and countermeasures. Even the door into this small chamber required a special black keycard with a holographic Σ embossed on it.

Painter lifted his phone and stepped aside. He held off exiting the private vestibule. "Kat, how is Dr. Delgado doing?"

"She seems to have shaken off the worst of the sedative."

Painter pictured the attempted kidnapping of the Librarian of Congress from the streets of Tallinn. Though the woman had been saved, the reported attack at the Estonian National Library raised all manner of concerns.

Kat continued, "Thanks for expediting a medical team to the tarmac. Monk was worried about her blood pressure, but she seems to have shaken off the drug's effects. She insists that she's good to keep going."

"I'm not surprised. The woman didn't strike me as a shrinking violet."

"Oh, she's about as purple as a violet, but out of anger. I think I learned a few new Spanish curse words." Kat sighed. "I also heard Director Tamm is in surgery. His condition remains critical. If it wasn't for him and his daughter's help . . ."

Her words trailed off, wrought with guilt. Painter knew that particular misery all too well. "Then let's make sure we put their hard work and sacrifice to good use. When are you scheduled to depart for Gdansk?"

"We'll be wheels-up in five minutes. But I wanted to touch base one more time before we left. To see if you or Jason had made any headway as to *who* attacked us and *how* they knew we were in Tallinn."

Painter heard the frustration in Kat's voice. Her expertise was in intelligence gathering. Out in the field, she was cut off from her resources and clearly chomping at the bit to take control.

"Jason is still chasing some leads. The kid's good. You concentrate on learning what you can in Gdansk about where James Smithson acquired that artifact. We need some answers. Hawaii is becoming more chaotic by the minute."

"What's the status?"

"The death count is now over two hundred. But more and more people are flooding hospitals and medical centers, hauling in patients in a half-comatose state."

"Like the four who Gray pulled off of Haleakala?"

"Seems so. The number of people parasitized is rising by the hour. Medical personnel are struggling to find a way of treating them. Kowalski's girlfriend, Maria, has joined a task force in Hana, to lend her genetic expertise in studying the organism."

"Shouldn't she have already been evacuated?"

"She refused. Even knowing the risk of being trapped on the island as quarantine measures are being instituted. As she said, *I'm trusting you all to put out this fire.*"

"Sounds to me like Kowalski better put a ring on that woman's finger before she wises up about him."

Painter smiled. "That's certainly true."

"How's the quarantine going?"

"Right now, it's simply adding to the panic and chaos. A riot broke out in Honolulu as the National Guard was mobilized. Soldiers are doing their best to cordon off the nesting areas, but the colonies seem to be moving constantly and splitting into multiple territorial *leks*. It's like trying to catch butterflies with a net full of holes."

"I heard they were testing a bunch of different insecticides."

"So far, those attempts have only succeeded in riling the wasps up and scattering the swarm. Even worse, there are now reports of wasps being found on Molokai and Lanai."

"So they're already hopping between the islands?"

"It would seem so. But either way, there's no telling how many parasitized birds and animals have recovered from the neurotoxin and are on the move, which will only further entrench this colonization across the islands." Painter struggled to grasp the enormity of the danger, both to the islands and to the world at large. "Flights have already been grounded, which is adding more fuel to the panic out there. And a naval blockade is currently being set up around the islands to keep anyone from entering or leaving the area."

"That still might not be enough," Kat warned. "A quarantine over such a large area is untenable. Eventually something or someone will break out and carry this scourge to the mainland."

Painter knew she was right. He remembered Ken Matsui's warning about the drastic measures that might be necessary.

You'll need to nuke those islands.

He prayed it didn't come to that. But he had already heard rumblings up the various chains of command, as this scenario was being judged and weighed.

One strategy being actively considered was to evacuate the populace via airlifts and aircraft carriers to the abandoned military site at Johnson Atoll, some eight hundred miles to the west—then sterilize the Hawaiian Islands with tactical nuclear strikes.

Still, such a plan presented a mountain of problems. Johnston Atoll was only three thousand acres in size, hardly large enough to hold Hawaii's entire populace. And some people would likely refuse to evacuate. Then, afterward there was the question of what to do with the relocated population.

If any of them had been parasitized and were incubating larvae, the whole cycle could begin again. Did that mean those islanders could never be let off of Johnston Atoll? Would their relocation be a lifelong prison sentence?

"We need a better solution," Painter mumbled to himself, but Kat heard him.

"We'll do our best to see if there are any answers at the end of Smithson's trail," she promised. "But what about Gray and his team?"

Painter knew she feared the other team was walking into a trap, one possibly laid by Aiko Higashi. After being ambushed in Tallinn, Kat seemed certain her mission to Estonia was leaked to the enemy by someone in Japanese intelligence.

"So far, I've not heard anything from Gray," Painter said with a sigh. "But he went radio silent before heading to the island. Jason has his ear to the ground, awaiting any update."

"I hope he's safe, but even more, I hope he finds something out there."

As do we all.

Painter checked his watch. "I need to sign off. Simon Wright is waiting for me. Let Jason know when you land in Gdansk."

"What does the curator want?"

"That's an excellent question."

Painter ended his call, pocketed his phone, and headed out the door of the security vestibule. The museum had opened less than an hour ago, so a few clutches of people hung around various exhibits. No one gave him a second look as he exited the nondescript door.

He headed toward the Castle's north entrance. Simon asked Painter to meet him in a small chapel-like alcove to the left of the entrance. It held Smithson's memorial and crypt. Painter had visited the place many times over the years. It seemed only fitting to pay his respects to the man who had founded this institution to science, history, and knowledge.

Ahead, Simon waited at the chapel's threshold. He wore a crisp suit and his shoulder-length white hair was combed back, exposing the lines of worry creasing his forehead. He spotted Painter and lifted his arm.

"Thank you for allowing me to impose on your time once again. But I thought this might be important."

"What did you want to show me?"

Simon waved him into the chapel and stood before the towering tomb with his hands on his hips, admiring it. Painter had to admit it was impressive. A giant white stone urn rested atop a decorated marble sarcophagus, which in turn sat upon a case that currently held Smithson's remains.

"I've walked past this crypt countless times," Simon admitted, "but now I wonder if Smithson was trying to tell us something. Maybe preserving something in stone, something that couldn't be burned in a fire like his journals."

"Tell us what?"

Simon glanced back. "About what he hid in his tomb."

Painter frowned. "I don't understand."

"Not only were James Smithson's *bones* brought over here from Italy by Alexander Graham Bell, but nearly a year later, this monumental *crypt* was packed up and sent here." Simon patted its side affectionately. "This is his original tomb that once sat in the San Beningo cemetery overlooking Genoa, Italy."

Painter knew that was the case, but not why this was significant.

"Smithson's nephew—Henry James Hungerford—arranged for this monument to be built for his uncle's grave, but the symbolism that decorates it has remained a speculative mystery. Some believe it was

Smithson himself who designed these specific symbols to mark his tomb, a nod to his interest in classical knowledge. Look at these lion's paws supporting the urn. Such decorative features can be found throughout the ancient world. Greece, Rome, even Egypt. The paws are supposed to represent strength."

Simon waved at other carved elements. "The laurel branch symbolizes the Tree of Life. The bird is the soul ascending to Heaven. The scallop shell, with its ties to the sea, signifies eternity and rebirth."

The curator raised an eyebrow at Painter.

Painter understood what the man was inferring. "You think he put that scallop shell on his tomb to indicate his crypt held something that could be reborn, that could be immortal. That's a fair stretch, Simon."

"Maybe." He pointed to the top of the urn. "See that pine cone finial atop the urn? It represents *regeneration*. Seems like a theme to me."

Painter crossed his arms, unconvinced.

Simon noted his posture, smiled, and shifted attention to the row of designs under the lid of the urn. "Notice the three figures to the right of the central scallop shell. Again, a shell that symbolizes *rebirth*."

Painter stepped closer, peering up at those three symbols. A cold shiver crested over his spine. *Why didn't I see this before?*

The three carvings next to the shell were a serpent, a chunk of rock, and a winged insect.

Painter lifted his hand and ran his fingers over the stone in the center. "You're thinking this is supposed to be the chunk of amber." He moved to the snake. "And this reptile depicts the dinosaur bones trapped in the stone. And on the other side, the winged insect—"

"Most believe it's a moth," Simon said. "Born out of a cocoon, it epitomizes life after death. But maybe the symbol is meant to have a dual meaning. Representing not only rebirth from death—but also depicting the very creatures that could perform that miracle."

Painter ran his fingertips across the symbolic line, as if reading a message left in Braille by the Smithsonian's founder. "Wasps born out of amber from the bones of a reptile."

Simon stepped back, returning his hands to his hips. "If he carved this warning on his tomb, it begs the question—"

"What else has he written here?"

Painter's gaze swept the fanciful decorations. Could there truly be some answer here? If not a cure, then maybe at least some hint as to where he acquired his artifact?

He clapped the curator on the shoulder. "Simon, I may have to recruit you."

"Thanks, but I like my job as it is. Especially as I don't get shot at while doing it."

Painter pointed to the crypt. "Can one of your staff photograph this tomb—from top to bottom and all sides—and forward them to me?"

"I'll do it myself right away."

"Thanks."

Painter turned and headed away. He wanted Kat to get her eyes on those pictures as soon as possible and prayed it might offer some clue on her search. He also wanted Gray to view them, as the man had an uncanny mind for seeing what was hidden in plain sight.

Unfortunately, there was one big problem with this plan.

Where the hell is Gray?

23

Ken shivered as the elevator descended into the island. He wore only his swim trunks. Still, it wasn't his near-nakedness that chilled him. It was the sight of the assault rifles pointed at their group. Four guards, all Japanese, shared the large cage, their weapons aimed at the captives' chests.

Aiko stood next to Ken, stripped to her one-piece swimsuit. Gray and Kowalski flanked them both, also only wearing trunks.

After being captured, the party had been marched to the west side of the island, where a cluster of cement-block Coast Guard buildings with rusted metal roofs topped a set of hills. The outpost overlooked a dark airstrip of crushed coral that paralleled the shoreline. A small jet and a larger-bellied transport plane were parked at the nearest end.

As the group was herded toward the largest of the Coast Guard buildings, a sleek white boat swept into view in the cove below. It skated atop a pair of tall hydrofoils until it neared a long pier, where it slowed and sank to its keel.

Ken could guess where it had come from. A column of smoke still obscured the stars to the south, marking all that was left of the fishing catamaran.

Once inside the cavernous Coast Guard building, the group had been stripped of all their gear, including their wetsuits. They were taken to where a shaft had been jackhammered through the concrete foundation. The cage of a freight elevator hung in a frame. It was the size of a one-car garage. The upper half was open, framed by bars.

Unable to face the black-eyed stares of the rifles any longer, Ken focused on the rock walls sweeping past the cage as they descended. The upper layers of the island had been compressed coral, but now they were dropping through a core of dark volcanic basalt. The history of the island was written into its geology. Born long ago of volcanic eruptions along the mid-Pacific ridge, the islands had been slowly drifting to the northwest, pushed by tectonic forces. Over time, the islands rose higher, pushed up from below, exposing their aprons of coral to the sun.

Ken tried to draw strength from the hard stone around him—but then the elevator came to an abrupt stop. Jarred, he bumped into Gray, who grabbed his elbow. The man's iron grip steadied Ken's balance.

Maybe that's the strength I need to count on here.

A guard posted outside the elevator pulled the gated door open. Ken and the others were marched at gunpoint into a tunnel cut through the island.

As they were forced along, Aiko studied the

shaft. "They must have used the shelter of the Coast Guard buildings to hide their mining operations."

She sounded calm, almost impressed.

Ken's heart pounded in his throat. He wiped sweat from his forehead. He realized how much he didn't fit in with this bold group.

The tunnel ended at a circular steel door, thick enough to seal a bank vault. It stood half-open. Ken was the last of their group to pass through. Despite his terror, he gaped at the sight that opened before him.

A glass tunnel extended out into the dark lake, lit by a strip of LED lights running the length of the arched roof. No starlight reached this depth. The illuminated complex was a world unto itself. Its interconnecting tunnels and rooms—set amid a maze of three levels—looked like a space station lost in some starless void.

One member of their group had a different reaction. "Looks like a Habitrail," Kowalski commented drily. "Only we're the stupid hamsters stuck in here."

A gruff voice growled behind them, "Keep moving."

As they continued into the complex, Ken noted an order to the sprawl. They were entering the middle level of the facility. The floors above and below appeared to be subdivided into sections, each of which was centered on a glass-domed chamber. The layout suggested the work here must be highly compartmentalized.

Perfect for maintaining quarantine.

The reason for that precaution became immediately clear. They passed a side tunnel that led to one of those domed chambers on this level. An airlock sealed its entry, but through a glass window, a black mass could be seen churning over every surface inside. Dark streamers swirled through the air.

Ken squinted and slowed his steps to get a better look, but he was prodded to keep going.

Aiko glanced at him, her brow knit with concern.

"I . . . I think those were all soldier drones in there. The big crimson-and-black ones." He stared across the glowing complex toward the other chambers. "Maybe they've divided the swarm into its component parts to study each one separately."

Elsewhere in the glass tunnels, technicians in white lab jackets hurried about. Ahead, men in blue maintenance coveralls pushed a line of heavily laden carts toward them, requiring their group to flatten to either side to allow them to pass.

"Must be preparing to clear out of here," Gray mumbled as they rolled past.

Ken feared what that implied.

What does that mean for us?

Once the parade of trolleys passed, the group was led to the end of the tunnel, where a central core connected all three levels. As they reached the hub, stairs spiraled up and down, but they were marched toward a room at the heart of the entire complex.

The lead guard pressed a button next to a set of double doors and leaned his lips near a speaker. He spoke rapidly in Japanese, too low for Ken to pick out any words.

As the man stepped back, the doors glided open, revealing a circular office centered around a wide desk made of polished teak. Shelves of the same wood swept across the back of the room, framing the desk in the center—along with the man who sat behind it.

The stranger stood as they were all forced inside. He looked to be no more than thirty. He was dressed in a business suit, tailored to accent his toned, muscular physique. Dark eyes, as black as his trimmed hair, narrowed as they entered, taking in each of them for one long breath, clearly sizing them up.

Though his expression was stoic, a cloud of anger hovered over him, evident from the twin lines between his brows and the hard edges to his lips.

Surprisingly, Aiko was the first to speak. She gave the smallest bow of her head. "*Kon'nichiwa*, Masahiro Ito."

The man's lips hardened, the lines deepened. He was clearly irritated at being named outright like this. After a distinct lapse, he collected himself and spoke. "Ms. Higashi."

"You know each other?" Gray asked, casting a sidelong look at Aiko.

"*Hai*." She gave a deeper bow toward the man, then lifted an arm. "May I present Masahiro Ito, vice president of research and development for Fenikkusu Laboratories."

Ken had already noted the gold corporate logo centered on the wall behind his desk. It depicted a fiery circle enclosing a stylized bird with wings of flames. A ruby the size of a thumbnail served as the eye of the phoenix, the mythical namesake for the pharmaceutical company.

Aiko spoke in Japanese to Masahiro. "How is your grandfather's health?"

Masahiro slowly sat, answering in kind, a formal dance ingrained into all Japanese businessmen, this courteous acknowledgment of ancestry and heritage between peers. "He is well."

"I'm pleased to hear it." Aiko gave another slight bow of her head and ended this brief ritual by switching back to English. She fixed the man with a steely gaze. "Then perhaps you'd like to explain your family's attack upon the Hawaiian Islands."

Ken flinched at her abruptness.

Masahiro did not react. "I don't believe any explanation is necessary nor required, considering the circumstances." His gazed flicked to the armed guards. "But all is going according to my grandfather's plan. Except for one detail."

His eyes narrowed, shifting to Gray. "Where is your partner?"

Gray glanced over to Kowalski, feigning bewilderment. "He's standing right here."

Masahiro stood again and leaned forward. "The woman . . . *your* woman. The treacherous *kisama* who brought down the *Kage*."

Kowalski tilted over to Gray and spoke out of the side of his mouth. "I think he's talking about Seichan."

Gray gave the smallest shake of his head, then

straightened, shedding any semblance of subservience. He matched the other's gaze, unblinking and cold, letting anger creep into his voice—all to add weight to his next lie.

"She's back in Maui. Quarantined and sick after being parasitized by whatever you bastards unleashed on the island."

Masahiro locked eyes, trying to judge his truthfulness.

While the team had failed to escape this ambush, their midnight swim and landfall on the dark side of the island must have helped mask their true number.

Ken felt a flicker of hope.

Masahiro settled back into his seat. "Then perhaps my efforts on Maui were not a total failure. Even if only indirectly, my actions have doomed your woman to a miserable and painful death."

Gray didn't have to feign looking distressed at this news.

Then a cold voice rose behind them. "The prisoner is lying."

Ken turned to see a striking figure stalk across the threshold, escorted by a cadre of armed men. The woman had snow-white hair, only a shade lighter than her pale skin. A prominent black tattoo marred one side of her face, forming the broken half of a wheel.

Piercing ice-blue eyes swept the room and settled on Gray.

The man's entire body tensed, as if coiling to lunge at her.

He clearly recognized her.

2:34 A.M.

Valya Mikhailov . . .

Gray clenched his fists to hold back from attacking her outright. After events in Africa last year, he had known this ghost of an assassin still lived. She'd even had the gall to leave a white rose with one black petal on her twin brother's gravestone.

Gray stared at the black wheel covering one side of her face, depicting a *Kolovrat*, a pagan solar symbol from Slavic countries. But her cheek bore only *half* the symbol; her pale brother had carried the other. Last year, Anton had died in the Arctic, far from his sister. From the fury smoldering in her eyes now, he knew whom she blamed for her brother's death.

As she spoke to Masahiro, her gaze never shifted from Gray. "The woman was not aboard the boat. We searched it thoroughly."

Past the door, a pair of familiar figures stood with their shoulders hunched, their faces glowering. It was Palu's cousins, Makaio and Tua.

Gray felt a measure of relief. Though far from safe, at least the brothers were still alive. Valya must have raided the catamaran and blown it up after grabbing Palu's cousins.

Masahiro scowled with disdain at the woman. "Then perhaps she was left back on Maui after all."

"No," Valya said firmly. "She's here on this island. Somewhere."

"You can't be certain of—"

"She's here." Valya cut him off with a glare, then pointed to Gray. "And he's going to tell us *where*."

Masahiro looked both doubtful and irritated. Clearly there was no love lost between this pair. "What does it matter? We're scheduled to be off this island in forty minutes, burning everything behind us."

"Because your grandfather—*Jōnin* Ito—will want to know she is dead. Especially after your earlier failure."

She let that barb sink in, then faced Gray. "Besides, forty minutes is more than enough time for me to break him."

Gray simply stood straighter.

Try me.

Accepting his silent challenge, she turned to the men behind her and pointed to Palu's cousins. "Take them where I told you. But we'll need one more. Someone to make him more pliant." She turned back around, her gaze settling on Aiko. "Perhaps a woman . . ."

Masahiro stood up. "No. According to my grandfather, Ms. Higashi is not to be harmed. She has been useful in the past and may be again."

Gray glanced to Aiko.

What did he mean by that?

Aiko remained expressionless, both at Valya's threat and Masahiro's insinuation.

"Then a civilian." Valya nodded to Ken. "An innocent in all of this."

"Again no." Masahiro stalked around his desk to confront her. "During his brief work with the wasps, Professor Matsui has accomplished far more than any other researcher. My grandfather even found his name for the species—*Odokuro*—to be an inspired choice, harkening to our mythology and heritage." He faced Ken. "*Jōnin* Ito believes, with the right persuasion, he might be convinced to join us."

From the professor's aghast expression, this seemed doubtful.

"Then that leaves me little choice." Valya turned to the only other member available. "Take him."

Kowalski groaned, but a poke in the ribs by a rifle got him reluctantly moving toward the door.

Gray took a step forward. "Where are you taking them?"

Valya's lips thinned, showing an edge of teeth, her version of a smile. "To test how strong your will is." She turned and headed out. "And your stomach."

2:58 A.M.

With Aiko at his side, Ken followed Gray up the sweep of stairs. Behind them, two guards pointed assault rifles at their backs. Ahead, the pale woman led the way, accompanied by another pair of armed guards.

Masahiro Ito stalked beside her, his every motion stiff and impatient. He checked his watch twice as they climbed to the top level of the lab complex.

Once there, the group was guided into one of its four sections. A pair of men in white lab jackets noted their approach and turned down a side tunnel to get out of their way. Both kept their gazes low, but one glanced over his shoulder toward where they were headed, where Kowalski and Palu's cousins had most likely been taken.

As the lab tech turned back around, Ken caught a glimpse of his fearful expression.

That can't be good.

After another crisscrossing of tunnels, the group reached a wall of glass that looked into a small steel room. Chains were bolted to the floor. Inside, guards snapped cuffs onto the wrists of the three prisoners who stood there, pinioning their arms out to the sides.

Makaio and Tua wore matching expressions of wide-eyed terror. Kowalski simply glowered under dark brows, looking like he wanted to punch someone really hard. Unfortunately, he was staring through the window at Gray, as if blaming his partner for his current predicament.

Valya also faced Gray. "I will give you three chances to reveal where your woman is hiding. This is the first. Before matters get messy. Cooperate and your friends' deaths can be swift and merciful."

Gray's face remained stoic, but his eyes flashed with barely constrained fury.

Valya shrugged. "So be it."

After the three men were secured, she tapped a knuckle on the glass. The armed guards hurried out of the room and into the hallway. They sealed a door behind them, wheeling a locking mechanism closed, similar to a hatch on a submarine.

Ken noted the perforated steel floor beneath the bare feet of the trapped men. He pictured seawater surging up from below.

Are they going to be drowned in there?

Instead, motion drew Ken's attention to the far wall. Next to a low windowless hatch, a row of seamless drawer fronts rotated open, hinged along the bottom, forming small shelves.

A flow of darkness spilled out from them and washed into the sealed chamber.

But it wasn't *water* threatening the men.

Ken realized this cubicle must adjoin one of those glass-domed test chambers. Only the neighboring pen here didn't house soldier drones armed with agonizing stings.

It held something far worse.

Each of the wasps flooding into the chamber was wingless, about the size of a pecan. Though small, they made up for their size by their sheer numbers—along with the strength of their robust mandibles.

Back at his lab in Kyoto, he had witnessed what these drones could do when loosed upon a rat.

I can't watch this.

He wanted to retreat from the window, but a rifle barrel pressed against his spine and held him in place.

Gray noted his distress, glancing over to him for some explanation.

Ken couldn't speak. Before him, the horde poured out of the neighboring pen and pooled onto the floor. The mass then swept outward along the room's edges. He recognized this pattern from before, as the drones encircled their prey in order to trap it.

To the side, Valya spoke and lifted two fingers toward Gray. "This is your second chance to speak."

Gray ignored her, his attention still on Ken. "What are they?"

He had to swallow to answer. "Harvesters."

HARVESTER

It was truly *they*.

The small drone bumped carapaces with its neighbors. Long antennae tangled. Countless legs rubbed all around, making it difficult to tell where an individual ended and the horde began.

Strengthening this bond, their bodies were covered in tiny hairs. For many in the greater swarm, those fine filaments simply gathered pollen. For the horde, the hairs had adapted long ago into tools of communication. Through the brushing of those hairs, chemicals and pheromones continually passed across the mass of their bodies, merging one into many.

As the group flowed into this new landscape, their finely attuned senses identified the presence of prey. This detection was amplified a thousand-fold by the rest of the horde. Hormones responded, firing the thick muscles woven around sharp mandibles.

Likewise, a gland between their eyes excreted a droplet of oil into their mouths, containing 2-hepatnone, a paralytic agent. Unfortunately, the poison of a single drop was only strong enough to incapacitate a caterpillar or some other small insect, but when working together, combining their strength, the horde could take down much larger prey.

In addition, their saliva held a potent slurry of digestive enzymes, strong enough to soften the hardest tissues. It was a trait that had evolved back when their meals were covered in armored scales.

Driven by behavior locked into their genetic code, the horde spread outward into two pincers, intending to snare their prey within their midst.

All the while, they continued to gather information about their meal, mostly gauging levels of threat. Still, the horde had little to fear. Their bodies were protected by hard shells, designed long ago to withstand tremendous forces, like the crushing footfalls of ancient giants. Within moments, estimates of risk were collected and shared.

As a consensus began to build, calculations became instructions.

Targets were selected, dividing the feast before them.

Finally, several groups within the horde snapped their hind legs, clacking them loudly and rapidly. Others took up this chorus. It was both a signal to be ready and a means by which the horde could more deeply analyze the quality of the meal before them.

Their reverberations echoed all around, returning with additional details.

First, only form, shape, and size.

But as the cacophony increased in volume, magnified by their great numbers, it succeeded in penetrating through the outer surfaces of their prey to reveal the feast within.

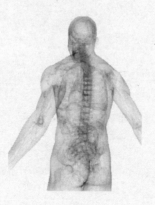

Around a core of hard bone, meat flexed, blood pumped, and viscera knotted. Electrical potential flowed throughout all, churning most strongly inside the skull.

At the sight of such a rich bounty, hunger flared

throughout the horde, stoking an insatiable longing to strip the prey bare, to leave nothing behind but bones. The ravenous crescendo built until it could no longer be denied.

Moving as one, the horde descended upon the feast.

Nothing would stop them.

Nothing *could* stop them.

FOURTH

RIPTIDE

24

A man hung in shackles in the open-air courtyard.

"Well, that can't be a good sign," Monk commented wryly, as they neared the prisoner.

Kat didn't put any stock in omens or portents, but considering all that had happened in Tallinn, she kept her guard up.

Ahead, the prisoner giggled as his photo was taken by his companion, both tourists to Muzeum Historycznego Miasta Gdańska, a museum dedicated to the medieval history of Gdansk. The institution occupied a complex of Gothic buildings dating to the fourteenth century. Back then, the site had served as both the city's jail and pillory. One of the museum's towers still contained intact prison cells. There, old torture devices were currently on display in all their bloody glory.

But that wasn't their group's destination.

Past the historic courtyard decorated with leg irons and hanging chains, a majority of the museum's five floors was dedicated to what the city called "the gold of the Baltic." Over a pointed Gothic arch, a sign read MUZEUM BURSZTYNU.

"The Amber Museum," Elena translated as they headed toward the archway. Gawking up, she stumbled on a cobble, but Sam caught her arm.

The entomologist had been sticking close to her side after they had landed in Gdansk. Though Elena seemed to have shaken off the effects of the sedative from her attempted kidnapping, Sam hovered next to her, especially as they traversed the length of Dluga Street, a picturesque pedestrian thoroughfare that cut between rows of tall historic buildings.

Kat had also kept a close watch as they'd walked— not on Elena, but on the surroundings. The street was packed with tourists, making her uneasy. To either side, the rows of old homes had been converted into shops, boutique hotels, and cafes. But many of the buildings' cellars had been turned into jewelry shops or galleries specializing in the city's "gold," a constant reminder of Gdansk's former glory as the amber capital of the world.

After paying at a small desk to enter, Kat led the group up a steep stairway into the museum proper. On the first floor, a sprawl of illuminated glass cases displayed examples of artwork sculpted out of amber. As they headed through this section, Kat's attention divided between watching for any threat and gawking at the wonders glowing behind the glass. A tree with leaves of amber rose from a landscape of flowers with petals of the same gem. A medieval sailing ship, sculpted of ossified resin, had masts of raised amber sails. Lamps with polished pebbled shades glowed in their cases, adding to the room's golden sheen.

Elena paused before a prominent case holding a

Fabergé egg made of amber that spun atop a turning pedestal inside. Its webbed gold top was hinged open to reveal a polished orb of the same gemstone.

"Beautiful," she mumbled, holding her reading glasses up to better examine it.

Sam bent down beside her. "Must be worth a king's ransom."

Elena nudged him with her shoulder. "You're right in more ways than you know. I wager this egg, a gift from the tsars, represents the industry's ties to Russia where a majority of amber—both in the past and today—is mined."

"And where James Smithson was headed on his cross-continental journey," Sam added pointedly.

Until it was cut short, Kat thought.

Elena simply nodded. "The Russian mining region is known as the Kaliningrad Oblast. But it was formerly called *Königsberg*, meaning the King's Mountain."

Sam straightened, rubbing a kink in his back. "So then this egg really has a royal history."

"A history that goes much farther back in time than just the Russian tsars." Elena squinted at the small polished orb inside the egg. "If you look closely, you can see a small fly floating in the amber."

She shifted upright and eyed them all. "It's as if the amber of this region has preserved this land's entire history. Culturally, politically, and even biologically."

"Unfortunately for Hawaii," Monk added, "maybe it preserved *too* much."

Reminded of this fact, Kat checked her watch.

"We should keep going." She directed them to a narrow staircase that led up one level. "This way."

Before leaving Tallinn, she had contacted the museum director here. She had employed the same cover story as before: that her team was looking to rebuild James Smithson's lost mineral collection, starting with a particular large chunk of amber mined from this region. The director had been happy to offer his assistance, especially upon hearing that the U.S. Librarian of Congress was part of this research team.

Kat only hoped the man's cooperation did not end as tragically as it had for Director Tamm. The last she heard, the man was out of surgery, but his chances of surviving remained critical. His daughter, Lara, kept a vigil at his bedside.

As she climbed the stairs, guilt ate at Kat. She hated to put others at risk, but with the situation worsening by the hour in Hawaii—where millions were threatened—she had no choice.

They reached the next floor, which dealt with the history of amber. A large medieval map hung on the brick wall to the right. Similar to what Lara had shown them, it highlighted a historic trade route running along the Baltic coast from St. Petersburg to Gdansk, then coursing south through Poland until eventually ending in Italy.

The Amber Road.

Somewhere along that path, Smithson had obtained his artifact.

But where?

"Dear," Monk said at her side, "I believe that man is trying to draw your attention."

On the other side of the chamber, a short man in a suit that looked too tight for his ample belly waved to them. It was the museum director. He stood behind a velvet rope that closed off a neighboring room. He must have recognized Elena Delgado. This was confirmed as the man called over to them.

"Dr. Delgado, what an honor!"

The scatter of tourists looked between the man and their group.

Kat held back a groan. She had asked the director to keep this visit secret, but clearly her words had fallen on deaf ears. She herded her group quickly across the floor. As they reached the man, he lifted away the rope to allow them access to the cordoned-off room.

"What a pleasure," the director effused, "a *true* pleasure to host the Librarian of Congress at our humble institution."

Elena took this professional adoration in stride. She smiled warmly and shook his hand. "Thank you, Director Bosko. We appreciate your help . . . and your *discretion*."

She emphasized this last word, while casting Kat an apologetic glance.

The director bobbed his head. "*Oczywiście* . . . of course. Come inside where we can discuss this privately."

Kat followed Bosko into the neighboring chamber. Partitions divided the space, and several display cases stood empty. It appeared the room was being prepped for a new exhibit. The director drew them to the back wall. While the location was out of the direct line of sight of the entry, it was far from *private*.

Several items rested haphazardly on the table, all of them amber.

"I gathered these to perhaps assist you with your search," Bosko said. "I hope that wasn't too presumptive of me."

"Not at all," Elena assured him.

Kat frowned at the collection. She saw no documents, journals, or books. "Were you able to find any evidence concerning the travels of James Smithson to your city?"

Bosko pursed his lips and shook his head. "Alas, no. We searched all records leading up to the date when Mr. Smithson boarded the merchant ship and headed to Tallinn." His sad expression quickly dissolved away, replaced again with his ebullient personality. "But perhaps with more time, we could still discover some reference."

More time was not a luxury they could grant him.

Kat had a sinking feeling they were wasting valuable time.

"Look at this," Sam said, as he stooped over one of the items on the table. "This is amazing."

They all drew closer. A magnifying glass had been positioned over a fist-sized chunk of amber. It was lit from behind and polished to better reveal what was frozen inside.

Elena took a turn looking through the glass. "It's a lizard."

"This bit of scientific curiosity is from our collection," Bosko said, puffing his chest proudly. "It's rare to see such a creature perfectly preserved in its entirety, from the tip of its tail to its narrow nose."

Kat also appreciated it as a stark reminder of what it was they pursued. This apparently was not lost on the director.

"When you described the artifact obtained by Mr. Smithson—a large boulder of amber holding the bones of some ancient reptile—I couldn't help but think of this exhibit piece." He lifted both eyebrows. "And perhaps a way to help you in your search for its source."

"How?" Kat asked.

Bosko waved to the lizard in amber. "That little fellow is thirty-two million years old, which is typical for the age of the amber found in this immediate area. The deposits in Russia and around the edges of the Baltic Sea are quite *young*. They formed during the Tertiary Period, some thirty to fifty million years ago. In fact, despite looking rock solid, our amber has not yet fully set."

Monk studied the collection on the table. "You're saying this stuff is still hardening."

"Indeed." Bosko smiled broadly, his cheeks blushing pinker. "It's why I know Mr. Smithson's artifact did not come from our Baltic coast."

Kat's lingering despair settled back to her shoulders.

Have we been on the wrong track all along?

Bosko continued: "For the truly ancient amber, you have to look elsewhere. Deposits scattered around the world. Like over in your country or in Spain—where amber can be found that is two hundred million years old."

"But what does any of this mean?" Kat asked. Her question came out a bit sharply as her patience wore thin.

The director noted her tone and tamped down some of his natural exuberance. "Yes, I'm sorry. You mentioned in your call that the bones in the artifact were believed to be those of a small *dinosaur*."

"That's correct."

"Then Mr. Smithson must have collected his sample from a deposit of amber that was very old. If you assume the creature came from as recently as the late Cretaceous Period—when the dinosaurs started to go extinct—then the amber would still have to be somewhere between eighty to a hundred million years ago. That's twice the age of the amber you'll find around the Baltic Sea."

Kat pictured the medieval map on the wall outside. "So the artifact couldn't have been found along the Amber Road?"

Monk cursed under his breath. He fiddled with the wrist of his replacement prosthetic. From past experience, he always brought along a spare, which he had left on the jet. It was a nervous gesture, as if he were trying to wear in a new pair of shoes.

"I didn't mean to suggest that," Bosko corrected her. "I only meant it didn't come from *our* coastline. But once upon a time, a prehistoric sea—the Tethys Ocean—covered all of southern Poland. Back then, forests along the Tethys's coastline oozed thick resin that would eventually harden into amber."

Kat followed his logic now. "So the farther south you go"—she pictured the map again—"the older the amber."

The director's subdued manner brightened again. "Old enough to perhaps preserve the bones of a dinosaur."

But where?

"You're probably wondering where that could be," Bosko added, as if reading her thoughts. The man was clearly sharper than his clownlike enthusiasm suggested. He moved over to the table. "I've laid out samples of amber here, from oldest to youngest. Note how the amber darkens as it ages, eventually becoming a deep reddish-brown. Most of the oldest amber is found in blue earth."

Monk frowned. "Blue earth?"

"The scientific term is *marine glauconitic sand*. Basically, salty sandstone that forms at the edge of retreating seas."

Monk nodded. "Like would've been deposited as the Tethys Ocean dried up."

"Precisely. So the oldest and deepest deposits of blue earth are found in southern Poland."

"A region through which the Amber Road runs," Kat said.

She suddenly wanted to get a closer look at that map. Something nagged at her, but she couldn't put her finger on it.

Bosko's grin turned mischievous. "That's why I took the additional liberty to—"

A loud bang cut him off, making them all jump and turn toward the room's entry. One of the metal stanchions holding up the velvet rope had toppled over. Footfalls hurried in their direction.

Kat reached for the weapon holstered under her jacket.

4:20 P.M.

Elena retreated to the table as Monk and Kat simultaneously pulled out pistols and pointed their guns toward the doorway. Sam moved to her side.

The director looked aghast at the exposed weapons, but he finally collected himself and lifted a palm. "Don't shoot. This is what I was about to tell you."

From around a partition, a tall, stooped figure hurried into view. His long coat billowed like a cape from his bony shoulders as he rushed forward. He clutched a worn messenger bag protectively to his chest. Though the man was likely only in his forties, his gaunt face made him look both older and more dour. As he noted the raised guns, he seemed unfazed, his expression merely gloomy, as if he had somehow expected to be ambushed.

"This is Dr. Damian Slaski," Bosko introduced, stepping between the newcomer and the weapons. "He's a colleague. From our sister Amber Museum that opened recently in Krakow. He was already here when you called, to borrow some of our pieces for an exhibit on amber manufacturing during the eighteenth century."

"How many amber museums are there?" Monk mumbled.

Bosko heard him and took his inquiry seriously. "There's one in Copenhagen, another in the Dominican Republic, and of course, in Kaliningrad to the north."

"Do not forget the Palanga Amber Museum in

Lithuania," Slaski added solemnly, then shrugged dismissively. "But it is just a division of the Lithuanian Art Museum."

Kat cast Monk a scathing look for distracting the pair and tried to get the conversation back on track. "Director Bosko, I'm assuming you must have solicited Dr. Slaski's help."

"Yes, yes, that's right. If you are seeking sources of *old* amber, deposits hundreds of millions of years, then my good friend, Damian, is our best resource."

Bosko clapped Slaski on the shoulder; he simply sighed in response. The pair made an odd couple. One short, the other tall. One round, the other thin. But it was their personalities that were the true polar opposites. The ebullient Bosko seemed incapable of forming a frown, whereas Slaski's lips seemed perpetually frozen in one.

Still, Elena sensed a true friendship between the two men, something more than just a professional relationship.

"Damian oversees the Amber Laboratory at his museum," Bosko extolled. "His lab has Krakow's only spectrometer for analyzing the authenticity of amber artifacts. His expertise is in *dating* amber. There is no one better."

Bosko grinned at his colleague, who only shrugged, as if acknowledging the authenticity of the compliment but taking no pleasure in it.

"Krakow is not far from Poland's southern border," Bosko explained. "That's where you'll find very old layers of blue earth, those strata of salty marine sandstone left behind as the Tethys Ocean receded. And that's where, in rare cases, deposits of ancient amber have been found."

"How *rare*?" Kat asked.

Elena knew the importance of her question. If such deposits were few and far between, it would help narrow their search.

Dr. Slaski answered, "I have most of those discoveries—past and present—compiled on my office computer. The project was only possible because of a history museum outside of Krakow, which houses an extensive cartography collection. I spent many months searching their collection. Several of the maps, some dating back to the fourteenth century, mark the sites of old amber deposits."

"If you could share what you learned," Kat said, "it could greatly assist us in pinpointing where James Smithson obtained his artifact."

"Or at least limit the scope of our search," Elena added.

"I'm not sure that would help," Slaski said. "I've mapped over three hundred sites across southern Poland."

Kat winced, but refused to let this lead go. "Maybe if we narrowed the search parameter down to the time frame of Smithson's travels along the Amber Road, we might be able to—"

The dour doctor shook his head. "There is no need to go to that trouble. I was rushing over here because I believe I know where Mr. Smithson could have discovered his sample of ancient amber."

Kat blinked at this claim. "How?"

Bosko simply clapped his palms together. "Did I not tell you that Damian is your man?"

4:32 P.M.

"What am I looking at?" Kat asked.

She struggled to understand how this had anything to do with Slaski's claim from a moment before. The group was gathered around a laptop that the doctor had removed from his leather bag and set up on the table. The image on the screen looked like a very old map.

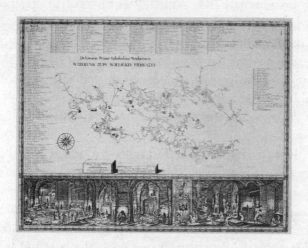

"This is from the museum's cartography collection. The map was drawn by Willem Hondius back in 1645, though it is believed he based his map from the previous work done by cartographer Marcin German."

"Yes," Kat pressed him, sensing each passing minute, "but what's its significance?"

"It's one of the maps I used in building my compilation. There are two amber sites noted here. But that's not why I wanted to show you this." Slaski stared hard at her. "You have to understand that amber sites in southern Poland are rare, relatively small, and scattered wildly. So no mines were established to solely dig for amber. The discoveries were haphazard and by sheer chance."

Monk straightened from his hunch over the laptop. "You're saying these deposits were stumbled upon during other mining operations."

"Which matches Archibald MacLeish's account in his journal," Kat added. "Smithson had claimed over drinks with a geologist that some miners accidentally broke into a rich vein of amber."

She restrained from sharing the rest of the tale, how something was unleashed in that mine. A horrible disease carried by stinging insects.

Born right out of the bones of the rock, Smithson had asserted.

Kat suspected what had truly happened was that those miners cracked through prehistoric bones trapped in the amber, bones full of the *Odokuro*'s cryptobiotic cysts. Once aerosolized, those spores were inhaled or ingested by the workers. After that, they'd be dead men walking, with the hatched larvae eating them from the inside out, until finally adult wasps came bursting forth from their corpses.

No wonder they firebombed the tunnels with the workers still down there, then sealed it all up.

Slaski, of course, knew none of this, but he came to a conclusion on his own. "I had already assumed the amber deposit must have been an accidental discovery at an already established mine. During Mr. Smithson's time, there were many active mines across Poland. Digging for copper, sulfur, silver.

But in southern Poland, the largest operations were all salt mines."

He pointed to the map on the screen. "Like this one Hondius drew. He even included etched vignettes of those operations along the bottom of his map, showing the huge scope of the operations at this particular mine."

"What mine is it?" Elena asked, as she peered at the drawings along the bottom through her reading glasses.

"It's one of Poland's most famous sites. The Wieliczka Salt Mine. It was established in the thirteenth century and continued operations until 2007, after which it was declared a UNESCO World Heritage Site."

Monk frowned. "Why was an old mine chosen for that honor?"

Bosko chimed in, his voice bright with excitement. "Oh, you must visit it. It is quite wondrous. Over the centuries, generations of miners had taken to carving and sculpting the subterranean chambers with elaborate decorations, most of them religious in scope, as the miners sought the good graces of God to keep them safe."

"For ages, the sights have drawn countless visitors to Wieliczka," Slaski said, a rare edge of pride in his voice. "The famous astronomer Nicolaus Copernicus toured the place in the sixteenth century. The Polish composer Frédéric Chopin did the same in the nineteenth. More recently, a few U.S. presidents have visited the site, as did the current pope."

Kat got an inkling as to the origin of Slaski's earlier claim. "Such a reputation would have certainly reached a geologist traveling along the nearby Amber Road."

"How could he resist?" Slaski said, with the faintest ghost of a smile. "That is why I went and called the mine and had them check the visitors roster from the window of time when your Mr. Smithson was in the vicinity."

"And you found his name?" Monk asked.

Slaski nodded.

Kat stared at the map glowing on the laptop's screen. "And according to this old account, amber had been found there in the past."

"Correct. It is in such strata of salt where you'll often find amber deposits."

Kat felt they were drawing close.

Sam cleared his throat. As an entomologist, he likely didn't have much to offer to this historical trail, but from his crinkled brow, he must have a concern.

"What is it?" she asked.

"It was something I remember from reviewing Professor Matsui's research notes concerning the . . ." His voice trailed off as he glanced at the two Polish men, plainly reluctant to speak too openly.

Kat wanted to dismiss such precautions with time running out, but she drew him aside and kept her voice low. "What?"

"Professor Matsui attributed the amazing death-defying properties of the wasps' life cycle to genetic properties they borrowed from other insects and possibly what he described as the *dark matter of life*, those Lazarus microbes that seemingly could lie dormant for hundreds of millions of years yet come back to life."

Kat vaguely remembered those speculations. "What about them?"

"Professor Matsui made a list of those Lazarus microbes in his notes. *Natronobacterium*, *Virgibacillus*, *Halorubacterium*, *Oceanobacillus*. All of them were discovered encrusted in crystal formations. And not just *any* formations. They were all found in the *same* type of crystals."

Though Kat could not recall the details, she could guess. She glanced back to the map on the laptop. "Salt."

Sam nodded. "Perhaps it was the wasps' proximity to those salt-loving buggers that allowed the insects to be infected by them. And over time, some of the microbes' genetic code was incorporated into the wasps' genome, gifting them with the power of cryptobiosis."

Or life after death.

"If you're right, that would further support that we're on the right track." She checked her watch. "Only one way to find out."

As she gathered everyone up, Slaski stepped forward. "I was going to return to Krakow today. Perhaps I should accompany you."

She wanted to refuse, remembering the blood seeping through her fingers as she struggled to keep Director Tamm alive.

Slaski was persistent. "I'm both familiar with the mine and its operators. I'm sure I can convince them to cooperate with your search."

With time running short, how can I refuse this offer?

She glanced to Monk. He looked worried, mirroring her own trepidation, but he ultimately shrugged, coming to the same conclusion as her.

"Thank you, Dr. Slaski. We'd appreciate your help."

After also thanking Director Bosko, the group was soon out of the museum and traveling down Dluga Street again, passing jewelry boutiques and tiny cafes. The congested foot traffic forced them to wend between throngs of tourists and locals.

Kat came to another conclusion, sharing it with her husband. "I guess I owe Aiko Higashi an apology."

"It seems you do," Monk acknowledged.

Before leaving Tallinn earlier in the day, Kat had asked Painter to lay a false trail, to tell Japanese intelligence services that their group was headed next to St. Petersburg. The strategy of hopping to the northern end of the Amber Road made logical sense and should have been convincing. If there had been a leak out of Japan, the enemy should've been looking for them in northern Russia.

That wasn't the case.

"How many?" she asked.

"I count five."

They were being followed.

Kat kept going, primed to act if the enemy made any move, but from the pattern of the tail, that seemed unlikely. Whoever had targeted them must have learned from their failure in Tallinn and now sought simply to draft behind them, to try to learn what they knew.

She weighed whether to lose the tail or simply let the others believe they were undetected. Either tactic had its advantages and disadvantages.

For now, a greater worry nagged at her.

How did they know we were in Gdansk?

She came to one final conclusion.

Whether back in D.C. or out here . . .

We have a traitor in our midst.

25

Powerless, Gray watched the black tide encircle the three trapped men. His jaw ached from clenching his teeth in frustration. There was nothing he could do to stop what was about to happen.

Professor Matsui's descriptive name for this variation of the wasp drone—a wingless carnivore he called *harvesters*—foretold the fate of the three trapped men.

Inside the sealed chamber, one intrepid scavenger broke away from the mass and shot toward Kowalski's toes. With his arms pinioned to the side by chains, he could only stamp a foot at the threat. The man ground his heel atop the insect, his face scowling in disgust. His lips moved in a curse silenced by the room's insulation.

Kowalski lifted his foot to inspect the damage. There was none. The wasp's tanklike body had withstood the assault. The harvester sprang upward, landing on his broad foot, then skittered to his hairy ankle.

It latched there.

Kowalski tried to rub it away with his other foot, but he couldn't budge it.

Then his grimace turned into a shocked, silent gasp.

Gray imagined razor-sharp mandibles biting deep.

Blood dribbled down the edge of the big man's foot.

Palu's cousins—Makaio and Tua—noted the damage. They were trussed to the right of Kowalski. They drew away from the horde slowly closing down from all sides, pulling their chains taut. The three men bunched in the room's center.

"Please don't do this," Ken begged. The professor was held at gunpoint at the window next to Gray. Another trio of armed men stood guard behind their group.

"Then tell me what I want to know." Valya lifted a palm to a large green button, likely an emergency switch to subdue the threat. "And I can stop the torment to come."

Ken glanced to Gray.

He shook his head, telling the professor to keep quiet.

Valya swung her cold gaze to Aiko. "Any of you may speak."

Aiko's face was slightly turned away from the window. It looked like she wanted to squeeze her eyes closed, but she fought not to. Perhaps out of some obligation to the beleaguered men: *if they must suffer, so will I.*

To answer Valya, Aiko returned to fully facing the window.

Valya lowered her arm. "So be it."

Masahiro stood at her side with his arms crossed, his expression disdainful—not out of disgust at Valya's tactics, but because he clearly believed it was in vain. "The woman may very well *not* be here."

"She's not," Gray growled. "She's back on Maui, like I told you from the start. You're torturing these men for no reason."

Masahiro cast a withering glance at Valya, as if to say *I told you so*, then checked his watch. "We should already be evacuating the island." He waved an arm dismissively at the window. "My grandfather has no interest in these three, so leave them here. But we should take the others and go now."

Valya turned her back on him. "Not without Seichan."

Masahiro scowled and mumbled a curse under his breath. "*Baka mesu . . .*"

She ignored him, plainly content to play this out.

It didn't take long.

Inside the room, the tide finally broke, likely drawn by the dribble of Kowalski's blood. The harvester horde descended on the three men chained inside.

Tua rose on his toes, as if to escape the rising threat. His brother, Makaio, even lifted both feet off the floor, but it was to no avail. As he hung from his wrists, the cuffs cut deeply into his flesh. He was forced to drop a leg back down. His foot vanished into the leading edge of the black mass. At his side, Tua danced in his chains as harvesters reached him, too, and climbed both legs in black streams.

Kowalski used his big feet like a pair of brooms, attempting to sweep the floor clear around him. But the wasps' numbers were too great. He lost the battle as the horde fully converged on their group.

In a matter of seconds, the men were covered from the waist down in a thick mat of biting wasps. The three contorted in their chains—not in a vain attempt to shake their attackers loose, but in clear agony.

Mouths were open in silent screams.

Gray knew it would only get worse from here.

More and more harvesters pushed upward. So far, they seemed to be sticking to the men's legs and midsections. As Kowalski tried to kick them off, blood spattered outward, striking the window.

Aiko finally broke, turning her head away and closing her eyes.

Gray refused, knowing he owed these men that much.

But how long will this last?

As if hearing his question, Professor Matsui offered an answer. "Harvesters are like the parasitizing larvae. They'll spare the vital organs." He spoke dully, likely trying to use a researcher's clinical detachment to shield him from the horror. "They'll keep their food source alive for as long as possible. Eating their way from the periphery to the core—from outside to in."

Gray stared at the tortured men, wishing Ken had remained mute.

But the professor wasn't done. "Harvesters carry a paralytic venom in their bites. In these great numbers, it will subdue most prey."

Aiko had listened with her eyes still closed. "Will the paralyzing stop the pain?"

"No," Ken said, the word coming out like a moan. "Though unable to move, they'll feel every bite as they're eaten alive."

Past the blood-spattered glass, the three men still fought, still writhed. But if the professor was correct, their struggles would soon end.

But not the pain.

Valya spoke with a dreadful calmness as she stared at Gray. "I warned you that I'd give you *three* chances to tell me the location of Seichan. This is that third chance."

She again lifted her palm to the green button.

Gray remained silent, but the muscles between his shoulder blades tremored. By now, he could discern faint cries from inside, loud enough to pierce the room's insulation.

She let him stand there for another long breath—then she reached her other hand and flipped a switch beside the window. Hidden speakers suddenly burst forth with screams, transmitting the men's agony in full volume.

Gray swore he could hear blood in those cries.

Inside, the horde had crested over the men's waists. They streamed up their flanks and along their chained arms, consuming their meal as Ken had described.

From outside to in.

Gray could take it no longer. "She's here," he gasped out loud.

Valya cocked her head, while flicking a glance at Masahiro. "What was that?"

Fury burned through him, giving him the strength to face Valya. "Seichan's sick. Parasitized, like I told you. But she's on the island."

"Where?"

"I don't know." He scowled. "I lost sight of her in the lake. She may have been too compromised to make the crossing."

Valya narrowed her gaze on him.

"It's . . . it's the truth," Ken said.

Even Aiko nodded, her eyes open again.

Valya studied each of them before coming to a conclusion. "I actually believe you." She lowered her palm without pressing it. "But it's not good enough."

She waved to the armed men, stepping away from the glass.

"We're finished here. Take them to the plane."

Inside the room, three men thrashed in their chains, like slabs of meat on hooks. Agonized screams followed Gray and the others as they were forced at gunpoint away from the window.

He stumbled as he turned, numb with the knowledge there was nothing he could do for the men inside, but a new purpose focused him.

He stared at Valya's back, making a silent promise.

I will make you scream even louder when I kill you.

3:55 A.M.

It's taken us too long to get here. . . .

Seichan questioned her course of action as she

released ballast and floated her stolen submersible toward the station's pressurized docking chamber. The steel-floored glass dome abridged the lowest level of the complex, a glowing barnacle on the underside of the research station.

On her approach, she had noted another two matching domes, along with a larger one. The conning tower of a midget submarine poked up into the bigger dock. Its bulk looked like a giant lamprey latched on to the facility. Past its length, her sub's cone of light revealed the black eye of a tunnel, which likely led out to the open ocean.

Seichan craned her neck as her tinier craft rose toward the circular pool at the center of the docking chamber. The pressurized air inside the dome must hold back the lake from flooding into the rest of the station.

When the sub breached, she ducked her head low over the controls.

Palu crouched behind her on the open deck in back.

As the craft surfaced into open air, salt water drained from his body and off the glass hood over the pilot seat. As it cleared, she spotted the watery image of a dockworker coming toward them.

She scowled at his presence. She had hoped to find the place empty.

No such luck.

The worker waved an arm impatiently. "*Hayaku-siro!*" he demanded, urging them to hurry, believing they were the returning crew.

She and Palu had disguised themselves in the

dead men's face masks, so it was an easy enough mistake to make.

The worker pointed to his radio headpiece and spoke rapidly in Japanese. "The evacuation order was just transmitted. We have fifteen minutes to clear the station."

Palu hopped off the back of the sub, but he immediately stopped at the pool's edge and turned his back on the dockworker. He pretended to be waiting to help Seichan.

The worker grabbed Palu's arm and tried to steer him toward the exit. "Get to the airlock."

Unfortunately, Palu didn't speak any Japanese.

Seichan rolled out of the pilot's seat and over to the back deck. As she stood up, she tossed off her scuba gear.

Upon seeing her, the worker's pinched expression changed to open-eyed shock.

She expected this reaction. Her lithe form was impossible to hide in a snug wetsuit. Before the man could take a step, she leaped at him, a dagger already in hand.

Palu stumbled out of her way.

She knocked the worker flat onto his back. Her blade sliced his throat, cutting above the larynx so he could not shout into his radio. She covered his death gurgle with her free hand. She watched blood run in a crimson trail across the steel floor and spill into the docking pool.

Palu quickly shed his own gear and moved to the airlock. He kept to one side, away from the door's porthole-like window. A green light shone above the frame, likely indicating the airlock had already been pressurized to match the docking dome.

Seichan rose from the dead man. Before she could take a step, fresh pain burst through her body. She hunched against it, her legs suddenly weak. She breathed heavily through the flare, willing it to subside back to its steady smolder.

Palu hurried to her side. "C'mon."

He hooked an arm around her and helped her to the airlock. Each step was like walking through fire. He got the door open, pushed her into the cramped space, and followed her inside, slamming the door behind him.

An illuminated timer above the exit door began counting down from three minutes as the airlock depressurized to match the main station. She cursed the delay but recognized the slow process was to help acclimate divers as they transitioned from the docks, lessening the risk of the bends from nitrogen bubbles forming in the blood.

Impatient, she moved to the tiny porthole in the outer door. She inspected the glass tunnel that extended from the dock. It was thankfully empty.

Small bit of luck there.

Her relief was short-lived.

A Klaxon suddenly sounded. It was ear-shatteringly loud in the small space. She hunched from the noise, trying to judge its significance.

Was it an evacuation siren? Or had they been spotted?

Palu answered it by pointing back into the docking dome, toward its roof.

A mounted camera swiveled there.

Distracted by the worker, addled by pain, she had failed to spot its presence.

She turned back to the other door. Through the porthole, she watched three men in helmets and body armor appear at the far end of the glass tunnel. They rushed toward the airlock, the butts of their rifles fixed to their shoulders.

She checked the timer.

Another two minutes to go.

They were now trapped in a cell of their own making.

She shared a glance with Palu, silently asking him.

Are you ready?

He shrugged, knowing they had no other option.

4:04 A.M.

As the siren continued to blare, Ken stood with his back to the tunnel wall. The others flanked him to either side. Rifles remained fixed on the group, while the chaos was sorted out.

Ken stared back down the tunnel toward the blood-spattered window five yards away. The group had been forced to stop in the tunnel when the Klaxon sounded. Even above the alarm bells, the men's screams could be heard. By now, harvesters coated their arms and legs and lower abdomen. Their bodies appeared to be struggling less as the paralytic agent in the wasp's bites began to take effect.

Gray stared back there, too, his face dark with rage.

Aiko simply studied her bare toes.

A few steps away, Valya and Masahiro huddled over radios. He could not make out what they were saying due to the noise. But the pale woman turned her icy stare onto Gray. Her lips thinned, one edge curling up with what could only be satisfaction.

Gray noted her attention.

The siren suddenly cut off, leaving Ken's ears still ringing.

Valya returned to them. "It seems all our questioning has proven to be moot."

"Seichan's here," Gray said.

"And we have her all boxed up and ready to be delivered to Masahiro's grandfather."

Gray showed no distress at this news. Instead, he stood straighter and narrowed his gaze on Valya. "I wouldn't be so sure of that."

4:07 A.M.

Through the airlock window, Seichan stared at the trio of armed men as they guarded the tunnel. Above her head, the timer ticked down the final seconds of depressurization, marking when the safety lock on the door leading into the station would be released.

Palu leaned against the wall, accepting the inevitable.

Finally, the timer read 0:00 and its red glow switched to green.

Time's up.

The three men outside had taken up position. Two of them hung a few yards down the tunnel with rifles leveled at the door. The third shouted through the window.

"Hands on your head! Where I can see them!"

Seichan obeyed, as did Palu.

"When I open the door, you wait. You only step through when I tell you. Do you understand?"

Seichan nodded for them both.

Agony racked the muscles of her legs and arms, making it hard to hold this position. She pictured the tiny larvae carving paths through her flesh, leaving fire in their wake.

Get on with it already.

The guard glared at the trapped pair, then shifted to the side, pulling the door open. He used its steel bulk to shield himself in case they tried anything. His two partners leaned their cheeks to their rifles' stocks, aiming into the airlock.

Satisfied, the guard at the door yelled, "Exit slowly. Your hands move from your head, you die."

Seichan led the way, stepping out first. The air inside the station was cooler. She could also feel the difference in pressure. Even this small movement apparently aggravated the larvae. Fresh pain shot down her legs.

Still, she kept her pace slow and steady, her fingers entwined atop her head.

Palu followed, matching her pace and posture.

The guard shifted from the door to cover them from behind with his weapon. "Keep going," he ordered. "Slowly."

With no other choice, Seichan allowed the men to herd them down the tunnel toward the main bulk of the station. In her head, another timer was running. Her training with the Guild had taught her this discipline, of compartmentalizing her thought processes.

It was more challenging due to the pain etching every muscle fiber.

By the time they reached where the tunnel turned into the main station, her brow was pebbled with sweat. Her breathing had become gasps. She stopped at the turn, panting, half-hunched. Though her arms now trembled, she kept her hands atop her head.

"Keep going!" the man in back shouted.

Palu twisted and growled back. "She's sick, brah. And pregnant. Let her catch her breath."

The guard scowled back, studying her trembling breaths. "Ten seconds."

Only need another two.

As the timer ran out in her head, she leaped headlong toward the side tunnel, pulling a blade from a wrist sheath.

Palu followed her through the air.

Before the guards could react, an explosion rocked the entire station. Her ears popped from the pressure. She landed atop the nearest guard, who had been knocked off his feet by the blast. She jabbed her knife under his chin until she hit bone, then wrested his rifle away. Still on the floor, she fired at the man who had been behind them, catching him in the throat.

Palu had barreled into the third guard and punched his meaty fist three times into the man's nose. His body went slack.

Seichan snagged the snub-nosed assault rifle and pointed toward the bulk of the station. "Go, go, go."

She had studied the rough layout of the station during her approach to the docking berth and fixed it in her head, where it turned like a 3-D model. But it hadn't been her only precaution before arriving here. In addition, she had readied a stratagem not taught to her by the Guild, but by Gray.

To improvise on the fly—to utilize old resources in new and unexpected ways.

What Seichan had chosen to utilize had certainly been *old*—going all the way back to World War II. Earlier, before leaving the graveyard of Japanese bombers, she had sought out and found an intact torpedo in the sand. She and Palu had carefully strapped and hidden its length on the underside of their stolen submersible and affixed a demolition timer packed with a small C4 charge to its nose.

At the time, she hadn't known if the ordnance preserved in these hypersaline waters was still intact.

She certainly had her answer now.

Behind her, as she sprinted with Palu, a massive throaty gurgle grew louder, chasing them. She recognized and expected this threat. She pictured the airlock doors blown off—if not the entire dock. No longer held back by the pressurized dome, the lake was flooding into the station.

She risked a glance over her shoulder. Past Palu's bulk, water blasted into view at the turn. It struck the corner with enough force to rattle the tunnel. The churning jet swirled around the turn and roiled toward them, pushing a tangle of bodies before it.

"Seichan!" Palu yelled at her, his eyes huge, his voice full of panicked warning.

She turned her attention back around. Ten yards ahead, a steel iris was pinching closed across the tunnel. The explosive decompression must have triggered the automatic closure of emergency hatches, designed to seal off flooded sections of the station.

She dug her toes into the perforated steel floor and sprinted with all her breath, using the fiery pain in her leg and belly muscles to fuel her.

She reached the iris before it closed and dove headfirst through it. She rolled off a shoulder and back to her feet.

Palu . . .

The large Hawaiian had been unable to match her speed. Water frothed and growled behind him, tearing up sections of steel flooring. The ballistic polymer glass splintered around him. The iris closed tighter and tighter.

Seichan recognized the truth.

Palu did, too—the terror of that certainty shining in his eyes.

He's not going to make it.

26

Chaos was opportunity.

Gray reacted with an instinct drilled into him by the Army Rangers and honed from his years in the field for Sigma. As the explosion shook the station, knocking everyone helter-skelter, Gray lunged to the nearest guard and grabbed the barrel of his rifle. He yanked the weapon, then punched the steel stock hard into the man's nose.

As bone crunched, the rifle fell loose. Gray spun it around, dropped to a knee, and shot another guard in the head. To the side, Aiko moved as swiftly, dropping another gunman with a snapped side kick into his jaw. She rolled over his body, coming up with a rifle, and shot the last armed guard.

The action had taken four long seconds—and unfortunately, he wasn't the only one taking advantage of the moment.

Gray swung his weapon toward the greatest threat, but Valya had Ken hugged to her chest, an arm pinned around the man's neck. Her other arm pressed a pistol against his temple. Using the man as a human shield, she dragged him to a side tunnel. She herded Masahiro behind her.

They vanished around the corner.

Gray glared after them. "Hold here," he ordered Aiko. "Cover my back."

"*Hai*." Aiko took a firm stance, her stolen rifle at her shoulder, aiming toward that corner in case reinforcements were sent.

Gray turned the other way and ran down the tunnel toward the three trapped men.

Their screaming had ominously stopped.

His heart pounded. He feared he was already too late.

When he reached the window, he saw their bodies hanging slack in their shackles. He swung his arm wide and slapped his palm against the green emergency button. An alarm sounded and thick streams of highly pressurized white foam sprayed from hundreds of jets in the ceiling. The men's bodies were immediately coated. From the force of the spray and whatever insecticide was in the foam, black bodies shed from their arms, legs, and bellies. As the mass was washed off, the draining white foam turned bright crimson with the men's blood.

The three continued to slump in their chains, their limbs limp and lifeless.

The foaming ended with a final sputtering, and the alarm went off.

Responding to this signal, Gray rushed to the door. He spun the locking wheel open. His breath heaved from the effort and the terror.

Am I too late?

4:22 A.M.

"Move it!" Seichan hollered.

She crouched to the side of the closing iris. A tempest of water and torn steel churned violently toward Palu as he crossed the last of the distance to the emergency hatch. As it tried to close, gears ground against the stolen assault rifle she had wedged lengthwise into the center of the iris a second ago, holding the way open for Palu. The force of the hatch's motor vibrated the weapon, struggling to pop it free.

The barrel began to bend.

C'mon.

Palu reached the hatch and dove headlong through it. His hip caught against the obstruction of the rifle, requiring him to twist and claw himself free. He finally rolled into the tunnel behind her.

Seichan yanked on the assault rifle, trying to free it, but the iris had closed tightly against it. If the hatch remained open, they would never escape the water's rage.

Palu came to her aid, clearly recognizing her struggle and the danger.

Together, they tried to rip the rifle out.

It refused to budge—then it was too late.

The wall of water hit the hatch, shooting like a fire hose through the pinched opening. Seichan tried to maintain her grip on the weapon, but she was washed down the tunnel. She caught glimpses of Palu. The Hawaiian still clung to his post, his legs braced against the hatch, impossibly withstanding the water's force.

Then a loud *clang* rang out, and Palu came rolling toward her.

Seichan sputtered for air, trying to break her tumble.

Then, after several harrowing, breathless seconds, the force of the riptide faded around her. She sloshed a few more feet and came to a stop. Water continued to spill forward, but with little power.

She turned to find a waterlogged Palu crawling toward her. He clutched the rifle in one hand.

"How . . . how did you . . . ?" It hurt too much to speak, so she nodded to the gun.

He looked down at its bent barrel and tossed the useless weapon aside. "Not me, *kaikaina*." He glanced back to the sealed hatch. "Big piece of the steel floor smacked into it on the other side. Popped it right out."

She nodded, relieved but still concerned.

And for good reason.

The station groaned under the weight of the flooded section. Around the edges of the sealed iris, the ballistic glass began to splinter.

It's not going to hold.

Confirming this risk, she watched the docking dome break away and slowly fall toward the lakebed.

Time to get out of here.

She hauled to her feet, while Palu did the same with a loud groan.

"Where to?" he asked.

She simply headed away, avoiding the question as much as the truth.

I have no idea.

4:33 A.M.

Gray wheeled the door's locking mechanism until it released. He took a deep breath, then pulled the steel hatch open. Residual foam spattered into the hallway, bringing with it a stench that immediately churned his stomach. It was a cloying sweetness mixed with rotted meat.

Grimacing, he stared at the trio of slack bodies hanging from cuffs. Blood and foam ran down their legs and dripped from their fingertips. From this distance, it was impossible to tell how much damage had been inflicted by the horde of biting wasps.

Only one way to find out.

He climbed inside. His bare feet crunched over the dead or listless carapaces of the wingless wasps. As hard-shelled as they were, it was like walking on marbles—marbles with sharp edges. The bottoms of his feet were sliced by mandibles that could no longer bite but remained razor sharp.

As he reached Kowalski, a thick-knuckled hand weakly lifted, then dropped, as if waving Gray off. Relief flooded through him. He noted the two cousins' chests heaved shallowly up and down as they hung.

Still alive . . . but for how much longer?

He hurriedly released the clasps on their cuffs and soon all three men were slumped on their sides in the slurry of foam, blood, and dead wasps. Through the window, he spotted Aiko, who still guarded the tunnel leading here. Gray knew he had only moments before reinforcements would arrive.

When that happened, Aiko could only hold them off for so long—certainly not long enough for him to move the three paralyzed men to safety by himself.

Past the window, he spotted his only hope.

He rushed back outside, skating treacherously over the slick, wasp-pebbled floor. A white metal box hung on the wall outside with a red cross emblazoned on it. He prayed the presence of the emergency first-aid kit at this location was significant.

Like eye-wash stations positioned near toxic chemicals.

He yanked open the kit's door. Inside, half the contents were a row of self-injectors. They looked like EpiPens, and maybe they were. Back on Maui, epinephrine had been used as a counteragent to the sedative effects of the egg-laying wasps' venom.

He grabbed a handful of the injectors and raced back into the room.

He knelt first next to Kowalski, ripped off the syringe's wrapper with his teeth, then jabbed the needle into the man's neck. The contents spurted through Kowalski's skin—the little that was left of it on his body.

As he repeated the emergency treatment with Makaio and Tua, he finally took notice of the damage wrought. It looked as if the skin had been flayed from their arms and legs, along with large swaths across their backs and lower bellies. Closer inspection, though, showed the skin was relatively intact, pocked by thousands upon thousands of pea-sized bites. Blood pooled and spilled from the countless wounds, but at least nothing showed overt arterial spurting.

Their chests, necks, and heads had also been mostly spared.

He remembered Ken's description of the harvesters avoiding anything vital, keeping their food source alive and fresh as long as possible.

Still, the men were far from safe. Exsanguination from so many bites remained a significant threat. All three men needed medical treatment, possibly blood transfusions, as soon as possible.

A guttural groan drew his attention back to Kowalski. The man slowly lifted his head, then sat up, wobbling dazedly. For him to already be moving, those syringes must have held something more potent than simple epinephrine. Likely some antagonist to the harvester's paralytic poison.

Moments later, Makaio and Tuo also stirred.

"My . . . my head's spinning," Kowalski complained.

"How much pain are you in?"

He stared groggily at the bloody ruin of his splayed legs. "Don't feel much of anything?"

If that was true, the injectors must have had some type of analgesics mixed in with their load, possibly opioid pain relievers.

"Can you stand?" Gray asked.

"Do I have to?"

A spatter of gunfire answered him.

Gray faced the window. Aiko retreated down the tunnel toward the chamber, firing at the far corner. She must have spotted someone and sought to hold them at bay.

In the room, Kowalski tried to stand, but he looked like a bull trying to roller-skate. Makaio and Tua were only beginning to sit up.

They were in no state to move yet.

Aiko fired off another three rounds, then dashed to the open door. "We must go now."

Gray glanced over to the slowly reviving men.

I will not abandon them.

4:44 A.M.

Ken stumbled down the last of the stairs to the middle level of the hub. He was dragged by strong pale fingers digging into his forearm. Valya threatened him with a black pistol in her other hand. The retreating party had also gathered a pair of armed security guards in helmets and body armor, who flanked Masahiro protectively.

And for good reason.

This section of the hub was in chaos. Evacuating lab techs and maintenance workers had fled the upper and lower levels. They all crowded toward the main tunnel back to the island, resulting in a bottleneck, which only added to the panic as everyone tried to escape the threatened station.

Valya nudged one of their armed escorts with her pistol. "Clear a path for us. We're leaving now. Shoot if you must."

The guard nodded and began to leave Masahiro's side.

"Stop," Masahiro ordered. He pointed to the

open doors to his office. "I'm not taking any chances. Follow me."

He led the group through the doors into his teak-paneled office. Ken again noted the fiery phoenix depicted in gold on the wall behind his desk, the logo for Fenikkusu Laboratories. If Ken survived the next hour, he knew that was where he would be taken, where he'd either agree to cooperate or be killed.

Valya scowled at Masahiro. "Why are you wasting time?"

"A fail-safe," he snapped back at her and crossed behind his desk.

"What fail-safe?"

"In case of an enemy intrusion." He reached a palm up to a glass rectangle below the phoenix symbol. It bloomed to life with his touch.

"Why wasn't I informed of this?"

As his palm was scanned, he cast her a withering glare of disdain. "This is *my* facility. Despite my grandfather's trust in you, I'm not so gullible as to share everything with a *gaijin*."

Valya's features hardened.

Ken imagined the woman's albinism had always made her a *gaijin*, an outsider, someone always held as suspect due to a genetic trait beyond her control. Plus, she was not Japanese. He knew how much heritage mattered in such a closed culture. Even his mixed blood—half Japanese, half German— had cast him a shade lower in the eyes of his fellow researchers in Kyoto. He remembered bristling against this age-old prejudice.

Valya clearly also rankled at her lower status, forever destined to be considered *less than* by her Japanese superiors. To have Masahiro cast this aspersion now plainly inflamed her.

The fingers still clutching Ken's elbow dug deeper into his flesh.

As the scan of Masahiro's palm completed, a hidden teak panel swiveled open, exposing a single red button. "We'll have four minutes," he warned. "Trust me, we'll want to be beyond the station's blast doors by that time."

He punched the button with a fist, his aggravation showing.

Valya frowned as he turned back around. "What's going to—?"

Masahiro cut her off and pointed to the door. "*Now* we can go."

The man stalked around the desk and ordered the two guards to clear a path ahead of them. Such an order was no longer necessary. Beyond the doors, the outer hub had mostly emptied as the earlier bottleneck finally broke. The final stragglers fled down the long tunnel.

But they were not the last.

A spatter of gunfire echoed down the stairs from the level above. Valya had sent an armed team to deal with Gray and Aiko. Apparently, the firefight was still under way.

Ken stared up, willing them to hold out.

But in the end, what good would it truly do?

He pictured the red button under the fiery phoenix.

They had less than four minutes.

Valya looked up also, her expression wary. It was that wariness that saved her life. She suddenly swung around, yanking Ken to her chest as a pistol blast rang out behind them. A round whistled past the side of his head, burning through the edge of his left ear. Pain flared, momentarily blinding hm.

As his vision cleared, he saw Seichan running toward them, her pistol raised, the barrel smoking.

5:02 A.M.

How could she be here?

Upon seeing the witch's tattooed face, Seichan had reacted hastily. She had fired immediately at the impossible apparition, knowing it was her best chance to eliminate this dread threat. But in her desperation, she must have given herself away—maybe the scuff of her feet on the steel stairs, the strained panting of her breath—or maybe it had simply been the woman's innate sense of danger.

The Guild had taught them both to be forever on guard, to draw every detail from their surroundings at all times and be ready to act.

Cursing the woman's preternatural senses, Seichan fired at one of the gunmen. The round struck his shoulder and sent him spinning away, the rifle flying from his fingertips.

The second gunman grabbed a Japanese man dressed in a business suit and rushed him out of the line of fire and into a side tunnel. From the map turning in her head, she knew it was the main passageway leading from the station to the island.

She ignored the fleeing men and concentrated on Valya Mikhailov.

The woman continued to use Professor Matsui as a human shield. Seichan fired two more rounds, not intending to hit her target. She couldn't risk striking Ken. Instead, she used the shots to drive the woman away from the exit tunnel, to keep her from escaping. Simultaneously, she ran for the only cover: the open door of an office.

Valya fired back at her, but Seichan had been just as well trained to anticipate danger and react. She responded mindfully but instinctively to the woman's body movements and to her gaze. She slipped through the rounds, the bullets ricocheting off the steel behind her.

Just keep focusing on me.

From the corner of her eye, she spotted Palu bolt from the lower stairwell. Cleaver in hand, he fled across an open gap of floor to the steps heading up, where spats of gunfire still rang out.

Minutes ago, while traversing the station toward the central hub, she had heard those same shots. She paused long enough to strip and clean her waterlogged SIG Sauer, readying it for use again. All the while, the compromised station had creaked and groaned around her, reminding her to hurry.

As did every gun blast echoing from above.

There could be only one source of that firefight.

Gray . . .

Knowing that, she had finally rushed up the central hub toward the fighting—only to discover Professor Matsui on the middle level being dragged toward the exit by a ghost from Seichan's past. She had only moments to attempt to rescue Ken, while also sending Palu off to help Gray and the others.

As she ran for cover now, Valya finally shoved Ken to the floor, frustrated by the man's thrashing, which confounded the woman's aim. Unencumbered now, Valya fired two fast shots. One sailed past Seichan's head, the other grazed her hip.

Fiery pain bloomed, but she ignored it and kept running.

Almost there . . .

Once she was safely shielded in the office and Valya was exposed on the open floor, she could either eliminate the witch or drive her off.

But before Seichan could reach her goal, both of her legs broke.

Or at least, that's what it felt like.

The burst of exertion had finally roused the horde inside her. Pain racked through her, cramping the muscles of her legs into unpliable stone. Her limbs refused to cooperate and sent her crashing to the floor. Agony narrowed her vision and weakened her control.

As she hit, the impact knocked the pistol from her palm. It bounced, then skidded into the office. She tried to follow it, struggling to get her legs under her.

Then a presence loomed over her.

She glanced up, knowing who was there.

Valya had collected Ken again. She had a fist knotted in his hair, pulling his head back. Blood ran down his neck from his ear.

Her pistol pointed at Seichan.

"I've waited a long time for this," she said.

"Tracking you and that bastard halfway around the globe, almost losing you twice."

Through eyes watery with pain, Seichan glared back.

So that's how the enemy knew we were on Maui.

Valya shoved her pistol closer.

Ken moaned. "Don't . . ."

His plea fell on deaf ears.

He tried again. "She's . . . she's pregnant."

Valya froze for a moment—then laughed, a chilling, hollow sound. "That's perfect . . . just perfect. Better than I could've hoped for."

She lifted her pistol high and brought its steel butt crashing down, cracking Seichan across the temple. The world turned bright white—then faded to darkness.

Final words chased her into oblivion.

"If you survive long enough, I may keep the child for myself."

5:18 A.M.

Numb with shock, Ken shambled down the tunnel toward the exit. Hot blood trickled from his wounded ear. He was followed by the gunman who had fled with Masahiro during the brief firefight. The man returned after sending his charge to safety.

Ahead of them, Valya led the way. Two workers behind her dragged Seichan's unconscious body. They all moved quickly.

Twenty yards away, the glass tunnel ended at the thick blast doors.

Masahiro stood there, arms crossed. "Twenty seconds," he hollered over to them. "And this door closes."

Valya moved no faster, defying the man even in this regard.

Ken suspected Masahiro would've already sealed them inside, but he must have spotted Valya's prize in tow. The man had been humiliated by Seichan back on Maui, and from the vengeful glint to his eyes, he wanted her in hand before they fled this island.

In his head, Ken counted down the final seconds.

They neared the threshold as his internal timer reached zero.

A series of chained detonations blasted behind him. He swung around, noting flashes of fire throughout the station. Closer at hand, smoke and flames burst into the glass tunnel from a side passageway to the right. A bent steel door crashed into view.

"Get through here!" Masahiro ordered.

Ken hurried, following the others, while still staring back into the tunnel.

The true purpose of the timed explosions came into view.

The smoke darkened as a frenzied swarm burst into the passage, coming from the test chamber he had spotted earlier when they had arrived. He remembered the room had been crawling with soldier drones. Angered by the noise and the flames, the wasps hummed through the smoke, seeking a target.

"Now or never," Masahiro warned.

From the other blasts throughout the station, all of the glass-domed test chambers must have had their doors blown off.

After years of captivity, the *Odokuro* were free at last.

But the wasps were not the only threat.

The station rumbled and shook. Water flushed into the tunnel from the direction of the test chamber.

Ken recognized the truth.

It's all coming down.

27

Deafened by the nearby blast, Gray crouched in the hallway outside the foamy ruins of the torture chamber. Smoke choked the room. The hatch that opened into the harvesters' neighboring pen had blown off its hinges and sailed across the chamber, crashing through the observation window on the far side.

A few stray harvesters who hadn't joined the others for the feast wandered out through the smoke, but once they crawled into the foam, their pace slowed, then stopped, poisoned by the insecticide.

It was by sheer luck that Kowalski and Palu's cousins had revived enough to crawl or stumble out of the chamber into the hall before the blast happened. The three men were on their feet but still needed the wall to support themselves.

Blood seeped from their limbs, but the flow was less as their bite wounds clotted.

On Gray's other side, Aiko leaned against the wall next to him. She hugged her rifle to her chest. Around the corner, two men lay dead in the next tunnel.

It was the only way out of this section.

Still, Aiko had proven herself to be a crack shot. She was the only reason they were all still alive.

But for how much longer?

Aiko held up one finger, indicating she was down to her weapon's last round.

He prayed it was enough. After the blast, the gunfire from the far side of the tunnel had stopped. He didn't know if the others fled or if they were waiting to ambush them, hoping the explosion would send their targets scurrying into view.

When the blast had first occurred, he had considered that option, believing they were doomed if they stayed. And that was certainly still a possibility. Water rained down in the harvester's pen, pattering against the steel floor. The explosion must have cracked the pen's glass roof.

It would not be long before the pressure at this depth imploded the dome and flooded this section.

Aiko glanced to him, her expression easy to read.

What do we do?

A pounding of many feet drew both their attentions back to the tunnel. The enemy was attempting a final full-on assault. Aiko dropped to a knee and peeked around the corner, leading with her weapon.

One bullet against how many?

To find the answer, Gray stayed high and leaned over her to gauge the threat. Two figures raced toward them, single-file, about five yards apart. The one in the lead was attempting to free a sidearm from a hip holster.

It was odd that he didn't already have his weapon in hand.

Perhaps recognizing this, Aiko restrained from shooting, reserving her one shot.

The lead runner finally yanked his pistol free, twisted sideways, and pointed the weapon behind him. Before he could fire, something struck his back leg. He crashed against the wall, turning enough to reveal a wide steel blade impaled in his thigh.

Still, the gunman had the wherewithal to keep his pistol leveled at the second assailant. Before he could fire, Aiko's rifle cracked. The man's head exploded.

The second figure skidded to a stop, hands up, showing no weapons.

Palu.

Aiko and Gray both tumbled into view. Palu's raised arms were soaked in blood. Gray recognized the blade in the dead man's leg. It was from Seichan's arsenal. He must have fought his way through the small force still on-site, using both the element of surprise and the explosion to take them all down, except for this last one who had tried to flee.

Gray reached him. "Where's Seichan?"

Palu grimaced. "Taken. When coming up, I saw her through the glass below being dragged toward the exit to the island. They had the professor, too."

Gray was already moving. "Then let's go get them."

Palu blocked him with a thick arm. "No. Never make it."

Aiko agreed, lifting her rifle and reminding him. "Out of bullets."

"We can find more ammunition, other weapons. If we hurry before they seal—"

A deep boom cut him off. The trickling of water in the neighboring dome became a heavy torrent. Water flooded out of the pen and into the torture chamber.

They were out of time for debate.

The flooding flushed Kowalski and the other two men into view. Palu did a double take upon seeing his cousins here—and in their condition. The Hawaiian must not have known about the raid on his men's catamaran.

Gray didn't have time to explain. "We have no choice now. We'll have to make for the exit."

Palu refused to lower his arm. "Not that way."

"Then where?"

He finally dropped his arm and pointed down. "All the way to the bottom of this damned place."

"Why? What's there?"

Palu turned and led them. "Hopefully a way out."

5:30 A.M.

Masahiro stood beside the open blast doors as the unconscious woman was finally dragged out of the station and into the rock-hewn island tunnel. He stared at the blood dribbling from her left temple. Someone must have pistol-whipped her.

Serves her right.

He wished the same fate had befallen her captor, the pale Russian. As if flaunting her prisoners, Valya had deliberately taken her time moving her party out of the station.

She gave Masahiro a smug look as she strolled past him.

Fury stoked inside him, knowing this *gaijin* would take full credit for the captures.

He stepped back as smoke rolled from the station into the outer passageway, carrying with it the angry hum of the freed wasps.

"Close it up," Masahiro ordered, turning his back on the station.

My work is done here.

He was wrong.

Valya nodded to the two guards, both part of her personal team.

One grabbed Masahiro by the lapels of his jacket and shoved him back through the blast door into the station. Masahiro tripped over the edge and landed on his backside. The other guard leaned a shoulder against the thick steel door and began to close it.

No . . .

He tried to get up, but something landed on his cheek. He swatted, panicked. The sting felt like a burning coal jabbed into his flesh. Then the entire side of his face ignited with fire. He patted a hand there, as if trying to put out those flames. He expected to find his skin melting off his cheek.

Through tears of pain, he watched the blast doors slowly shut. Before it sealed, Valya stared back at him from the other side, her eyes shining with cold victory.

Then she was gone.

In that last moment, Masahiro knew his ultimate failing: underestimating the depths of the woman's ambition.

Behind him, the humming grew louder, drawn by his frightened breath and pounding heart. As the swarm swept over him, he closed his eyes. His body was pelted from every side, like the hard hail that frequently assailed the heights of Mount Fuji.

Only here ice was fire.

Screams ripped from his throat, which only opened himself further. Wasps crawled into his mouth, crowding inside, pushing deeper, stinging all the way down.

Their sheer numbers choked his wails to whimpers.

Until finally fiery pain chased him into oblivion.

5:38 A.M.

Gray followed the others in a mad dash down the stairs of the central hub. They paused only long enough to collect weapons along the way, removing them from dead bodies, the grim handiwork of Palu and his cleaver.

By now, the entire station trembled and shook.

The footing on the steps was treacherous as the staircase had become a waterfall. Other domes in the upper tier must have collapsed. The lake was rapidly flooding into the station from multiple directions. Gray felt the pressure in his ears building as the remaining air was squeezed by the closing walls of water. It was also harder to breathe as smoke was compressed into those same tightening spaces.

And it wasn't just the smoke.

As they reached and ran out onto the middle level of the hub, he smacked a stray wasp from his hair. Still, he felt a mule kick to the side of his head as it stung his ear. Between them and the sweep of stairs to the lower level, a dark swarm hovered at the mouth of the main exit tunnel. The wasps milled and churned. In the enclosed space, their humming sounded like an electrical fire.

With no other choice, the group skirted the swarm's edge.

"Don't slow," Gray warned. "Keep running."

The group hugged the outer walls of Masahiro's office. Still, as they passed the cloud of wasps, the swarm was drawn by the wake of their passage. The buzzing intensified as the wasps finally found targets to vent their fury.

"Faster!" Gray urged the others.

He knew he asked the impossible. Aiko led the way with Palu, who supported Makaio, all but carrying his cousin. A step behind them, Kowalski tried to do the same with Tua.

The swarm closed in on their group, a dark wave threatening to crash over them.

Gray did his best to herd the others toward the stairwell to the lower level. Wearing only swim trunks, he felt exposed. His skin pebbled with anticipation of more stings.

Kowalski suddenly swore, crashed to one knee, and swatted at his neck.

Gray rushed to his side. He grabbed Tua with one arm, while offering the other to Kowalski.

The big man simply glared and pushed up on his own.

Together, they chased after the others.

Gray felt strikes against his right leg, his left arm. Fire burst from those spots. He forced himself onward. Adrenaline fought against the pain. Tears coursed his cheeks. His legs stumbled under him.

Kowalski must have noted his distress and shifted to half-carry both Gray and Tua. Gray was in awe of the man's constitution, especially noting the number of wasps perched on his shoulders and back. The man's muscles twitched and shuddered as he was stung multiple times.

Maybe it was the antidote in the syringes or the opioid analgesics that kept Kowalski moving, but Gray suspected it was the guy's sheer stubbornness.

Ahead of them, Aiko and the others had reached the stairwell. They vanished into the smoke billowing up the steps.

Like a long-distance runner spotting the finish line, Kowalski grunted and hauled harder for the stairs. As they finally shoved into the thick pall, the leading edge of the swarm retreated from the smoke.

Even the wasps on their bodies fled.

Gray quickly understood their precaution. He coughed on smoke that smelled of scorched rubber. He tasted burning oil on his tongue. He tried to hold his breath but pain and exhaustion forced him to keep gasping.

Finally, the group splashed into the lower level. The floodwaters were knee-deep down here. Once free of the stairwell—which had been funneling the smoke upward like a chimney—the air grew clearer. Smoke continued to flow along the roof of the tunnels, but by ducking their heads, they found a stratum of breathable air.

The ice-cold water also helped reduce the pain from the stings.

"This way," Palu said, pointing to a tunnel on the left.

The Hawaiian set off, wading swiftly.

The surface of the water was full of debris, all covered by a dense layer of drowned wasps of every iteration: tiny scouts, larger egg-laying breeders, and others he did not recognize.

"Should be just down this next tunnel," Palu promised them. "If it's still here . . ."

The next passageway was long, extending to a remote corner of the station.

He prayed such isolation had kept this section undamaged and intact.

As they traversed its length, the water quickly crested their waists. It became easier to half-swim, floating and kicking off the floor with their feet. This method also kept their heads away from the layer of smoke above.

Finally, the tunnel ended ahead at a sealed door.

An airlock.

Just as Palu had promised.

The Hawaiian had told them how he and Seichan

had spotted a small submarine docked down here. It had likely been used to ferry in supplies, maybe even sections of the station while it was being constructed.

Now it was their only hope of escape.

And not just *their* only hope.

A trio of station workers shivered in front of the airlock. They looked like drowned rats. It seemed their group wasn't the only one trapped in the flooded station.

Aiko pointed a rifle at them and spoke rapidly in Japanese. She then turned to Gray. "It's the sub crew. They were assigned to move the vessel."

Gray felt a surge of relief. He had planned on doing his best to figure out how to operate it. This was even better.

But Aiko did not look happy and explained why. "They've been trying to get inside, but the airlock mechanism is damaged. There's no way to get through."

Gray shifted forward, waving the crew out of his way. He peered through the double set of windows to the dry dock beyond. The conning tower of a small submarine poked from a pool inside, just waiting to be used.

Despondent, he rested his forehead against the glass.

So close, yet so far.

5:49 A.M.

Ken braced himself in the cargo hold of the transport plane as it took off from the island's airstrip. Due to the short runway, the aircraft accelerated powerfully—then lifted skyward at a steep angle.

From the Cyrillic script stenciled on the inside of the hull, the plane was likely former Russian or Serbian military. Its design was simple. The flight deck was enclosed behind a door. The rest of the aircraft was a hollow shell. Jump seats lined the inner walls, but the bulk of the hold was empty space.

Not that it was *empty* now.

The hold was packed with crates, boxes, and barrels, all tied down or covered in netting. It was everything salvaged from the station.

As the plane tipped at an angle, circling around, Seichan's head lolled in her restraints. The blood had dried on her temple, but she remained unconscious. Still, their captors were taking no chances with her. Her wrists and ankles were secured in steel cuffs and chains. She was belted into her jump seat. A guard sat next to her with a pistol in hand. Another sat across with an assault rifle across his knees.

A door slammed, drawing Ken's attention.

Valya left the flight deck and pointed to two other men. Ken eavesdropped as she spoke in Japanese. "You and you. With me."

The men snapped out of their seats to follow.

Ken knew all the crew were loyalists to her ambitions. None of them had questioned her when she had abandoned Masahiro in the station. She had also taken additional steps to cover everything up. When their group had reached the former Coast Guard building, Ken discovered the place had been turned into a slaughterhouse. It appeared others on her team had ambushed everyone as they evacuated via the freight elevator, mowing them down with submachine guns. The bodies had been dragged to the side and rested atop a lake of blood.

Valya had barely given the pile more than a dispassionate glance.

Ken recognized a coup when he saw one.

Confirming this, a loud explosion shook the craft. Ken craned around to a window behind his seat. The rusted tin roof of the Coast Guard building sailed high into the air, propelled by a column of smoke and fire.

Definitely erasing her tracks.

Winds suddenly howled into the cargo hold. Ken flinched, fearing some flying shrapnel had struck their aircraft. Instead, he spotted a hatch at the rear of the plane hinging open.

Valya stood back there and pointed below.

Two men rolled an orange barrel to the door once it was fully open. Upon her signal, they shoved the large canister out the back of the plane.

Ken turned his attention to the window. He followed the barrel as it tumbled down. It struck the island's pier, where the station's hovercraft was docked. Upon impact, a fiery blast mushroomed skyward. Fountains of flame swept outward, covering both the wooden pier and the boat.

As the plane circled the island, more of the incendiary charges were dropped. Smoke and flames spread over the atoll. It was all too reminiscent of the destruction he had witnessed at the Brazilian island of Queimada Grande.

They're going to burn it all down to the bedrock.

But they had one additional step.

Valya pointed again, hollering to be heard over the wind. Ken couldn't make out all she said, but he did hear the word *mizūmi*.

He cringed, suspecting what was about to happen.

The plane swung out over the ocean, then tilted around for a final bombing run. Only this time the barrels were not going to be used to set anything on fire.

Instead, they would serve as makeshift depth charges.

For *mizūmi* meant *lake*.

5:55 A.M.

"This is friggin' nuts," Kowalski noted, but he bore a savage grin on his face.

Gray couldn't argue. But if they died in the next seconds, Kowalski would do so happily. There was nothing Sigma's demolition expert liked more than blowing stuff up.

Gray and the others sheltered behind a pried-up section of steel floor. They were positioned some twenty yards away from the damaged airlock. Earlier, Kowalski and Palu had rigged a cube of C4 to a timer. It was the last of the fireman's supply from the cache they had obtained back on Maui.

This either worked or they were all dead.

The plan was to blow the airlock and gain entry to the docking dome. But so much could go wrong. If the charge was too weak, they would fail to blast their way through both doors. If it was too strong, they risked damaging the submarine or even collapsing this section of station.

Still, they had to take the chance.

As the two men had prepared the charge, Gray had listened to blasts echoing through the water from above. From the dull glow overhead, he knew the enemy must be firebombing the island on their way out.

"Get ready," Kowalski warned. He studied Palu's wristwatch and counted down the final seconds by holding his fingers outstretched and curling each digit, marking the time.

By now, the floodwaters swirled chest-high—which was a good thing.

Gray knew the docking bay must be pressurized to keep the lake from flooding though the pool inside there. When they blew the doors, the violence of the decompression could immediately let the lake rush in. Their only hope was that the trapped air in the flooded station was compressed enough to somewhat match that pressure.

Just one other detail that could go wrong . . .

Kowalski curled his last finger, forming a fist.

Gray had warned everyone to open their mouths and expel their breaths, to help them withstand the blast's concussion. It failed miserably. The explosion slammed his eardrums and squeezed his rib cage to the point that he didn't know if he'd ever breathe again.

Then it was over.

He gasped along with the others.

Ahead, both doors were gone.

Past the airlock, the pool around the conning tower welled upward, meeting the waters flooding out of the tunnel and into the chamber.

He sighed.

The pressure seemed to be holding for now.

So far so good.

They lowered their section of flooring and allowed the current to drag them all into the docking bay. As they all washed into the chamber, sheets of water started jetting from the domed roof. The force of the blast had splintered the glass.

As Gray watched, the cracks spread and widened.

He pointed to the conning tower. "Inside! Now!"

One of the crew swam to the tower's ladder and clambered to the top. Once there, he crouched and twirled the locking mechanism to open the hatch.

The others climbed up. When the door was heaved open, the perched crew member helped them all—one after the other—down into the safety of the small submarine. Gray went last, making sure everyone was aboard.

He matched gazes with the terrified man atop the tower.

Together in this, they were no longer enemies.

Movement through the glass wall drew Gray's attention. A bright orange barrel fell past their position.

No, no, no . . .

Gray lunged forward, grabbed the crew member, and rolled him headfirst through the opening. He then swung down to the ladder inside and slammed the hatch behind him as an explosion rocked the sub sideways.

The conning tower struck the edge of the docking pool with a loud clang.

He hung on to the ladder with one hand and spun the lock on the underside of the hatch with the other. He then dropped down. He was relieved to see that the man he had tossed below had landed on others, cushioning his fall.

Gray shouted. "Get us mov—"

The engines engaged with a rumble, cutting him off. Clearly the other two crew members had already rushed into position.

Gray stalked forward, ducking his head from the low roof. He recognized the small vessel. It was a *Una*-class submarine built by the Yugoslav navy. The midget sub had been engineered to lay down mines in or deliver Special Forces into waters too shallow for larger vessels. It had clearly been decommissioned and modified for private use. The solid nose cone in front had been replaced with polymer glass.

Seated in front, the pilot lowered the sub away from the station.

Gray joined him in time to witness the final destruction of the station. The concussion of the depth charge had shattered one side of the facility. Air bubbled upward, while broken tubes tumbled toward the lake bed. In slow motion, the rest all came down. With a last flicker, the emergency lights died, turning the lake dark again.

One of the crew flicked a switch and a beam of light shot forward, revealing the dark eye of a tunnel to the open ocean. The pilot guided the vessel toward it. Even taking into account the small displacement and draught of the midget sub, it looked like a tight fit.

Gray noted another crew member, acting as navigator, bent over a Krupp Atlas sonar array. The sensor suite could run active or passive.

Worried, he leaned to Aiko, who had joined him. "Tell them it's okay to use the light to traverse the tunnel, but once in open water, they'll have to douse it and run on passive sonar so we're not detected."

She nodded and transmitted his orders.

He looked up as the nose of the small sub entered the tunnel. Whoever had dropped those depth charges could still be up there, monitoring the surrounding seas.

As the tunnel fully swallowed the sub, he drew his attention back to the crew. "Are the batteries fully charged?"

One of them spoke enough English to answer with a thumbs-up.

"Then once free of here, make for Midway. Max power."

He got a nod.

Grimly satisfied, he followed the beam of the sub's light as it pierced the darkness ahead and made a silent vow to Seichan.

I won't stop until you're back in my arms.

28

The world slowly returned, bringing pain with it.

Seichan's left temple throbbed, and her limbs burned. Agony knotted her guts. She wanted to vomit but feared it would only make matters worse. She blinked her eyes against a glaring brightness that spiked through her skull.

Groaning, she tried to shield herself from the radiance, but her wrists were cuffed and bound by chains to her ankles.

It took her another few breaths to recognize she was in a cargo plane. From the timbre of the engine's whine, probably a turboprop. She swiveled her head, which set the world to spinning.

Still, she spotted Ken strapped in the jump seat next to her.

"How are you feeling?" he asked.

She simply scowled and forced her dry tongue to form a few words. "Gray . . . the others . . ."

Ken looked down at his bound hands. "Don't know. Still down there." He glanced sorrowfully at her. "She firebombed the entire island. The station is destroyed."

Seichan twisted enough to stare out the bright window. The sun had finally risen and shone brightly across a calm ocean, revealing the damage wrought overnight.

Behind the plane, the island burned, cloaked in smoke.

She stared back there, refusing to accept that Gray was gone. She grasped on to that hope, trying to make it certainty. But pain and exhaustion confounded her. Tears welled, which only made her angrier.

As she faced forward, that knot of pain in her gut exploded.

She cried out, doubling over her bound hands. She closed her eyes and panted, as if trying to blow out the fire inside her. After what felt like tens of minutes, it finally subsided enough for her to sit back up.

As her gaze focused, she found a familiar tattooed countenance staring back at her. Valya was down on one knee.

"So you're awake?"

Seichan didn't bother answering her.

Valya turned to Ken. "You're the entomology expert. What stage is she in?"

He winced at Seichan. "By now, from the pain she is experiencing, it suggests the larvae are likely beginning to molt into their second instars."

"So that means the *real* agony is about to begin."

Seichan could not help but quail at such a thought.

Ken looked with pity on her. If her hands were free, she would've punched him. She did not want pity—not from anyone.

"She has another day," he continued. "Then the third instars will begin migrating into her bones."

Seichan knew what that meant.

Valya stared at her belly. "And her child?"

Ken shook his head. "I don't know."

Ice-blue eyes studied Seichan with a calculating look. "Then we'll discover her status when we land in Japan. A pregnancy could prove useful to Fenikkusu Laboratories' plans. If that ends up being the case, it looks like I'll be arriving with *three* prizes, instead of just two."

Valya glanced at them both as she straightened.

Before she could turn away, one of her men came rushing from the back of the plane. "Spotters have identified the submarine from the air. It just exited the island and is crossing the shallows."

Valya's fingers curled into fists. "I knew that rat would find some way to escape the sinking ship."

Gray . . .

Seichan grasped this thin hope with all her heart.

"It could be our people," the man warned.

"Doesn't matter." She pointed to the plane's rear. "How many barrels do we have left?"

"Ten."

She twirled a hand in the air. "Bring us around and open the rear hatch. We'll drop half the load to soften them up, then swing back and dump the rest."

"*Hai!*" The man ran back to pass on her orders.

Valya faced Seichan again. "There are miles of shallow waters aproning the island. There'll be nowhere they can run where we can't spot the vessel from the air."

Seichan's hope began to crumble.

Valya must have noted her despair. "Fear not, at least you'll have front-row seats to the death of the father of your child."

6:32 A.M.

Gray cursed the new day.

He leaned on the back of the pilot's chair. The *Una*-class sub glided low over ridges of reefs. Schools of fish flashed out of their way, their scales reflecting the morning sun's brightness.

Though the midget submarine had been specifically engineered to traverse such shallow water, he felt exposed.

"How deep are we?"

The pilot, a man named Nakamura, spoke English. "Thirty meters."

Gray knew they needed to find depths of at least two hundred to be able to sink into the shadows of the deep sea. From Gray's constant gaze upward, the pilot must have guessed his worry.

"There's a deep trench that we usually run along to stay hidden. About ten klicks ahead."

Perfect.

"Get us there as fast as the engines will allow."

"*Hai.*"

Aiko stood at Gray's side. She still had her rifle, but it was hung over her shoulder now. There was no need to coerce the crew's cooperation. After their own people had tried to kill them, they were happy to switch allegiances.

Palu crowded up to them, his head bowed from

the low roof. He had spent the past twenty minutes using a first-aid kit to bandage the bloody limbs of the three injured men. In addition, he had taped gauze sponges over the wounds on their backs and lower abdomens.

"How are they doing?" Aiko asked.

Palu grimaced. "They lost a lot of blood. And Tua's too pale. He's slipping into shock."

Aiko turned to Gray. "Midway is still eighty miles away. Even at top speed, it'll take us seven or eight hours to get there."

She glanced at the men in back, her thoughts easy to read.

They won't last that long.

Gray recognized this, too. "Once we're well enough away from here, we can risk raising an antenna and sending a mayday to the station at Midway. Get them to dispatch an airlift to us."

Palu nodded. He squinted at the seas, at the spread of reefs. "We better not wait too long."

Understood.

Weighted down by the press of time, Gray followed Palu's gaze.

"It's beautiful out here," Palu mumbled, his voice mournful, as if reflecting on all that had already been lost. "We should be entering the waters of Papahānaumokuākea soon."

Gray recognized the name of the protected marine monument that surrounded these remote islands. As if mirroring Palu's mood, a dark cloud swept over the bright waters.

It took Gray a breath too long to realize the truth.

The *cloud* was moving too fast, aiming straight for them.

Aiko grabbed his arm. "Plane."

Gray jerked forward. "Hard to port! Now!"

The pilot responded immediately. He heaved on the boat's rudder, while trimming the dive planes in opposite directions—raising one, lowering the other—to cut sharply away. The sub listed hard into the turn, tossing everyone sideways.

Kowalski groaned in back. From the sudden maneuver, he must have known they were in trouble.

Gray leaned forward, looking up through the glass nose cone as the shadow passed overhead. Through the water, he could make out the silhouette of a cross sweeping the sky.

Definitely an airplane.

But was it the enemy?

The question was answered as a rain of dark objects plummeted into the sea off their starboard side. As the plane's shadow swept away, fresh sunlight revealed orange barrels.

"Brace yourselves!" Gray yelled.

The cascade of blasts pummeled the sub. Shattered bits of reef and coral pelted their flank. The concussion rolled the boat. Gray held his breath, willing them not to go upside down. If that happened, with the ballast doors open under them, they would sink.

As the explosions faded, the sub righted itself.

Gray gasped with relief.

But they were far from safe.

The strain had stressed the seal between the nose

cone and the sub's body. Water seeped through. Even more concerning was a noticeable crack in the glass. It appeared to be holding, but if there was another attack . . .

He searched the waters. Off to the starboard side, the seas had vanished, obscured by blasted silt and rock. He craned all around for the return of the black shadow, not knowing from which direction it would come, only certain that it *would*.

They were sitting ducks out here.

"How long until we reach that trench?" Gray asked the pilot.

"Still another eight klicks."

Too far.

They would never reach the trench's dark harbor before the plane overtook them.

Gray searched the seas again—not for the enemy, but for some answer.

"Maybe we should return to the island," Aiko suggested. "Perhaps we can hide in the tunnel until it's safe."

Gray shook his head.

Even if they could turn around and reach that shelter in time, he didn't like the idea of being trapped there. A few well-placed charges and they'd be sealed in their own grave. But her words gave him another idea, another place to hide.

He placed his hand on the pilot's shoulder. "Forget the trench. Power to the southwest." He pointed in that direction. "With everything your engines have."

He turned to Palu, silently thanking him.

The Hawaiian's confused frown suddenly brightened into a knowing smile. "Like I said before, you be one lolo buggah."

6:49 A.M.

"Where the hell are they going?" Valya asked.

Seichan took satisfaction in the woman's frustration. The witch leaned over a window next to her, plainly wanting to stick close to savor Seichan's pain when the submarine was destroyed.

Only the tables had been turned.

It had taken the large plane too long to circle back around and search the bright waters for their target. By the time they had returned, the first bombardment had cast up a silty cloud that spread far over the seas. At first, it was unknown if the initial barrage had already destroyed the vessel. It could be sunk under that cloud, resting dead on the bottom.

As a precaution, Valya had ordered the plane to search a path out to some trench. When that failed to reveal them, she seemed to grow more confident in its destruction. Still, she had them circle back and make sure the sub hadn't retreated to the island.

Again no sign.

Afterward, Valya had loomed over Seichan with her hands on her hips. She wore a self-congratulatory smug expression.

"One down," she gloated, casting her gaze from Seichan's face to her belly. "*Two* to go."

Then the radio cut in as the pilot called from the

flight deck. *"Target acquired. Running to the southwest."*

As the plane banked in that direction, Valya's expression hardened. She cursed in her native tongue and swung back to the window. "Where the hell are they going?"

Seichan twisted around, too. She ignored the flare of pain, using the woman's irritation as a balm. She caught Ken's eye, reading the hope there. She refused to match it. Not yet. Gray may not even be aboard the submarine.

Suddenly Valya shoved away from the window, her eyes wide with fury. She grabbed the closest man and pushed him toward the flight deck. "Tell the pilot to dive at them. Now! Get us as close as possible."

The man looked baffled, but he nodded and ran.

Valya turned in the opposite direction and rushed for the open rear hatch, where the last five orange barrels waited to be dropped. As she left, she mumbled under her breath in Russian, a clear sign of the woman's agitation.

Seichan pretended not to hear her or understand, but she did both.

"I can't let the bastards get there," Valya had said.

Curious, Seichan returned her full attention to the window. Sunshine stung her eyes as she strained to discover what had so angered Valya.

"Look!" Ken said. "Across the ocean ahead."

She squinted into the glare—then saw it, too.

A mile off, a flotilla of wide rafts and small islands rode the swells and waves. They spread across

the breadth of the horizon. As the plane raced in
that direction, the clogged seas seemed to stretch
ever onward.

"What is it?" Seichan asked.

6:54 A.M.

Palu had supplied Gray with the answer, a possible
source of shelter in the open ocean. Back aboard the
catamaran, the Hawaiian had warned Gray of the
danger lurking at the fringes of the region's marine
reserve, threatening both the islands and the surrounding sea life.

Even now as they raced toward it, evidence appeared in the water: a black tire resting on the seabed, a knotted tangle of plastic bags swirling like
a frond of pale kelp, a lost fishing net waving from
where it had snagged on a branch of coral.

But the true bulk of their refuge lay directly
ahead.

It was known as the Great Pacific Garbage Patch,
a morass of floating refuse larger than Texas, where
marine debris was funneled into this spot by a vortex of ocean currents. The surface was dotted with
small islands of accumulated trash: plastic bottles
and bags, Styrofoam cups, barrels from oil rigs,
crates from ships. But the real danger lurked below.
To the depths of several meters, a toxic slurry of
photodegraded tiny bits of microplastic fogged the
waters.

While such pollution was a growing environmental disaster, for their group it offered a hope for shelter from the coming storm.

As they sped toward this refuge, Gray sensed time was running out. He crouched low beside the pilot. Though he had no way of knowing for sure, he could picture the shadow of that airplane closing in behind him.

His fingers dug into the back of the pilot's chair.

"Almost there," Aiko whispered, as if fearing the enemy above might hear her.

Palu scowled, matching her whisper. "Don't jinx us."

The nose cone of the midget sub aimed for the darker waters ahead, where the debris field shielded the sun.

And soon hopefully us.

Gray held his breath, willing the engines more speed. Then at long last, the sub glided under the thick layer of soupy microplastics. The world grew immediately dimmer. Ahead, darker patches of the ocean marked trash piles on the surface.

He let out a rattling sigh.

Made it.

Then a muffled *BOOM* shook the back of the boat. The vessel momentarily lifted up on its nose as a shock wave struck their rear.

Gray crashed against the pilot's seat. "Hard to starboard!" he hollered and pointed to a shadow-mottled section under the garbage patch. "Max power!"

The pilot expertly drove the boat into a sharp turn as more bombs smashed through the trash and filth, exploding like fiery stars in the night. A darker shadow enveloped them as the plane passed over the debris field. More charges exploded in its wake, but the barrage was scattershot and spread out.

They're shooting blind, he realized.

Even better, the explosions blasted up sand and silt, further obscuring the path ahead.

A moment later, the ocean went silent, marking the end of the initial bombing run.

But would they come around again?

Knowing they needed somewhere to hide, Gray spotted and pointed to a large carpet of debris ahead—and the dark shadows beneath it.

"Bring us to a stop under there."

The pilot nodded sharply. He slowed the sub and glided it to a hover under the protective blanket of garbage. The underside was woven together by a tangle of nets. Several draped lower, hanging from above like Spanish moss.

The nose cone brushed alongside one, setting the net to twirling. As it turned, the carcass of a seal revealed itself caught inside. The flesh had mostly been picked clean, leaving rubbery fins and bones.

Aiko gasped.

In the murk, even Gray shuddered at the sight.

"We call it ghost fishing," Palu said, nodding to the carcass. "Hundreds of tons of nets find their way to the Patch. While carried by the currents, they trolled the seas on their own, catching and tangling prey, carrying their ghostly cargo here."

Gray stared up at the netted mass of debris and bones.

Let's hope we don't suffer the same fate.

7:12 A.M.

Seichan enjoyed the exasperation on Valya's face as she stalked forward from the back of the plane. Behind her, the rear hatch was already closing after the last of the barrels had been dropped overboard.

As Valya approached, Ken whispered over from the next seat. "Do you think they survived?"

Seichan only had to stare at the woman's face to know the truth. Valya glowered darkly. Storm clouds hung over her head. Even the tattoo on her face stood out more starkly.

"I'd say so," she whispered back.

Valya stopped and barked to one of the crew in Japanese. "Tell the pilot to head away. I want to be wheels-down in Tokyo before sunrise."

Ken leaned toward Seichan. "Is it over? Are they giving up?"

"I don't think they have much choice."

Valya heard their whispering and crossed to them. "Another word and I'll have you both gagged."

Seichan did her best to shrug in her shackles. "Seems you were wrong earlier."

"About what?"

"About being *one* down and two to go," Seichan said, throwing the woman's words back at her. "Something tells me your score is back to *zero*."

Valya balled a fist and turned away—then, unable to help herself, she swung back around and punched Seichan in the mouth.

Seichan's head bounced back and rang off the hull. She tasted blood as those knuckles split her lip. Pain flared, but it was nothing compared to what raged inside her. The abuse also failed to quash her amusement, her certainty.

Through bloody lips, she laughed.

Valya scowled and continued toward the flight deck.

Seichan continued to laugh, unable to help herself. Only one person would think to find salvation in garbage.

She now knew for certain who was alive and aboard that sub.

The father of her child.

8:22 A.M.

"Do you see anything?" Kowalski asked.

Gray studied the sky through the raised periscope. He had waited an hour before feeling confident that the plane had vacated the area. Either the enemy had exhausted their arsenal, or they had run out of time. He knew the plane couldn't circle around forever, not without risking exposure. The burning island would eventually draw attention, most likely from the U.S. military.

"Skies clear in all directions," Gray announced. He backed from the scope, which had been raised through the raft of debris overhead, and turned to the crew. "Let's get that radio antenna up."

He glanced over to where Palu sat with his cousin Makaio. Both looked on Tua with concern. The man was trembling, his lips cyanotic. Exposure, blood loss, and terror had taken their toll.

Aiko stood next to Kowalski, who huddled under

a blanket. "What's the plan after we get these men to a hospital on Midway?"

For Gray, there was only one option, one path from here.

His eyes settled on Aiko.

"We're going to take the fight to them."

29

"I'm sorry, *Jōnin* Ito."

Takashi knelt at his *kotatsu* table. He no longer felt the warmth of the coals hidden under the antique quilt covering the frame. His morning cup of green tea, roasted with brown rice, sat cooling and forgotten in his palms.

His head remained bowed, ignoring the pale woman's face on the screen of his laptop. Her words from a moment ago were still a knife in his heart.

Those bastards killed your grandson.

He needed to let that sentiment sink to his bones, to settle there, before speaking. She had told him of the midnight raid upon the island base, of Masahiro's bravery, of the cunningness of the man who took his grandson's life. The details were irrelevant; only the outcome mattered.

He wondered as he did many times during his long life.

Am I cursed?

He had lost his beloved Miu in a burst of gunfire in a dark tunnel. Then many years later, his new wife—a kind woman with sweet lips—had succumbed giving birth to Takashi's only son. He had named the boy Akihiko, meaning *bright prince*, hoping such a blessing would balance his tragic entry into this world. And how Takashi had loved the young man he grew into, straight as a reed, with an intelligence that surpassed both his parents. Eventually Akihiko gave Takashi his only grandson—and with this duty done, promptly died a year later with his wife in an automobile accident.

Afterward, Takashi had raised Masahiro as if he were his own son. But there was always a bitterness in the boy, a darkness in his blood, as if the tragedy of the family had taken root in his heart. Despite all his efforts—both gentle and firm—the two of them had never deeply bonded. There had remained an aloofness between them.

Still, one fact was undeniable.

He did love his grandson.

He finally lifted and sipped his tea. He woke each morning at four, using these early hours to meditate with his tea, to watch the sun rise over Mount Fuji from the vantage of his office. The ritual prepared him for the day.

Even this day.

He whispered his breath over the edge of the cup, "*Ichi-go ichi-e.*"

The origin of the old phrase was ascribed to the sixteenth-century tea master Sen no Rikyū, roughly meaning *one time, one chance*. It was a reminder to appreciate those who crossed your path, since they might never do so again. It was a testament to life's impermanence.

It was a lesson Takashi knew all too well.

As the tea wet his lips and loosened his tongue, he stared over the rim of his cup. The early spring morning was cold, etching the flanks of Mount Fuji in frost. Sunlight reflected off the thin ice, setting fire to it.

Both echoed to his heart.

Ice and fire.

He allowed his heart to remain cold, while fury heated his blood.

He spoke with his cup still at his lips. "The bastard who killed my grandson. Where is he?"

"I do not know," the woman admitted.

His eyes flashed back to the screen, letting some of the fire show.

Valya Mikhailov acknowledged his anger with a bow of her head. "But I know where he will be. I have his woman." She lifted her gaze, her own eyes flashing. "And his unborn child."

Takashi lowered his cup to the table. He pictured Miu's smile, her hand on his cheek, her lips on his own. "He will come for them."

"*Hai*." Valya's lips formed a hard line. "She is also sick, parasitized by what Masahiro unleashed back on Hawaii."

He sat straighter, finding satisfaction in this small measure of revenge exacted by his grandson.

Valya continued, "So, yes, he will come for her, for his child—but also for a cure to her affliction."

"Then he will fail."

Takashi stared down into the cooling depths of

his tea. He touched the ice in his heart and admitted a secret he had not even shared with Masahiro. Despite decades of research, one outcome had become clear.

He spoke it aloud.

"There is no cure."

FIFTH

CHRYSALIS

30

"If we keep holing up in medieval buildings," Monk warned, "I'm going to go rent a suit of armor, so I'll fit in better."

Kat smiled, while trying to cover a yawn with her fist. They were all seated around a table in a tiny research library. The chamber was located in the north tower of a quaint thirteenth-century castle. Bookshelves towered all around, so close they loomed above the group, as if peering over their shoulders at the sprawl of old maps on the table.

Kat rubbed her tired eyes.

It was after midnight, and they'd all been running on very little sleep. After resolving a few details in Gdansk, the team had left the Baltic coast and flown to southern Poland, landing in Krakow four hours ago. While they were in the air, their newest teammate—Dr. Damian Slaski—had contacted the management of the Wieliczka Salt Mine and arranged for them to have access to the underground labyrinth after it was closed.

Unfortunately, they were not the first ones to make such a petition. Slaski learned that a subterranean chapel in the mine—the Chapel of St. Kinga—had been rented for a private Midnight Mass. It apparently was not a rare event. Regular church services were held there every Sunday. In addition, the chapel was also available for private weddings, even concerts.

Upon learning of the midnight mass, Slaski had suggested they wait until the ceremony was over before venturing into the mine. At first, Kat had balked at his suggestion, not wanting to lose any more time. To help convince her, the researcher had recommended a short detour.

In hindsight, she now recognized the wisdom of his counsel.

After landing in Krakow, they had traveled twenty minutes to the location of the mine complex. But rather than going directly to the tourist offices, Slaski had led them a couple hundred yards away to the city's history museum. The Muzeum Żup Krakowskich Wieliczka occupied an ancient set of fortifications known as *Zamek Żupny*, or the "Saltworks Castle." For more than seven centuries, the medieval complex of stone-and-timber buildings had been the headquarters for the mine's management board. The Castle oversaw not only the Wieliczka Salt Mine but also its neighbor, the Bochnia Salt Mine.

Clearly, salt had been big business back then. According to Slaski, the mines had once accounted for a full third of the royal income for Polish kings. Even the word *salary* came from the Latin *salarium*, which meant the amount a soldier was paid to buy salt.

Under the tutelage of Dr. Slaski, it did not

take long for Kat to learn the full scope of this industry—along with the challenge ahead of them.

That's why he wanted us to come here first.

She stared across the table at the collection of maps and charts, some dating back to the founding of the mine. Slaski had selected them from the museum's extensive cartography collection, which held more than four thousand maps. A good portion dealt with the area's mining industry. It was here that Slaski had conducted his research into the region's amber deposits for his own museum.

Starting with the oldest maps and moving forward, Slaski had been illustrating the mine's history, basically rebuilding its labyrinth of tunnels and chambers layer by layer. The sheer scope of the place grew to be daunting.

"Let me show you this for some perspective." Slaski laid out a newer map. "This chart was drawn by my dear friend Mariusz Szelerewicz. It offers visitors to the salt mine a vision of what lies underground."

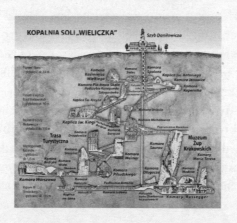

Kat studied the chart's maze of tunnels, shafts, and chambers that made up the complex.

Elena shifted closer, peering through her reading glasses. Despite the late hour, the librarian seemed energized, her eyes flashing with interest, sometimes clucking her tongue as a new map was presented to the group. She was clearly in her element here.

Contrarily, Sam sat across the table, his chin bobbing occasionally as he struggled to stay awake. For an entomologist, the history of mapmaking and mining in the region must hold little interest, plainly not enough to stave off his exhaustion.

Elena traced her finger over the map, her voice worried. "I see how it would be easy to get lost down there."

"Indeed," Slaski said. "And this chart just represents the tourist route through the mine's upper levels. The lowest level depicted on this map is only some hundred meters deep, but the mine delves three times that into the earth."

Elena let out a slight groan. "So over a thousand feet." Her expression was sickly. She clearly did not like the thought of traveling so far underground.

Slaski's next words offered her no reassurance. "Many areas of the deep mine are off-limits due to old collapses and flooding."

Kat frowned. "Flooding?"

Slaski nodded. "When the mine broke into the water table, it created a whole series of lakes and pools at the lowest levels."

Kat began to share Elena's misgivings.

This just gets better and better.

Slaski wasn't done. "The tourist route through the mine is about four kilometers long. But there are actually four hundred kilometers of tunnels." He placed a palm on his friend's map. "This only represents *one percent* of the actual mine."

Monk sighed and leaned back in his chair. "That certainly does give us the *perspective* you promised."

Elena shook her head. "How can we ever hope to discover where Smithson found his amber artifact?"

"And what if we're wrong about this mine?" Sam mumbled, then yawned. "Smithson could've found it at the neighboring mine. Or someplace else entirely."

Kat refused to believe that.

Slaski supported her. "By the eighteen hundreds, tourists were already flocking to Wieliczka. The workers here tolerated the intrusion, but that wasn't the case with other mines."

"Still, even if this is the right place," Elena said, "where do we even begin to look? I mean how many rooms or chambers are even down there?"

"Over two thousand."

Kat closed her eyes, overwhelmed by the magnitude of this salt mine. She was also nagged by the sense that she was missing something important. She'd had the same impression back in Gdansk.

What am I not seeing?

Frustrated and exhausted, she could not pinpoint the source of this feeling.

Slaski waved a hand over the scatter of charts on the table. "As you can see, all the tunnels and rooms are meticulously numbered or named. From the first excavations near the surface to the later ones at the greatest depths."

Kat had noted this on the maps, as generations of mapmakers carried this information forward through the centuries. For some reason, this realization stirred up that nagging sense, but it still failed to bring any enlightenment.

Slaski shrugged. "If only your Mr. Smithson had left behind some clue for us to follow . . ."

Kat sat straighter, abruptly enough to draw everyone's attention.

Could that be it?

Monk stared at her. "Honey, you got that look on your face."

Kat reached over to her satellite phone and tapped and swiped to bring up the photos that Painter had sent of James Smithson's crypt at the Smithsonian Castle. Before they had landed in Gdansk, she had briefly reviewed them. The director was convinced there might be some hidden clue incorporated into his tomb. Painter had highlighted the carving of a serpent, a rock, and a winged insect found on the lip of the crypt, as if Smithson were using such hieroglyphics to hint at what was hidden in his coffin.

On the flight to Krakow, she had even briefly wondered about the scallop shell positioned next to those three symbols. She had toyed with the idea that Smithson might have ordered it placed there as some vague clue pointing to the salt mine, a mine that dug into layers of salt deposited after the ancient Tethys Ocean dried up.

A seashell to represent that ancient sea.

She had eventually dismissed this thought as too fanciful. And even if she were right, how did it help? She was already confident from Smithson's name being found listed as a visitor here that they were on the right track.

But Slaski's mention of numbered rooms— more than two thousand of them—reminded her of a mystery surrounding Smithson's tomb, an error found on his grave that both amused and confounded historians.

She pulled up the photo of the prominent inscription on the marble crypt.

Sacred
to the
Memory
of
James Smithson, ESQ.
Fellow of the Royal Society
London
who died at Genoa
the 26th June 1829.
aged 75 Years.

"Look at this," she said, sharing the picture. She read the last three lines concerning the date of Smithson's death. "... *who died at Genoa, the 26th June 1829, aged 75 Years.*"

"What about it?" Sam asked.

Elena, of course, immediately understood. She removed her reading glasses, her eyes huge. "What's written there is *wrong*. While the date of his death is correct, James Smithson was born June fifth, 1765."

Monk calculated the discrepancy. "That would make him only *sixty-four* when he died, not *seventy-five*."

Sam frowned. "Still, what does a difference of eleven years make?"

"Hopefully all the difference in the world," Kat said. "It's baffled historians that Smithson's beloved nephew should make such a glaring error and have it carved onto his uncle's gravestone. But what if it wasn't a mistake? What if, like the serpent, rock, and wasp, Smithson ordered this error to be inscribed on his tomb?"

"As a clue," Monk said.

Kat turned to Slaski. "You said that by the time the mine closed there were over two thousand rooms. I'm assuming that even when Smithson came here that count had to be pretty close to that number, give or take a couple hundred."

"You are most correct."

Monk understood. "So, Kat, you're thinking Smithson left the room number on his grave, like an address, identifying the spot where he found his artifact?"

"If you subtract seventy-five from the date of his death, you get the year 1754, which we know was *not* the year he was born."

Elena's voice grew hushed with awe. "But maybe it points to the room or tunnel in the mine."

They all turned to Slaski.

"Can you show us on a map where chamber number 1754 is?"

"Of course." He turned and drew his laptop

closer. "I have such information all compiled and cataloged. It should only take a moment."

He tapped for a few seconds, then stepped back. A familiar map glowed on his screen.

"You showed us this before," Elena noted. "Back in Gdansk."

"Yes, it's the map of the mine drawn by Wilhelm Hondius. Only I've highlighted the section of the map designated as 1754."

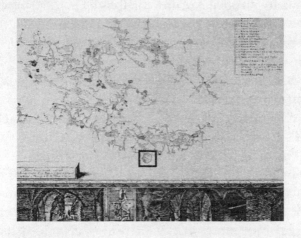

He leaned closer to read the handwritten notes in the map's margin. "This section of the mine also had a name assigned to it. For a rather obvious reason."

"What's the name?" Sam asked.

"*Kaplica Muszli.* Polish for *Chapel of the Seashell.*"

Kat gasped out loud, picturing the prominent scallop at the center of Smithson's tomb.

Slaski zoomed into the highlighted section. "Like I said, the choice of name is fairly obvious."

The map showed an interconnecting loop of tunnels radiating out from a central cavern in the obvious shape of a scallop shell.

"That must be the place," Kat murmured.

Sam seemed less sure. "Why did the miners carve tunnels like this? It doesn't seem very practical."

Slaski shrugged. "When we go down there, you'll better understand."

"Then let's get going." Kat checked her watch. "It's after one. Surely the private mass is over."

Slaski raised a hand. "First, be warned." He pointed at the image on the laptop screen. "The Chapel of the Seashell may look tiny on the map but it actually covers a full square kilometer. Very large. And most of it is in ruins—crumbled into pieces after it was abandoned."

"Why abandoned?" Kat asked, wondering whether this could be another connection to what was reportedly unleashed there.

Slaski had a different explanation. "That section of the mine flooded." He zoomed out the image of the map and circled a section of the neighboring tunnels. "This is all now a lake."

Kat pictured the vast body of water—and the giant seashell resting on its bank, as if washed ashore there.

"We still have to go," she said, looking around to see if anyone objected.

Elena's face shone with trepidation, but she nodded.

With the matter settled, they set off. They were soon hiking across the castle's parklike grounds toward a sprawling structure glowing through the trees. The lights illuminated a yellow building roofed in red clay tiles with an industrial tower looming high above it. The steel erection was the old head frame for the mine, positioned over the Danilowicz Shaft, which drilled down into the heart of the excavation.

As they crossed the park, the night had turned chilly, requiring them to bundle into jackets. Kat kept a close watch for any sign of a tail. Whoever had been following them in Gdansk had never revealed themselves again once they reached Krakow. Earlier, she had only informed Painter and Jason of her intentions to head to southern Poland. She had asked the director to keep her destination secret, even from U.S. intelligence services.

Perhaps such a cover had helped them lose the tail.

But Kat remained wary.

During that call, Painter had also updated her on the situation in Hawaii. As chaos continued to spread, an evacuation plan had been settled upon, though the logistics were still being worked out. The exodus was scheduled to start in half a day. The plan was to start moving the populace via both airlifts and an armada over to Johnston Atoll. It would be a monumental undertaking, requiring international cooperation, but they dared wait no longer, not if they hoped to contain the situation and keep it from spreading globally.

Monk must have noted her consternation. "If anything's here, we'll find it."

We'd better—and soon.

31

This must be the place.

Seichan fought through a fog of pain to study their destination. She sat in the back of a light transport helicopter—a Fuji-Bell 204B. The namesake for this Japanese variant of the American helicopter filled the skies ahead of them. The snow-frosted cone of Mount Fuji stood out starkly against a stack of dark thunderclouds, as if the mountain were holding back the storm.

A lake below reflected that battle.

She recognized Lake Kawaguchiko. The helicopter descended toward a village along its banks. She struggled to remember the town's name, but each beat of the aircraft's rotors pounded in her head, making it hard to concentrate.

Once near the shore, the helicopter swung toward the town's outskirts. As it turned, morning sunlight blazed into the aircraft's hold. Dazzled, Seichan squinted her eyelids to slits, refusing to look away, absorbing every detail below.

The lines of a cable car climbed from the town to the summit of a neighboring peak behind it, where the panoramic views must be stunning. On the lower slopes of the same peak, a multistoried pagoda towered above the treetops. Its glass-and-steel structure reflected and shattered the sunlight, looking like a sculpture of ice and fire.

From the helicopter's angle of approach, she knew it was their destination. She studied the surrounding area. The modern pagoda sat dead center of a walled-off square, easily encompassing a thousand acres. A score of outbuildings dotted the grounds, none taller than two stories, as if refusing to challenge the height of the shining temple.

The aircraft circled to the back of the compound where a helipad blinked with lights. Seichan noted a Japanese garden behind the pagoda, trickling with streams and waterfalls, all surrounding a large koi pond decorated with flowering lily pads. A small wooden bridge arched over the water to a tiny teahouse at the center of the island. The rest of the garden was artfully decorated with maples, cherry and plum trees, and patches of swaying bamboo. In one corner, a rock garden dotted with a plethora of bonsais framed the raked sand of a meditative space.

Seichan tried to absorb the peace and serenity of those gardens, knowing the challenges ahead. She still tasted blood on her tongue, oozing from her lip, split and swollen from Valya's fist. Her attacker sat up front with the pilot. The woman had ignored her during the five-hour flight to Tokyo, allowing Seichan a couple of hours of fitful sleep. She appreciated the short amount of rest. The hop from Tokyo to this lakeside town had taken only twenty minutes.

From here, she suspected there would only be pain.

Even now, she felt Ken Matsui studying her from the next seat, silently evaluating her every wince, flinch, and gasp. Twenty-four hours had passed since she was parasitized. By now, thousands of larvae had molted into their second instars. In another twenty-four, they would do so again. At that point, the hungry legion would begin migrating into her bones, where they would continue their feast, while also seeding her marrow with cystic clones of themselves.

In twenty-four hours . . .

As they landed, a gust of wind struck the helicopter. The skids hit the pad hard. The impact jarred through her, enough to awaken the horde inside her. Pain burst in her lower belly and radiated through her limbs. She tried to ride out the agony, but it only grew worse. Pain rebounded from her limbs back to her stomach, stoking the flames inside her—then back out again.

Stop . . . please stop . . .

It didn't.

At some point, she simply passed out. She woke to a clap of thunder and the icy spatter of raindrops on her face. She was on her back, strapped to a gurney near the helipad. Overhead, half the sky was bruised and dark, the other sunny and blue. The storm was sweeping in fast, propelled by cold winds.

Her gurney was rushed toward the open steel doors of a squat cement-block building. Once inside, she was escorted down a ramp to a subterranean tunnel. Fluorescent lights ran along the ceiling, blurring together as she hovered on a razor's edge of agony. Each bump of the gurney jacked the pain up another notch.

She fought to compartmentalize that torture, to bottle it into a corner of her mind.

It proved impossible.

The pain was too variable. It was a tiger ripping through her insides, lashing out, then going quiet, only to spring again somewhere else in her body.

Hot tears ran down her cheeks. Her breath heaved in and out.

She tried to focus on where she was going, mapping a layout in her head. She suspected she was being whisked toward the pagoda, toward its subterranean levels.

At some point, she slipped into a hazy delirium, only to be snapped back by Ken's sharp voice. "Where are you taking her?"

She blinked and let her head fall in the direction of his voice.

Valya had Ken's arm in her pale grip. As the gurney was roughly jerked into a passageway to the left, Ken was being dragged the other way.

Separating us . . .

Valya's voice carried over to her. "Med ward," she answered. "She'll get a full physical. Including evaluating her pregnancy. With a little luck there, she'll become our prized guinea pig."

Apprehension swelled through Seichan, holding back the pain. It wasn't fear for herself—but for her child. Despite the peril of the situation, she was more than willing to undergo a thorough examination. Throughout the ravages of pain, one question persisted.

Is my baby still alive?

Up until now, with all the strife and mayhem, she had pushed that worry deep down, where it had burned like a hot coal. As each hour passed since leaving Maui, the pressure of that unanswered question mounted.

She needed to know the answer.

Unfortunately, the intensity of that desire could only stave off the agony for so long. As she was shoved into an elevator, the gurney hit the back wall. The jolt struck through her like an electrical shock, amplifying the pain into a crescendo.

The world went gray—then black.

When she woke again, she had no idea how much time had passed. She was now in a hospital bed, her wrists and ankles cuffed to the frame. Someone had stripped her and placed her in a hospital gown, which was folded up to her breasts.

A pair of blue-smocked medical personnel—maybe a doctor and nurse—flanked the bed. The nurse finished swiping an icy lubricant over her exposed abdomen. The sudden chill on her heated skin must have stirred Seichan back to consciousness. The doctor held the wand of an ultrasound, while he calibrated the unit at her bedside.

"All set here," he said quietly in Japanese and turned to the bed. His gaze noted her open eyes. "Ah, and it seems our patient is awake. She has quite the constitution to withstand Level Two pain without meds."

Seichan ignored the compliment and merely

glared at him. He was a small man with delicate features and a thin mustache. She could've broken him in two in a heartbeat, but even if free, she would've held off. For the moment, he was the most important man in the world, the only one who could settle the question aching inside her.

"Should I administer a fentanyl patch?" the nurse asked. She was a round-faced older woman with a stern expression worn into her features. "Her temperature is hovering at a dangerous level, most likely due to the pain."

"Let's hold off for the moment." He shrugged. "She's already gone this long without analgesics, and I don't want any opioids in her system if she's pregnant. If this scan proves to be positive, we can always induce a coma afterward."

"*Hai*, Dr. Hamada."

The nurse shifted over to the ultrasound unit, while the doctor reached across Seichan's body with the wand of the transducer probe. As it touched her skin, the doctor turned to her, addressing her directly for the first time.

"I'm afraid this will hurt."

"Do it," she said.

"Very good." He nodded to his nurse, who flipped a switch.

Seichan braced herself, balling her fingers into the bedsheet under her. At first, there was only a sharp pressure on her abdomen as the probe was rolled across her belly. Then the wand suddenly became a scalpel, carving deep into her core. She screamed, unable to restrain herself. She stared over the edge of her folded gown, expecting to see her bowels bursting from a gaping wound.

There was nothing.

The doctor's shoulder hunched against her outburst. "The larvae are sensitive to sound waves," he explained. "It sends them into a frenzy. What you're feeling is them fleeing from the ultrasonic waves."

His explanation—while intended to be helpful—only made the experience a hundredfold worse. She pictured masses of larvae ripping through tissue and muscle in a roiling panic.

"Do you need a break?" he asked.

Unable to speak, she whipped her head back and forth, like a wild horse trying to shake off a bit.

Keep going . . .

He nodded and continued his examination, drawing and quartering her with his probe. Sweat and tears flushed her cheeks. Pain blinded her. Nails dug through the sheets into the skin.

Then suddenly—when she was certain she could take it no longer—the agony ebbed. She gasped with relief, half-sobbing, too anguished to care.

"There we go." Dr. Hamada leaned back so Seichan could see the screen. With his free hand, he pointed to a fluttering of gray pixels. "Your baby's heartbeat."

Still alive . . .

An indescribable joy flooded through her.

"We know second instars avoid their host's vital organs, like the heart and brain," Hamada said. "Luckily, your pregnancy must be far enough along for the fetus's tiny heartbeats and minuscule brain waves to stave off the larvae. At least for now."

Hamada must have noted her deep frown at his last words and explained: "Third instars are not as forgiving. Once they've ensured their genetic continuance by seeding a bone's marrow with their crytobiotic clones, they are less concerned with the host's survival."

A countdown began to run in a corner of Seichan's mind.

Twenty-four hours . . .

Hamada lifted the wand away and the ultrasound screen went dark, erasing the thin fluttering. She would have traded her right arm for another few seconds of seeing her baby's heartbeat.

Losing the anchor of that heartbeat, she could no longer hold on. The room faded around her.

As she sank away, she heard Hamada speaking to the nurse.

"Her fetus looks vital and unharmed."

She felt relief at his prognosis, but he was not done speaking.

"It should make an ideal specimen for the next stage of our experiments."

8:32 A.M.

If I wasn't so terrified, I'd be impressed.

Ken gawked at the sprawling underground lab. It dwarfed his own facilities back at Cornell, which had taken him a decade to construct through the judicious cobbling together of university grants and funds from corporate sponsors.

His tour guide—Dr. Yukio Oshiro—stood a head taller than Ken, but so thin-limbed, he looked spidery, which was fitting considering Ken was familiar with the man's published papers on arachnid venoms.

"We're already moving forward with Phase One clinical trials for an ion-channel blocker to treat muscular dystrophy," Oshiro extolled, ending with an exasperated sigh. "This way."

The man plainly resented being assigned this role.

As they continued across the circular space, Oshiro nodded every now and then to a fellow scientist, who stopped to bow more deeply in a sign of respect, which the man clearly demanded.

"Of course, we have groups working on other drugs." Oshiro pointed them out. "Alpha Team is studying a promising analgesic. Beta, an antitumor medication. Gamma, an agricultural pesticide. I could go on and on. The potential here is nearly bottomless. We've barely scratched the surface."

"And all of these compounds were culled from the venom of the ancient wasps?"

"The *Odokuro*, as you named them." Oshiro gave a small dismissive shake of his head. In Japanese corporate culture, it was the equivalent of raising a middle finger at Ken. "We received a memo to start using that name. Seems you've won a measure of respect from Takashi Ito."

And likely why I'm being given this grand tour.

Ken knew he was being groomed to join the staff. From Oshiro's cold manner, the man must feel threatened.

Ken studied the place with a discerning eye. He didn't have to pretend to admire the facility. Banks of equipment and tools filled the room. Most he knew; some he didn't. Besides being larger than his own lab, it was far better equipped.

He quickly noted a pattern to the space. It was divided into two distinct halves, each doing different work on the venom collected from the many incarnations of these wasps. From his own experience, he knew typical poison glands contained hundreds of different chemicals and molecules.

One side of the lab seemed devoted to studying the *proteomics*—the proteins and peptides—of the wasp's venom. This was evident from the many humming banks of mass spectrometers, along with a trio of huge gel electrophoresis machines used to separate out proteins.

Still, other pieces of equipment were a mystery.

Oshiro must have noted his puzzled expression. His voice took on a gloating tone. "Over there, Alpha Team is doing flow cytometry, employing femto- and pico-second lasers to inspect and separate out advantageous-looking proteins."

"Impressive," he said and meant it.

"And *necessary*, as you know when faced with such small samples."

He nodded. It was one thing to milk a snake for its venom, which generally produced a decent investigative sample, but it was another matter when trying to do the same with a spider—or in this case, a wasp.

Ken turned his attention to the other half of the lab, a space clearly devoted to *genomics*. Here, nucleotide sequencers were being used to study the RNA and DNA associated with venom production, along with gathering valuable transcriptomic data.

He knew from his own experience how tricky venom could be. What was found in a poison gland could vary greatly depending on the sex of the species, the type of food, even the ambient temperature. Sometimes it was easier to sequence the DNA and reverse-engineer the toxic peptide, rather than hunting it down.

Ken nodded over to where Gamma Team was working on a sequencer. "You've got some serious next-gen tech. Your lab must be capable of performing some incredible high-throughput analyses of the venom."

"Certainly, but it's not like we don't hit walls." Oshiro stared over at the group. "For example, Gamma has discovered fragments of a promising RNA transcript, including the gene that produced it—but they've been struggling to *find* the actual protein it's supposed to synthesize."

"Like discovering a shadow but not the object casting it."

"Exactly." Oshiro offered a rare smile, warming up to Ken, as competing colleagues sometimes do when talking shop. "The gene is ubiquitous across all incarnations of the species, but the protein it encodes still escapes us. It's why we need the best minds."

Off the cuff, Ken could already think of several different reasons for the missing protein, but he stayed silent. Especially as he felt Oshiro was dancing toward an invitation to work here . . . an invitation that Ken dared not refuse. So instead, he quickly changed the subject, pointing to the back of the lab, to a set of prominent red steel doors.

"What's through there?"

Oshiro put his hands on his hips, his features hardening into a scowl. "Nothing for us to worry about, apparently. All I know is that the team leader on that side—Dr. Hamada—frequently commandeers our entire lab, shooing us out of here like so many flies. It's very aggravating and disruptive."

"What are they researching?"

He shrugged. "All I know is that it has something to do with the evolutionary history of the *Odokuro*."

Ken frowned. "Why? To what end?"

Another dismissive shrug, as if to state *It's not my research, so why should I care?*

Ken allowed himself to be led away. In the past, he had run into such narrow-mindedness among other scientists. It was an easy trap to fall into, one that led to mistakes and missed opportunities. Over the years, he had learned it was better not to suppress scientific curiosity in any form.

A lesson that was especially important here.

As Oshiro continued his tour, Ken kept a sidelong focus on the red doors.

What's really going on behind there?

8:35 A.M.

Kneeling at his office table, Takashi tented his fingers before his lips as he studied the camera feed on his laptop. The view was into a locked hospital ward, with the lens focused on a single bed. The woman secured there slipped into and out of delirium, occasionally thrashing in her restraints, mostly sleeping. Her brow shone with fever sweat, her lips dried and cracked.

Still, he recognized the beauty behind the illness. Her mixed blood—Asian and European—had seemed to draw out the best of both heritages. Her bruised lips, if painted, would form a perfect bow. Her cheekbones, arched high and wide, narrowed to a perfect chin. Her black hair was cut straight and sharp, both efficient yet accenting her features with a simplicity that reminded him of his beloved Miu.

There was a soft knock on the door before it swung open.

His personal secretary bowed and stepped aside to allow the woman Takashi had summoned into his office. Valya entered like a storm, her ice-blue eyes flashing with lightning. The rain-heavy clouds rolling over Mount Fuji greeted her with a clap of thunder that rattled the windows.

This time, the woman cast aside any pretense of masking her pale features. He was momentarily unsettled. She looked so ethereal, ghostly. It was as if the black tattoo were all that was holding her to this plane.

She bowed deeply and upon his signal, knelt opposite him.

"*Chūnin* Mikhailov," he greeted her, using her new title, a position she had inherited from Masahiro.

She kept her chin down. Her head bowed incrementally at this acknowledgment of her raised status.

He returned his attention to the laptop screen and to the captive strapped on the bed. "She is with child?"

"*Hai*. Dr. Hamada has confirmed her pregnancy."

"Very good."

He studied the woman on the screen. She and the others had cost him his grandson. It was only right for him to repay them in kind.

He pictured what would happen next.

Back during the war, he had visited the Imperial Army's research camps at Zhongma Fortress. There, too, pregnant women—Chinese mothers forcibly removed from nearby villages—were experimented upon with chemical and biological weapons. Afterward, their babies were cut from their wombs without anesthesia. He could still hear their screams, see those weak arms reaching for bloody children before death claimed them.

Back then, new to the *Kage*, he had to hide his revulsion at such atrocities.

Now I will relish it.

He intended for another to suffer as much.

"The American?" he asked.

"No word. But if he survived, he will come for her." The woman paused too deliberately, clearly refraining from speaking.

"What is it?"

She glanced to the screen, then back down. "You said before that there was no cure for what afflicts her."

He understood the question behind this statement. "You wonder why we took such a risk in releasing something we could not control."

"*Hai, Jōnin* Ito."

"It is not out of madness, but calculation," he assured her. "What was released in Hawaii was only an example. Once the world comprehends the threat, only then will we move forward with the second phase."

She glanced up, her brows pinched. "Second phase?"

"Ikikauō Atoll was not our *only* staging ground."

Her eyes widened with shock.

"Other locations are ready to move upon my order. To spread the *Odokuro* across Europe, Russia, China, Australia. Unfortunately, we lost control of our site off the coast of Brazil, almost exposing our plan for South America. Still, by our conservative calculations, the world will be overrun in two years."

She looked aghast, anger threading her words. "So you mean to destroy the world?"

"No." He matched her anger with cold command. "Like I said, it's not madness, but calculation."

He read her confusion and sighed, lowering his voice as if quieting a child. "What drugs do you think are the most profitable?"

She was taken aback by the abrupt change and simply shook her head.

"It is not a medication that can *cure* a disease.

There's limited profit in such one-time fixes. Instead, consider those drugs needed to treat the *symptoms* from an incurable disease. That is a guaranteed lifelong revenue stream. It is a lesson I learned long ago as the founder of this company."

"And you're applying this lesson here?"

He didn't bother acknowledging the obvious.

"But how?" she asked.

"I don't intend to destroy the world, but simply bring it to its knees."

"Still, if there's no cure . . . ?" she asked haltingly, trying to understand.

"In a year, when the world is suffering and in chaos, our corporation will offer a palliative for their symptoms. While we have no cure for the parasitized, we have developed an aerial spray that will kill the adult wasp populations. It took us over two decades to perfect. It's extremely toxic, nearly impossible to duplicate, and will do great damage. Still, it will allow countries to survive, to limp along."

Comprehension slowly dawned in her eyes. "Yet, they'll never be safe. With their environment contaminated and parasitized, the *Odokuro* will rise again and again."

"An incurable disease that only *we* can knock back down and hold in check."

"So, in the end, the world will become dependent on Japan, on your corporation."

"And if anyone resists," he said with a shrug, "we hold back the spraying for a few months until they fall back in line."

"But what about Japan?"

"We will remain unscathed during the initial overrun. We already have the natural advantage of being isolated and quarantined by our surrounding seas, but a secret program of spraying will commence immediately to protect our shores. We will be the only country standing strong in a year, ready to offer relief to those who bend a knee to a new Imperial Japan."

She sat back on her ankles, absorbing this all. "You'll have taken over the world without firing a single shot."

"After nine decades, I've learned armies rise and fall. From the Tokugawa shoguns who succumbed to Japan's emperors long ago, to those same emperors who were brought low by Allied forces. True strength is not found at the tip of a sword or the barrel of a gun, but in ingenuity and innovation."

Chūnin Mikhailov stared back at him, her eyes unreadable now, reflecting the dark storm beyond the windows. Finally, she closed her eyes and lowered her forehead to the floor.

He accepted her deference by folding his fingers in his lap, knowing soon . . .

. . . *the entire world will be forced to bow before us.*

32

"Off to the salt mines, we go!" Monk said cheerily.

Elena cringed at the clank of the large red elevator doors as they were slammed closed. She concentrated on breathing through her nose and out her
mouth, a calming technique she had learned from
the old *Oprah Winfrey Show*. While growing up as
the daughter of migrant workers, that was all her
family could afford as "therapy."

Ever since she was a young girl, she could never
tolerate cramped spaces. Her parents believed it was
a buried memory from when her family was led
through a tunnel from a warehouse in Tijuana to
San Diego. It was a route used by the Sinaloa Car-
tel to move drugs—and for the right price, workers and families could buy passage through to the
United States.

"How are you holding up?" Sam asked her, keeping close by her side as the elevator sank into the
bowels of the earth.

Her fingertips tapped the two crucifixes hanging
from the chain of her reading glasses, a nervous tic.

She forced her hand down. "I keep telling myself we're just heading into the basement of a library."

"Then this place has a pretty darned deep basement," Sam said with a wry grin.

She scolded him with a look that said, *You're not helping.*

"Sorry." He held out a hand. "Maybe this will serve as an apology."

She wanted to decline, refusing to be seen as the sort of woman who needed to lean on a man.

Screw it.

She took his hand. His palm was dry and warm. He squeezed with a generous amount of reassurance. She refused to be embarrassed. On the way here, she had made no effort to hide her fear, preferring to be frank with everyone in case she had to abandon the mine and leave this hunt to the others.

Her plan forward was to ignore the bigger picture—like being buried a thousand feet underground—and concentrate on moving one step at a time. Of course, she couldn't do that while stuck in an elevator. The enclosed space trapped her anxiety, amplifying her fear.

Across the cage, Kat turned to their two escorts. After arriving at the mine, Damian Slaski had introduced them to the mine's public relations officer, a young pretty blond woman named Clara Baranska. From the way the dour-faced Slaski kept looking doggedly at the woman, he was plainly infatuated. Elena suspected the man's frequent visits to the nearby museum weren't entirely based on research alone.

"Dr. Slaski," Kat said, "you mentioned before that the Hondius map had *two* amber sites marked on it. Were either of them anywhere near the Chapel of the Seashell?"

Elena focused on his answer, using the conversation to distract her from the descent into the mine.

"No, that does not appear to be the case. Both sites were small and emptied of their deposits long before Mr. Smithson visited here."

Clara nodded. "No mine would let such a discovery go to waste. While salt was valuable in the past, amber was much more so. Even today, a modest amber bracelet costs the equivalent of a Rolex watch."

"Because of such value," Slaski added, "many sites were pillaged by black miners."

As a Hispanic woman, Elena had a knee-jerk reaction to such casual racism. "What do you mean by *black* miners?"

Slaski clarified his statement. "I'm referring to miners who raid other excavations or secretly pocket a portion of their own load, then sell the stolen gain on the black market. In fact, two out of every three pieces of amber sold today were acquired illegally."

The bump of the elevator interrupted the conversation. As the doors opened, music flowed inside, solemn and melancholy. Upon hearing this, Elena felt a chill that had nothing to do with the cool sixty degrees of the mine. The melody had a foreboding quality to it, as if marking all their funerals.

Clara had a more mundane explanation as she stepped out of the elevator. "The midnight mass must be just concluding. I heard they started late."

Monk followed with a smile for his wife. "So I guess that would make this an *after*-midnight mass."

Kat shoved him forward, while Sam urged Elena along with an encouraging tug on her arm. He still held her hand—or rather, she clutched his.

As she exited into a tunnel that stretched to the right and left, she was struck by the salty tang to the air, along with the clammy humidity. It felt like walking along a seabed, where the water had dissipated, leaving only its salty spirit behind.

Still, she breathed harder, as if drowning down here.

Any pretense that she was in some basement was dismissed when she stared up the throat of a wooden staircase that paralleled the elevator and climbed eight hundred steps back to the surface.

Thank God we didn't have to climb down those like the typical tourist.

"We're only ninety meters deep here," Clara said.

Only?

Elena fought not to scoff.

Their guide pointed to the stretch of the tunnel to the left. "That way leads to a chamber dedicated to the astronomer Copernicus. You'll also find St. Anthony's Chapel, the oldest in the mine, going back four hundred years."

Slaski waved in the opposite direction. "But we'll be going this way, as it's a more direct path to the chapel we're seeking."

Clara nodded. "I've sent three men ahead of us, all the way down to the lake to prepare matters for your crossing." She smiled over at them. "They're my three older brothers."

"Sounds like it's a family affair down here," Monk said, meaning it as a joke.

Clara took it seriously. "Of course. Salt is in our blood. My father and grandfather before him worked here while the mine was still operational." She waved them to follow, like a young schoolmarm herding her pupils. "Come, we have far to go."

As they set off, the music slowly grew louder. Low voices eventually could be heard, singing along with the hymn, echoing up from below. The tunnel transected a series of rooms, chambers, and niches, mostly depicting dioramas of mining life, including full-size models of workers, even horses.

Slaski nodded to one of the four-legged miners. His mood grew even more glum. "Horses spent their entire lives down here. Never seeing the sunlight."

"And in the early centuries," Clara added, "so did some miners."

Slaski shrugged, plainly more concerned about the horses.

As they clambered down a series of wooden stairs into other chambers, some of the original mining equipment was shown to be still functional, including a giant horizontal wheel geared to winches that was used to haul material up and down shafts. Natural forces were also utilized here, as evidenced by a huge waterwheel still turning under a steady stream. It looked like it had been churning there for centuries.

Sam still had hold of Elena's hand. She didn't care how it looked. While the mining history was interesting, it wasn't distracting enough from the weight of rock overhead.

Sam stared up there, too, but his concern was different. "I don't understand," he said. "Where's all the salt?"

She had wondered the same. The rock here was shades of dark gray, offset by whitewashed timber and logs supporting the walls and roof.

Clara smiled at his question and waved an arm. "It's all around you. Everything you see is salt in its natural form. Go ahead and scrape a finger and taste it."

Sam matched her grin. "My momma taught me never to go licking walls. So I'll take your word for it."

"Why's all the wood around here painted white?" Monk asked.

"Mostly to better reflect the light from the miners' oil lamps." She pointed to the hard hat she wore outfitted with a modern battery-powered lamp. They were all similarly equipped, though they wouldn't need the lights until they reached the off-limits area of the mine.

Clara patted one of the logs with clear affection. "Over time, salt has impregnated the old wood, making it harder, almost like stone now. Besides its strength, wood was also good because it would talk to the miners."

Monk raised an eyebrow. "Talk?"

"Logs would often groan when under too much pressure, warning of a pending collapse, offering workers time to escape." She gave the timber a final pat. "Of course, they've grown silent over the years."

Elena stared at the logs, willing them to continue to remain quiet.

As they delved ever deeper, some of the rooms and niches began to reveal the miners' artistic handiwork. Sculptures carved out of salt appeared, from fanciful dragons to even Snow White's seven dwarves. Several of the statues were backlit, making them seem to glow with an inner warmth.

Clara stopped at the entrance to one chamber and clicked on her helmet's lamp, casting her light across the dark threshold. Her beam lit up the bust of a crowned figure with a prominent beard.

"It is only fitting we acknowledge Casmir the Great," Clara said. "Especially as it's considered bad luck not to do so."

If that was the case, Elena was happy to stop.

"Casmir was the last Polish king of the Piast dynasty. He was a very liberal king. He encouraged science and the pursuit of knowledge, even founding the University of Krakow. In addition, he was the only European leader who openly welcomed and encouraged Jews to settle in Poland, which they did in great numbers."

Her voice trailed off. She avoided recounting the fate of the descendants of these settlers centuries later when Nazi Germany invaded Poland.

In a more somber tone, she added, "Let's move on."

After a steep descent down a long tunnel, they began to run into clutches of people heading up. The men were dressed in dark suits, the women in matching dresses. The music they had been following into the mine had stopped at some point as the midnight mass ended. The parishioners were starting to leave. Voices grew louder ahead, carried by the salty acoustics.

At last their party reached the source, stepping out onto a wide balcony that overlooked a cavernous three-story space.

"The crown jewel of the Wieliczka mine," Clara announced. "The Chapel of St. Kinga."

Elena gaped at the wondrous site. It was more a cathedral than a mere chapel. Massive chandeliers, glowing with crystals of rock salt, hung from a vaulted roof. At the far end, a giant crucifix loomed over a stone altar, all sculpted of salt. Illuminated niches along the walls to either side shone with great masterworks from generations of miners. There were biblical scenes of Mary and Joseph arriving in Bethlehem, a nativity crèche lit by a tiny salt-carved baby Jesus. Even the walls and floors had been cut and polished to look like bricks and octagonal tiles.

The majority of the parishioners still milled below, easily numbering two hundred—though the room looked like it could hold twice that. A few people trailed up the two sweeping stone staircases on their long journey back to the surface.

For the moment, Elena didn't even envy their leaving. She let go of Sam's hand and wandered up to the balustrade to better view this crystalline cathedral, a Sistine Chapel made of salt.

"The chamber is named after St. Kinga," Clara explained. "Legend has it that Lady Kinga, a Hungarian princess, was betrothed by her father to the

Prince of Krakow. Before leaving Hungary, she cast her engagement ring into a salt mine in her home country. Then upon arriving in Krakow she ordered a group of miners to dig. In that new excavation, the workers discovered a large lump of salt—and inside it was Lady Kinga's ring. Since that time, she has become the patron saint of miners."

"She should've just filed an insurance claim for the lost ring," Monk whispered. "Would've saved a lot of backbreaking labor."

Clara scolded him with a deep frown.

Clearly one didn't disparage a saint—especially in her own domain.

A bit miffed, Clara led them away from the balcony and back into the tunnels heading deeper into the mine. As they descended through a labyrinth of caves, tunnels, and sculpted rooms, they began to reach chambers flooded with emerald-green pools. Wooden catwalks bridged the still waters, reflecting their scatter of lights. Along the bottom, a layer of coins shone like some lost dragon's horde, left behind by centuries of visitors casting prayers and wishes into those depths.

"Have we already reached the water table?" Kat asked. "Is that why they're flooded?"

"No, these small pools were formed from ages of rainwater seeping down here. The much larger lakes lie *twice* as far down from where we are now."

Elena groaned. She meant to do so softly, but the acoustics of salt and water amplified her complaint. Sam found her hand again. She did not object.

Clara led them through the last of the tourist route until she reached a long traverse that inclined steeply down. The passageway ahead had no strings of lights or gently glowing salt statues, only a stygian darkness that seemed to go on forever.

"We'll need our own lamps from here," Clara said, switching on her helmet light.

They all followed her example. As backup, they also carried flashlights. With her free hand, Elena clutched hers in an iron grip.

As Clara led the way, Monk leaned to Kat and quoted from Dante's *Inferno*, reciting the words said to be inscribed at the entrance to hell.

"Abandon all hope, ye who enter here."

3:42 A.M.

Kat stood at the bank of a wide lake. The scatter of their helmet lamps cast spears of light over the dark water. The beams reflected off its mirror-flat surface and flickered across the low vault of rough stone above. The air here was damp with the seaside scent of saltwater.

The lake stretched so far that she could not make out the far bank.

Its sheer breadth boggled.

Clara shared an anecdote to put the size in perspective. "We entertained windsurfers on this lake a few years back. It was amazing to see their sails sweeping across the dark cavern."

"Propelled by what wind?" Monk asked. He held up a finger as if searching for that breeze.

Clara smiled. "They brought in big fans powered by generators."

"In other words, they cheated," Monk grumbled.

"We sometimes have to *improvise* to accommodate guests," Clara corrected. "Like tonight."

She waved to where her three brothers stood along the bank beside a small Zodiac pontoon boat and a Sea-Doo Jet Ski. Dressed in waterproof gear, the trio—all as blond as their sister and as muscular as wrestlers—had collected the watercraft from elsewhere in the flooded levels of the mine and ridden them here to meet up with Kat's group. Evidently these lower levels had become series of pools, lakes, and twisting canals, all interconnecting to form a watery labyrinth.

"My brothers have also brought along some excavating tools in case you should discover this lost amber deposit and desire to collect a sample for your museum's collection."

Clara nodded respectfully to Elena Delgado.

Kat checked her watch, all too mindful of the passing of time. "Then we should be going."

It had taken them more than ninety minutes to traverse the lower half of the mine after leaving the tourist route. The paths through these levels were less maintained, frosted with rills of salt. They had to climb down rickety stairs, even a series of ladders that were white with encrusted rime.

Everything looked strangely intact, preserved over the decades, if not centuries, due to the high sodium atmosphere.

Along the way, they also found further evidence of the miners' artistic bent: a tiny niche shielding the figure of a Madonna with child, a handful of biblical quotes inscribed into the walls. And they crossed the path of many standing figures whose features were blurred by ancient runnels of white salt. They stood like ghostly sentinels along their route, as if warning them back.

Kat was happy to climb into the pontoon boat for this final leg of their journey. According to Dr. Slaski, the Chapel of the Seashell lay on the far side of this lake.

Clara's brother Piotr untethered the boat and then hopped in the stern. Another brother, Anton, manned the Zodiac's engine and yanked it to life. Gerik, the last sibling, waded to the Jet Ski, mounted it, and added its engine to the chorus of rumbling.

The noise reverberated off the low ceiling, strong enough to be felt in Kat's rib cage.

Once ready, the group set off across the lake, led by a swivel-mounted lamp at the bow end of the pontoon. Piotr took up position there, watching from the front for any obstructions hidden beneath the surface.

Slaski interrupted the vague tension by turning to Sam. "Back at the museum, you asked *why* the miners should dig out such a unique structure as the Seashell Chapel. Perhaps now you understand after all you've seen. After spending their lifetimes down here, they sought to leave some trace of themselves behind, a legacy for those who would follow."

Clara concurred. "Besides the sculptures and decorations, you'll find other chambers of the mine that were transformed through their labor into pieces of art."

"Like back at the Chapel of Saint Kinga," Elena said.

"That's correct."

The conversation died down again, as if squashed to silence by the weight of the roof. It also didn't help that the stone ceiling slowly lowered upon them as they crossed. By the time the boat's lamp pierced the darkness to reveal the far shore, Kat could have reached up and brushed her fingertips along the salty ceiling.

Everyone instinctively hunkered down.

At first, it appeared this side of the lake ended at a solid wall, but then Piotr guided the boat to the left, revealing a channel exiting the lake and curving out of sight. They were soon off the main lake and idling slowly along the narrower canal. It made an S-shaped path, which ended at a smooth slope of rock.

The bow of the pontoon bumped into it and rode slightly up onto that stone beach.

The slope rose up into a large cavern, though it was only a quarter of the size of the cathedral to Saint Kinga.

Slaski stood and pointed ahead. "The entrance to *Kaplica Muszli*."

Kat pictured the map that the museum director had shown them and imagined this cavern must be the pelvis of the scallop shell. Even from here, she could see the dark outlines of passages exiting one side of the cavern, radiating out to form the veins of the shell.

Relieved to have safely reached here, Kat got everyone moving. They clambered out of the boat and scaled the slope into the cavern. Upon seeing the condition of this section of the mine, Kat's relief quickly faded.

Their lights revealed half the tunnels were filled with rubble from old collapses. Even in the intact passageways, water dripped and leaked from cracks and fissures in the ceiling.

Kat pictured rainwater seeping all the way down here. The dissolved salts had hardened into crusts, caking everything into a snow-white landscape. Frozen sheets of rime covered the walls. Long, fragile-looking crystal icicles hung from the roofs of the tunnels.

She despaired of ever finding the source of Smithson's artifact. For all anyone knew, it was already buried under tons of rock from the old cave-ins.

"We have to go look," Monk reminded her, reading her as he always did.

She nodded and clicked on her flashlight, adding its light to her helmet's shine. Others followed suit.

Sam frowned at the number of tunnels. "I guess from here it's a matter of eeny, meeny, miny, or moe."

"Maybe we should split up," Monk said. "We can cover more ground."

Elena scowled. "When is that ever a sound plan?"

"She's right," Kat said. "For now, we stick together. We don't have time to waste hunting down anyone who gets lost."

With the matter settled, Kat set off down the far right tunnel, planning to proceed systemically through this maze. Anton and Gerik stayed behind with a radio, ready to ferry any tools they might need from the boat.

The group forged down the dark passageway. It was wide enough for two people to walk abreast. Still, they had to often break through blockades of salt stalactites to pass. All the while, streams of water ran underfoot, trailing a slow path toward the flooded labyrinth behind them.

Kat searched all around, sweeping both her flashlight and helmet lamp across the walls and ceilings, looking for any clue that Smithson had been here.

While she failed to find anything, she had at least chosen wisely. Though it took them nearly a half hour, they reached the end of the passageway. It had easily been a quarter-mile long. She remembered Slaski's description of the size of the Seashell Chapel.

A full square kilometer.

They still had a lot of ground to cover.

The tunnel ended at a thin cavernous arcade that swept across what would be the large rim of the scallop. It was here where all the radiating passageways ended. The cavern's roof sloped from overhead and slanted to the floor, forming the sharp edge of the shell.

Kat started to turn toward the next tunnel, ready to circle back to where they started, intending to crisscross back and forth until she had covered as much of this "shell" as humanly possible.

"Look at this," Elena said.

The librarian was down on one knee, pointing her flashlight up toward the low roof as it slanted to the floor. Like in the tunnels, salt had formed a blockade of stalactites, spikes, and pillars that barred off the back half of the long cavern. It looked like a frost-coated prison gate that ran the length of the arcade.

Kat and the others joined Elena.

Her beam splashed across the low roof. The light revealed a riotous bas-relief carved into the salt. Kat added her light, as did the others as they spread out along the barrier.

Though rimed in salt and crumbled in places, the surface appeared to depict a great battle. Winged angels flew across the upper half, wielding spears and bows. Below, twisted demons tried to scrabble out of the underworld, with gnashing teeth and clawing limbs. The Gothic grotesqueness of the motif reminded Kat of a Hieronymus Bosch painting, but one sculpted out of salt.

"Did you know this was here?" Kat asked, not taking her eyes from the sight.

Slaski moaned, "No . . ."

Clara was less firm. "I had heard rumors of some hellish artwork in the deep mine, but few travel this far. Due to the flooding and the risk of cave-ins, I doubt anyone has been to this section in years, and considering all the salt we had to break through to get over to this side . . ." She shook her head. "I doubt anyone's set foot back here in decades, if not longer."

Kat straightened and pointed her flashlight along the curving cavern. It had to stretch a half mile. She knew they had no choice.

"We'll need to search its entire length."

No one argued, sensing the magnitude of the discovery.

"Keep an eye out for anything that might be significant or out of the ordinary."

Sam grimaced as he stared down the length of the macabre decoration. "Like any of this is *ordinary*."

They set off single file, with Clara leading. Their flashlight beams bobbed and played across the Gothic masterpiece, adding additional shadow and substance to the battlefield.

Seven pairs of eyes scanned for every detail.

Kat noted the anomaly first, almost skipping past it. She backstepped into Monk to fix her light there.

He spotted it then, too, and whispered to her, "We've seen this little bugger before, haven't we?"

Everyone joined them, adding their lights.

It was hidden among the angels, just another winged figure, hovering above the demon horde.

Kat recognized the symbol—as it had also graced Smithson's tomb.

It was a winged insect, maybe a moth, but she knew better.

It was a wasp.

"We need to get a closer look," she said.

In short order, the group smashed through the salt icicles and columns to reach the symbol. Like much of the sprawling artwork, it was crusted with a rime of salt, smudging its details.

Kat reached for her water bottle, intending to try to dissolve and wash away the salt.

Piotr pushed next to her and held out a thermos. "*Gorąca herbata.*"

None of the brothers spoke English, so Clara translated. "He says to try his hot tea. It should work better than cold water to remove the salt."

Good idea.

She soaked a handkerchief with the steaming tea and did her best to splash more over the image. To give time for the salt to dissolve, she draped and pressed her sodden cloth over the winged figure.

She turned to Monk as she waited. "Hopefully there's something under the salt, maybe a message left here by Smithson. If we could only—"

Still pressing against the symbol, she felt it shift as its salty crust gave way. The bas-relief of the wasp sank into the stone. A sharp *crack* followed as something far larger released behind the wall.

She stumbled back, dropping the cloth and pushing everyone away.

Before her, the entire section of the roof broke loose. It swung down, crushing the stalactites under it. As it opened, the sound of rushing water echoed out, accompanied by the groaning of mighty gears.

She pictured the giant waterwheel she had seen earlier, turning far above.

Apparently it wasn't the only one still operational.

As the roof's edge lowered and touched the floor, it formed a ramp going up.

She peered into the beckoning darkness.

Monk turned to her. "Now look what you did."

33

"Two minutes to go," Gray warned the others.

He sat astride a Yamaha PES2 motorcycle, powered by an electric motor. Like him, the other four members of the strike team wore smart helmets outfitted with radios. The group was hidden in the woods behind the research campus of Fenikkusu Laboratories.

From the perch of his seat, Gray focused on their target rising from the center of those fenced-off grounds: a glass-and-steel pagoda known locally as *Kōri no Shiro*, or the Ice Castle.

Though it was midday, the sky was dark. A thunderstorm had rolled down the slopes of Mount Fuji, hammering its flanks with hail. Lightning crackled overhead, reflecting off the Ice Castle.

The storm should serve them well, offering cover for the mission to come. Inside Gray's helmet, he received visual feed from the main assault force as it raced down the main road and headed toward the campus's front gates.

"One minute," he radioed to his group.

Aiko crouched over her cycle to one side, Palu on

the other. Aiko had also brought along two other men—Hoga and Endo—to fill out the small team. Both had been handpicked from her personal task force at the newly formed Japanese intelligence unit. Under their helmets, Aiko and her men wore black face masks, showing only their eyes, like a trio of modern-day ninjas. Gray didn't even know what the two men looked like, only that they were lithe, muscular, and heavily armed.

As Gray counted down the final seconds, his heart pounded in his ears; he was anxious to get moving. Their group had lost valuable time getting here. After surviving the barrage of depth charges, they had radioed for help. Helicopters were immediately dispatched from Midway Atoll to their location in the middle of the Pacific's garbage patch. Once safely on Midway, Kowalski and Palu's cousins had been transported to a small hospital to undergo emergency treatment. Tua's condition remained critical.

Unable to wait, Gray and the others had immediately taken off in a private jet, redlining its engines to cross the remainder of the Pacific to reach Japan. While en route, Aiko had coordinated this assault, alerting authorities in her unit of the involvement of Fenikkusu Laboratories in the attack on Hawaii, pinpointing this research building as the likeliest target due to Takashi Ito's presence here and the secretive nature of the facility. She had kept this knowledge limited to only a handful, fearing word might reach the enemy. Aiko had expressed concern that Fenikkusu Laboratories might have bribed or blackmailed a few members of the newly formed agency, taking advantage of this transitional period as the country's various intelligence services were reorganized.

On a phone call earlier, Painter had shared that same worry. He had also updated Gray on the evacuation of Hawaii. Two words exemplified those efforts: *panic* and *chaos*. The situation was rapidly deteriorating out there.

Recognizing this, Painter had stressed the priority for this current mission: *to discover what countermeasures the enemy had against this threat.* Gray had also understood the implied command underlying this order. *Even if it means sacrificing Seichan and Ken.*

Too much was at stake for this to be a rescue mission.

Hundreds of thousands of lives were in jeopardy.

Through his helmet feed, Gray watched the main Japanese security force reach the campus's main gate. The group was led by an armored urban assault vehicle. The mini-tank didn't slow. Equipped with a battering ram, it smashed through the steel gates, opening the way for the brigade that followed. Sirens suddenly flared across the sweep of motorcycles and military police jeeps.

As if responding to the noise, the storm broke overhead. Thunder boomed, and forked lightning ripped open the clouds. A cold rain fell like a heavy drape from the sky, smothering the commotion below.

"Go, go, go . . ." Gray radioed.

Using the cover of the storm and the distraction of the raid occurring at the front of the compound, Gray and the others swept from the heights above the rear of the campus. They raced through the dark woods with their headlamps extinguished. Pelting rain further obscured their sight. But the head-up display inside the helmet transmitted a night-vision view of the rough mountain trail they descended. Unfortunately, lightning flashes occasionally whited out the views, which was unnerving, but no one slowed.

Not even Palu.

The Hawaiian had already informed Gray of his experience with trail bikes back on Maui. The fireman proved to be a man of his word, impressing Gray with his skill atop the cycle as it bumped and slid across the rocks and thickening mud.

Not having to worry about Palu keeping up, Gray increased their pace the last quarter mile through the woods. With attentions focused up front, no one at the compound raised an alarm as the five bikes crashed out of the forest and braked into a skid before the rear fence.

Hoga leaped off his bike before it had fully come to a stop, letting the cycle topple as he flew forward. He unstrapped a canister at his hip and lifted it to the fence. A nova-bright blue flame shot a few inches out. He swept it across the chain link fencing, melting a way through with a single swipe of his arm.

The tool was no ordinary acetylene torch, but something concocted by Aiko's new agency, which Gray suspected was in all likelihood a Japanese version of Sigma.

Not that Aiko would admit as much.

With the way open, the group slipped into the grounds and ran low across manicured lawns and through a copse of trees. They aimed for a helipad. According to specs obtained by Aiko, the nearby building had a tunnel into the basement levels of the main tower.

Their goal was to reach the labs buried under the tower before the frontal assault triggered a purge of the facilities. They couldn't risk evidence being erased or destroyed.

With a final dash through the rain, the group reached the concrete-block building next to the helipad. Sirens could be heard blaring on the far side of the tower, punctuated by orders barked through bullhorns.

Upon Gray's signal, the strike team burst through an open door into the small hangar. A pair of workers in beige jumpsuits flinched at their sudden appearance, already tense from the commotion of the raid.

Hoga and Endo rushed forward with weapons raised, silently picking separate targets. Hoga fired first. A scatter of thin darts struck his target's chest. As they hit, a chain of electricity frazzled between them, jolting the worker into a cataleptic seizure, then stillness.

Endo shot at the other worker, striking him in the neck with what looked like a quarter-sized black steel spider. The implant pumped in a load of swift-acting sedative. The target took two steps, then crumpled to the floor.

The attack took all of three seconds.

As Gray rushed past the prone men, he glanced

at Hoga and Endo's handiwork. He admired their weaponry, recognizing that Sigma needed to up its game . . . or at least compare notes with Aiko's burgeoning agency.

He faced forward again as they reached a ramp heading down.

He focused on his goal, knowing how much was at stake. While the raid was not primarily a rescue operation, Gray knew the two objectives were likely intertwined.

As they reached the bottom of the ramp and entered a long tunnel, Gray sped faster, leading the team, driven by a fearful question.

Are we already too late?

12:08 P.M.

Time must be up.

Ken watched Dr. Oshiro stalk across the room toward him. At the moment, Ken was seated at a workstation in Gamma Team's corner of the lab.

As the lab director approached, his very posture was one of dominance, demanding subservience in his little fiefdom. From the hard scowl to the man's face, Ken could no longer delay the inevitable. This was made even clearer when Oshiro waved a guard at the door to close in on Ken, too.

They want my answer.

Cooperate with them or die.

Earlier, to delay answering, Ken had asked the director to allow him to study some of their research firsthand, to help make up his mind. From the raw suspicion on Oshiro's face, he had not been deceived by this explanation, sensing Ken was stalling. Nevertheless, the director had allowed it, apparently more than happy to end his role as tour guide.

Still, over the past two hours, Oshiro kept eyeballing him from across the room, studying him, evaluating him, as if this were a working interview.

And maybe it was.

If so, it was a test he dared not fail.

Earlier, Ken had picked Gamma Team to shadow, sensing there was something significant to their research. He sat with a folder in front of him. The label read 農林水産省, or *Nōrin-suisan-shō*, which was the name of the Japanese Ministry of Agriculture, Forestry, and Fisheries. The file contained a petition for a research grant, including an abstract about the promising attempts by Gamma Team to bring a new pesticide to market, a toxin derived from one of the myriad peptides found in the venom of the *Odokuro* wasps.

Oshiro reached Ken's workstation, standing with his hands on his hips. "So have you gleaned any insights concerning Gamma Team's research? Something to prove your worth to me?"

Ken leaned back. "Only that this work is a dead end."

Oshiro's brows shot up at the boldness of his statement. Even the members of Gamma Team looked upon him with dismay. He felt sorry for disparaging their work, but the conclusions were self-evident.

"How so?" Oshiro challenged him.

"I've reviewed the DNA analysis of the ghost peptide."

That was the colorful term the team had been using for the missing protein they had been hunting for, the one that held such promise as a pesticide. While the group had identified a series of genes that potentially could produce such a peptide, they had failed to find any of it in the species' venom sacs.

"Gamma Team has indeed been chasing a *ghost*," Ken explained. He waved to a computer where he had reviewed the code, reading the sequence like a textbook. "The group was correct in its genetic analysis. The series of genes do seem to code for a biolytic enzyme that targets arthropods and insects. Any prey injected with this toxin would dissolve from the inside out."

"Exactly," Oshiro said. "Such a compound would make a perfect agricultural pesticide."

Ken didn't back down. "But remember the *Odokuro* eventually learned it was better to keep their prey *alive*. What Gamma accidentally discovered was a fragment of junk DNA, old code that is no longer viable but remains cached in the wasps' DNA. Didn't you ever wonder why the team failed to actually find this protein?"

Oshiro stammered, mumbling about difficulties and challenges.

Ken cut him off, beyond caring if he insulted the man and the work. "Like most species on the planet—including us—the *Odokuro*'s DNA is a hodgepodge of active genes, junk, and pieces of code gained from exposure to viruses and bacteria.

In fact, it was infections in the wasps by ancient Lazarus microbes that gifted the species with its ability to hibernate for ages."

Oshiro shrugged. "And what's your point?"

"The missing protein—this ghost peptide—can't be found because its code is an evolutionary dead end." He pointed to a member of Gamma Team. "You showed me the methylation of the DNA in those genes, how the gene sequence is locked up by epigenetic markers."

"*Hai*," the man nodded.

"Those epigenetic markers—which decorate the DNA like Christmas tree lights—regulate whether that code is ever expressed, whether the DNA will ever produce a protein like the one you've been hunting." Ken stared across the group before settling his gaze on Oshiro. "In other words, this old bit of useless code was locked up long ago and the key thrown away."

Oshiro visibly swallowed.

Ken shrugged. "Without that perfect key, this sequence will never produce any protein. And to forge such a key—one that basically has the equivalent of a million facets and permutations—is all but impossible."

Oshiro looked at the worried faces of the group. None of them would meet the director's eye. "If you're right . . ."

"This research is a dead end," Ken concluded.

The muscles along Oshiro's jaw visibly tightened. He spoke as if each word pained him. "Perhaps Takashi Ito was right about you. Maybe you have some use after all."

Oshiro nodded to the guard. Apparently after passing this test, Ken was about to be offered a permanent position, one he could not refuse.

Still, how could I ever work for this group?

Steel coursed up his spine as he prepared to accept the inevitable.

Then a loud siren burst across the space, ringing with alarm and urgency.

Everyone froze, momentarily stunned.

Ken was the only one to let out a sigh of relief.

Talk about saved by the bell.

12:28 P.M.

As the Klaxon continued to blare, Gray crouched atop the landing of a basement stairwell. Above his head, large steel blast doors closed off the way into the tower's upper levels. He imagined similar doors were sealing all other exits.

They're buttoning this place up.

While Gray's strike team had managed to slip inside here in time, what could they do now?

Aiko sought to gain that information. She knelt over the cowering form of a lab tech on the landing. Hoga held a blade against the frightened man's neck, while Aiko spoke rapidly in Japanese. While she interrogated the man, Endo guarded the outer hallway, firing three-round bursts to encourage any evacuating personnel to seek another exit.

Both of Aiko's men had removed their helmets but continued to wear their black masks, still looking like faceless ninjas. The team had encountered very little resistance getting here. As they had hoped, most of the building's security had been drawn to the firefight at the main entrance.

The alarm suddenly fell silent.

The resulting quiet was unnerving.

Aiko finally straightened and sent her captive scurrying out into the hallway. She turned to Gray. "He said a man matching Professor Matsui's description was taken to subbasement four." She pointed down the stairs. "To a toxicology research lab."

"And Seichan?"

Aiko shook her head. "He didn't know."

Gray had no choice but to accept this, knowing Aiko had done her best. He could only hope that Ken and Seichan were still together. "Let's go."

They ran down three more flights to reach the fourth level. Access to a fifth was blocked by a set of locked red doors. They ignored that mystery for now and continued out into this level.

Aiko gave curt directions, following the intel gained from her interrogation. They crossed through a series of empty corridors. Occasional faces peered out of rooms, then ducked away at the sight of the guns.

"At the end of the hall." Aiko pointed to a set of double doors emblazoned with a biohazard symbol. "That should be the place."

Gray increased his pace. He reached the doors first and burst through into a large biolab full of high-tech equipment and instrumentation. He kept his SIG Sauer leveled, sweeping the room as the others spread out to either side.

The place had been hastily abandoned. Papers

were scattered across workstations, and glassware was shattered on the floor. One computer station smoked, as if someone had fried its hard drive.

Gray turned to Aiko, a cold stone weighing down into his gut.

They're not here.

12:32 P.M.

Ken ran low along one wall of a darkened hallway.

What am I doing?

Four minutes ago, he had made a rash decision. As the evacuation siren sent the lab into a state of panic, Ken had sought to get out of everyone's way, fearing he might be trampled. For that brief spell, he was the least of anyone's concern. Even Oshiro had claimed the armed guard for himself, drawing the man in his wake as he crossed to a tall wall safe.

Ken took advantage of the distraction to shift to the set of red double doors at the back of the lab. Since arriving here, he had wanted to get a look behind there, to discover what research was being kept hidden from Oshiro.

Still, at that moment, a new motivation spurred him.

As he had hoped, someone inside responded to the Klaxon and burst out those doors. Ken had imagined there must be other exits, since no one had come or gone during the hours he had spent in Oshiro's lab. But for at least one tech, the red doors were the closest exit.

Ken used the chance to duck through the entrance behind the fleeing man. As the doors shut behind him, a lock engaged with a buzz of gears. He knew Oshiro did not have the clearance to follow him. With a barricade now between him and his captors, he set off into this secure area.

As he snuck down the corridor, he heard voices rising from an open doorway ahead. Light spilled into the hallway. He approached cautiously. With the sirens ominously quieted, he feared being heard.

Once he reached the doorway, a quick peek revealed a tiny room lined by a bank of sinks. Shelves held packs of green gowns and boxes of gloves. The place smelled strongly of soap and iodine. It was clearly a surgical scrub room.

Past a window into the next room, a broad lamp illuminated a pair of gowned and masked figures working around an operating table. From their hurried motions, the evacuation alarm must have caught them in mid-surgery.

Ken was about to continue past, not wanting to be spotted, when the taller of the two stepped aside, revealing the patient draped on the table.

Seichan . . .

Fearing the worst, he slipped into the scrub room and peered through the window.

"We have no time to induce a coma and prep her," the surgeon said with clear exasperation. "We'll have to abandon using her as a test subject."

"*Hai*, Dr. Hamada," a nurse responded. "What about the fetus?"

"If we're quick, we should be able to harvest it. She's already passed out from the pain. While she's strapped down, we'll simply perform a hysterectomy without anesthesia. We'll remove the uterus and fetus as a whole. It's not ideal, not what I had hoped, but the fetal stem cells will still be of great use."

"I'll prepare a surgical pack."

"Be quick. The bunker below could become compromised at any moment. They'll only hold the exit through there for so long."

"*Hai.*"

As the nurse shifted over to a set of shelves, Dr. Hamada loomed over his patient, still plainly frustrated.

"I hate to lose this opportunity," he told the nurse. "But maybe it doesn't matter. The MRI showed signatures in her musculature suggestive that the second instars are beginning to thicken, preparing to molt into the third instars. Some larvae probably have already started the process early." He shrugged. "It's a shame. Though in all likelihood, we'd have been hard-pressed to learn much from the viable embryo before it was consumed by the next hatching."

Aghast at these plans, Ken searched the small room, looking for a weapon. He kept one eye on the operating room. The nurse returned with a sealed pack, placed it on a stainless steel tray, and ripped it open.

Out of time . . .

He grabbed what he could, swallowed hard, then slammed into the room. The nurse was closest to the door. She jumped around, crying out in surprise. He lifted the nozzle of the fire extinguisher and blasted her in the face. Blinded, she clawed at her eyes, stumbling backward.

He swept past her and swung the extinguisher by its handle. He clubbed the doctor in the side of the head. Metal clanged against skull, and the man went down to his knees, then crashed headlong to his face.

Ken returned his attention to the nurse. The woman had cleared her eyes enough to see her boss on the floor. He took a threatening step toward her. It was enough. She turned tail and ran for the exit. Ken didn't have time to chase her down. He could only pray the chaos of the evacuation would delay her ability to raise any significant response.

Still, he hurriedly undid the straps binding Seichan to the table. Her head lolled drunkenly as he freed her ankles, her lips twisting in a rictus of pain. For now, she remained lost in a delirium of agony and exhaustion.

He moved next to the IV line that ran from a fluid bag to a catheter in her arm. His fingers closed over the line, about to rip it away. His initial plan had been to drag her bodily off the table and over to some hiding place.

But what then?

He realized such a scheme would likely end with them either recaptured or dead. So instead, he turned to a crash cart standing nearby. He yanked open the top drawer, revealing an array of emergency drugs. His fingertips ran over the bottles as he read the labels. He paused at an ampule of morphine, weighing the effectiveness of the pain reliever against the risk to the child.

Not yet . . .

He moved on, settling instead on epinephrine.

He had to trust that if he could jump-start Seichan out of her pain-induced fugue, she could handle the torment on her own. At least long enough for them to escape from here.

He loaded a syringe, crossed to Seichan, and poked the needle into the injection port of her IV. He clamped the line and pushed the plunger. He didn't know how much to administer, so he titrated the drug in slowly.

Such caution was excruciating.

He breathed through clenched teeth.

C'mon . . .

On the floor next to him, Dr. Hamada groaned, echoing Ken's own sentiment. He remembered the doctor's warning about the pending threat to Seichan's unborn child, how the larvae inside her were already beginning to transition from the second to third instars.

He stared at Seichan's exposed belly.

Dear God, please be wrong.

SECOND INSTAR

The larva moved slower through the macerated muscle. Its gut was distended, packed full, unable to hold more. It had grown tenfold since its last molt—now a healthy half a centimeter in length—but its segmented exoskeleton could stretch no farther and had begun to darken. The strain in the underlying epidermis triggered glands behind its brain to excrete a hormone, ecdysone, to ready the larva to shed its skin once more.

Compromised, it moved slower now, feeding less—both because it could no longer use the fuel to grow and because its mandibles had begun to harden, making it difficult to chew. A thick lubricating gel built up between its soft epidermis and tough outer cuticle. Glands in its head and thorax swelled with liquid silk, readying for when it would weave a bed upon which it would imbed tiny claws. At that point, it would grow quiescent for several hours, until it was ready to split out of its old skin and wriggle free.

Still, the time was not quite right. Its body was still undergoing changes. Faint white patches—imaginal discs—had formed along its flanks, marking where wings would eventually grow. Silvery strings wound through its length, waiting to become future trachea.

As it slugged dully through the tissues, it bumped into something hard. Mandibles tested and probed the obstruction in its path, defining the oblong shape.

It identified the dense packet of silk in its way. Smelling through that woven mat, it sensed what was hidden there.

As it squirmed around the obstruction, more details emerged, revealing the metamorphosis that was under way inside that silk nest. Another larva lay rooted inside there.

This other was quiet and unmoving—but only on the surface. Inside that dead husk, life continued to change and incubate. A fresh layer of cuticle formed under there. A new set of mandibles grew, designed for drilling through bone.

Once the larva was past this obstruction, its progress continued to slow, approaching the moment when it, too, would spin a nest and begin its own transformation.

As it forged ahead, an evolutionary certainty grew.

It would not be long now.

34

Seichan woke with a stab of pain between her eyes, bright enough to blind her. Decades of brutal training with the Guild had taught her to control her autonomic reflexes. Despite the throbbing in her head and confusion, she remained still, forced her breathing to remain even, to give no sign she was awake.

She slivered her eyelids open once the initial flare died away.

Bright lights hung over her head. A hard, cold table chilled the bare skin of her back. The strong tang of antiseptic struck her nose. Her heart pounded fast—*too* fast—racing when it shouldn't be.

A frantic voice whispered a mantra to her left: *"C'mon, c'mon, c'mon . . ."*

She recognized Professor Matsui's accent, heard the urgency and panic in his voice.

Still, she remained quiet, taking in her environment for another breath. Using her peripheral vision, she absorbed every detail in a glance.

I'm in an operating room.

Ken stepped fully into view. He held a syringe

in one hand and fumbled with a glass bottle in his other. "Can't risk giving her too much," he mumbled to himself as he stabbed the needle into the bottle.

She again noted the unnatural flutter to her racing heart.

Drug-induced.

Adrenaline . . .

Realizing the man must be trying to wake her, she shifted her face toward him. As she did so, a shadow rose behind Ken. The figure's features were masked, his form draped in a surgical gown.

Still, she recognized him.

Dr. Hamada . . .

Hands reached for Ken's throat.

Seichan moved.

With her agonized muscles already tensed, she sprang off the table, shedding surgical drapes from her half-naked form. Without ever taking her eyes off of Hamada, her hand lashed out and grabbed a scalpel from an open surgical pack. An IV pole toppled over, ripping the catheter from her arm. As she leaped, her other arm pushed Ken out of her way, then hooked around Hamada's throat.

She whipped behind the doctor and pressed the tip of the scalpel under the angle of his jaw, positioning it against the man's pounding carotid.

A drop of blood formed there.

"Do we need him?" Seichan asked through cracked lips.

It took Ken a moment to collect himself and realize the intent of her question. His gaze flicked between the scalpel and her captive's face. Hamada tensed in her grip, clearly recognizing that his life balanced on Ken's next words.

"I don't . . . maybe . . ." Ken searched back toward a set of swinging doors leading out of here. "There was a siren, an evacuation. I heard him mention something about a way out, through some bunker."

"You're going to show us," she hissed in the doctor's ear. She kneed him in the back of the legs and dropped him to the floor, then passed the scalpel to Ken. "Guard him."

He took the blade with trembling fingers, but his grip firmed quickly.

She dashed over to a discarded pile of gowns in a bin marked with a medical waste symbol. She quickly donned one, ignoring the dried spray of blood across the front. She tucked her hair under a surgical bonnet and tied a mask around her neck, letting it hang loose to her chin. She could always lower her face into it to further obscure her features. She hoped her half-Asian heritage would allow her to pass as part of the Japanese medical staff.

Once ready, she had Ken do the same. The professor dashed to the next room and returned in less than a minute in surgical scrubs.

She forced Hamada to his feet. "Show us the way out of here—and you might live."

The doctor nodded vigorously. "There's an elevator at the end of the hall."

They set off in a tight group. She balled a fist in the back of Hamada's gown and pressed her scalpel into his side. She trusted the doctor to recognize that a stab and twist into his right kidney would produce a mortal injury.

As they headed off, blood dripped from her wrist, flowing from where her catheter had ripped away.

She felt little pain—suspiciously so.

She turned to Ken. "Did you shoot me up with something? Morphine, fentanyl?"

She remembered Hamada's concern about the risk of strong analgesics to the child inside her.

"No," Ken answered. "Just epinephrine. Why?"

"Doesn't matter. Pain's just not as intense as before."

Ken and Hamada shared a look.

"What?" she asked, noting the worry on the professor's face.

"Before molting into the third instars, the larvae will grow quiet for a short spell. That might be what you're experiencing. But when those new instars hatch . . ."

His voice died away, speaking volumes to the pain and threat to come.

She understood. Right now, she was experiencing the calm before the storm.

Any further discussion ceased as they reached the elevators at the end of the hall. She used the key card hanging from Hamada's neck to call the cage. Once the doors brushed open, they hurried inside.

Seichan noted the elevator only went *down* one level—not *up* toward the surface. She had Ken block the doors from closing and dug the scalpel through the cloth of Hamada's gown until the doctor winced.

"Is this a trap?" she asked.

"No, no," he insisted with a pained expression. "In case of an enemy incursion, the basement labs are all locked down. Only top personnel have access to Sublevel Five. The research bunker below has its own evacuation route, to ensure the survival of critical assets to the company."

Seichan glanced to Ken to see if he had any additional insight.

He looked worried as he nodded to Hamada. "I overheard him say the exit down below might not be open for long."

"That's true," the doctor warned.

With no other recourse and time running short, she moved deeper into the elevator and nodded for Ken to do the same. As the doors closed, a loud explosion echoed down the hallway, as if trying to stop them.

Too late now.

12:48 P.M.

Gray waved smoke from his face. He crouched halfway across the circular lab, shielded behind a stout workstation. Aiko and Palu flanked him. The team's other two masked members, Hoga and Endo, were closer to the damage after slapping charges onto the locking mechanism of a set of large red metal doors.

As Gray watched, the doors toppled into the room, falling through the smoke.

"Get up!" Palu ordered, speaking to the man crouched at his side.

His name was Yukio Oshiro, the head of the research lab. Several minutes ago, after they had discovered the lab was empty, the man had rushed into the room, yelling in Japanese that all the exits from the basement levels had been blocked. His tone was demanding, believing them to be members of the facility's security unit.

That misconception was quickly dismissed when weapons were leveled at his chest, and Aiko ordered him to his knees, with his hands on his head.

She took two minutes to efficiently interrogate him. She quickly learned of his role here and forced him to open a wall safe where research files had been stored per evacuation orders. The safe's lock required a retinal ID. The man's right eye was already swelling from where Endo had slammed the scientist's face into the reader when he tried to resist.

After all the files had been gathered and secured in the team's backpacks, they continued their hunt for Ken and Seichan. Oshiro knew nothing about Seichan, but from his deep scowl, he knew Professor Matsui. It seemed Ken had slipped away during the confusion, locking a door between him and any pursuers.

Smart . . .

Gray waved toward the blasted doors. With the way now open, they set off into the secured section of the facility. Oshiro had no clearance beyond those doors, so he likely could offer no guidance from here, but Palu dragged him along anyway. The scientist surely knew more about the ongoing research than could be found in the files alone.

So for the moment, he was of value.

As they continued down the hallway, they passed

a series of empty surgical suites and medical labs. They called out furtively for Ken but got no reply.

Gray grew concerned, knowing they had only a limited window to execute a rescue. The files and Oshiro were too important to risk. If there was any information in them that could help with the *Odokuro* scourge, it had to be brought to light.

Aiko seemed to recognize this and cast a hard glance at Gray, her concern easy to read. They still had enough explosives to blast their way out of the sealed basement. But with every minute they delayed down here, they risked everything—all for a hunt that might be futile.

What if Ken had been caught and was already dead?

Hoga paused a few yards ahead and dropped to a knee. He lifted a pair of fingers in the air, the tips wet and dark.

Blood.

Despite the risk to their mission, Aiko pointed forward, willing to follow the trail for now. The hallway ended at a set of elevator doors. They were painted red, like the ones they had blasted through to get here.

Endo waved to a small door off to the side. A thin window revealed a series of stairs leading down.

Not up.

If Ken had made it this far, there was only one direction to go from here.

Unfortunately, the door was locked.

As Hoga and Endo prepared another charge, Gray confronted Oshiro. "What's down there?"

The researcher shook his head. "I don't—"

"There had to be rumors," Gray said, cutting him off. Even in top-secret government facilities, everyone whispered and wondered. "What have you heard?"

Oshiro looked down.

Palu shook him by the collar. "Tell him."

The man's answer was meek with shame. "Human . . . human experimentation."

12:50 P.M.

"Proceed with Phase Two," Takashi ordered over the scrambled phone line.

"*Hai, Jōnin* Ito." The speaker was the commander of the company's island base in the Norwegian Sea. "It will be done."

As Takashi knelt at his desk, he pictured a dozen planes lifting off from icy airstrips. In a matter of hours, the fleet would spread far and wide, seeding their colonizing loads of wasps across major cities throughout Europe.

With the command given, he ended the call.

It was his seventh and final.

Already planes should be rising from the other islands owned or leased by Fenikkusu Laboratories around the globe. With the exception of Antarctica, no continent would be spared.

Satisfied nothing could stop the wrath he had unleashed, he rose slowly from his desk. He needed his cane to support him. He reached to where it rested against his low desk. His thin fingers clasped hard to the fiery rose-gold phoenix crowning the cane's head. The sharp feathers and beak of the symbol pinched the thin skin of his palm as he leaned on the cane's length, taking deep breaths.

Even this small effort taxed him.

Once he caught his breath, he thumped across a series of tatami rugs that covered the teak floor. The mats were made of woven dried rushes, wrapped around a core made up of a traditional rice stalk, unlike the cheaper modern versions that used synthetics.

He reached the wall of his office and slid aside a shoji screen to reveal his personal safe. It took him two tries to use his right palm to unlock it. He silently cursed the new security system his grandson had insisted on installing.

Look where such caution got you, Masahiro.

Feeling suddenly older, he opened the thick door and removed the lone contents of the safe. Sealed in a chunk of Lucite was a broken piece of amber, which in turn trapped the bones of a prehistoric reptile. The creature had been identified as a juvenile *Aristosuchus*, a small crocodile-headed dinosaur from the early Cretaceous Period. Its bones and skull were found to be rife with cysts from the wasps.

Still, Takashi preferred the original, more elegant name for the relic.

The Demon Crown.

He leaned his cane against the wall, knowing he would need both hands to carry the treasure to his desk. Though heavy, it was only a fraction of the original artifact stolen from the tunnels under Washington, D.C. The rest had been consumed over the decades by the research into its deadly mysteries.

He cherished what remained, knowing the blood spent and the life lost to bring it to Japan. Finally, a promise made long ago, one frozen in amber, had been fulfilled. The operation realized these last days served as both personal vengeance and a long-overdue national triumph.

Once at his desk again, he glanced over to his abandoned cane.

He stared at the phoenix, a symbol of the wasps' eternal nature, of the *Odokuro*'s ability to rise from their own ashes, undying and eternal.

As will be the new Japanese Imperium.

It was his gift to Miu, for her sacrifice, for her love.

Even from the heights of his office, he could hear the continuing battle on the ground floor as Japanese forces attempted to assault the Ice Castle. Explosions and gunfire echoed to him, but they sounded so distant, so petty and small.

Instead, he stared out the window toward the summit of Mount Fuji. Lightning played across the mountaintop, illuminating vast piles of black clouds. The storm's force made a mockery of the feeble fight below.

Still, it would not be wise to linger any longer.

He retrieved his phone and made one last call before he headed to his personal helicopter atop the pagoda. It waited to whisk him to a secure facility. He was done here. He needed nothing more from this place than what rested on his desk, representing a piece of Miu's broken heart.

He placed his palm atop the Demon Crown.

It is done, my love.

He heard the telltale click on the phone as the connection was made. The head of the facility's security answered curtly. The man had been awaiting this call, ready to receive Takashi's final command. He gave it, ordering the incendiary charges built throughout the structure of the pagoda to be ignited.

It was time for the Ice Castle to burn.

35

Abandon all hope . . .

Elena remembered Monk's words from when they'd first entered the mine. She could not help but think of Dante's warning as she followed the others up the ramp and into the cavernous space beyond.

Tension and a vague sense of dread quashed any conversation. Clara's brother Piotr remained at the entrance, in case the secret door decided to close on its own.

As the rest of the group ventured inside, their lights pierced the darkness, the beams scattering away in all directions. The sound of splashing water drew Elena's attention to the left. A giant wooden waterwheel hung high on the neighboring wall, turning in a stream of water flowing from the roof and draining down a hole in the floor.

She pictured a secret lake above her head and noted the open hatch in the roof through which the water poured. The hatch must have been triggered when Kat pressed the wasp-shaped button, setting the wheel and wooden gears in motion to lower the ramp.

The old mechanism was frosted white, suggestive that the passing ages had petrified the wood with salt, like the logs Clara had patted earlier.

Only this wood still *talked*—or more aptly *moaned*.

The gears creaked ominously, while the revolving wheel groaned a low complaint.

The mournful tone sent a shiver through her. Or maybe it was the sudden chill. The air in the cavern was far colder, smelling of salt and dampness, along with something bitter and acrid.

Like an old campfire doused with water.

The team continued across the threshold into the cavern. The roof arched three stories overhead. The space's volume easily matched that of the Chapel of St. Kinga, but within a few steps, it became clear this chamber was no cathedral to a saint.

The stone underfoot grew darker, blackened by old fires.

A number of piles dotted the floor.

Kat examined the closest. "Charred bones," she concluded and cast her light across the scores of other mounds. Some were curled tightly; others stretched longer.

"Must be the remains of the miners who were trapped here."

Monk had stepped over to a larger heap. "Their horses, too," he added with a sad shake of his head.

Elena remembered the story of the miners and their horses, how they seldom, if ever, saw the light of day. Such an arrangement was a ready-made isolation ward. It was no wonder the mine had been able to contain the contagion released here.

And keep it secret.

As they tread carefully through the grave mounds, Clara made the sign of the cross, tapping her fingertips to her forehead, chest, and shoulders. Elena followed her example a second later, praying for protection.

Kat stopped to scuff a toe on the oily layer of soot surrounding a tall pile of ash. "To purge this place, they must've stacked wood in here, then flooded the chamber with lamp oil, before torching and sealing the cavern."

Elena tried to imagine those trapped workers, studying the pattern of the mounds. She could read no panic in the spread, no rush toward the door. From what she could glean from Clara, the miners were a close-knit family. Most were probably too sick or recognized the threat they posed to the rest of the mine and sacrificed themselves for the greater good.

Elena made the sign of the cross again—only this time out of respect for the dead, knowing their suffering had saved the world back then by keeping this scourge from escaping the mine.

She looked across the bodies.

Here are the mine's true saints.

"Come see this!" Sam called over from one side.

After entering, he and Dr. Slaski had chosen to avoid the graveyard and had shifted to the wall instead. A layer of soot obscured the lower quarter of the wall, as if those old flames had crashed like waves against there, blackening the stone.

As the rest of the group angled closer, the two men concentrated their lights higher. The bright beams seemed to penetrate the wall, igniting the stone to a rich ruddy glow.

Kat let out a small gasp, while Monk whistled sharply.

The two men stepped back, sweeping their lights higher and farther to either side.

"Amber," Slaski said, glancing back to them. "It's *all* amber."

The shock of the sight drew everyone to splay their beams across the walls and roof. Everywhere they pointed, the stone absorbed the light and shone it back out with an inner fire.

"It's like we're in a bubble of the gemstone," Elena whispered.

"Maybe we are." Slaski traced his fingertips along the wall. "Feel how smooth it is."

Elena did. "It's as if the amber melted and cooled."

"Exactly," Slaski said. "Amber softens at 150 degrees Celsius. It becomes moldable. Modern fabricators use this trait to heat slivers and small pebbles of amber. Once soft, they fuse the rubble under high pressure into larger pieces."

Kat stepped back and craned around at the huge expanse. "You're saying that's what happened here?"

"Only on a far grander scale." Slaski's voice grew awed. "If this cavern is truly the source of Mr. Smithson's artifact, it would make this deposit hundreds of millions of years old, formed before tectonic forces pushed the continents into their current positions, when this region was a pine-covered coastline of the ancient Tethys Sea. Heat and compression from those tectonic forces could've squeezed the soft amber along this stretch of the coastline, until gas and pressure molded it into this giant bubble."

"That's all well and good," Kat said. "But if this is indeed where James Smithson acquired his sample, where was it excavated from?"

Clara pointed her flashlight toward the back of the cavern. The wall there was all dug out and crumbled. They headed in that direction.

As they traversed the cavern, iron cartwheels and the heads of pick-axes appeared half-buried in mounds of ash. Elena pictured the abandoned mining equipment being set aflame, burning away until only these iron skeletons were left behind.

Next to her, Sam and Slaski continued their examination of the wall. It seemed the cavern had preserved other remains, ones far more ancient.

Sam's footsteps slowed as he pressed his flashlight against the amber, setting it aglow. He came to a sudden stop, his voice hushed by awe and excitement. "My god, I think that's an intact *Cyllonium*."

They all clustered around him.

Floating in the amber was a fist-sized winged insect.

"It's a giant cicada," Sam explained. "From the early Cretaceous Period."

They barely had a moment to examine it before the entomologist hurried forward.

"And look over here. A whole flock of *Austroraphidia*, an extinct species of snakefly from the same period."

Elena stared across the stretch of wall, where the creatures appeared to have taken flight through the amber. Each fly was five inches long, carried aloft by wings twice that length.

Sam continued, moving along in fits and starts, his flashlight flicking here and there. "*Kararhynchus*, a genus of beetle from the late Jurassic . . . *Eolepidopterix*, an extinct giant moth . . . *Protolepis*, one of the first true butterflies . . ."

He led them through this prehistoric terrarium frozen in amber: lines of massive ants, a centipede as long as Elena's arm, a giant spider that was the stuff of nightmares. Amid this encyclopedia of extinct bugs, beetles, flies, and moths were also preserved pieces of ancient forests. Twigs and branches. Primitive cones. Giant broad leaves. Elena paused at a huge flower, whose snow-white petals appeared as fresh as the day they had first budded.

But that wasn't all.

Kat pointed her flashlight at a leathery skull the size of a bowling ball, with a pointed crocodilian jaw lined by shark's teeth. "Definitely saurian," she whispered.

Monk nodded. "It's like someone took a blender to a piece of Jurassic history and preserved it all in amber."

"And all of it appears to date back to the same time period as Smithson's artifact," Kat added.

Sam waved from a few yards ahead. "Over here," he said, his voice now grimmer.

As they joined him, Elena caught his eye, noting a flicker of fear there. Her heart began pounding harder.

He pointed his flashlight's beam deep into the

amber, revealing the horror hidden there. Captured in the stone was a dense swarm of familiar shapes, their carapaces striped in black and crimson.

Soldier wasps.

"The *Odokuro*," Sam pronounced. "They're here."

6:04 A.M.

So this is definitely the right place.

Kat was both relieved and horrified. For the past three minutes, she and the others had followed the curve of the wall. With every step, more and more incarnations of this infernal species appeared, from tiny males to huge breeders. As the group progressed, the number of competing species receded, replaced by the ravaging horde, until only the *Odokuro* were left.

And it was plain to see why.

"Ugh." Elena turned her face from the sight of a small lizard whose belly had been ripped open, bursting forth with a frenzied mass of wasps.

The *Odokuro* had clearly burned through its prehistoric environment, consuming and utilizing all the biomass before it.

Two members of the party showed little interest in this alarming tableaux. Instead, Slaski and Clara had ventured farther ahead. The museum director had stopped, dropping down to one knee.

As Kat approached, she heard him speaking angrily in Polish to Clara, plainly aggravated. "What's wrong?" Kat asked.

Slaski stood with a final spat of Polish that had

to be a curse. He quickly collected himself and pointed to the next expanse of wall. Several blocks had been crudely hacked free, cutting through the blackened section near the floor to reveal the fresh amber beneath.

"This was *not* the handiwork of the miners who died here," Slaski explained. "But thieves who came later."

Kat understood. Someone had come here after it was all burned. Opportunists who must have heard of the priceless deposit and risked coming here in secret afterward.

"Black miners," Clara explained, sounding as upset as Slaski. She glanced back to the entrance. "Maybe it is why someone went to such efforts to seal this place later."

Monk leaned to Kat. "It could also explain how James Smithson had acquired his artifact. Maybe he bought it off one of these black miners."

She nodded.

If so, Smithson probably learned of the tragedy here from the same source.

Kat pictured the first group of miners here, imagining their horror as they cracked through the prehistoric bones trapped in the amber, releasing and aerosolizing the cryptobiotic cysts. The men's deaths must have been agonizing as those cysts hatched inside them, releasing a scourge of larvae— until finally their hollowed-out bodies burst forth with adult wasps.

While Kat stopped to inspect the damage along the wall, Sam continued past, sweeping his light high and low. From the corner of her eye, she noted him stop, back up a step, then lean closer to the wall, checking several spots with his flashlight.

He finally called over to them. "Guys, something . . . something's wrong here."

Now what?

Kat led the others to him, drawn by his dismay. As they joined him, their combined illumination brightened the section of amber before them, revealing swaths of *Odokuro* in all their horrendous incarnations.

She frowned, unable to fathom what so distressed the entomologist.

He drew closer to the wall, fixing his beam upon a few specimens. "I think these were already dead before they were trapped in the amber."

"Why do you think that?" she asked.

"If you study them closer, you can see they're malformed. Look at this soldier. Its exoskeleton has collapsed. The surrounding amber is stained."

Kat squinted, while Elena lifted her reading glasses into place.

He's right.

The wasp looked *crushed*, its shell cracked. A vague wisp darkened the surrounding amber, as if it were the insect's spirit leaving its dead corpse.

"I think that's blood," Sam said. "As if the wasp bled out before it died."

Monk peered closer, too. "Could it have been crushed by the pressures that molded and formed this bubble?"

"No." Sam stepped back. "Look how all the wasps throughout this section show the identical damage, while the few other species found in this same section—*Palaeolepidopterix* over here, *Tektonargus* over there—show no such mutilation or injury."

Sam faced them, his expression firm with certainty. "Whatever killed them did so *before* the amber preserved their bodies."

Kat slowly nodded, accepting his conclusion. "If we could find out what that was . . ."

She stared across the group. She didn't need to state the obvious. Here was the very purpose of this journey. Something in the prehistoric past had kept this apex predator from spreading, from completely dominating the ancient world.

But what could it be?

They continued forward as a group. Even Slaski and Clara followed, frowning at them, perplexed by their sudden urgency and distress.

Their lamps lit up the neighboring amber wall, revealing the ongoing destruction of the *Odokuro*. No incarnation was spared. Tiny scouts by the thousands formed mountainous piles of carcasses. More soldiers lay broken and shattered. A score of breeders hung in mists of their own blood.

But what was the source of this damage?

Several yards ahead, a flash of color on the floor caught Kat's attention. She swung her flashlight in that direction. By now, others had noted it, too, adding their lights.

It was a body—but not the charred remains of a miner.

The dead man's clothing was intact, his skin pale and sunken, contrasting with his coarse dark hair and beard. His expression—forever preserved by the high-sodium atmosphere—was one of shock and horror. A pick-axe lay nearby, long abandoned. Not that the man could have wielded it as his wrists were bound by rope.

The cause of his death was easy enough to discern.

His throat had been slashed open.

The reason for his execution was also evident.

Not far from his body stood a waist-high cube of amber, hacked from the nearby wall. It would have been worth a king's ransom back then.

"One of the black miners," Slaski said.

Clara shook her head sadly. "Such thievery was dealt with harshly."

Sam had shifted over to examine the damaged section of the wall, which appeared to be darkly discolored, but not from the old fire. He then crossed over to the block of amber that matched that hue. He rested his flashlight atop the cube and began to kneel beside it—then he cried out, stumbling backward, falling on his rear end.

Under the glow of Sam's flashlight, the block glowed like a lamp. The shine revealed the treasure inside. No wonder the dead miner had attempted to steal such a huge piece. How could he not with what was preserved inside it?

Sam rolled to his knees, never taking his eyes from the sight. His words were forlorn and dismayed. "Professor Matsui was wrong . . . everyone was wrong."

36

"We're far deeper down than just *one* floor," Ken said as he stepped from the elevator onto Sublevel 5. He had felt the pressure change in his ears during the minute-long descent from the fourth subbasement to this lowermost section.

Even the temperature down here was several degrees cooler.

He checked the short corridor that led to a set of steel sliding doors.

Empty.

He waved for Seichan to follow him out. Dressed in a surgical gown and loose mask, she brusquely escorted Dr. Hamada by the arm. She had her other fist pressed against his side, where she threatened him with a hidden scalpel.

"How far down are we?" Seichan asked their captive.

"Seven . . . seventy meters," Hamada stammered.

Ken inwardly cringed. That was equivalent to a twenty-story building buried underground. "Why so deep?"

"To serve as a bunker for our most sensitive

work. It's said this level could withstand a tactical nuclear strike. But it was also chosen for the natural insulation offered by the unique geology of this location."

"What do you mean?" Seichan's forehead shone with sweat, revealing the level of pain she was still experiencing—even after the larval load inside her had grown quieter.

"You'll see for yourself." Hamada waved to the sliding doors. "It's on the way to this level's emergency escape station."

As they crossed the short distance, the doors glided open before them, revealing a circular lab identical in size to the one above. It had already been evacuated. A blinking green arrow pointed to another exit on the far side, likely leading to Hamada's promised emergency exit for this level's key personnel.

As they hurried toward it, Ken searched around him.

To the right and left were adjoining rooms holding banks of caged laboratory rats and rabbits. The workstations in the center held rows of centrifuges, thermocyclers, and autoclaves. Shelves were stacked with all matter of glassware, pipettes, and bottles of molecular enzymes, reagents, and buffers.

Ken's feet slowed as he noted two significant labels: *CAS9* and *TRACRRNA PLASMID*.

He turned to Hamada. "You're performing Crispr/Cas here."

Hamada shrugged.

Seichan looked questioningly at Ken.

He explained: "It's a technique for ultrafine genetic engineering. With this equipment, you could cut and splice DNA as accurately as cutting letters out of an encyclopedia. And nearly as effortlessly."

"What are you experimenting with here?" Seichan asked, drawing them momentarily to a stop. From the urgency in her voice and glint in her eye, she clearly hoped it had something to do with a cure.

"We're doing a deep study on the wasps' genetics," Hamada said. "To tease out the secret to their astounding longevity."

Cold dread iced through Ken. "You mean you've been experimenting with the section of the insect's DNA that they borrowed from the Lazarus microbes that infected them ages ago."

"Precisely. Over the past decade, we've had the chance to thoroughly study the borrowed fragments of DNA and found the *Odokuro* utilize them in a unique and amazing manner. The discovery holds great promise not only for life *extension*, but possibly even *resurrection*."

Ken cast a harsh look at the man. "You're insane."

"I prefer forward-thinking," Hamada countered. "Unfortunately, it's taken until the development of sophisticated genetic tools—like the Crispr/Cas technique—before we could proceed with clinical trials."

The doctor nodded to a bank of dark windows near the doors leading out.

Seichan pushed Hamada forward. Ken didn't want to look through those windows, but he couldn't stop himself. The edges of the glass were lightly frosted with ice on the far side, as if the neighboring room was kept at or below freezing.

Beyond the window, muted lighting revealed a long line of hospital beds. The patients were men and women, ranging in age from pubescent to elderly. They lay lifeless, hooked to all manner of monitoring equipment, IV lines, and EEG machines that traced their brain activity, which even from here looked leaden.

Hamada confirmed this. "They're all in an induced coma. We're not monsters. We maintain strict guidelines for pain and stress management of our subjects."

Ken wanted to argue, but he could not talk.

Each patient exhibited signs of extreme brutalization. Both arms of one man had been burned, his skin blackened and cracked. Another's abdomen lay open, the viscera inside dried like jerky. The closest woman had her lower half frozen in a block of ice. Everywhere Ken cast his gaze, the horrors compounded: mutilations, weeping boils, stripped skin, radiation burns.

He had remembered reading about Japanese camps in China during World War II, where scientists had performed ghastly biological experiments on prisoners and local villagers. Clearly someone had updated that program for the new millennium.

Hamada tried to justify his work as they passed along the windows, but from his halting manner, he could not fully hide his shame. "We're performing stress challenges. On tissues, on organs. Establishing baselines before we begin testing in earnest the ability of the Lazarus genes to repair damaged bodies."

Seichan had seen enough, her face a mask of fury.

She knew this was where Hamada had been planning to take her, to be experimented upon—along with her unborn child.

Hamada gasped as Seichan jabbed him with the scalpel to get him to take the last steps to the exit. Ken was more than ready to leave. They had delayed long enough and learned nothing that would help Seichan.

Through the next set of doors, a maze of hallways led through offices and smaller labs. Blinking green arrows indicated the emergency evacuation route. The hallways grew colder as they went. With each turn, they began to move more quickly, sensing time was running out.

Finally, another set of red doors opened at the end of a hall.

A wintry rush of icy air washed over them.

They hurried through the doors and into what could pass as a pristine Japanese subway station. The long tubular chamber stretched before them, with a narrow platform running beside a sleek chain of seven white pill-shaped cars. Through tiny windows, figures could be seen standing there, packed inside.

Must be the last of the evacuating crew of this level.

Ken also spotted men with rifles slung over their shoulders. He kept his face down, his eyes diverted as they crossed toward the caboose of this train. Seichan did the same, balling her fist tighter into the back of Hamada's scrub gown.

As they crossed the platform, the lead car suddenly zipped away, shooting silently down the dark tunnel. It was clearly electrically powered, but

JAMES ROLLINS

rather than running on a rail system, small spiked wheels on the undercarriage propelled it, stabilized by pairs of large skates on top and bottom.

Only then did Ken realize that the surfaces of the tubes were lined by polished ice. He remembered Hamada's comments about the site being chosen for its *natural insulation offered by the unique geology.*

He now understood.

This was one of Mount Fuji's many lava tubes. Colleagues back at Ken's lab in Kyoto had shown him pictures of their trips to the Narusawa Ice Caves, on the volcano's slopes, where caverns and tunnels were forever covered in ice and draped in crystalline stalactites. It was said the entire mountain here was riddled with such perpetually frozen passageways.

Clearly Fenikkusu Laboratories had taken advantage of this natural feature of the mountain, both for its constant refrigeration and for its ready-made tunnel system, perfect for engineering a secret escape route. He pictured the vanished car shooting under Lake Kawaguchi to some distant place of safety.

Now if only we could get there, too . . .

As they approached the last car, the doors opened before them. It appeared only half-full, offering plenty of room for three remaining stragglers rushing to safety.

Unfortunately, the *half* inside were heavily armed.

And led by a familiar figure, who stepped out to greet them.

Valya Mikhailov.

She was dressed in a white parka, the hood thrown

back. Along with her pale face and snowy hair, she looked the queen of this icy station. Her haughty smile added to her guise of royalty and power.

Seichan drew Hamada in front of her, using the doctor as a shield. "Get back," she warned Ken, urging him behind her.

Ken didn't bother, remaining where he was.

Behind Valya, a team of hard-faced men and women, all armed, backed her up. He recognized a few from Ikikauō Atoll. These were her handpicked team, loyal and merciless.

Ken also recognized another face.

Valya held a large pistol in one hand, but clutched an older woman in blue scrubs. It was the nurse who had escaped the surgical suite. It seemed the woman had found someone to alert during the evacuation after all.

A muffled Klaxon sounded as another of the cars zipped away.

Ken glanced back and saw the last of the illuminated green arrows start to blink rapidly in red.

Valya noted the alarm and his attention. "It seems our illustrious leader has ordered the final destruction of this pagoda dedicated to science." She leveled her pistol at them. "Not that it'll be any concern of yours."

She aimed and fired.

1:11 P.M.

That can't be a good sign.

Gray led the others at breakneck speed down

an endless flight of steps. After Hoga and Endo had blown the red stairwell doors on the fourth subbasement level, they'd discovered a descent that appeared never-ending. He had already counted a dozen flights when the series of green glowing arrows they'd been following suddenly began blinking an angry red and a Klaxon rang out.

"Faster!" Gray goaded the others. He leaped steps, colliding off walls and bouncing around turns in the stairwell.

Aiko raced ahead, proving more fleet-footed. Hoga and Endo kept at her heels. Palu trailed behind them all, compromised by his panicked captive, Dr. Oshiro. The Hawaiian half-carried the researcher, with a thick arm around the man's thin waist.

Then the expected *BOOM* . . . a whole series of them.

Gray crashed across the next landing as a cascading series of explosions rocked the tower's foundation. He twisted around to check on the others.

Palu was sprawled headfirst down the stairs. He had saved himself from a concussion by snatching the handrail, but he had lost hold of his prisoner. Oshiro sat on his backside on the upper landing. The man's eyes were huge with panic, but he also looked at his hands, as if acknowledging he was free.

Gray read the man's next move. "Don't!"

Oshiro hopped to his feet and bolted like a jackrabbit up the steps, fleeing his captors. The man quickly vanished around a turn.

Palu began to stand, ready to pursue him.

"Forget it." Gray pointed down. "No time."

This was confirmed as Oshiro howled above, his scream echoing down the stairwell. Gray felt the pressure change in his ears.

"Run!"

They fled again, even faster now, leaping from landing to landing, crashing around turns. The air grew hotter and denser. Each breath soon scorched. He heard a dragon roar behind him.

Gray pictured a wall of flames closing upon them from behind.

Then they finally reached the bottom of the stairs. The group banged out its lower doors and into a short hall.

"Keep going!" Gray hollered.

They raced in a tight group. A set of steel sliding doors opened before them, as if welcoming them into the security beyond. They fled through into a lab. A low *whoosh* drew Gray's attention around.

The dragon had caught up with them.

Flames shot into the circular space, blistering the air as they leaped out of the way. Then the steel doors clamped closed again, stanching the flames, trapping the inferno outside. Sprinklers overhead responded to the blast and began spraying the space.

Better late than never.

Gray gathered everyone together. "We should—"

A volley of gunfire drew him around, echoing through an exit on the far side of the lab. His heart clenched in his chest.

Without him needing to order it, they all ran for the door.

With each step, the firefight grew louder.

1:15 P.M.

Fight or die.

That had been Valya's order as she slapped a SIG Sauer into Seichan's palm. Seichan still didn't understand the situation, and for the moment, she didn't need to.

Seconds ago, Valya had fired her pistol at them. Her first shot dropped Dr. Hamada with a slug to his chest. Seichan had tried to hold him up as he collapsed, using his dead weight as a shield. Then Valya's second shot blew away half the skull of the stunned nurse in her clutches.

As Valya shoved the body aside, she pointed her smoking weapon toward the last car. "Get inside."

Seichan hadn't moved, too pain-addled and surprised to make sense of it all.

Then doors opened along the chain of neighboring cars and armed gunmen came barreling out, more than two dozen, drawn by the blasts and murder. At first the security force—who were likely assigned to protect the key members of the research staff—had milled around in confusion.

Valya's team took advantage and fired at them, taking down half in a savage volley. During the ensuing firefight, Valya had grabbed Ken and shoved him into the protection of the car and passed Seichan a weapon.

She crouched at Valya's side now. Both of them sheltered in the open door of the last car. Valya braced high, Seichan low, down on one knee. Together they fired at the remaining handful of guards.

Valya had lost four of her crew, who were sprawled on the platform. Others were wounded behind them in the car. Four more hid behind poles outside, trying to flank the enemy.

Valya cursed with every shot she popped off.

Seichan smelled the sweat and gunpowder wafting off her. Clearly Valya had underestimated the vigorous response from the security force down here. It had cost her dearly and put them all in jeopardy.

Another of her men tried to dash from his hiding place to get a better angle, but a crack shot dropped him before he could take four steps.

Valya growled her frustration, clearly recognizing this was becoming a stalemate. And time was not on their side.

Then the doors into the station opened. A new group burst forth between the two entrenched forces.

Seichan stared at the impossible sight.

Gray and Palu slid low across the platform, accompanied by a masked trio. They fired at the train of cars, aiming for the obvious threat of the armed guards.

Taking advantage of the newcomers' arrival, Valya hollered to her remaining three men. "To me!"

They immediately obeyed and pounded into the car. Valya continued to offer fire support for Gray's assault, picking off another guard. Seichan did the same.

In seconds, the fierce battle ended.

As if this were some signal, the lead train car jetted away down the tunnel, then the next, whisking on sharp blades across the ice.

Gray and the others came running toward the last car, weapons bristling.

He immediately spotted Seichan, relief shining from his face, but his eyes never left the pale form of the woman beside her. He leveled his weapon at Valya as he closed the distance.

Seichan stood up, blocking his shot, shielding the woman.

"Get out of the way," Gray warned.

Seichan faced his fury. "Not yet."

1:18 P.M.

Gray scowled, baffled by Seichan's reaction. When he had first burst in here, he had watched the pair firing in tandem from their shelter in the caboose of this sleek train. Apparently, with a common enemy to fight, the two adversaries were temporarily working together.

But that was over.

Gray's group trained their weapons on the clutch of men inside, some wounded, others unharmed. The enemy, in turn, threatened them in the same manner.

What the hell was going on?

Valya holstered her pistol. With exaggerated care, she reached to a pocket and removed a small thumb drive. She tossed it at Gray, who caught it one-handed, while never lowering his gun.

His fingers closed over the drive. "What's this?"

"A ticket out of here for me and my team." She nodded to the device. "It contains the location of a warehouse holding barrels of gas canisters."

"Gas?"

"Insecticide. Developed by Fenikkusu Laboratories. Effective against the wasps, but highly carcinogenic and toxic to many other species. It'll cause a lot of heartbreak and environmental damage on its own, but it'll get the job done." She stared over at Aiko. "Fenikkusu Laboratories was planning to use that storehouse to protect these shores in the coming months and years, but it should do the same for Hawaii."

Gray was suddenly glad he hadn't shot Valya outright, especially with her next words.

"The drive is quantum-encrypted and will destroy itself upon any attempt to jailbreak it." Valya glared at Gray. "I'll send you the code once I'm safely gone."

"And how can we trust you'll do that or that there's anything even on here?"

"I don't want the world to end any more than you do. It doesn't suit my own plans for the future. So I need *you* all to save it for me."

Gray understood.

The cunning bitch intends for us to be tools for her own ambition.

He studied her crew. He recognized their hard countenances, having seen shadows of the same with Seichan at times. These were all former Guild. To have survived the worldwide purge of their organization, they had to be its most dangerous core.

Led by a woman with a heart as icy as her skin.

How can I let them leave, a seed that'll grow into something far worse?

He sighed, knowing the answer.

That's tomorrow . . .

He lowered his gun and waved for the others to do the same.

Valya's lips thinned into a self-satisfied sneer. "As a sign of goodwill, I already sent an auto-destruct signal to a fleet of planes rising from islands around the globe, destined for major cities with their deadly cargo."

Gray understood, picturing the trio of Cessnas flying pilotless toward the Maui coast.

"So you see," Valya continued, "I've generously taken care of that problem so you can concentrate on the situation in Hawaii." She shrugged at Seichan. "Unfortunately, the pesticide has no effect on the parasitized."

Gray had feared as much. He reached over and took Seichan's hand, feeling the feverish heat in her palm and fingers.

"Which means," Valya said, "the threat already entrenched in Hawaii will rise again and again. Requiring constant retreatment with the toxic gas to stamp it back down. The cumulative environmental damage will be severe, and a quarantine will have to be maintained to protect the rest of the world."

Gray glanced over to Palu, whose face had gone ashen. Such a course was not the best solution, but it was the only one they had.

By now, the three remaining train cars had already zipped off, leaving only the caboose. Knowing he had no choice but to cooperate, Gray waved his team inside with the Guild.

As the doors closed, Valya turned her gaze up. "Oh, and I granted you one additional parting gift."

1:22 P.M.

Takashi Ito stood before the windows of his office, staring out at the storm raging over Mount Fuji. Flashes of lightning crackled through dark clouds. He listened to the thunder, felt it through his palms pressed to the glass.

It echoed the rage inside him.

When he had first stepped to the window, the pane had been cold, swept by rain and thin patters of hail. Already it had become warm, heated by the flames in the tower below as the incendiary charges burned their way through the pagoda's steel infrastructure. Fires raged below. Glass shattered in bright shards, reflecting the flames.

Behind him, smoke poured under the door from the hallway behind him.

No one had come for him.

When he had tried to leave, he found the door blocked on the far side.

He pictured his private secretary dead, likely the same with the helicopter crew atop the tower. Even prior to that, he had watched on his laptop as calls came in from various installations, passing on feed from the dispatched fleet. Video showed plane after plane exploding in midair and raining down into seas around the world.

He knew only one hand could have orchestrated all of this.

A hand as white as the finest porcelain.

Chūnin Mikhailov.

He now suspected the woman had not been entirely truthful about the fate of his grandson, Masahiro. Even still, he respected her ambition, which was apparently boundless. From her actions, she clearly refused to settle for a world in ruins, one where her options would be limited, her future confined and forever restricted by Japanese overlords.

Still, she must be punished.

He had already taken measures to ensure that, knowing the most likely route she would take to escape. The facility had been engineered with one last fail-safe, intended for a worst-case scenario. But it would not be a cleansing fire this time.

Instead, something equally purifying.

Contented in this matter, he turned from the window and headed back toward his low desk. Smoke fogged the room, making it difficult to breathe.

He dropped to his knees, meaning to do so gracefully, but he struck the floor hard, jarring his bones. He ignored the pain and sat before his desk. As he stared out at the storm, knowing it would be his last, he reached for a thick piece of paper.

Without looking down, he made one crease, then another. His fingers moved from memory. He studied the storm, but he could no longer echo its rage. Fold after fold, he worked. Slowly shape took form.

When he was done, a white origami lily rested on his desk.

Miu's favorite.

He gently lifted it and placed it atop the block holding the last fragment of the Demon Crown. For him, a fractured piece of his wife's heart.

Flames now crested the windows, dancing brightly.

It will not be long now.

Smoke already choked his throat and lungs. His body would soon burn, becoming one last offering of incense to his beloved.

Miu . . .

The nineteenth-century words of Otagaki Rengetsu returned to him now, speaking to the wonders and mysteries of incense.

> *A single line of*
> *Fragrant smoke*
> *From incense stick*
> *Trails off without a trace:*
> *Where does it go?*

He prayed now, dropping his eyes from the ferocity of the storm to the gently folded blossom, to what it represented.

Please let me go there.

1:43 P.M.

Ken clutched a strap hanging from a rail overhead. As the car whisked through the frozen lava tube, the inside of the cab remained starkly divided.

Valya's group took up residence at the front, their team at the back. No one spoke; no one took their eyes off the others.

The only noise was the rattle of the car and low whine of its electric engine. The sound grew grating after the first few minutes.

He shouldn't have complained.

The car suddenly went dark, and the engine died.

The sudden deceleration threw everyone forward, forcing the two parties together. After a moment of confusion and jostling, lights mounted on assault rifles flashed on, illuminating the dark cab.

"What happened?" Palu asked, climbing to his feet.

Gray craned around. "Someone must've shut us down."

"But who?" Seichan asked.

Valya had a two-word answer. "Takashi Ito."

The car began to move again slowly—but *backward*. Without power, the car was sliding down the sloped tunnel toward the station.

Gray had crossed to the door. "If we can pry this open, we could still hop out and go on foot."

"We'll never make it," Valya said, cocking her head. "Listen."

Ken strained to hear past the pounding of his heart. After a breathless moment, he heard a low rumbling coming from behind them. "What is that?" he whispered.

Gray's posture stiffened. "Water."

"*Lake* water," Valya corrected.

Earlier, Ken had imagined the path of this subterranean train, picturing it passing under Lake Kawaguchi.

Valya scowled. "Ito must have drilled and planted charges along the lava tube. Right under the lake above our head. Engineered to flood the place in case of emergency, to wash away any evidence of his activities below the tower."

Including us, Ken thought.

The car continued sliding toward certain doom.

Gray ordered Valya's men. "Help me with the door." Then he turned to Aiko's partners. "Hoga and Endo, how many demolition charges do you have left?"

One held up four fingers, the other two.

"It'll have to do."

With Palu helping, Gray and the others forced the door open. Walls of ice glided past. Gray addressed the entire group. "Out. We'll need everybody's weight and strength to stop the cab while we still can."

No one argued.

Ken followed everyone out. As the car slowly picked up speed, they all edged to the back of the car and hurried to positions behind the lower skates. As one, they shouldered into the car, bracing with their legs.

Their boots slipped on the ice underfoot. They were like ants trying to halt a tantalizing morsel from rolling downhill. Even with the car mostly made of a lightweight plastic composite, it was still too heavy to stop.

Then Ken had a thought.

He fell out of position and dropped onto his back. He let the car roll over him, its large spiked wheels passing ominously to either side. He searched the undercarriage.

C'mon . . .

Then he saw it.

A hatch near where he imagined the engine block was located.

He quickly yanked the releases but hung from the door's edge as the car continued to slide. As he had hoped, row after row of battery packs filled the compartment. With his free hand, he began prying them out, letting them drop to the ice, leaving a trail in the sliding car's wake.

Each weighed thirty pounds.

By the time he had freed fifteen or so, lessening the cab's weight by a quarter ton, the car began to slow—then finally stop.

Sighing with relief, he shimmied back to the others. Palu grabbed his ankles and dragged him the rest of the way out, giving him a bear hug.

"Quick thinking," Gray acknowledged.

"I . . . I own a Prius," he said with a shrug. "Swear half its weight is batteries."

He glanced several yards back. Hoga and Endo were quickly planting their charges around the circumference of the tunnel. As the pair worked, Gray instructed Valya's men to collect several of the abandoned battery packs and jam them against the rear wheels to hold the car in place.

Once everything was ready, Gray waved. "Everyone back in!"

He had to yell to be heard above the approach

of rushing water. By now, the draining lake must have flooded the lower level of the tower and it was shooting toward them.

Breathless with fear, Ken followed the others into the cab.

As the doors closed, Gray pointed to Aiko's partners. "Blow it."

A button on a detonator was pressed.

The explosion rocked the car forward a foot. Even through the insulation of the cab, the blast was deafening, pounding eardrums and chest. Ice and rock pelted the car's stern and rattled past the windows.

As it ended, Ken stared back. "I don't understand. Will the cave-in be enough to dam all that water?"

Gray shook his head. "Not a chance."

"Then what—?"

"Think of a cork in a champagne bottle."

Before he could imagine it, the raging waters struck the blockage of ice and rock with a thunderous strike. The plug only held for a fraction of a second—then was blasted forward.

The mass hit the rear of the car like a battering ram and drove them forward hard. The two groups tumbled to the back, tangled together.

The force of the flood pushed the cab up the tunnel. Water splashed alongside the window, but so far, the car continued to race in front of the worst of the deluge.

No one tried to get up, remaining on the floor.

Finally, their flight slowed—as equilibrium was reached between the draining lake and the elevation of the tube. No longer propelled by the force of the water, the car came to a halt. Gray herded everyone out again. A hundred yards ahead, lights beckoned.

They hurried in that direction, carrying the wounded.

Even Gray had one arm around Seichan and the other around the waist of one of the enemy.

The tunnel emptied into a long concrete-block warehouse. The other cars waited there, having arrived safely before the power was cut. They were all empty, abandoned by those fleeing.

Their group headed outside into a sullen rain.

The storm was dying down, rumbling with some final complaints. Off to the side, Gray conversed with Valya, their heads bowed together. He was likely exacting a promise from her, to keep her word.

Her response reached Ken as she stepped away with her men. "This is not how I wished matters to end." She cast a hard, pitying look at Seichan, who only glowered back. "Better it be a bullet. But at least, you'll be able to say your goodbyes."

As they left, Gray hooked an arm around Seichan. She leaned her tired head on his shoulder. It seemed the two had already begun their long and painful road to that goodbye.

Unable to watch, Ken wandered away. They were somewhere high up the slopes of Mount Fuji, which offered a panoramic view across Lake Kawaguchi. Its waters were now banded by wide, muddy banks as the lake drained below.

Beyond its far shore, a fiery beacon glowed under low storm clouds.

It was all that was left of the Ice Castle.

As Ken stared at the burning structure, a suspicion nagged at him, growing slowly into a certainty.

We missed something.

And now it was too late.

37

Elena crouched with the others around the giant block of amber. Sam's flashlight still rested atop it, setting the stone to glowing.

"What is it?" she asked as she peered inside.

Sam stalked around the group, as if physically seeking a solution to the mystery presented. "It's a chrysalis," he answered. "A cocoon."

Elena had already guessed as much. Preserved in the stone was a large, densely woven mass that was plainly a pupa of some sort. A darker halo of amber enclosed it, as if trying to hide the horror inside.

From a rupture along one side of the chrysalis, a creature the size of a small dog pushed out. Long antennae lay curled atop its bowed head. Huge black faceted eyes stared out at the party gathered around. Long-veined wings, which looked damp, remained forever folded over its arched back. A pair of jointed front legs perched at the top of the chrysalis.

Elena imagined it struggling to drag its body out of the cocoon before sap from some prehistoric pine trapped and consumed it.

Clearly it had lost that struggle.

Kat nodded to the monstrous beast. "Sam, I think Elena meant *what's* emerging from that cocoon."

He glanced at them as if the answer should be obvious. "It's clearly *Odokuro*. Look at the characteristic pattern along its abdomen. Black and crimson. Even the mandibles—which are as unique as fingerprints in the insect world—mark it as a member of that species. A genetic analysis would confirm it, but I'm already sure."

Monk rubbed his chin, loudly scratching his beard stubble on the plastic of his prosthesis. "I read Professor Matsui's dossier on the *Odokuro*. He reported nothing like this."

"Because this incarnation never made an appearance in his lab."

"But what is it?" Elena pressed him again.

Sam gave her an apologetic look. "Sorry. I think we're looking at a never-before-seen *Odokuro* queen."

"Wait." Monk frowned. "I thought Professor Matsui said the *Odokuro* had no queen."

"Not that he knew of. He had already determined that *Odokuro* were an intermediary species between ancient solitary wasps and their more social descendants, those who learned to swarm and evolved a variety of multipurpose drones."

Monk nodded. "But Professor Matsui believed the *Odokuro*'s breeding was based on the behavior of older solitary wasps. That the species propagated through a *group* of egg-laden female wasps, instead of a *lone* queen."

"But he must've been wrong," Kat said.

"Maybe not entirely." Sam continued to circle the amber block, examining the creature from every angle. "Professor Matsui was right that this species *does* share characteristics of both solitary and social wasps. He just never thought there was a version of a swarm *queen* in their lineage. Maybe such a creature only arises in a natural environment, versus a lab."

"But why?" Elena pressed. "What's its role with the swarm?"

"I don't know, but it must be important. Maybe the answer to everything."

Elena thought so, too. She straightened from her crouch, too anxious to remain so still. Her knees complained, and she almost lost her balance.

But Sam was there, catching her hand, steadying her.

She turned to him. "Thanks for—"

He yanked her before him, startling her. He hooked an arm around her waist and pressed the cold barrel of a pistol against her neck. "No one move."

He tilted his head and spoke rapidly in Japanese.

Behind them, lights flared. Dark shadows rushed into the cavern. Boots pounded on rocks. Thin red beams pierced the darkness, rising from laser sights mounted atop assault rifles. The crimson spears danced wildly, then quickly settled upon the group standing stunned beside the block of amber.

"Down on your knees," Sam ordered. "Hands on your head."

Elena gaped at the arriving force, then back to the others. One by one, they dropped to the floor, empty hands rising and clasping the backs of their head.

Kat was last, glaring menacingly at Sam, murder in her eyes.

Then she, too, lowered slowly to the stone floor.

6:22 A.M.

"Why?" Kat asked after her weapons had been stripped from her.

I'll at least know that.

She had already figured out the seven-man assault team must have hidden themselves among the parishioners at the midnight mass, sent there in advance by this traitor as their group had reviewed the old maps at the history museum. From the way Sam cocked his head and ordered the force in here, he must have a sophisticated radio buried deep in the canal of his right ear, advanced enough to both communicate and allow him to be tracked.

"Why?" Sam asked, focusing on her, stalking through his men. With the assault force now guarding them, he had shoved Elena forward to join them. "I call it payback. Against a government that would rip away the heritage of a hardworking American. Between inheritance taxes and a backlog of property taxes, the ranch owned by my family in Montana for four generations was about to be foreclosed upon by a bank—a bank that when they were in crisis was bailed out with *my* tax dollars. So what do I owe such a government?"

Off to the side, two men lifted the block of amber. It seemed an impossible feat of strength, until Kat remembered how light the low-density stone actually was. The pair began to haul it across the cavern, intending to leave with the treasure.

She frowned after them.

It seemed the dead miner on the floor wasn't the only thief here.

Sam noted her attention. "Fenikkusu Laboratories came calling after Matsui emailed me about his discovery in Brazil. They were already keeping tabs on him. There is very little that escapes Takashi Ito's attention or reach. He cleared all my debt for no more commitment than keeping his corporation abreast of any developments in Matsui's work." He shrugged. "Then you all called me, and the offer became much more lucrative."

Kat nodded toward the block of amber. "What do you hope to gain there?"

"Considering what Takashi Ito is planning, to be in his good graces when this is all over will be payment enough."

"What is he planning?" Kat pressed.

Sam laughed, retreating step by step, following after the two men and his prize. "Oh, trust me, you'll be happy for a quick death." He turned to one of the other five men and spoke rapidly in Japanese, clearly fluent—but so was Kat. "Once we're clear, shoot them and blow the entrance on your way out. We don't want their bodies found too soon—not that it will matter shortly."

The leader of the assault force nodded. "*Hai.*"

Kat cursed herself for not vetting the entomologist more thoroughly before including him on this mission. In her haste to leave, pressured by the time constraints, she had put too much trust in a scientist working for the National Zoo, a part of the Smithsonian Institution.

She watched Sam exit with the two men carrying the prize. As their lamps illuminated the ramp out of here, Kat spotted a body sprawled at the foot of it.

Piotr . . .

She feared the same fate had befallen Gerik and Anton at the shore of the lake.

Kat glanced to Clara, who had also spotted her brother. The woman was shaking, her eyes shining with tears. Slaski's normally dour face had purpled with fury. Elena simply looked stunned and shell-shocked, both at the situation and at the betrayal. Kat knew the librarian had warmed up to the duplicitous entomologist.

Her eyes finally settled on Monk.

She nodded, signaling him.

Sam may have fooled her prior to the expedition, but a moment ago he had inadvertently given himself away, letting his mask slip at the shock of the discovery of an *Odokuro* queen. *Professor Matsui was wrong . . . everyone was wrong.* His choice of words had struck her as odd. Who was this *everyone*? Sam had only been in contact with Ken about this species.

Still, she couldn't be sure, so she had stayed silent, hoping to lean on his expertise regarding this discovery before challenging him. She knew this never-before-seen incarnation of the species had to be significant. Though, in hindsight, perhaps she should've been more cautious. She hadn't expected the man to grab Elena so suddenly.

Not that I don't have a backup plan.

6:34 A.M.

Elena knelt on the ground, sitting on her ankles, too weak to even hold herself up. Despair and regret hollowed her out. Her arms trembled as she continued to hold her hands atop her head. She wanted to lower one of them, to touch the pair of crosses hanging from the chain of her reading glasses, to cast one last prayer to her daughter and two grandchildren, to wish them a long and fruitful life.

She found it hard to concentrate on such a last plea to God, not with five rifles pointed at the group. She caught Kat's small nod to her husband, a final silent expression of love and affection, which the two had amply demonstrated throughout this journey. She also knew the pair had two children and added those girls to her prayers.

After acknowledging his wife, Monk faced their executioners, his hands clasped behind his head. She blinked, realizing her mistake. There was only *one* hand cradling the back of his skull. The fingers of that hand fiddled with the titanium wrist cuff, where the man's prosthesis was normally attached.

It was gone.

When Sam had ordered the assault team to strip the group of their weapons, he had forgotten in the rush of events to inform them of a hidden threat. She also suspected Kat had kept attention on herself by questioning Sam, distracting everyone so Monk could detach and drop his prosthesis.

But where and how—?

Then she spotted movement behind the legs of

the armed men: the skittering of a pale plastic spider across the burnt amber floor.

She remembered back at Sigma headquarters in D.C., how Monk had demonstrated his ability to remotely control his disarticulated limb. He clearly had some skill. His disembodied hand danced on its fingertips and drew closer behind the line of men.

Elena also remembered the library museum in Tallinn.

Monk whispered one word, "Boom."

On this signal, Kat leaped at Elena, while Monk flung himself at Slaski and Clara. The concussion of the explosion deafened her; the flash in the near-darkness blinded her. She landed hard on her side, shielded by Kat. Even before the blast echoed away, Kat's weight rolled off her.

Elena remained on the floor, blinking away the flare. Before her, Kat slid on a hip across the stone, scooping up a rifle from one of the armed men whose back was cratered and smoking. From the ground, she fired nearly point-blank at another, who was climbing to his feet. He sprawled backward.

The farthest gunman, relatively unscathed, had only been knocked to his knees. He leveled his weapon at Kat—then his chest exploded, the point of a pick-axe protruding out his shattered rib cage. His body slumped forward, revealing Monk standing there, holding the handle of the salt-mummified miner's axe.

The other two members of the assault team, both closest to the explosion, were already dead.

Monk hurriedly collected two rifles and shoved one at Slaski. "Do you know how to use this?"

He backed up a step, shaking his head.

Elena had gained her feet already and stepped forward. She took the weapon, did a quick check, then nodded. "Not a problem. I grew up in the barrio of East L.A."

Monk grinned at her. "You are a librarian of many skills."

Kat remained cold and serious. "Follow us out, but stay near the ramp."

"What are you going to do?" Elena asked.

She nodded to her husband. "We're going to work."

6:39 A.M.

As the group exited the accursed cavern, Kat quickly changed tactics.

The surrounding mine groaned around them. The ground trembled underfoot. Fragile stalactites of salt broke from the roof and shattered. The concussion of the blast must have destabilized this fragile corner of the mine. Half of the scallop shell had collapsed in the past, and now the rest threatened to do the same.

Still, Kat paused at the bottom of the ramp long enough to check on Piotr, noting the blade imbedded in the back of the poor man's neck. Monk drew Clara to the side, keeping her from the sight.

Kat gritted her teeth as she stood. "Okay, new plan. We're all getting out of here, but Monk and I'll take the lead. You all follow but hang several yards back."

She didn't wait for confirmation. She firmed her grip on the stolen rifle and set off down the passageway they had used before. She set a hard pace, knowing Sam and his men would've heard the explosion. But would they believe it was just their teammates blasting the cave opening, as Sam had ordered?

She had no way of knowing, but she could not let that traitor escape with the treasure stolen from here. If there truly was an answer to be found preserved in that block of amber, they had to acquire it.

As they traversed the quarter-mile-long tunnel, the quaking continued, jolting ever stronger. The blast must have set off a cascade effect, as one section undermined the next, spreading throughout the area. The air filled with fine salt crystals, shining like diamonds in the beams of their headlamps.

The ground suddenly bolted violently under Kat's feet, throwing her against the wall. The others suffered the same, but at least kept upright. A wash of smoke and more salt dust flowed over them from behind.

The tunnel must have collapsed back there.

"Faster," Kat urged.

They set off again at a near run. She sensed they must be nearing the exit—when the shine of her headlamp revealed a jumble of rock blocking the passageway ahead. It had already caved in.

Monk drew alongside her as she stopped. "What now?"

"I don't . . ." She shook her head, despairing.

He hooked his arm around her waist. "Use that big brain of yours to get us out of here."

She stared down at her toes—not out of defeat, but to note the flow of water running past. It was fast and heavy. Even as she watched, the flow increased.

She glanced back, waving a trace of salt dust from her nose. The earlier jolt had clearly collapsed the tunnel behind them, but if water was continuing to flow . . .

"Back," she said. "We have to go back."

She got everyone retreating along the passageway.

In less than a minute, they reached where the tunnel wall had collapsed. But rather than fully blocking the passageway, the break had cracked through into the tunnel that paralleled this one. Water flowed underfoot from that neighboring vein of the shell.

"Go, go, go," she urged.

As she scrambled with the others into the next tunnel, she thanked the old miners for their engineering skills. Once together, they set off again. Their progress through the new tunnel was slowed by blockages of old salt formations, but the quaking had shattered enough of the brittle and delicate formations to allow them to move briskly.

At last, they reached the pelvis of the shell. Kat proceeded cautiously, her rifle raised, fearing Sam might have left one of his men behind. But her search revealed no hidden sniper, only an empty cavern. Two bodies lay near the shoreline of the canal that led out to the lake.

Gerik and Anton.

Her fingers tightened on her weapon.

The Jet Ski was still beached beside the bodies, but the Zodiac pontoon was gone, taken by Sam to transport his prize. She also noted a pile of discarded scuba tanks, knowing now how the assault team had made their silent approach to ambush Clara's brothers.

Kat waved the others out. "Elena, stay here with Clara and Dr. Slaski." She nodded to the rifle in the librarian's hand. "Stay hidden. If anyone besides us returns—"

Elena hefted her weapon higher. "Oh, the bastards will regret it."

Good.

Kat turned and headed to the Jet Ski. She silently apologized to Gerik as she unsnapped the watercraft's keys from his vest. She and Monk then pushed the Jet Ski back into the dark water and quickly mounted it. Unable to pilot the craft with his missing prosthesis, Monk climbed in back. He cradled the SIG Sauer he had recovered from their captors in his other hand.

Kat dropped behind the controls, resting her rifle across her knees.

Monk leaned forward. "Hon—"

"I know. We have no element of surprise."

Out in the open water, it would be an all-out assault.

"No, I just wanted to say I love you."

"Oh." She leaned back and pecked him on the cheek. "Me, too."

Monk settled back. "Now let's go shoot us some bad guys."

She leaned down.

That's why I love you . . . we're always of one mind.

She ignited the engine, squeezed the throttle,

and shot forward down the canal. She didn't slow through the S-curve of the waterway. She gained speed with every turn. By the time she hit the lake, the craft flew across the water, all but skimming above the flat surface.

Ahead, she spotted her target: a lone light racing across the black lake. She had already doused her helmet lamp and raced her craft dark toward her quarry. The others closed in on the far shore, but they appeared to be proceeding slowly, having to balance their cargo aboard their craft.

Kat had no such disadvantage and sped faster, the needle of the speedometer cresting toward sixty. The pool of light ahead grew swiftly. Though she ran dark, there was no masking the scream of the Jet Ski's engine.

By the time the enemy decided the approaching watercraft might not be piloted by one of their own, the Jet Ski was nearly atop them. Rifle blasts pierced the engine's roar, but Kat wove the ski back and forth, challenging their aim at the small craft.

Monk returned fire, his SIG Sauer's retort deafening in her ear. Luckily he had a much larger and brighter target. He dropped one sniper and drove the other down with the first volley of shots, emptying his weapon. He then reached around and took the rifle from her lap.

He lifted it one-handed, balanced it across his other forearm, and sprayed a barrage of automatic fire—strafing the pontoon along one side, ripping it to shreds. The boat quickly foundered, spinning toward the damaged side.

The second gunman tried to drive them off, but

he lost his balance as the dragging pontoon suddenly sank, jolting the boat. As he toppled toward the water, Monk shifted his aim and plugged him twice in the chest, a parting gift before sending him to a watery grave.

But the gunman wasn't the only passenger to lose balance.

Kat watched the block of amber teeter, then crash on its side. Momentum rolled it over the deflated pontoon. It vanished with a splash into the dark depths of the deep lake.

Panicked at the loss, Monk shoved his rifle at her, then leaped off the back of the Jet Ski as it raced past the foundering boat.

She didn't have time to tell him it was a wasted effort.

Instead, she hunkered down and continued toward shore. At the start of the attack, she had spotted a splash near the bow of the boat. A rat leaving a sinking ship. From the corner of her eye, she had followed Sam's path as he swam for safety.

By now, he had already reached the far shore and clambered out. He sprinted for the tunnel leading out. She sped toward him, but he had the wherewithal to douse his helmet lamp. His figure was a slightly darker mote against the inky darkness.

Once he reached the tunnels, it would be nearly impossible to catch him.

The Jet Ski struck the sloped bank at near-top speed. She rode it far across the rock, keeping her seat by squeezing her thighs. She lifted the rifle and emptied her weapon in a final barrage—but she didn't bother aiming for such a small target.

Instead, she fired at the huge array of salt stalactites hanging along the roof near the opening to the cavern. The formations rained down in a wide swath of sharp spears.

A sharp, startled scream followed.

As the Jet Ski slowed, she hurtled off the seat and ran toward the source. She kept her own lights doused, knowing Sam was armed. She ran low, trying to discern where he was. Her boots crunched through sharp shards of broken salt.

Then a sharper cry erupted ahead, agonizing and tortured.

She easily followed it to a body writhing on the ground. She flicked on her light. Sam struggled with a broken lance of salt through his neck, another pierced his shoulder, a third impaled his upper left thigh. His struggles weakened as blood pulsed from his wounded throat—but the pain plainly grew worse.

His agonized screams echoed across the cavern.

She knew what tortured him—something beyond the certainty of his impending death.

Salt in the wounds.

She turned her back and let him scream. By the time she reached the lake, the last of his strangled cries died away.

Good riddance.

Out in the dark water, she saw Monk paddling back and forth near the half-sunk boat. He noted her approach and hollered.

"I can't find the block! We'll need divers."

She cupped her mouth and called over to him. "Just wait!"

"For what?"

She searched the lake. After another breath, a large object burst to the surface, startling her husband. It rocked in place beside him.

She shouted across the water. "Amber floats!"

Its density was less than salt water. It was why so much amber was found along the Baltic coastlines, where waves washed floating bits to its sandy shores.

"Now you tell me," Monk groused.

He swam to the block and began pushing it toward her.

She sighed with her hands on her hips. They had secured the prize, but what had they truly accomplished? She pictured the queen frozen in amber.

What did it mean?

38

Two hours after escaping the destruction of the Ice Castle, Gray paced the length of a conference room at the Public Security Intelligence Agency. Their headquarters was located in central Tokyo, in the Chiyoda ward, the city's equivalent to the U.S. National Mall. Out the window was a commanding view of the Imperial Palace. Elsewhere in the same ward stood their Supreme Court and the prime minister's official residence.

He awaited a videoconference call with Painter Crowe. Earlier, Gray had updated the director on all that had happened. Now there was this sudden new request. He feared the worst. Prior to this summons, he had been working with Aiko and a cadre of her inner circle. Shortly after arriving in Tokyo, Valya had fulfilled her promise, transmitting the code to unlock the thumb drive. Aiko had sent a military force to secure the identified warehouse, discovering a vast stockpile of the pesticide developed by Fenikkusu Laboratories.

An airlift of those canisters—accompanied by a Japanese squadron of tanker planes to distribute the pesticide—was already en route to Hawaii. Though the chemical should eradicate the adult populations of the colonized wasps, it promised no relief for those already parasitized: human, animal, or insect.

Aiko had also translated some of the corporation's feasibility studies and toxicology reports found in the documents they'd recovered. According to the findings, the pesticide was highly carcinogenic and toxic to a wide spectrum of other arthropods. Use of the chemical would wreak havoc on the island's delicate ecosystem. But worst of all, the Hawaiian chain would be forever contaminated, needing constant monitoring and retreatment as the larval stages rose again and again.

Maybe it would be better if the place was simply nuked, Gray thought grimly.

And he wasn't the only one advocating this.

Aiko had shared some confidential communications between the U.S. military and various intelligence agencies. While the pesticide put a thumb in this proverbial dike, the threat of the contagion breaking loose and spreading remained. For many countries, this was still too much of a risk.

And now this sudden call from Painter.

Gray studied those gathered in the room. The director had asked for Professor Matsui to be present, along with Seichan and Palu. The Hawaiian still looked shell-shocked upon learning the grim future of his native lands. Seichan sat stoically, but from her haunted eyes and tight lips, she knew she was mere hours at best until the pain returned tenfold, marking when the third instars would begin ravaging her body. Ken kept glancing her way, as if trying to read her every twitch and breath for some warning of the end.

Finally, the large screen on the wall before the table bloomed to life, drawing everyone's attention. Gray stiffened, surprised. He had expected to find the director staring back at him. Instead, the crystal-clear image revealed a slim figure leaning against what appeared to be a table in a small laboratory.

"Kat?" Gray stepped closer. "Where are you? What's this about?"

"I'm in Krakow, at a small amber museum. Painter arranged this call, knowing the urgency."

"Why?"

"We found something out here. Something that makes no sense. But it's beyond any of our expertise. The only man who could've helped . . . well, I killed him. So I was hoping Professor Matsui might offer some insight."

Gray scrunched his brow. "What did you find?"

Kat quickly explained the events in Poland, about a salt mine, a vast amber deposit, and a block of stone holding a unique specimen. "Let me show you." She waved to the video operator. "Monk, bring the camera over to the table."

The image jiggled as the view swept high, then lowered to a wide table holding a giant cube of glowing amber. It was lit from multiple angles to reveal what was frozen inside.

A chair crashed behind Gray.

"My god . . ." Ken rushed around the table to join him before the screen. He leaned closer, his hands rising as if wanting to grab the object. "That's a prehistoric chrysalis. Captured in the process of hatching."

Kat returned to the edge of the screen. "Professor Matsui, could this be the birth of an *Odokuro* queen?"

"What? No. There's no such—" He stepped closer again. "Wait."

He studied the image for a long breath, then asked Monk for different angles, for the lights to be shifted.

"Ken," Gray pressed, needing him to reach a conclusion. "Is it or isn't it?"

The man licked his lips, his voice hushed. "Yes . . . yes, it must be." He searched the screen and found Kat. "Tell me again in more detail about what you saw, about the state of the dead wasps."

She repeated her story, answering questions from Ken along the way. "Sam thought they had bled out," she finished. "Or at least *something* had oozed out of their bodies."

"Dissolved from the inside out," Ken mumbled to himself.

Kat heard him. "That sounds about right."

Ken retreated and fell heavily into a seat. "I was wrong. Wrong all along."

"About there being an *Odokuro* queen?" Gray asked.

He nodded. "That certainly, but I suspect such a queen would never appear in a laboratory setting. She would rise only within an established swarm, one in a natural environment."

"But why?" Kat asked. "What does it mean?"

He stared at her. "It means I was also wrong

about Gamma Team's research. They had the answer all along. The lock, but not the key."

"What are you talking about?" Gray asked. "What team's research?"

"One of Fenikkusu's drug groups was investigating a series of genes for a missing protein, what they named a *ghost peptide*. They called it a *ghost*, because they found the genes, but never the protein it coded for. Analysis of the sequence suggested it was a strong biolytic agent capable of dissolving a prey's tissue."

Kat glanced to the block of amber. "From the inside out."

Ken nodded. "I thought it was a piece of old code, ancestral junk from a time when the *Odokuro* killed their hosts. I believed, once the wasps evolved out of this behavior, they had set aside this toxic peptide, locking it away with a bunch of epigenetic markers. I thought Gamma Team had been wasting their time, that they'd never in a million years find the key to that lock."

"And now?" Gray asked.

Ken shrugged. "At least I was right in one regard. The key is actually *two hundred million* years old." He pointed to the screen. "She's the key."

"How?" Kat stared at the block. "What are you talking about?"

"I should've seen it, or at least suspected it." Ken shook his head. "I sensed I had missed something. What I forgot was basic *Hymenoptera* behavior, whether you're talking wasps or bees."

"What behavior?" Gray asked.

"In social wasps—those that have a queen—it is only the queen that survives winter. The rest of the swarm dies during the harsh freeze. Only she hibernates and overwinters, waiting for the warmth of spring to awaken her. Already pregnant, she rises and brings the hive back to life."

Gray remembered Ken explaining this behavior back at the cottage in Hana, when he revealed the true horror of this species.

Ken stood again and approached the screen. "It's why none of us saw such a queen before. She only appears when conditions are harsh, when the colony is threatened. She is the colony's means of moving to a new home." He turned to Gray and the others. "But only after she first makes sure the old colony is wiped out. If a freeze doesn't do it, she takes matters into her own hands."

"How?" Kat asked.

"I can't be sure yet, but I suspect she releases a potent pheromone. Didn't you mention that the amber surrounding the site where the block was excavated was *darker* than elsewhere? Even in this block, I can see the stone around the queen is several gradations richer in hue."

Gray understood. "You're thinking the chemical she was emitting stained the amber."

"A chemical that I believe is the key to unlocking the genes of the ghost peptide. With the key in the lock, the genes would begin producing this biolytic protein. Before I thought the peptide was meant as a weapon against *other* prey." He shook his head. "Instead, it's a suicide pill for *this* species.

Once exposed to this chemical, every incarnation of the *Odokuro* that carries this sequence of genes would die."

"And all the wasps carry these genes?" Kat asked.

Ken ignored her and turned to Seichan. "Even their larvae."

Gray felt a slight surge of hope but stamped it back down, not wanting to get his expectations up.

On the screen, Kat called to someone out of view. "Dr. Slaski, as I recall, your lab is one of only two in Poland equipped with a sophisticated mass spectrometer for analyzing the authenticity of amber artifacts."

"That's correct. We can judge quality, analyze impurities, even date samples."

"So if you cored a sample of the *stained* amber, could you determine what chemical is in there?"

"With enough time and resources, certainly."

"I can supply you with all the *resources* you need, but *time* . . . that I can't give you."

The speaker seemed to understand. "I'll do my best."

Gray turned to find Seichan standing next to him. She took his hand.

To hell with it.

He squeezed her fingers, and with all his heart, he allowed himself to hope.

For her, for him, for their unborn child.

8:37 P.M.

"That's it," Ken pronounced.

He shook his head as he stared at the molecular diagram on the laptop screen.

Of course, that's the chemical.

Ken was still in the conference room. None of them had left. They all clustered around the laptop. On the wall, the video feed from Poland continued to run. The lab in Krakow was packed with all manner of experts summoned by Kat: molecular biologists, genetic scientists, organic chemists. New equipment had also been hauled into the lab.

Still, the sepulchral figure of Dr. Slaski had orchestrated the chaos with an iron hand—until four hours later, the group had finally teased the answer from the amber.

"Are you sure that's the right chemical?" Gray asked. "Not some other impurity."

"I'm sure," Ken said.

"How can you be certain?" Gray pressed, anxiety straining his voice.

"Because I recognize this organic compound. It's a derivative of 9-keto-2-decenoic acid." Noting Gray's confused expression, Ken explained. "It's also known as *queen substance*."

Gray glanced over to the creature aglow in the amber.

"So, yeah, I'm pretty sure," Ken said with a tired

grin. "The compound is very much like the aromatic ketone released by honeybee queens. Many other *Hymenoptera* species release some variant of this same pheromone."

"What does it do in bees?"

"When a new queen flies off to establish her own hive, she casts a pall of this chemical over the old hive, where the hormone sterilizes all the workers left behind."

"Why?"

"So the queen ensures her own genetic legacy, erasing the lineage behind her." Ken nodded to the screen. "What the *Odokuro* queen does is not all that different. But as this species has *multiple* subqueens who are capable of breeding and parasitizing—like the big wasp that attacked Seichan—a more aggressive tactic is employed, a nuclear option if you will. When a swarm is threatened, she clears the genetic slate and moves on to perpetuate the next generation based on her own genes."

Ken shrugged. "While sounding callous, it makes sense from an evolutionary standpoint. When an environment is threatened, the best chance for a species is for one individual to pack their proverbial bags, erase any trace of its existence, and move on to greener pastures with a new set of genetics. For countless millennia, some version of this strategy has worked for all manner of wasps, where their swarms are killed off every winter to start anew. Or in the case of bees, they simply sterilize their way to a new genetic heritage."

"And this pheromone? Will it be effective as a treatment?"

"Exceedingly so. Not only should this derivative be safe, it's *specific* to the *Odokuro*. It shouldn't harm any other species. Plus the aromatic nature of the ketone will draw the swarm to the pheromone. Like moths to a flame."

Ken leaned back. "Best of all, any lab should be able to easily manufacture this organic compound in vast quantities. And once it's sprayed across water, spread over plants, and soaked into dirt, any parasitized creature that drinks, eats, or grooms the chemical will absorb the compound into its bloodstream, where it should destroy the internal larvae."

"What about people?" Gray reached over and took Seichan's hand.

Ken noted her eyes shining with the threat of tears—not from resurgent pain, but from the agony of hope. "No different," he assured them. "I wager a single intravenous or intramuscular injection should be enough. Though I'd recommend repeating this a few days in a row to be sure."

Gray leaned into Seichan, sighing loudly. "So this *is* the cure."

Palu grabbed Ken by the shoulder. The Hawaiian's grin demonstrated he understood what this meant for his native lands. "Brah, it's not just the *cure*. It's our motherfucking *salvation*."

Ken matched his grin.

You'll get no argument from me.

39

Kat sat beside Monk in the Chapel of Saint Kinga. The subterranean cathedral was packed for the memorial mass. Above the altar, a salt cross glowed with an inner fire. A children's chorus sang a hymn that echoed from the walls, seeming to defy the tons of rock to rise to heaven.

Clara sat in the front row, draped in black, her head bowed. The caskets of her three brothers rested before her. Each was sculpted of amber, priceless in their own right, more so from the men inside, who gave their lives so the world might have a future. They were to be buried here, new saints for this holy place.

"Piotr, Gerik, Anton," Kat whispered, acknowledging them aloud, intending never to forget their names.

Monk squeezed her hand. They had flown in last night from D.C. for the service and would leave again this evening.

Though two weeks had passed, there was much still to be done. Hawaii was recovering, treated daily with aerial sprayings of the organic compound. As Professor Matsui had predicted, the queen substance had eradicated the *Odokuro*, the fragrant ketone drawing the wasps out of every nest and colony. Hospitals across the state were treating everyone with intramuscular injections as a precaution. Ecologists and biologists were monitoring wildlife for signs of any resurgence.

With Hawaii safe, Kat had concentrated her attention on tracking down the other research installations run by Fenikkusu Laboratories. She worked closely with Aiko to coordinate an international response. In addition, such work helped Aiko solidify her covert intelligence agency in Japan, which she had christened TaU—or *Tako no Ude*—which stood for "Arms of an Octopus," an apt name for a new spy agency. But Kat also knew that *tau* was the next letter in the Greek alphabet after *sigma*, a clear shout-out to their American counterpart.

While the choir sang, she glanced over to Professor Matsui. He was seated down the row next to Dr. Slaski. Ken had been working closely with the museum director to examine the mysteries frozen in the amber below. It was proving to be a treasure trove of prehistoric life. In addition, Ken had been offered a new position in D.C., one he was still debating to accept, to fill a certain seat left vacant, as head of the entomology department at the National Zoo.

She hoped he took it.

Slaski leaned down and whispered to Ken, who nodded. They both glanced to Clara. Kat knew the two had been doing their best to console the bereaved woman, but only time would dull such a pain. Kat was relieved another woman did not have to experience that particular agony. She had heard news yesterday out of Tallinn that Director Tamm was out of the hospital, back at home with his daughter, Lara.

She sighed heavily.

Thank god . . .

Kat settled back as the choir finished the hymn in a transcendent chorus. A lone boy then strode to the balustrade beside the coffins. He was blond, apple-cheeked, like a young ghost of the dead brothers. He sang "Ave Maria" in Polish, without accompaniment. His single sweet voice spoke to the loss here more powerfully than any words.

As the boy sang with all his heart to the heavens, Kat lowered her face.

Monk drew her closer.

Tears fell from her eyes . . . to the hands of her husband clasped to hers.

She held tightly to him.

Don't ever let me go.

8:05 A.M. EDT
Washington, D.C.

"Now remember," Elena warned, "we don't touch anything without asking first."

Her two granddaughters nodded vigorously as she held open the door to the Smithsonian Castle. "*Sí, abuela,*" they sang in unison.

The fragrance struck Elena as soon as she followed them inside. A sweet perfume of roses, lilacs, and lilies filled the marble hall, drawing her to the crypt not far from the door.

She herded the two girls toward the men waiting for her there: Painter Crowe and the museum's curator, Simon Wright. At their feet and spilling across the floor were bouquets of flowers and scatters of loose stems. The small room that housed James Smithson's crypt was full of even more.

"And who might these young women be?" Painter asked, bending down as she joined him.

The girls slunk bashfully behind her legs. Once safely out of view, the older of the two risked pointing to her young sister. "That's Olivia. And I'm Anna."

"Are you both librarians like your grandmother?"

Olivia giggled. "No."

Anna stamped a foot. "But I'm gonna be."

"Going to be," Elena corrected.

"I don't doubt it," Painter said as he straightened. He glanced back at the overflowing crypt. "But I wonder which of you could collect the most yellow flowers. I really like *yellow*."

"I can, I can," the girls chimed together, pausing to confirm with their grandmother that they could *touch* things.

Elena shrugged. "Go ahead. But be careful of rose thorns. Can't have your mother calling Child Protective Services down on me."

The girls dashed into the pile of flowers, trailing giggles.

Elena shook her head. "They're a handful."

"That I also don't doubt." Painter waved to the bounty. "Clearly your op-ed in the *Washington Times* had quite the response."

"Or maybe it was your appearance on *Good Morning America*," Simon added with a grin.

Elena blushed. "Just trying to get your founder some publicity."

"That you did," Simon concurred.

After arriving back in the States, she had shared her story of their adventures in Europe, how they had followed what were literally *cryptic* clues left by James Smithson to save the world. She had ended her piece in the paper by suggesting the man be properly honored: *He should be showered with flowers.*

It seemed the curious who had come to view the symbols for themselves had followed her directions.

Painter nodded to Simon. "We thought you deserved a small reward yourself. It's why we asked you here before the Castle opens. It only seemed proper to do that here."

"That's silly. I don't need—"

"Dear god, woman," Simon said with an exasperated sigh, "let the man give you what he's got."

She rolled her eyes. "Fine."

Painter reached to a pocket of his suit jacket and took out a small box, no larger than a deck of cards. He held it out. "For a lady who has everything . . . including two rambunctious grandchildren."

Curious, she took the gift.

"Open it," Simon urged, bouncing a bit on his toes.

She hinged back the lid to reveal an obsidian-black metallic card resting atop a red silk cushion.

As she tilted the box, a holographic silver symbol rose from the card's surface.

It was a single Greek letter.

Sigma.

"Keys to the kingdom," Simon explained.

"In case you ever tire of being a librarian," Painter said. "And want a little adventure."

She cast him a jaundiced eye.

He shrugged. "Or maybe you just want to come down for a cup of coffee. With that key, my door's always open."

She snapped the lid closed. "Director Crowe, coffee sounds like plenty enough adventure for me."

"I don't know. You've never tried Kowalski's brew. It'll make you wish you were being shot at."

She grinned. "I'll take my chances."

8:08 P.M. EDT
Takoma Park, Maryland

With crickets burring and fireflies flickering in the neighboring hydrangeas, Gray stood before the FOR SALE sign posted in the yard of his parents' craftsman bungalow.

A smaller SOLD! sign rested atop the crossbar.

He headed across the expanse of yard. He remembered mowing the lawn, the fresh smell of cut grass, shoving a push mower around because his father had been too cheap to buy a gasoline-powered one. He reached the driveway. At the end of it, the garage at the back of the house stood closed and dark, but he could still hear his father hammering away inside, cursing, as he tinkered with his vintage Thunderbird, which was still parked there. He pictured his mother watching her husband work from the kitchen window, burning the family dinner, preferring her books and grading papers to learning how to cook properly.

Everywhere he looked, there were ghosts.

It was why nine months ago he had decided to take a sabbatical with Seichan. More than needing a break from Sigma and its responsibilities, he had fled from *here*. A month ago, he had finally agreed to allow his brother Kenny to list the house.

What do either of us need with this place?

With no reason to remain any longer, Kenny had returned to California, chasing a new job in the tech industry. The only people through the house these past weeks were real estate brokers and potential buyers.

Since arriving back in the States, Gray had avoided coming here. He hadn't even stepped foot inside. But with the pending sale, he needed to inventory what was left in the house. He didn't know what to do with all the old furniture and the lifetime of accumulated knickknacks that seemed so important. He considered charity, using an estate sale service.

He sighed.

He knew a large part of the reason behind his foot-dragging and hesitation.

Promise me . . .

He could still feel the pressure of the syringe as he induced the fatal overdose. He remembered his father's fingers relaxing as he held his frail hand, the feel of his calluses, the thinness of his bones. As much as Gray accepted that it was the right decision at the time, he still could not escape the guilt.

Even traveling the full breadth of the globe, he could not escape his ghosts.

And now I've come full circle.

No wiser, no less guilty.

He accepted this was a burden he would carry with him the rest of his life. Unable to delay any longer, he headed toward the front door. Seichan was already inside, needing to lie down. Her treatments were finished. Though the larval load was dead, it would take her body some time to clear what was inside her, challenging her immune system. But at least the tests this morning seemed to indicate the baby inside was faring well.

Despite his melancholy, he smiled softly, remembering the tiny flutter of a heartbeat on the ultrasound.

Our baby . . .

He shook his head at the impossibility of it all.

Both were safe. Even Kowalski was recovering from his injuries, as were Palu's cousins. Earlier in the day, Gray had spoken to the big man, who was still on Maui. *Gonna finish my goddamn vacation*, Kowalski had told him. He had joined his girlfriend, Maria, who was helping with efforts out there. They were staying with Palu's family.

Kowalski had only one major complaint about his care: *They got me wearing pantyhose.* Maria had explained, trying to calm the man's dismay. Apparently Kowalski had been ordered to wear medical compression stockings for six weeks, to help heal his many bite wounds. Gray had insisted that Maria send him photos. In case he ever needed to blackmail the guy.

Gray reached his parent's front door and tugged on it.

It didn't budge.

He was about to knock when the door opened.

Seichan stood there, cocking an eyebrow. She dangled a key from a finger. "I changed the locks."

"What? Why?"

She stepped back to let him inside. In his mind's eye, he knew exactly what his parents' home looked like.

But with a blink, it all vanished.

The furniture was gone. The carpets had been ripped up and replaced with hand-scraped hardwoods. The large fireplace had been re-rocked. Even from the doorway, he could see the kitchen had new granite counters and cabinets.

"Seichan . . ."

"Shut up." She grabbed his hand and drew him toward the stairs leading to the second floor, but not before she nodded outside to the yard, to the sign posted out there. "Who do you think bought this place?"

Before he could respond, he was hauled up the stairs.

Everything was changed. The wood banister was now wrought iron. The wallpaper stripped. Everything was freshly painted.

"Don't worry," she said. "Your father's Thunderbird is still in the garage. Wasn't about to part with that beauty. Plus there are boxes of personal items. You can go through those later. But first . . ."

She stopped at a closed door. "It's time to stop running from your ghosts."

Gray felt a chill at how well she could read him.

She opened the door and pulled him inside. The tiny bedroom was as empty as the rest of the house. Only a single item of furniture stood there.

A pure white crib.

"While you can't escape those ghosts," she said, "you can invite them into your life, let them share your joys and sorrows."

Gray felt a sob rising up and fought against it. He looked around, breathing deeply. "All this effort . . . and I didn't even have a clue."

She shrugged. "You're not *that* difficult to fool, Gray. Besides, for me, doing all this was more of a vacation than hopping around the world."

He shook his head, smiling now, tears rising. "Then we'd better enjoy it while we can. This peace won't last for long."

"You're right." Her face grew grim. "Valya's out there. No doubt plotting something."

Gray turned to her, dropped to his knees, and lifted the lower edge of her blouse. He kissed her stomach and whispered to her belly.

"That's not what I meant."

EPILOGUE
HALEAKALA, MAUI

QUEEN

She knows it is time.

A biological clock, fueled by hormones, triggers her new body to writhe in its black chrysalis. Mandibles reach up to snip at the cap of silk she had spun as a larva. A hole is chewed through, softened by saliva steeped in the queen substance excreted by glands in her maw.

One antenna uncurls and extends out, probing the world beyond. Fine sensillae test the moist cool air. Once satisfied, she batters her triangular head through the opening and uses hooks in her forelegs to split the pupal case. The thin chrysalis crumples under her weight as she wriggles around and perches there.

She pauses to groom herself in the darkness, readying herself to be revealed. She cleans her unblinking black eyes and brushes each antenna with fine combs on the underside of her forelegs.

All the while, haemolymph pumps through the long veins of her damp and crinkled wings. They slowly spread and expand. Once the wings are draped long and sturdy, she flutters them dry.

Only then is she ready.

She crawls off her perch to the damp rock of the tunnel. It is here she had spun her cocoon months ago, safely hidden in the dark. Now she follows the rock, escaping *away* from where she had come, seeking a new home in a new direction.

Her abdomen is already heavy with eggs, pluripotent clones of herself, capable of becoming every caste of her new swarm.

She carries the very future inside her.

As she travels, she leaves an aromatic path in her wake. The alluring scent will draw any of the old swarm still in the area, a sweet trap that will kill, erasing that genetic lineage behind her. Only her code must survive, unchallenged by the past.

She moves relentlessly. She will not stop until she has found a suitable home. But as she continues, the stone under her feet grows colder. Still, she presses onward, driven by a millennia-old drive to survive. She smells fresh air far ahead, promising a new opening to the upper world.

Before she can reach there, the stone grows a layer of ice.

She pauses, casting out her senses in snaps of her hind legs and testing the air with her antenna. An image forms in the knotted ganglions of her brain.

The tunnel ahead shows ice covering every surface. Drapes and spikes and waves. Despite the danger, she continues forward, unable to turn back, incapable of defying her genetic instinct. She heads into the cold, timeless and patient. She will not change. Instead, she will wait for the world to do so.

If not now, her time would come again.

Knowing this, she marches into the cold tunnels, until her wings frost over and her legs stiffen. Her body grows cold. She only stops when the pads of her feet finally freeze to the ice.

There, she will remain.

There, she abides.

Awaiting her chance to rise again.

AUTHOR'S NOTE TO READERS: TRUTH OR FICTION

We've come once again, you and I, to that moment when I must separate fact from fiction. Of course, I would prefer it if you simply believed every word—as that's any novelist's goal. But sometimes *truth* is as fascinating as any *fiction*, so let's go ahead and separate that chaff from the wheat.

I thought I'd start with the past and work my way forward. This book is full of interesting characters out of history, including the mysterious founder of the Smithsonian Institution. Perhaps it's best we start with him.

James Smithson

Considering this British chemist and geologist founded our nation's greatest institution of knowledge, he remains vastly underappreciated. I hope this novel helps correct this egregious oversight. Almost everything written here about the man is factual. He was an esteemed member of the British

Royal Society, and he traveled throughout Europe collecting a vast mineral collection that was indeed bequeathed to the United States, along with his fortune (a collection that unfortunately was destroyed when a fire broke out at the Smithsonian Castle near the end of World War II).

After his death, Alexander Graham Bell and his wife did indeed sneak off to Europe and return with his bones. As to the tomb, the symbols found on his grave, along with the error about his age, are real. I suggest you go to the Castle and check out these details for yourself. And if you feel like it, please place a flower there in his memory.

If you can't make such a trip and want to know more about the man and his life, I recommend you read:

The Lost World of James Smithson, by Heather Ewing

Joseph Henry

The first secretary of the Smithsonian, Joseph Henry, oversaw the museum during the Civil War, including being present when the infamous fire broke out there. The arson was said to be due to the faulty installation of a stove and not the nefarious work of early members of the Guild. But rumors abound whether there might be more to this story, as Joseph Henry, a devout abolitionist, was secretly helping Abraham Lincoln during the war.

Archibald MacLeish

The investigative hero of this story was indeed a Librarian of Congress during World War II. In his role as the head of the Committee for the Conservation of Cultural Resources, he secured the nation's treasures. Fearing bombing raids during the war, he sent the Declaration of Independence, the Constitution, and a copy of the Gutenberg Bible to Fort Knox. Even the Smithsonian buried the Star-Spangled Banner deep in the Shenandoah National Park. But early on, Archibald had advocated for building a bombproof shelter beneath the National Mall to store national treasures in times of crisis. Unfortunately, Congress shot down his idea due to its expense.

Moving from the past to the present, let's look into the science behind the novel. Here is where fact is often stranger than fiction, especially in regards to . . .

Wasps, Wasps, and More Wasps

This novel explores some of the intriguing biology, behavior, and lives of *Hymenoptera* species. In the sections of the book written from the perspective of various wasp drones, all of their fantastical abilities, skills, senses, and horrors are all based on real species found in the wild. For a fascinating (and disturbing) glimpse into that world, I recommend the following books:

The Wasp That Brainwashed the Caterpillar, by Matt Simon

Planet of the Bugs: Evolution and the Rise of Insects, by Scott Richard Shaw

As to the science of venom and the search for new drugs, the following books are eye-openers in regard to the potential locked up in such toxic glands:

The Sting of the Wild, by Justin O. Schmidt

Venomous: How Earth's Deadliest Creatures Mastered Biochemistry, by Christie Wilcox

Finally, the novel posits a question: What role did insects have in the death of the dinosaurs? The answer: A lot! For great insight and a provocative argument, check out:

What Bugged the Dinosaurs? Insects, Disease, and Death in the Cretaceous, by George Poinar Jr. and Roberta Poinar

Throughout this book, there are thousands of other details about insect life and the part they play in our lives, all of which are real, but let me stress one final point. As horrific as the *Odokuro* seem to be, wasps play an important role in nature. Not only are they important pollinators, but they control the populations of undesirable insects. In fact, a single wasp nest is said to control five metric tons of garden pests within one year. So maybe a sting or two is well worth the price of having them around. Of course, make sure they're not the prehistoric *Odokuro*.

Lazarus Microbes and Tardigrades

I lumped these two topics together as both organisms address the subject matter featured in this novel: the amazing genetic abilities of some species to survive against impossible odds. As I was finishing this novel, *National Geographic* featured an article about tardigrades titled "These 'Indestructible' Animals Would Survive a Planet-Wide Apocalypse." And they're not wrong. Similarly, in the May 20, 2017, issue of *New Scientist*, an article titled "Wakey, Wakey" by Colin Barras recounts the astounding ability of Lazarus microbes to survive for hundreds of millions of years in salt crystals, their lives suspended in "a twilight zone between life and death."

It's also been well documented that many species "borrow" advantageous code from others, especially following viral or bacterial infections. So considering the advantages locked up in the DNA of Lazarus microbes and tardigrades, who can say if such miraculous traits aren't already being "borrowed" by some ambitious species?

Invasive Species

The crux of this novel is the environmental threat posed by foreign invaders. Gray mentions the damage wrought by the introduction of pythons in the Everglades, European rabbits in Australia, and Asian carp in our lakes. But other examples of invasive species are plentiful and global. In fact, one of the worries of homeland security is that some hostile power might weaponize such a species and use it as a means of waging war. Especially as such a threat is nearly impossible to defend against.

One of the joys for me of writing novels is to explore intriguing corners of the world. And this novel is no exception. So I thought I'd share how amazing some of these locations truly are. Feel free to book your next vacations.

Tallinn, Estonia

I had a chance to visit this city a few years ago. It was like falling back into a piece of medieval history. The Old Town, with its narrow streets and cobblestoned alleys, is a wonder. Yet, at the same time, the city is truly the Silicon Valley of Europe, where there are more tech start-ups per capita than anywhere on the continent. Likewise, their national library is an amazing edifice of both modern and medieval features, a true testament to the city. So I guess I should apologize for blowing up a good portion of it.

The Amber Road

This ancient trade route ran from St. Petersburg to Venice, Italy. It's so ancient, in fact, that the breastplate of Tutankhamen does indeed bear pieces of Baltic amber. The two amber museums featured in this novel—one in Gdansk, the other in Krakow—are real places and open to the public. And the museum in Krakow does indeed have a sophisticated lab for analyzing amber.

Wieliczka Salt Mines

While the mine is a UNESCO World Heritage Site, it truly should be one of the wonders of the world. Everything described in this novel concerning the beauty and majesty of the salt mine is factual. I had to move a few details around to focus the storytelling, but not much. The tourist map featured in the novel (drawn by Mariusz Szelerewicz and used by permission of his daughter Paulina) offers a glimpse into this amazing labyrinth. When the story ventures deeper into the mine, some of the geography and geology is of my own imagining. But the details regarding the sheer size of the lakes found down there—like how windsurfers have plied those waters, propelled by giant fans—are real.

Japan and Mount Fuji

The small resort town and lake featured in this book are real places. The campus and Ice Castle of Fenikkusu Laboratories are, of course, not. As to the frozen lava tunnels beneath Mount Fuji, they exist (and yes, surprisingly they can be found in Hawaii, too). Even the memorial shrine to martyred insects, where Takashi Ito burns incense in memory of his dead wife, can be found at the temple of Kan'ei-ji in Tokyo.

Concerning the state of Japanese intelligence services, it's true that they are in the process of revamping, consolidating, and extending their international reach. They are making this transition slowly and cautiously, likely for the very reason featured here: fearing infiltration and corruption. As to Akio's new covert group—TaU—that's also pure speculation. Though some of the weaponry they employ in this book is based on theoretical prototypes designed by DARPA. At least, they claim to be *theoretical*.

Maui and the Outer Hawaiian Islands

I tried to be as accurate as possible in regard to the geography of Hana, but some details of the story had to be slightly changed. Still, you can't go wrong visiting there and checking for yourself how much is real.

Moving on to the northwestern Hawaiian archipelago, I must admit I *did* create my own island out there (such is a novelist's power). While Ikikauō Atoll is pure fiction, it's actually based on details found on two neighboring islands. The island of Laysan goes by the Hawaiian name *Kauō*, which means "egg." Similar to my fictitious Ikikauō ("Little Egg"), Laysan boasts a large inland lake. As to the abandoned Coast Guard station, that's actually found nearby on Kure Atoll, not far from Midway. Still, it is true that sunken World War II–era wrecks litter the entire region.

Lastly, the existence of the Great Pacific Garbage Patch is unfortunately real, including its vast size and the threat it poses to the outer Hawaiian Islands. Even the small detail about "ghost fishing" is also tragically true.

So that brings us to the end of the story. A thousand other bits and pieces are also true, but as I mentioned from the start: *I'd prefer you believe all of it.*

Still, before I sign off, I thought I'd leave you with one additional poem from the Japanese Buddhist nun Otagaki Rengetsu. Her words convey my final wish to you all:

In the future,
happiness
and long life . . .
two sprouting leaves
to grow a thousand years.

So may you all live long and happy lives. As for the stalwart members of Sigma Force . . . well, only time will tell.

Arriving home on Christmas Eve, Commander Gray Pierce discovers his house ransacked, his pregnant lover missing, and his best friend's wife, Kat, unconscious on the kitchen floor. With no shred of evidence to follow, his one hope to find the woman he loves and his unborn child is Kat, the only witness to what happened. But the injured woman is in a semi-comatose state and cannot speak—until a brilliant neurologist offers a radical approach to "unlock" her mind long enough to ask a few questions.

What Pierce learns from Kat sets Sigma Force on a frantic quest for answers that are connected to mysteries reaching back to the Spanish Inquisition and to one of the most reviled and blood-soaked books in human history—a medieval text known as the *Malleus Maleficarum*, the Hammer of Witches. What they uncover hidden deep in the past will reveal a frightening truth in the present and a future on the brink of annihilation, and force them to confront the ultimate question: What does it mean to have a soul?

Keep reading for a sneak peek at the next Sigma Force novel. . .

CRUCIBLE

Coming Soon from William Morrow

"Eu non creo nas meigas, mais habelas, hainas."
<I don't believe in witches, but they do exist.>
—an old Galician saying

The coven awaited her.

Charlotte Carson hurried across the breadth of the darkened university library. Her rushed footsteps echoed off the marble floor to the bricked roof of the two-story medieval gallery. All around, ornate shelves housed books dating as far back as the twelfth century. With the vast space lit by only a handful of sconces, she gaped at the shadowy climb of ladders, at the elaborate gilded woodwork.

Constructed in the early eighteenth century, the *Biblioteca Joanina* remained a perfectly preserved gem of Baroque architecture and design, the true historic center of the University of Coimbra. And like any treasure house, it was a veritable vault. The walls were two feet thick; the massive doors that sealed the space were solid teak. The purposeful design maintained the interior at a steady sixty-five degrees, no matter the season, along with a constant low humidity.

Perfect for preserving the integrity of ancient books . . .

But such conservation efforts were not limited to the library's architecture.

Charlotte ducked as a bat whisked past her head and shot into the upper gallery. Unheard but felt, its ultrasonic whistle shivered the small hairs on the back of her neck. For centuries, a colony of bats had made the library its home. They were steadfast allies in the fight to preserve the work stored here. Each night, they consumed insects that might have otherwise feasted on the vast bounty of old leather and yellowed parchment.

Of course, when sharing this vault with such hunters, precautions had to be taken. She ran a finger along the leather blankets that covered the tables. They were draped each evening by the caretakers after the building was closed, shielding the wooden surfaces from the bats' droppings.

Still, as she stared up at the glide of dark shadows against the brick vaults, she felt a stir of superstitious dread—along with a modicum of amusement.

What's a gathering of witches without bats?

Even this night had been specially chosen. The week-long scientific symposium had ended today. By tomorrow, the participants would be headed home, spreading to the far corners of the globe to spend the holidays with friends and family. But tonight, the city was lit by countless bonfires, accompanied by the merriment of various musical festivals, all to celebrate the winter solstice, the longest night of the year.

She checked her watch, knowing she was running late. She still wore the same semi-formal outfit from the holiday party at the embassy: a loose black skirt that brushed her ankles and a short coat over a blue blouse. Her hair was styled smooth to her scalp. It had gone prematurely silver and remained short and sparse after the course of chemo nine months ago. Afterward, she had never bothered with dyes or extensions. After surviving the brutalities and humiliations of cancer, vanity seemed a foolish frivolity. She no longer had the patience for it.

Not that she had much free time anyway.

She frowned at her watch.

Only four minutes to go.

She pictured the sun on the other side of the world as it crested toward the Tropic of Capricorn. When the sun balanced at that latitude, it would mark the moment of the true solstice, when winter inevitably tilted toward summer, when darkness gave way to light.

The perfect time for this demonstration.

A proof of concept.

"*Fiat lux*," she whispered.

Let there be light.

Ahead, a brighter glow illuminated an archway that opened to a spiral staircase that led to the lower regions of the library. This topmost level was called the Noble Floor, due to its beauty and history. Directly below, the Intermediate Floor remained the sole domain of librarians, where a bulk of the rarest books were stored for safekeeping.

But Charlotte's destination lay one story deeper.

Sensing the press of time, she hurried toward the archway.

By now, the others would be gathered below. She crossed under the painting of King John V, the Portuguese king who founded the library, to reach the steps that spiraled all the way down to the bottommost level of the library.

As she circled around and around the tight staircase, a low murmur of voices rose to greet her. Upon reaching the last step, she came to a stout black iron gate. It had been left ajar for her. Fixed upon it was a sign that read PRISÃO ACADÉMICA.

She smiled at the thought of a prison being built under a library. She pictured recalcitrant students or drunken professors being locked up down here. Once a part of the original dungeons of the royal palace, this floor had continued to serve as the university's prison until 1834. Today, it remained the only existing example of a medieval prison in all of Portugal.

She slipped through the iron gate to enter the dungeon. A good section of this floor was open to tourists, while other locked rooms were used as additional book storage, but she headed toward the far side, where the modern age had infiltrated this medieval space. A new computer system had been installed in an unused back vault, including a system for digitizing books, offering a way to further safeguard the treasures stored above.

But on this winter's solstice, the computers would serve a new purpose—not to preserve the past, but to offer a glimpse into the future.

As she entered the vault, she was greeted by Lisa Guerra, the head of the Joanina Library. "Ah, *Embaixador* Carson, you made it in time."

Dressed in a crisp navy suit and white blouse, the petite librarian crossed over and gave Charlotte a peck on each cheek, along with a quick squeeze of her upper arm. The excitement all but bubbled through the librarian.

"I wasn't sure I would make it," Charlotte explained with an apologetic smile. "The embassy is short-staffed and in a state of chaos with the approach of the holidays."

As the U.S. ambassador to Portugal, Charlotte had a thousand responsibilities this night, including catching a red-eye back to D.C. to join her husband and two daughters. Laura was back from Princeton—which was Charlotte's alma mater—where she was pursuing a degree in biotechnology. Her other daughter, Carly, was more of a wild child, chasing a dream of acting at NYU, while also hedging her bet by studying engineering.

Charlotte couldn't be prouder of them both.

She wished they could be here to witness this moment. Her daughters were one of the reasons she had helped found this organization composed of women scientists and researchers. The charitable foundation was an offshoot of the larger Coimbra Group, a union of over three dozen research universities spread around the globe.

In an attempt to foster, promote, and network women in the sciences, Charlotte and the four women here had started Bruxas International, named after the Portuguese word for "witches." For centuries, women who practiced healing, or who experimented with herbal remedies, or who simply questioned the world around them were declared heretics or witches. Even here in Coimbra—a town long revered as a place of learning—women had been put to the torch, often in great grisly pageants called *Auto-da-Fé*, or Acts of Faith, where scores of apostates and heretics were burned at the stake all at once.

Rather than shy away from such stigma, she and

the others decided to lean in to it instead, to defiantly name their foundation *Bruxas*.

But the metaphor did not stop with the name.

Lisa Guerra had a computer station already booted up. The symbol for their organization glowed upon the screen, slowly spinning. It was a pentagram surrounded by a circle.

The five points of the star represented the five women here, the original coven who had founded the organization at the University of Coimbra six years ago. They had no set leader. All matters were voted upon equally.

Charlotte smiled past Lisa to the three others: Dr. Hannah Fest from the University of Cologne, Professor Ikumi Sato from the University of Tokyo, and Dr. Sophia Ruiz from the University of São Paulo. Though Charlotte had received her ambassadorship last year—not in small part due to her role in arranging this international organization based in Portugal—she had originally been a researcher like the others, teaching at Princeton and representing the United States.

Despite their differences, the five women—all in their fifties—had risen in their respective professions about the same time, enduring the same hardships due to their gender, experiencing the same discrimination and slights. Beyond their common interest in the sciences, they shared this bond. Their goal was to even the playing field, to encourage and help shepherd younger women into the sciences through scholarships, apprenticeships, and mentoring.

Their efforts had already produced great results around the world—especially here.

Hannah leaned toward a stick microphone resting beside the computer keyboard. "Mara, we're all present." She spoke in English, but her accent was thickly Teutonic. "You can start your demonstration when you're ready."

As Hannah stepped back, the screen split. The pentagram shrunk to one side, revealing the young face of Mara Silviera. Though only twenty-one, she had already spent the past five years at Coimbra, earning a scholarship from Bruxas at the tender age of sixteen. Originally from a small village in the Galicia region of northern Spain, she had garnered the attention of a slew of tech companies after publishing a translation app that outshone what was currently on the market. She seemed to have an innate ability both with computers and with the fundamentals of language.

Even now, raw intelligence shone from her eyes. Or maybe it was just pride. The dark mocha of her complexion coupled with her long straight black hair suggested a mix of Moorish blood in her family's past. She was presently across campus at the university's Laboratory for Advanced Computing, which housed the Milipeia Cluster, one of the continent's most powerful supercomputers.

Mara glanced slightly to the side. "I'll start cycling *Xénese* up. We should be online in a minute."

As the women gathered closer, Charlotte looked at her watch.

10:23 P.M.

Right on time.

She again pictured the sun perched above the Tropic of Capricorn, marking the culmination of the winter solstice, promising the end of darkness and the return of light.

Before that could happen, a loud iron *clang* made them all jump and turn.

A tight cluster of dark hooded figures poured past the black gate and across the prison floor. They all bore large glossy pistols in hand. The group spread out, trapping the five women inside the computer vault.

There was no other exit from this room.

With her heart pounding in her throat, Charlotte backed a step. She blocked the monitor with her body and reached blindly behind her. She shifted and clicked the computer mouse to collapse the image of Mara Silveira, both to protect the young woman and to turn the student into a silent witness. With the microphone and camera still broadcasting, Mara should be able to hear and see what transpires.

As the group closed in on the women, Charlotte willed Mara to call the police, though it was unlikely any rescue would arrive in time. She could not even be sure Mara was aware of the change in circumstance and was likely concentrating on her pending demonstration.

The eight assailants—all men—were dressed in black robes with crimson silk sashes tied across their eyes like blindfolds, but from their manner and stealth, they plainly could see through the cloths.

Lisa Guerra stepped forward, ready to defend her library. "What is the meaning of this? What do you want?"

An unnerving silence answered her.

The group parted to reveal a ninth man, clearly the leader. He wore a crimson robe with a black sash over his eyes, his garb a mirror image of the others. He carried no weapon, only a half-foot-thick tome. The worn leather binding was the same crimson as his robe. The gold gilt lettering on the cover was easy to read: *Malleus Maleficarum*.

Charlotte shrank back, hope dying inside her. She had prayed this was merely a high-stakes heist. Many of the library's volumes were priceless. But she recognized the book in the man's hand and despaired. It appeared to be a first edition, one of only a handful still in existence. One copy was preserved here at the Joanina Library. From the deep frown on Lisa's face, maybe it was even the same edition, snatched from the stacks.

The book was written in the fifteenth century by a Catholic priest named Heinrich Kramer. The Latin name translated as *The Hammer of Witches*. Devised as a guide to identify, persecute, and torture witches, it was one of the most reviled and blood-soaked books in human history. Estimates put the number of deaths attributed to this book at over sixty thousand souls.

Charlotte glanced to the others.

And now there will be five more.

The leader's first words confirmed this.

"Maleficos non patieris vivere."

Charlotte easily translated the Latin, recognizing the admonishment from the Book of Exodus.

Suffer not a witch to live.

The man continued in English, though his accent sounded Spanish. *"Xénese* must never be," he intoned. "It is an abomination, born of sorcery and filth."

Charlotte frowned.

How did he know what we attempted this night?

Still, the mystery would have to wait. Pistols were leveled intently at the group as two men carried forward a pair of five-gallon tanks. She read the lettering on the side: *Querosene.* She didn't need to be fluent in Portuguese to recognize the content, especially after the tanks were upended and oily fuel flooded across the floor of the confined space.

The smell of kerosene quickly grew suffocating.

Coughing, Charlotte shared a look with the other terrified women. After working in tandem for the past six years, they knew each other. No words were needed. They were not tied to wooden stakes. If this was their end, these particular witches would die fighting.

Better a bullet than the flame.

She sneered at the leader. "Suffer this, asshole!"

The five women splashed through the pool of kerosene and dove into the gathering of men. Pistols fired, explosively loud in the confined space. Charlotte felt rounds pelt into her, but her momentum still carried her to the leader. She lunged and clawed at his face, gouging her nails deep into his flesh, tearing down his cheek. She tore his blindfold free and saw fear and pain in his exposed eyes.

He dropped the accursed book and shoved her away. She landed on the stone floor at the edge of the pool of kerosene. Propped up on one arm, she glanced across the room in horror at the other four women sprawled and unmoving, their blood mixing with the oil.

Weakening rapidly, she slumped to the floor herself.

The leader swore and spat orders in Spanish.

A half dozen Molotov cocktails were removed from robes and quickly lit.

Charlotte ignored them as her body grew cold, draining any fear of the coming heat. She stared back into the room, where motion drew her fading eyes. On the computer screen, the Bruxas pentagram spun rapidly, far faster than before, as if agitated by all that had transpired.

Mystified, she stared at the blurring image.

Was Mara trying to signal her somehow?

Molotov cocktails were tossed into the room, shattering against the walls. Flames splashed high. Heat washed over her.

Still, Charlotte stared into the heart of the fire.

The symbol on the screen spun faster for another breath—then stopped abruptly. But the center could no longer hold. Fragments broke loose and scattered away.

The leader stepped closer to her prone form, likely studying the same mystery. Though she could not see his face as she lay on floor, she sensed his bewilderment. All that was left of the pentagram were two prongs of the star, like the horns of a devil.

As if recognizing the same, the man stiffened, clearly offended. He stumbled back, an arm lifted. His shouted in Spanish. "Des . . . destroy the *computadora*!"

But it was already too late. The image turned one final time, a full quarter turn.

Pistols cracked, and bullets pierced the fire. The computer screen shattered and went dark. Charlotte slumped and followed that darkness, searching for the promised light at the end, praying for Mara's safety.

Still one image accompanied her into the depths. It shone brightly in her mind's eye. It was the last image on the screen. The circle around the pentagram had vanished, leaving only a new symbol that grew to fill the monitor before it shattered.

It looked like a Greek letter.

Sigma.

She didn't know what it meant, but the purposefulness of it gave her hope as she died.

Hope for the world.

From #1 *New York Times* bestselling author James Rollins comes an electrifying short story, in which the battle over a lost treasure leads to murder, betrayal, and the revelation of a shocking mystery hidden aboard the . . .

GHOST SHIP

The discovery of a burned body sprawled on a remote Australian beach shatters the vacation plans of Commander Gray Pierce. To thwart an ingenious enemy, he and Seichan are pulled into a centuries-old mystery surrounding a lost convict ship, the *Trident*. The vessel—with a history of mutiny and stolen treasure—vanished into the mists of time, but nothing stays lost forever. A freak storm reveals clues scattered across the Great Barrier Reef, but following those clues will lead to bloodshed and savagery, for *where* this ghost ship is hidden is as shocking as the mystery behind its disappearance. It will take all of Gray's ingenuity and Seichan's deadly skills not only to survive—but to stop an enemy from destroying everything in his path.

Now you don't see that every day . . .

From the vantage of his horse's saddle, Commander Gray Pierce watched the twelve-foot saltwater crocodile amble across the beach. A moment ago, it had appeared out of the rainforest and aimed for the neighboring sea, completely ignoring the trio of horses standing nearby.

Amused and awed, Gray studied its passage. Yellow fangs glinted in the morning sun; a thick-armored tail balanced its swaying bulk. Its presence was a reminder that the prehistoric past of this remote stretch of northern Australia was still very much alive. Even the rainforest behind them was the last vestige of a jungle that once stretched across the continent, a fragment dating back some 140 million years, all but untouched by the passage of time.

As the crocodile finally slipped into the waves and vanished, Seichan frowned at Gray from atop her own horse. "And *you* still want to go diving in those waters?"

The final member of their group—who was acting as their guide—dismissed her concern with a wave of a darkly tanned hand. "No worries. *That* particular salty bloke is a mere ankle biter. Quite small."

"Small?" Seichan lifted an eyebrow skeptically.

The Aussie grinned. "Some of the males can grow to be seven meters or more, topping off at over a thousand kilos." He nudged his horse and led them across the beach. "But like I said, not much to fret about. Salties generally only kill two people a year."

Seichan cast a withering look at Gray, her emerald eyes flashing in the sunlight. She plainly did not want to fill that particular quota today. She tossed the length of her black ponytail over a shoulder in obvious irritation as she set off after their guide.

Gray watched her depart for a breath, appreciating the grace of her movements. The sight of her almond skin glistening in the sweltering heat drew him after her.

As he joined her, she glanced to the rainforest. "We could still turn back. Spend the day in the lodge's spa, like we'd planned."

Gray smiled at her. "What? After we came all this way?"

He wasn't just referring to the trail ride to reach this isolated stretch of beach.

For the past half year, the two of them had been slowly circumnavigating the globe, part of a sabbatical from their work with Sigma Force. They had been moving place to place with no itinerary in mind. After leaving D.C., they had spent a month in a medieval village in France, then flew on to Kenya, where they drifted from tent camp to tent camp, moving with the timeless flow of animal life found there. Eventually, they found themselves amid the teeming sprawl of Mumbai, India, enjoying humanity at its most riotous. Then over the past three weeks, they had driven across the breadth of Australia, starting in Perth to the east, traversing the dusty roads through the Outback, until finally reaching Port Douglas on Australia's tropical northeast coast.

Seichan nodded to their guide. "Who knows where this guy is really taking us?"

"I think we can trust him."

Though the two of them had been traveling the globe under false papers, Gray had never doubted that Sigma was covertly keeping track of their whereabouts. This became self-evident last night, when upon returning from a day hike into the Daintree Rainforest, they had stumbled upon a familiar figure holed up in their hotel's lounge, belting down a whiskey, trying to act inconspicuous.

Gray eyed the broad back of their rugged Aussie guide. The man's name was Benjamin Brust. The fifty-year-old Australian happened to be the stepfather of Sigma's young intelligence analyst, Jason Carter. The Aussie had also helped Sigma resolve a situation a year or so ago in Antarctica.

So to find the man seated in their hotel bar . . .

Ben had tried to dismiss the chance encounter as mere coincidence, quoting *Casablanca* at the time. "*Of all the gin joints in all the towns in all the world . . .*"

Gray hadn't bought it.

Ben had recognized this and simply shrugged it off, as if to say, *Okay, you caught me.*

From Ben's presence, Gray realized that Sigma's

director must have leaned on former colleagues and associates to keep an eye on the pair during their half-year sojourn.

Accepting this reality, Gray hadn't pressed Ben on his subterfuge. Exposed and apparently apologetic for agreeing to spy on them, the man had offered to take them on a guided tour to a few of the region's highlights, spots known only to the locals.

Judging by the scuba gear they carried with them, Gray expected they were likely headed to some remote dive spot. Ben had refused to offer any further details, but from the mischievous gleam in his blue eyes, he had some surprise in store for them.

"We can tie the horses in the shade over there." Ben pointed an arm toward a tumble of rocks amid a copse of palm trees.

Gray leaned toward Seichan. "See, we're already here."

She grumbled under her breath, while maintaining a wary watch on the beach and forest. He recognized the tension in her back. Even after months on the road, she refused to let her guard down. He had come to accept it. Trained from a young age to be an assassin, she'd had paranoia and suspicion incorporated into her DNA.

In fact, Gray shared some of that same genetic code, courtesy of his stint with the Army Rangers and his years with Sigma Force, which operated under the auspices of DARPA, the Defense Department's research-and-development agency. Members of Sigma Force acted as covert field agents for

DARPA, protecting the globe against various burgeoning threats.

In such a line of work, paranoia was a survival skill.

Still . . .

"Let's just try to enjoy this adventure," Gray said.

Seichan shrugged. "A hot stone massage would've been enough of an adventure for me."

They reached the tumble of boulders and dismounted. In short order, they had their horses secured.

Ben stretched a kink from his back with a rattling sigh, then pointed to a forested promontory jutting into the blue sea. "Welcome to Cape Tribulation. Where the rainforest meets the reef."

"It is stunning," Seichan admitted with some clear reluctance.

"Only place in the world where *two* UNESCO World Heritage Sites butt up against one another." Ben pointed to the forest. "You got the Wet Tropics of Queensland over there." He then squinted out to sea. "And the Great Barrier Reef stretching way out there."

Seichan kicked off her sandals and wandered farther along the beach, her gaze taking in the sight of the jungle-shrouded cliffs tumbling into the crashing waves. Birdcalls echoed across the beach, while the perfume of the fragrant forest mixed with the bitter salt of the Coral Sea.

Gray stared appreciatively after her, which Ben noted.

"Quite the sight," he said with a big grin. "You

should put a ring on that finger before you lose your chance."

Gray scowled at him and waved to the laden horses. "Let's unpack our gear."

As they worked, Gray nodded to the promontory. "How'd this place get the name Tribulation?" he asked. "Looks pretty damned peaceful to me."

"Ah, you can blame that on the poor navigation skills of Captain James Cook. Back in the eighteenth century, he ran his ship aground on Endeavour Reef." Ben pointed out to sea. "Tore out a section of the keel and almost lost his boat. Only through some desperate measures were they able to keep her afloat and manage repairs. Cook named the place Cape Tribulation, writing in his logbook *'here begun all our troubles.'* "

"And not just for Captain Cook," Seichan called back to them, plainly overhearing Ben's explanation. She pointed down the beach, drawing both men toward her.

As Gray cleared the rock pile, he spotted a mound half buried in the sand and draped in strands of seaweed. A pale, outstretched arm rested atop the beach.

A body.

They hurried over. The dead man lay on his back, his eyes open and glazed. His legs were covered by wet sand but his exposed chest was striped with blackened marks, as if he'd been lashed with a flaming whip.

Ben dropped to his knees with a sharp curse. "Simon . . ."

Gray crinkled his brow. "You know this man?"

"He's the reason we're all here." Ben gazed out to sea, plainly searching the waters. "He was a biologist working for the Australian Research Council. Part of the Coral Reef Study. He was out here monitoring the spread of coral bleaching. It's knocked out two-thirds of the reef. A bloody international disaster. One Simon was trying to prevent from spreading."

Seichan frowned at the blackened stripes across his body. "What happened to him?"

Ben spat into the sand as he stood. "*Chironex fleckeri.*"

"And that would be *what*?" Gray pressed.

"The Australian box jellyfish. One of the most venomous creatures on the planet They're as big as basketballs with three-meter-long tentacles full of stinging cells. It's why we call them sea wasps. You get stung by one of those and you can die an agonizing death before you reach shore." Ben shook his head, continuing to stare out to sea. "They've multiplied like crazy since the bleaching, thriving on these oxygen-deprived waters."

Gray studied the ravaged body, noting the rictus of pain frozen on the dead man's face. Seichan gently picked up his outstretched hand, examining the pliability of the fingers. She glanced significantly at Gray.

At these warm temperatures, with his body baking in the sun, rigor mortis would have set in within four hours. Which meant he'd died recently.

"Makes no sense," Ben muttered as he stepped away, rubbing the stubble across his chin and cheek.

Gray followed him, hearing the worry behind his words. "What makes no sense?"

Ben waved to their gear spread over the sand. "It's why I hauled in full wet suits. While the seas around here might be plenty warm enough to go skinny-dipping in, you don't go diving in these waters without covering yourself up."

While unpacking the gear, Gray had noted the set of Ocean Reef Neptune masks, meant to cover a diver's face and head. They even had integrated comm units to allow them to communicate with each other underwater.

"Simon would've known better than to go swimming in these waters without proper protection." Ben gave another shake of his head. "Something's bloody wrong here. Where's his catamaran? Where are the others?"

"Others?" Gray asked.

"He was working with a small team from ANFOG." Ben noted his confusion. "The Australian National Facility for Ocean Gliders. They're a group of oceanographers that deploy underwater gliders, unmanned drones that patrol the reefs. The devices can continuously sample water, monitoring temperature, salinity, light levels."

"To help study the coral bleaching," Gray said.

"There were four scientists from the University of Western Australia aboard his boat, along with a graduate student." Ben glanced with concern at Gray. "Simon's daughter, Kelly."

Gray understood.

The others wouldn't have abandoned the dead man, especially his daughter.

Seichan joined him, her brows pinched with suspicion. "You said the dead man was the reason we're here. Why?"

"Simon knew I was up in the Queensland area. He wanted to see if I might help him solve a mystery. One suited to my particular skill set."

Gray frowned. "What skill set?"

"At mapping and traversing tricky cavern systems."

Gray knew the man's history. He was formerly with the Australian army, specializing in infiltration and extractions. He had been recruited from a military prison to help with an operation in Antarctica two decades ago, one involving an unexplored cavern system and a missing team of scientists.

"What did Simon want with your skills here?" Gray asked.

"Three days ago, one of the group's gliders revealed the opening to an underwater cave, likely exposed from the cyclone that swept this coast last month."

Seichan crossed her arms. "And he wanted you to help explore it. Why?"

"Because of what he found in the sand at its entrance. A set of old manacles and a half-buried ship's bell. They recovered the objects and found a name inscribed on the bell. The *Trident*."

Ben glanced between them to see if they recognized the name.

Gray shrugged.

"The *Trident* was a convict ship that transported prisoners from Great Britain to Australia. While docked in Melbourne in 1852, a group of prisoners teamed up with a handful of the ship's mutinous crew. They commandeered the *Trident*, absconding with several crates of gold mined from the Victorian goldfields. After that, the ship vanished into history."

"Until now," Seichan commented drily.

Gray stared out at the promontory jutting into the sea. "Perhaps Captain Cook wasn't the only one who had trouble navigating these waters."

"That's certainly true. You can find plenty of shipwrecks out there. Like the ruins of S.S. *Yongala* farther south. It sank during a cyclone a century ago."

Seichan sighed. "So you brought us to the edge of a graveyard of ships."

"I thought you might like to do a little treasure hunting with us. I never thought . . ." His words died away as he glanced at the remains of his friend.

"If this is truly foul play," Gray said, "then someone else must have caught wind of Simon's discovery. What else did your friend tell you?"

"Only to meet him here, and if he was delayed, to head to the coordinates of the glider's discovery."

Gray frowned. "And where is that?"

Ben pointed to the promontory of Cape Tribulation. "On the far side of that ridge."

Before he could drop his arm, a sharp chatter of gunfire echoed from that direction. A startled flock of birds took flight from the forest near there.

Knowing what this implied, Gray cursed himself for leaving his satellite phone back in D.C., but the device was Sigma property.

"With no cell signal and no radio," Gray said, "we have no way of alerting authorities."

"So what do we do?" Ben asked.

Gray turned his back on the sea and stalked toward their gear. "We suit up and get to work."

9:51 A.M.

As Seichan swam from the shallows to the deeper water, her body shed the dulling months of relaxation. With each stroke and kick, an icy coldness suffused her limbs. It sharpened her senses, honing her reflexes. The weeks of leisure faded into a dream, proving how illusory those months had been.

She settled into that cold center of her being. Her true nature was as coldblooded as any shark in these warm waters, predators that needed to keep moving to survive.

It was a lesson she knew all too well.

She followed behind Gray and Ben as they glided over the bright reefs. She studied Gray's physique, the kick of muscular legs, the sweep of his arms. She remembered the glint in his eyes as he turned from the seas to prepare for this dive.

Like her, he was in his element.

After recent events back in the States, the two of them had attempted to flee, to vanish for a spell, to use the time to heal, to discover each other in new ways. And they had. But they both seemed to sense that such a sojourn could not last.

Not forever.

It wasn't who they were.

She felt that even more keenly now.

Accepting this, she took in her surroundings. Life stirred all around her, as rich as the densest jungle. The trio whisked through a school of sleek black-and-silver barracuda, scattering them like a flock of birds. Sea turtles hung motionless in the water, watching them pass with unblinking eyes, while gorgonian sea fans waved from ridges of hard coral. Elsewhere, eagle and manta rays glided out of their way with an unearthly elegance. For several yards, a googly-eyed grouper as large as a Volkswagen van paced alongside them before losing interest and lumbering away.

Across this wonderland, they slowly made their way along the promontory, intending to circle past its tip to reach the far side. Their only weapons were the element of surprise and one dive knife each. Seichan regretted their lack of firepower, especially after hearing those earlier rifle blasts.

"Slow up," Ben radioed through their comm units.

As they bunched together, Seichan reached a gloved hand to the sandy bottom to steady herself. Before she could touch the seabed, Ben knocked her arm away.

"Watch yourself," he warned.

The sand where she had been about to place her palm suddenly sprouted spines. A creature burst from beneath the silt—and swam away.

"Stonefish," Ben explained. "Most venomous

fish in the world. Get stung badly enough by those spines, you can die in seconds. Sometimes just from the sheer pain. Only safe place to grab them is by the tail."

She retracted her hand to her chest.

I'll pass.

"We've cleared the promontory," Ben informed them, while checking a wrist GPS. "I'll take the lead from here as we head back along the far side toward Simon's coordinates."

The coordinates of a dead man.

If that thought wasn't ominous enough, the terrain around them quickly changed—from multicolored splendor to gray desert. They had reached a section of the bleached reef. Sea life appeared to have fled the desolation.

"My god . . ." Gray mumbled.

Ben explained as they worked back toward shore, using the distraction to temper the tension. "It's not as hopeless as it appears. The bleached coral is still alive. It's just been stressed by the higher temperatures to expel the symbiotic algae that give the reef its vibrant colors. If left unchecked, the coral polyps will eventually die. But if the stressors can be eliminated in time, the reefs can return to life. Unfortunately, the Great Barrier Reef has suffered back-to-back bleaching events. If this continues, by some estimates, the entire reef could vanish in the next couple decades."

"Solving that particular danger will have to wait for the moment," Gray said, and pointed ahead.

Thirty yards away, two large shadows hovered

above, linked to the seafloor by taut anchor cables. One boat had a single keel. The twin hulls of the other marked it as the scientific team's catamaran.

Ben eyed the larger single-hulled craft. "Definitely unwanted company."

Gray drew closer to him. "How far off are we from Simon's coordinates to the sea cave?"

Ben pointed toward the promontory coastline. "Fifty meters farther along."

Gray nodded and turned his attention toward the surface.

Seichan could guess the question plaguing him. With no knowledge of the situation above, they faced a troubling choice.

Which boat should they attempt to board first?

The answer was taken from them—suddenly and violently.

The dark shadows beneath the catamaran suddenly erupted with a fiery explosion. The ship lifted out of the water for a breath, then crashed back down. Its shattered hulls crumbled in on themselves, then slowly sank as the sea flooded its compartments.

Seichan shook her head, expelling a breath.

The concussion of the blast ached in her ears and chest.

If we'd been any closer . . .

Ben swore as he gaped at the sinking wreck.

Seichan spotted a body rising off the broken deck, trailing blood.

One of the oceanographers.

The earlier gunfire echoed in her head. She pictured the ravaged body of Ben's friend. Whoever

these pirates were, they had moved beyond execut-
ing their prisoners. They were cleaning house.

But what did that mean? Were any of the other
scientists still alive? And what about Simon's
daughter?

Are we already too late?

Only one way to know for sure.

"Let's go," Gray said coldly.

10:10 A.M.

Gray hung in the shadow of the boat with Ben. The
craft appeared to be an old fishing charter with a
wide open rear deck, a small raised wheelhouse, and
a cubby cabin beneath the bow.

He and Ben had taken up position under the steel
dive deck at the stern. Across the length of the
twenty-foot hull, Seichan hovered near the bow.
She clutched one hand to the anchor cable. Over
her head, the line rose out of the water and up to a
bow roller and a winch. She would use the cable like
a rope to board the boat from that side.

At the moment, they dared not even use their radios, fearing that in such close quarters the enemy
might hear them. He couldn't risk losing their best
weapon.

The element of surprise.

Gray rose up until his palm rested against the starboard side of the dive deck. Ben followed him, taking a position on the port side.

Once ready, he eyed Seichan—then sliced his
free arm through the water.

They all moved at once.

Gray grabbed the edge of the dive deck and smoothly pulled himself out of the water and twisted around to land his backside on the steel. He kept his head below the stern rail. Ben mirrored his maneuver on the far side. With no alarm raised, they shifted to get their legs under them and freed their dive knives.

As he crouched, he heard low, furtive voices, one deep chuckle, and someone softly crying. All the sounds seemed to be coming from the open rear deck—but was anyone in the ship's wheelhouse or in the lower cabin?

Only one way to find out.

He waited for the right moment—and it came with a shout of surprise from the deck. Upon that signal, both he and Ben burst up and hurdled the stern rail. Across the boat, a figure stood exposed atop the bow deck.

While still underwater, Seichan had unzipped and stripped down the top half of her wetsuit. She stood now in her bikini top, leaning nonchalantly with her hips cocked, a hand leaning on the neighboring rail. With her bottom half still encased in her black wetsuit, she looked like a mermaid stranded atop the deck.

Her sudden appearance—along with her bored expression—momentarily baffled the two armed men guarding a pair of kneeling prisoners. Even before they could shift their weapons toward her, Gray came up behind and knifed the first man in the side of the throat. Ben was less lethal and clubbed his target with the hilt of his weapon, striking him expertly behind the left ear. Bone cracked, and the man crumpled limply to the deck.

Gray grabbed the Desert Eagle pistol carried by his target and focused on the empty wheelhouse, where a closed door led down to the cubby cabin. He collected the other weapon and tossed it to Seichan, who caught it one-handed.

She quickly crossed to the door to the cubby cabin, kicked it open, and surveilled the cramped space below. "All clear," she called as she retreated to join them.

The two prisoners were a red-haired young man and a woman in her late forties.

Ben knelt before them as they stared wide-eyed and stunned at the sudden assault. "We're friends of Simon," he assured them. "I'm guessing you're part of the ANFOG team working with him."

The woman took a shuddering breath, wiped tears from her cheeks, and nodded.

"What happened here?" Gray asked.

The story unfolded in stuttering bits and pieces, told by the pair of survivors, Maggie and Wendell. Three hours ago, the assailants had pretended to be a fishing charter. The ruse lasted long enough for the armed men to assault the catamaran. Simon had tried to fight them, but he was overpowered, stripped, and tossed overboard.

"Why?" Ben asked. "Why not simply shoot him?"

Maggie looked near shock with the retelling. "They were trying to get his daughter to cooperate."

"Kelly?"

She nodded. "Only Kelly knew the coordinates where the *Trident*'s artifacts had been found. We were all on a dive that day, leaving her, as our lowly student, aboard the ship to monitor a routine glider survey. It's mind-numbing work. While watching the feed, she happened to spot the bell and shackle. Excited, she free-dove down to collect the trophies. But when she recognized the name on the bell—and what such a discovery implied—she erased the glider's record. Though she told us about the discovery, she kept its exact location secret."

"But not from her father," Ben added.

Wendell looked startled. "What?"

"Kelly told Simon," Ben said. "Then he told me."

Gray suspected Simon shared this information with Ben for selfish reasons. He likely wanted to recruit Ben before his daughter tried doing anything even more foolhardy, like attempting to search those caves on her own.

"Kelly eventually broke and told the gunmen the coordinates," Maggie explained. "But before they could pull Simon out of the water . . ."

Ben grimaced. "He ran afoul of a box jelly."

She nodded. "Kelly witnessed it all. That poor girl."

"Where is she now?" Seichan asked.

The woman stared out toward the forested cliffs. "They forced her to go along with them. When she initially refused, they shot Tyler and threatened us."

Gray pictured the dead man floating amid the wreckage. "How many went with her?"

"Six, including Dr. Hoffmeister."

Ben frowned. "Dr. Hoffmeister?"

"Our team leader," Wendell elaborated with a bitter scowl. "He was the one who betrayed us to those murderous bastards."

Seichan snorted. "So much for the purity of scientific research."

Maggie looked down. "We'd all heard rumors he had a gambling problem, but I never imagined he could be so callous. Especially with those he worked alongside."

Gray was not as surprised. All too often greed trumped friendship or loyalty.

"You have to do something," Wendell said. "They'll kill Kelly once they find what they're looking for."

Gray knew he was right. And from the despair in the kid's voice, his interest in Kelly was more than merely collegial.

Seichan glanced toward the coast and shrugged. "Three against six. Not bad odds."

"And we still have the element of surprise," Ben added.

Gray began to nod when a crackling noise drew his attention to the dead assailant on the deck. The noise rose from a radio headpiece.

He quickly snatched it free and lifted the radio to his ear and lips. A trail of words reached him.

"... *late in reporting in. What's your status?*"

Gray had to take the chance. "All quiet here," he said gruffly.

There was a long pause before the voice on the line returned, angry and suspicious. "*Who the hell is this?*"

Seichan stared at him as he lowered the radio.

He shook his head.

So much for the element of surprise.

10:25 A.M.

"Let's give those blokes a wide berth," Ben radioed to them.

Seichan didn't argue as she followed the two men. A trio of bull sharks circled the wreck of the catamaran, likely drawn by the blood of the murdered oceanographer. Their group steered well clear of that wreckage and headed for the coast.

Earlier, before going overboard, they had briefly searched the guards for the boat's keys but had no luck. They also found the ship's radio disabled, requiring a digital code to unlock it. So as a precaution, they had ordered Maggie and Wendell to suit up and swim to shore, sending the pair out of harm's way with instructions to get word to someone in authority and let them know the situation.

Seichan knew better than to expect any help in time.

We're on our own.

Before leaving, Maggie had also informed them what they'd be facing. The crew had departed with spear guns and carried satchels of demolition charges.

Seichan glanced to the ruins of the catamaran, recognizing the handiwork of those explosives. The thieves plainly had come prepared in case they had to blow their way into that cavern system in order to search for the cache of gold.

She pictured the mutinous crew back in 1852 rowing into those same sea caves to hide their loot, perhaps fearing the *Trident* might be recaptured by British forces. But was the gold still here after so long?

As they neared Simon's coordinates, Ben waved for them to spread wider, making their group less of a target. They proceeded with great caution, using the ridges of reefs as cover. If the assailants suspected treachery after the aborted radio call, the enemy would likely have a guard hidden near the entrance to the cavern system. If any of their team flushed him out, the other two would still have a chance to take him down.

Unfortunately, once they drew closer to the coordinates, they realized the guard at the entrance was not what they expected. They almost missed it as the waters grew murkier, clouded by sand and silt stirred up by the waves crashing into the towering coastal cliffs.

Through the gloom, a yellow torpedo-shaped tube with fins hovered a couple yards in front of the black eye of a tunnel. Its nosecone pointed out toward the sea, its buoyant length gently bobbing in the current.

"One of ANFOG's gliders," Ben hissed.

The thieves must have left this electronic guard dog to watch the entrance to the cavern system. Someone was likely monitoring its feed from inside the sea caves.

"No way we can sneak past that glider's sensors," Ben said. "If we get too close, the enemy will know we're on our way inside."

"Then we find a way to blind it," Gray said.

"How?"

Gray reached to a webbed bag hanging from his weight belt. He pulled out one of the two demolition charges they had found aboard the boat during their search.

"If you try to blow the glider up," Ben warned, "it'll be as good as being spotted. They'll still know we're coming."

"That's not my plan."

Gray swam back several yards, then used his dive knife to remove three-quarters of the charge's load of plastic explosive, weakening its potential blast. He then quickly buried it a foot into the sand at the base of a ridge of bleached, brittle coral.

"Move well back." He waved them farther from the shoreline. "I set the timer for thirty seconds. Be ready to go on my mark."

With the charge buried, they retreated.

Seichan counted down in her head as she swam. When she reached zero, a muffled *whump* thudded into her ears and rib cage. She twisted back around as the section of the seabed where Gray had buried the charge belched upward with a massive flume of sand and shattered coral. The current immediately swept the cloud toward shore.

"Now!" Gray radioed. "Get into the debris field and stick close together."

Seichan understood. She swam with the others into the dense cloud of sediment. They quickly lost sight of one another, even when clutching an elbow or the edge of a neighbor's fin. Still, Ben guided them unerringly forward, swimming by instruments alone, following his wrist GPS. He skirted them to the side of the blinded electronic guard dog, then along the rocks.

Moments later, the Aussie was pulling them into the mouth of tunnel. Even from here, Seichan could not spot the glider through the stirred-up silt. It was as if the entire world had vanished beyond the tunnel.

Ben took her hand and drew her fingers to a length of rope staked along the seabed. It led deeper into the tunnel.

She understood.

Follow the line.

She set off behind Ben, with Gray behind her. She was soon grateful the enemy had left this path to follow. With each kick and paddle, their motion stirred up more silt in the tunnel. Not only could she barely see Ben's fins ahead of her, but being weightless in her gear added to her disorientation. It was almost impossible to tell up from down.

Once far enough away from the glider's sensors, Ben risked switching on a pair of small lights flanking his mask. "Okay, I love caving and I love scuba diving, but when you combine the two into *cave diving*," he groused, "it turns into bloody death sport. And even more so now."

Ben slowed and pointed to a blinking red light fixed to one side of the tunnel. It was one of the demolition charges. The enemy must be planning to blow the entrance on their way out once they secured the treasure.

As Seichan continued, following the staked line of rope, she oriented herself enough to realize the tunnel was less a passage drilled through solid rock than a winding, torturous path through and around a jumble of boulders and broken slabs.

"It's an old rock slide," Ben confirmed, scanning his lights around as he wriggled between two blocks of granite leaning against one another.

As Seichan followed, she sensed the precarious nature of this pile, suspecting it wouldn't take much of a blast to bring this all crashing down.

After another minute of kicking and squirming, Ben's voice dropped to a hissed whisper. "Got lights ahead."

He doused his own lamps and slowed to a crawl. The passage widened enough for the three to cluster together. The way opened directly ahead, illuminated by a figure floating weightless in scuba gear beyond the tunnel. The man's attention was on the glowing device he held in his hands. Its screen was as bright as a lamp in the dark waters.

Ben glanced significantly at them.

It must be the monitoring device and control unit for the glider outside.

Gray held up a palm, indicating the other two should hang back.

He then pushed off the tunnel floor and glided toward the man's back. Some warning eddy of current must have alerted his target.

The diver spun around, fumbling for his shouldered spear gun—but Gray was already atop him.

He plunged his knife under the man's chin and clutched him with his other arm. The body writhed for several seconds, then went slack. Gray deflated the man's buoyancy vest and let his weighted form sink into the dark depths, but not before relieving him of his spear gun and glider's control unit.

Ben and Seichan joined Gray as he doused the device, returning the waters to a stygian darkness—or at least, it should have.

They all turned their faces upward.

Through the waters overhead, a soft, shimmering glow beckoned to them. The diffuse light gave dimension to the flooded cavern around them. It had to be half the size of a football stadium. The glow also revealed the surface of the lake inside here. It stretched about ten meters overhead.

They slowly rose toward the shine.

With great caution, they risked peeking the edges of their masks above the water.

Ben gasped next to her. "Holy Mother of God . . ."

10:42 A.M.

Gray understood the Aussie's stunned shock.

The roof of the cavern glowed with what appeared to be swaths of stars, shining in hues from a deep blue-green to a bright silver. The glow revealed long filaments hanging from the roof, each lined by rows of pearlescent droplets.

"Glowworms," Ben explained.

Gray had heard of caves in Australia and New Zealand that harbored these bioluminescent larvae, but he had never imagined they could produce such a brilliant display. There had to be millions glowing throughout here, attempting to lure prey with their shine into their sticky traps.

But the true wonder was not found across the roof.

The glowworms had found a more convenient purchase.

The wreck of the *Trident*.

The three-masted sailing ship listed crookedly in the cavern, having run aground into a sandbar on the far side. The entire surface of the ship was draped in glowworms and their fine silk nets. It was as if the wreck of *Trident* had risen from ghostly seas, still draped in bioluminescent kelp and algae.

Despite the wonder of the sight, movement— both on the sandbar and atop the deck—drove Gray back underwater, drawing the others with him.

"Did you notice the ship's sails were furled and tied?" Ben said as he joined Gray. "At one time, this cavern must've been open to the sea. The crew likely sought to shelter here during a storm. Maybe even hiding from a cyclone."

Gray pictured the rockslide they had traversed to get here. "And in doing so, the bastards got themselves trapped here."

"Let's not suffer the same fate," Seichan reminded them.

Gray nodded. "We need to find Simon's daughter, secure her, and get the hell out of here."

"I spotted a blond woman with the group on the sandbar," Seichan said.

"That'd be Kelly," Ben confirmed.

Gray set off toward shore. "Then let's go get her."

As they traversed the lake, they kept deep. The lakebed slowly rose up under them as they neared the far side. Even here, life thrived. Centuries-old coral fluttered with sea fans. Brightly colored fish darted from their path, while albino lobsters as long as his forearm stalked the reefs.

Seichan swam beside him, carefully eyeing the sand and rocks for threats. Something caught her eye, drawing her to the side.

Before he could inquire about her interest, they reached the *Trident*. From here, they would have to work swiftly. At any moment, someone might try to radio the man they had taken out earlier. Gray knew they had only a narrow window before their presence in the cavern was exposed.

Hidden in the shadow of the wreck's hull, he worked quickly with the others, making sure everyone was prepared. Once satisfied, they set off again. They circled the bulk of the *Trident* and approached the sandbar, hugging the lakebed. Gray was counting on the gleam of the glowworms reflecting off the lake's dark surface to keep their group hidden for as long as possible.

As they reached the shallows, Gray could make out figures atop the sand, not far from where the *Trident* had run aground. The ship loomed above the small group, revealing a huge crack in its hull. A trio of wooden chests stood nearby. From the drag marks in the sand, it appeared the boxes had been hauled from the ship's broken hold.

Gray didn't doubt what they contained.

The *Trident*'s lost treasure.

Ignoring the wealth stored in those chests, he concentrated on the watery image of the three mercenaries standing guard over the treasure—and one lone girl.

Kelly knelt in the sand, her shoulders slumped, her face despondent.

One of the men had a pistol casually pointed at the back of her head, clearly awaiting the order to dispatch this witness. The other two were similarly armed. Their abandoned spear guns were propped on boulders behind them. It seemed the crew must have packed-in additional weapons in waterproof cases.

Gray cursed their preparedness, but there was nothing he could do about it. His team was committed now. He curled his body and got his legs under him. He glanced right and left to make sure the others were ready.

In his head, a countdown had been running, matching the timer he had set on the demolition charge. Moments ago, he'd attached his remaining device to the far side of the *Trident*'s hull. He even added the leftover plastic explosive from the earlier charge.

As the countdown reached zero, he burst out of the water.

At the same time, the explosion rocked the cavern with a deafening blast. Water and broken planks flumed high into the air behind him.

Gray already had his stolen spear gun at his shoulder. He fixed his aim and squeezed the trigger.

The steel spear shot through the air and struck the gunman looming over Kelly in the eye. The bolt pierced his skull and threw his body backward.

To his left, Seichan whipped her arm and deftly sent her dive knife flying from her fingertips. No one was deadlier with a blade than her. Her dagger impaled her target in his Adam's apple, dropping him into a gurgling heap.

With a knife in hand, Ben barreled out of the water to Gray's right. He aimed for the third assailant, who stood closest to the water's edge. The enemy—stunned by the blast and the sudden attack—still managed to swing his pistol toward Ben.

Before he could fire, Kelly lunged up from the sand and knocked his arm high. The pistol cracked brightly, but the shot went wild. Ben crashed hard into the gunman, which threw off his attack. His initial knife jab was blocked by an elbow.

Still, Ben was not done.

With a hard shove, the Aussie sent his target stumbling backward—straight into one of the spear guns propped against a boulder behind the man. The impact drove the loaded bolt through his back and out his chest. The man sank to his rear, his mouth opening and closing, gasping like a beached fish, before he finally sagged and fell on his side.

Before anyone could speak, a thunderous groan drew all their attentions to the lake. In slow motion, the glowing bulk of the *Trident* tipped sideways, falling toward the water, collapsing on the side blown out by Gray's charge. Its masts shook and its deck canted.

"Look!" Kelly yelled.

Two figures—one thin-limbed and spry, the other bulky with muscle—leaped over the rails on the far side and dove toward the lake. They hit the water together and vanished into the dark depths. Gray imagined these last two men must've been scouring the *Trident* for any last treasures.

"No, no, no . . ." Kelly said.

Gray turned to her, noting the bright terror in her face.

"That was the leader of these bastards," she explained. "And Dr. Hoffmeister."

The traitor.

"They won't get far," Ben assured her. "We'll find them."

"No, you don't understand," Kelly said. "Hoffmeister has the transmitter for the demolition charges."

Gray understood. "He'll blow this place behind him once he's safely clear."

Ben pointed to where a few brighter lines of sunlight pierced the glowing roof, marking the presence of cracks. "It could bring this whole place crashing down."

Knowing this to be true and with no time to spare, Gray stripped his body of nonessential weight, grabbed one of the spear guns, and sprinted into the water.

Seichan followed his example and dove alongside him.

They swam in tandem after the fleeing men. With the enemy already having a significant lead, it was likely a futile chase. Still, Gray refused to give up.

He glanced over to Seichan.

Behind her shoulders, the *Trident* sank into the depths, its bulk still aglow as it finally met its doom.

As he turned back around, something silvery flashed past his nose.

A spear.

The bolt shot between the two of them.

Ahead, a shadow rose from behind a ridge of a reef. It was the mercenary leader. He was already raising a second spear gun. Beyond the man, a small iota of light bobbled in the darkness.

Hoffmeister.

He was getting away.

10:55 A.M.

Seichan knew they had only one chance.

She lifted her spear gun with one arm and kicked hard. As she passed Gray, she shoved her free hand into his shoulder. "Go! I'll deal with this bastard."

Gray didn't hesitate or balk. It was one of the reasons she loved him. As exasperating as he could be at times, he trusted her fully. He did not suffer from some overinflated conceit of male bravado. Instead, they were a team. They knew each other's strengths and weaknesses—and Gray was the better swimmer.

Proving this, he twisted to the side and swam off. He vanished almost immediately as he circled around the threat.

Seichan continued on a straight path.

She lifted her spear gun.

The enemy did the same.

Let's do this.

When only yards separated them, they both fired. Spears flashed through the dark waters. Seichan twisted to the side, but the bolt grazed the length of her thigh, slicing her wetsuit and leaving a line of fire down her leg.

Her aim was better. But at the last moment, the mercenary leader deflected the bolt with the steel butt of his gun, sending the spear careening to the side.

So be it.

She closed the distance between them. She had suspected all along this battle would end in a knife fight.

She reached for the sheath at her waist—but her fingers came up empty.

Cursing silently, she pictured the blade impaled in the throat of her target on the beach. In her haste to depart, she had never collected it.

Her enemy was not so ill prepared.

He bared a foot-long dagger.

10:58 A.M.

Across the lake, Gray continued his chase after the fleeing light. It was a beacon in the darkness and became his sole focus as he kicked and swept his arms. He used it to distract him from his worry about Seichan.

Slowly the luminous speck grew before him, offering both encouragement and hope. He still had his spear gun over one shoulder.

If I can get close enough . . .

Then suddenly the light vanished ahead of him, blinking out entirely. Caught by surprise, he momentarily slowed—then realized what the loss implied.

Hoffmeister had reached the tunnel.

I'm out of time.

11:01 A.M.

Unarmed, Seichan fled from her assailant.

Like Gray, she was practical. She knew her limitations and recognized the skill of her adversary. Her only hope was to keep ahead of his muscular bulk. With that goal in mind, she headed back toward the sandbar, following the path the team had used earlier.

Her brutal training as an assassin had taught her always to memorize her surroundings, to weigh every variable at hand.

So she headed unerringly along their prior path.

She pictured the dive knife abandoned on the sandbar.

It was a stupid lapse.

One I'll not make again.

But first she had to live.

She was already slowing, both from exhaustion and from the blood trailing from her sliced leg. It was becoming harder to kick with her wounded limb. Still, if nothing else, her injury drew her attacker onward, like a dog after a wounded bird.

A glance over her shoulder revealed the man was almost on top of her.

Good.

She slowed even further as she neared the location fixed in her mind's eye, a spot that had drawn her attention earlier on the way to the sandbar, enough to draw her away from Gray briefly.

She crested over a coral ridge and dove down to a stretch of bare sand.

She had noted a weapon here earlier.

One of those many variables.

With her gloved fingers, she reached for it—just as a shadow loomed over her.

Following Ben's warning from earlier in the day, she grabbed the weapon by its tail. She whipped around as the mercenary plunged his dagger toward her back. She easily avoided the strike, taking advantage of the man's overconfidence.

She swung and struck the stonefish into the man's neck. Spines pierced his flesh. Venom pumped. The effect was instantaneous. His body stiffened. He dropped his dagger and pawed at his neck, knocking the impaled fish away—but the damage was done.

His body thrashed in the water. The pain so maddened him that he ripped off his mask and regulator. Fingernails clawed at his face. Then his limbs slackened, falling away leadenly. He hung in the water. His blind eyes stared back at her. She didn't know if the pain had killed him, or the poison, or if he'd simply drowned.

She knew only one certainty, picturing the ravaged body of Kelly's father.

Good riddance.

11:05 A.M.

Gray scrambled along the rope as it wound a serpentine course through the old rockslide. He hauled with arms and kicked off purchases with his feet. His shoulders remained hunched by his ears. At any moment, he expected the charges hidden along the passageway to explode, to send the pile crashing down atop him.

His only hope was that Hoffmeister would wait until he was well clear of the coastal cliffs before he risked using his transmitter. The oceanographer must know the blasts could cast off massive boulders that would pound into the water around him.

· But would the panicked bastard be that cautious?

Gray grabbed the rope with both hands and yanked his body around another turn in the tunnel. As he continued, the line suddenly went slack. The next pull only drew the rope toward him.

Gray cursed, knowing what this meant.

Hoffmeister had cut the safety line.

Gray took care not to pull on the rope. He needed its draped length to lead him out of here. Still, the stirred-up silt made it hard to see the line. He had to proceed with greater care—which slowed him down considerably.

I'll never make it now.

But then, impossibly, a light appeared out of the murk ahead.

Daylight.

He hurried again, rushing the last of the distance. As he burst out of the tunnel, he found Hoffmeister only ten yards away. He was crouched low to the seabed.

Gray was shocked to find the man so near. He quickly hauled the spear gun from his shoulder.

Hoffmeister had nowhere to flee.

Gray was wrong.

From the seabed, a yellow torpedo shot upward, jetting away from the oceanographer.

It was the ANFOG glider.

Suddenly, Hoffmeister was torn off his feet. His body flew after the glider, dragged in its wake. The man had clipped and tethered himself to the glider by a length of cable. He plainly intended to escape using his own tool, likely manually setting the glider's motor to maximum power a moment ago.

Gray fired after his retreating form, but his shot didn't come close.

He even tried to swim after the bastard but quickly recognized the futility. In less than a minute, Hoffmeister would be far enough out into open water to use his detonator.

It's over.

But as Gray watched, the yellow torpedo suddenly made a sharp left turn, banking quickly. It rolled Hoffmeister like a ragdoll through the water.

Confused, Gray swam out farther to follow its trajectory.

The glider aimed for the wreck of the

catamaran—and the frenzy of bull sharks drawn by the blood of Hoffmeister's murdered colleague. The oceanographer must have sensed the threat, even more so when the glider began to slow as it neared the wreckage.

Hoffmeister frantically tried to unclip his line from the glider before it dragged him into the sharks. As the torpedo decelerated, the oceanographer finally broke free and fought his way from the danger.

But sharks were not the only predators hunting these waters.

From the wreck below, a dark shape shot upward, jaws impossibly wide. Yellow teeth clamped on Hoffmeister's left arm and shoulder. A thick armored tail whipped in a circle, sending the crocodile's half-ton mass into a wrenching spiral.

Hoffmeister's body went flying away—minus his entire left arm.

Still, the man lived. With blood pouring from his shoulder, he kicked and pawed with his one arm. Then a bull shark swept down, snatched him up, and with a whisk of its powerful tail, vanished into the sea.

Aghast, Gray retreated toward the sea tunnel. He glanced to the passageway. He suddenly suspected the source for the glider's deadly turn.

Hoffmeister wasn't the only one who knew how to operate the glider.

So did a certain lowly graduate student.

11:11 A.M.

Poor girl . . .

Seichan watched Kelly drop the glider's control unit to the sand. Gray had left the device here before diving into the waters after Hoffmeister. It was Ben who had suggested the girl use her past experience with the underwater drones to monitor the seas beyond the cave.

Little did the Aussie know how fortuitous such a suggestion would prove to be.

Kelly remained on her knees. Ben was beside her. He hooked an arm around her shoulders and pulled her to his chest.

"Nicely done, Kelly . . . nicely done."

The only response from the girl was the shaking of her thin shoulders as she sobbed silently into Ben's chest. Though Kelly had exacted her revenge, it would not bring back her father.

Seichan stepped toward the water, leaving the girl to her mourning, knowing there were no words to ease that pain.

Instead, she stared up at the glowing stars, trying to find meaning. Long ago, greed had led a mutinous crew to a tragic end here in this cavern. And centuries later, it was greed again that led to more bloodshed and death.

Were some places simply cursed?

She remembered Captain Cook's name for this corner of the world.

Cape Tribulation.

She shook her head.

Maybe this place wasn't cursed, but it had certainly lived up to that name.

7:56 P.M.

A low groan drew Gray's attention to the left. He lifted his face from the padded doughnut of the massage table and stared over at the source of the complaint.

Seichan lay on the neighboring table. She was naked, covered only by a modesty towel over her buttocks and a row of steaming stones along her spine. He stared at the line of Steri-Strips closing the shallow laceration down her upper thigh.

"You okay?"

"More than okay," she said with contented sigh. "Like I said earlier, this is more than enough of an adventure for me."

He grinned and settled back to his table.

A heated stone was gently placed on the center of his lower back.

It was his turn to groan.

He allowed himself to drift in the pleasure of the attention. Earlier, Ben had facilitated their escape from Cape Tribulation, keeping them out of the ensuing limelight. Ben had also promised to protect Kelly in the weeks ahead, determined that the recognition for the discovery of the *Trident* go to her and her father—along with the gold.

In turn, Kelly intended that the treasure be used to finance her father's passion.

Protecting the reefs.

It would be the perfect way to honor the man's sacrifice.

Seichan made another noise—this time more thoughtful.

He glanced over again. "What now?"

She rested her cheek on the table, staring back at him. "I was just thinking about where we should go next."

"Any ideas?"

"Somewhere that's still warm and tropical." She lifted her cheek, staring pointedly at him. "But *without* box jellyfish, saltwater crocodiles, or stonefish."

"Like where."

"I was thinking Hawaii . . . maybe Maui."

"Really? Aren't those islands too tame and boring for you?"

She shrugged. "I've never been there. And right about now, boring sounds perfect."

"Then a Hawaiian vacation it is." He settled his face back into his doughnut. "Surely nothing can go wrong there."

WHAT'S TRUE, WHAT'S NOT

At the end of my full-length novels, I love to spell out what's real and what's fiction in my stories. I thought I'd briefly do the same here.

Cape Tribulation. I was lucky enough to spend some time in this area near Port Douglas in Queensland and always wanted to set a story here. It's truly a magical place, where the rainforest meets the Coral Sea. I also took a horseback ride to the beach featured in this story, where I watched a huge saltwater crocodile saunter across the sand and into the surf. While there, I also became enamored with the history of the region. The site was indeed named by Captain Cook after his fateful accident on the nearby reefs. So I thought it would be fun to tell a story of a ship that suffered a similar, if more tragic, fate.

The *Trident*. While the ship featured in this short story is purely fictional, I based its fateful tale on the histories of two real convict ships: the *Success* and the *Hive*. Their combined stories involved mutiny, gold, and lost shipwrecks. So I borrowed their tales for this adventure.

The Great Barrier Reef. As I was setting this

story here, I couldn't help but mention the tragic bleaching that is currently affecting two-thirds of the reef's coral, covering a swath almost nine hundred miles long. The reef is home to many endangered species, along with four hundred types of coral and fifteen hundred species of fish. It's an invaluable habitat, one that three hundred million people rely on for food, employment, and livelihood. So let's not lose it.

ANFOG Gliders. Yep, those yellow research torpedoes are real . . . though I may have stretched their capabilities a bit. But not by much!

What's Next?

At this story's conclusion, Seichan makes a fateful decision to head to Hawaii, specifically Maui. Gray has, of course, cursed them by declaring *nothing can go wrong*. Their sabbatical from Sigma Force is about to come to a crashing end—and nothing will ever be the same for the two of them. Already forces are in motion, fueled by an ancient horror known only as the Demon Crown. So hold tight, and I hope you enjoy the wild ride to come!

New York Times **bestselling author**

JAMES ROLLINS

SANDSTORM
978-0-06-201758-1
Twenty years ago, a wealthy British financier
disappeared near Ubar, the fabled city buried
beneath the sands of Oman.

ICE HUNT
978-0-06-196584-5
Danger lives at the top of the world . . . where nothing can
survive except fear.

AMAZONIA
978-0-06-196583-8
There are dark secrets hidden in the jungle's heart,
breeding fear, madness . . . and death.

DEEP FATHOM
978-0-06-196582-1
Ex-Navy SEAL Jack Kirkland surfaces from an underwater
salvage mission to find the Earth burning and the U.S. on the
brink of a nuclear apocalypse—and he is thrust into a race
to change the tide.

EXCAVATION
978-0-06-196581-4
For untold centuries, the secrets of life have been buried in
a sacred, forbidden chamber in the South American jungle.
Those who would disturb the chosen must now face the
ultimate challenge: survival.

SUBTERRANEAN
978-0-06-196580-7
A hand-picked team of scientists makes its way toward the
center of the world, into a magnificent subterranean
labyrinth where breathtaking wonders await—as well as
terrors beyond imagining.

JR1 0916